SKYBIRD SEVEN-TWO-THREE-WHISKEY-TANGO

ISBN-13: 9780578337050
ISBN-10: 1477123456

Cover design by: Nikitas Kavoukles
Library of Congress Control Number: 2018675309
Printed in the United States of America

For my family, with gratitude

Ann Mason
Thomas Mason
Tommy Foos
Mason Davis
Danner Davis
Clay Davis

CONTENTS

THANK YOU

Brilliant editing by:
Susan Fernandez
Webb Salmon

Editor:
Carol Gaskin,
www.EditorialAlchemy.com

Cover design:
Nikitas Kavoukles

Social Media:
Ann Mason

Production:
Thomas Mason

Special gratitude:

Thelma Danner
Mary Dusina
Tommy Foos
Cliff Gosney
Lindsay Hood
Jeanne Malmgren
Jim Melvin
Pat Owen
Jordan Paul
Pat Roush
Darryl Saffer
Kate Shellie-Stram
Charlie Schuette
Frank Sylvestri
Susan Hathaway Tantillo
Nancy Warren
Toni Van Pelt
Jim Voyles
Jill Whitfield
Ruth Whitney

AOPA (Aircraft Owners and
Pilots Association)
Amnesty International
Human Rights Watch

Walt Troyer
1946-2012

Walt, this is your book, too.
Thank you for always
believing in it,
for your aviation brilliance,
your wonderful pilot stories,
your world class humor.

BASED ON A
TRUE STORY

This story took place in 2000. It can only be told now.

Some of the people who assisted in this daring mission needed to become ghosts for at least twenty years. They asked little in return for risking their lives or for the gift of their time and amazing talents. All they asked was that everyone involved agree to keep the whole story secret until now.

Which we did.

PROLOGUE

Ready for takeoff at the gate at the Half Moon Bay airport, pilot Stan Grady waited in the cockpit of the Skybird S-5.

From the right seat, copilot Rich Cramer nudged him and pointed out the window. "There they are," he said.

A black Mercedes sedan was turning swiftly into the airport parking lot. Right on time, 8 a.m. The car pulled closely alongside the fence next to the gate. The car's windows were too darkly tinted to see how many occupants were inside, but the driver quickly got out and opened one back door on his side.

The first man to emerge had bushy hair the same dark color as his suit, which was too small, with sleeves that hiked up on his forearms. He bounded from the vehicle as if he was dismounting a horse. Then he bent back into the open door and reached in. His jerky back and forth motions suggested a struggle was going on inside the backseat.

Meanwhile, the driver got out of the other side of the car. This man was a slightly shorter but plumper version of the first. His suit, the same black-brown color, was also too tight, and he also had too much hair. He walked around the car and stood behind the first man, an arm extended as if to assist. But the first man had already won out over the stubborn occupant, dragging her from the car by a handful of arm and bunched up black sleeve. As she moved out into the open, she tried unsuccessfully to pull her arm out of his grasp.

The man leaned down and said something very close to the woman's ear, or where her ear probably was located under the black hood of the abaya she wore, and then still gripping her arm, he began marching her toward the gate. The other guy fell in on the other side and took hold of the other arm, but the woman wasn't struggling anymore.

Grady assumed that the guy had said something threatening, because even completely concealed, her body, her way of walking, the tilt of the hood all suggested the compliance that comes from fear. The second man carried a soft bag the size of a briefcase, and other than that, the group had no luggage.

Grady gave himself permission to wonder. Who was she? Cramer must have been thinking the same thing, because he muttered caustically, "C'mon, hoo-o-oney, you know you've always wanted to see the rocky coast of Maine."

How could this woman be a threat to these two big bubbas? She was quite a bit shorter than either of them, and she stepped from the car with a foot that looked small and delicate, even in the running shoe she was wearing. Grady would have expected a thin black slipper over a black stocking, or maybe a full-length boot.

Grady fantasized momentarily that she broke away from the men and started running, tearing through the gate and across the runway, toward the bluffs overlooking the Pacific on the west side of the field. The men would take off after her but their too-small suits would slow them down, and in her running shoes she would be faster than the wind, her black robes billowing behind her. As she ran she would shed the coverings—first the hood, tossing it up and out behind her, and then, still running, peel the robe from her shoulders, and it would float off of her like raindrops off the windshield at 300 knots.

Now down to cutoff jeans and a sweatshirt, she'd disappear over the bluffs, and the trees would move in together like Birnam Wood coming to Dunsinane, linking their branches in a circle of protection, shielding her escape.

The group passed in front of the plane to the entrance on the port side, where Elliot, the sole flight attendant, was waiting to help them board. The cockpit on the S-5 was separated from the passenger cabin and had its own lavatory, and it was customary during charters for the pilots to stay out of the passenger area. So that would be the last Grady would see of the woman.

Grady and his copilot exchanged a look, and Cramer shrugged. They would talk no more about it. The charter pilots' credo: Don't ask, don't speculate, don't tell. You were there to fly the plane, no more. Unless a passenger shot somebody or tried to hijack you, what they did was none of your business.

Grady heard the muffled thump of the hatch shutting, then a click as Elliot secured the latch. He nodded to Cramer, who lifted his headset from around his neck and settled it into place on his head. He pressed his microphone button.

"Half Moon Bay traffic, this is Skybird Seven-Two-Three-Whiskey-Tango, ready to taxi to runway three-zero."

Elliot stuck her head into the cockpit. "They're all on," she said. "And we're secure."

"Before taxi checklist complete," Cramer said.

Grady switched off the auxiliary generator. Cramer nodded. There was no response on the radio, indicating that no other planes were in the way of the Skybird's takeoff path. The engines were idling. Grady brought up the power on the left engine, then back down to half, checking the instruments before repeating the same procedure for the right engine, which hummed into synch like the second half of an orchestra for the full finale.

"Half Moon Bay traffic, Skybird Seven-Two-Three-Whiskey-Tango on taxi to runway three-zero," Cramer said.

Everything was going smoothly, Grady thought, and they sure weren't wasting a second. The thugs couldn't complain about getting their precious fast start. But Grady flew by the book, always, even when he was turning somersaults in his own little Pitts. He figured he had survived all those years flying out of Eglin, taking that old lumbering Hercy-bird, the C-130, all over the Third World, doing landing approaches in tight spirals to stay out of bullet-ridden no-fly zones, putting that baby down on dry, split dirt runways—he'd survived because he never skipped a step, never glazed over a checklist or gave anything up to chance.

"Flaps set to ten," Cramer said.

"Let's review takeoff speeds."

"Confirm V-1 at 125, rotation speed 131, V-2 at 144," Cramer said, finishing with "in case of return," the procedure for an aborted takeoff.

As Grady guided the airplane toward the departure end of runway 30, he again allowed himself to wonder. If they had some kind of trouble and had to abort the takeoff, what might happen to the woman in the black robe and veil, the woman who didn't want to be on this plane, the woman too small and too outnumbered to do anything but submit? Would she have a second chance to get away? Would there be someone just now turning into Half Moon Bay airport, someone who had been following the Mercedes, a rescuer who arrived minutes too late, but might, if the plane came back, have a second chance to save her?

Grady shook off the thoughts as dangerously distracting. His focus had to be completely on getting this plane in the air. By the book.

Cramer spoke again into the mike. "Half Moon Bay

traffic, Skybird Seven-Two-Three-Whiskey-Tango ready to depart on runway three-zero."

Grady eased the throttle forward, and the plane leaped forward like a champion racehorse caged too long in the starting gate. Within seconds they were at 80 knots.

Cramer announced, "V-1," which meant that the plane was going 125 knots and the takeoff was beyond the point of no return. If they lost an engine now, they'd still leave the ground.

"Rotation." Grady eased the yoke toward him and the plane lifted off the runway.

"Positive rate," Cramer said.

"Confirm, and gear up."

"V-2 plus 20," Cramer said, advising Grady of the air speed.

"Okay, flaps up."

The S-5 shot up at 4,000 feet per minute. As Grady initiated a right turn, he saw the ground, the single runway that nearly paralleled the Pacific Ocean, bluffs on one side and the terminal on the other, all swiftly receding, as if a camera were zooming back. If he had been in the passenger cabin gazing out the window, he would have seen the now-miniature black car, sitting where the men had left it, with its doors still hanging open; and as the empty parking lot got smaller and smaller, there was still not a person in sight, and no tiny rescuers arriving minutes too late.

CHAPTER ONE

Morgan had walked the beach every day, rain or shine, for seven years. Two miles, three miles, sometimes more. The first big decision she had to make every morning was whether to turn right or left, north or south. If only the rest was that simple.

As she walked, she tried to figure things out. As if there was some prescribed distance she was supposed to cover, and then she'd understand. *If I can just walk long enough,* she thought, *I'll eventually stumble on the answers, and maybe what I am supposed to do with the rest of my life.*

That morning on the beach, Morgan kept going and going. She had walked nearly three miles before turning to head home. The surf was mildly rough, and though the sun was bright and unclouded, the air was wet and brisk from the previous night's storm.

The Gulf of Mexico was, for the most part, a friendly body of water. Even when the surf was kicking up, it was rarely enough to knock you over, and sometimes the water was so calm and flat that the only movement was a gentle sloshing right at the edge, as though some force was tipping a huge tub just enough to disturb the water but not enough to spill it.

Ashton was twenty-five now, and it had been years since he'd surfed on this coast. Still, Morgan checked out the water anyway, making mental notes as if he was still at home, waiting for a report.

"How're the waves, Mom?" he would ask.

"About two feet, glassy, breaking offshore, and choppy closer in," she would say.

DIANE MASON

"Break?"

"It's right."

She had a love-fear relationship with Ashton's surfing. It was beautiful to watch him glide along on the frothy edge of a glistening blue-green swell. But that same lump of water was as unpredictable as a nightmare's monster, and could turn mean and reach out and grab his lanky little nine-year-old body and topple him over and churn him up like a piece of flotsam, indifferent as the sky. There was simply no way to protect him out there, and often she was scared.

Once she asked him if he could wear a life preserver when he surfed, and he looked at her as if aliens had just inhabited her body. *Ashton certainly didn't get his guts from me,* Morgan thought.

A half-hour from her house she saw Don walking toward her, as usual. On the beach on the small barrier island, you tended to see the same people every day at the about the same time and spot. Morgan didn't know his last name, but called him Don the Beachcomber. He had a nice smile and a big gut that his light blue spandex bathing suit failed to circumnavigate. Seeing him one day had prompted Meredith to ask, "Mom, how come all the men your age don't have butts?"

"Hey, Morgan," he said, waving.

"Hey, Don."

"So, you dating the police chief or something?" He winked.

"What do you mean?"

"Chief Bill. You got something going?"

Not because he didn't try, Morgan thought. Key Island was a small town, and the chief of the police department, Bill Conrad, was friendly with everyone. Especially women. He strutted around like an older, plumper Don Johnson, and fancied himself quite the lady magnet. His nickname was The Con. Actually he was kind of cute, with a boyish confidence, and probably scored about one in a hundred-fifty. Which was enough to keep him trying.

In the cozy resort town, the worst crimes were dogs off leash and rear-enders at the one traffic light, if you could call that a crime. A couple of years earlier there was a rash of jewelry thefts; that had been a very big deal. The department assigned two of its eight officers to a task force to solve the mystery. It turned out that the perps were pest control guys who were snatching necklaces and watches when they came into empty condominiums to spray for bugs.

One summer, when Morgan was coming out of the water after a swim, her way was blocked by a guy who was standing with his shorts down around his ankles. At first she thought he was hitting himself in the stomach, until she got a little closer and the water cleared out of her eyes, and she saw that he was masturbating vigorously. She found it disgusting. Also scary. She'd quickly turned back into the water, swam about two hundred yards down the beach, and then ran to her house and called Bill. He came over personally, along with two more officers, but of course the masturbator was gone when they got there.

Things were so slow down at the precinct that they had asked Morgan to come in and do a composite drawing on the computer. It was a brand new program, and the officer who was operating the keyboard kept putting women's hair on the beach masturbator's head and mustaches down on his chin. By the time the officer figured out which keys to hit to widen the mouth and make the eyes come closer together, Morgan had forgotten most of what the guy looked like.

They never caught him. But she'd been terrified for weeks. She berated herself for running right into her own house. Now he knew where she lived. She locked her doors for the first time and looked all around before getting into or out of her car. She jumped out of her skin when shade in bushes moved or a rabbit ran through the underbrush. At night, every noise had her diving for the light switch. God, how she hated that guy. He had violated her little safe haven, and for a while, ruined her life.

"Most of the time," Bill had declared, citing the police profile, "these guys are harmless. They don't ever hurt anyone."

Like she hadn't been hurt.

So that was Chief Bill Conrad. A nice guy, but not a clue.

And according to Don the Beachcomber, his squad car was now parked in her driveway. Don said that when he'd walked by a few minutes before, The Con was leaning against the side of his car, arms folded, waiting.

Curious, Morgan stepped up her pace a bit. She was still a half mile from home.

*   *   *

From about three hundred yards away, through the shaggy branches of the Australian pines that encircled the house, she could see Bill Conrad, leaning against the front of his squad car just as Don had described. Morgan waved, and he raised his hand, reserving any return gesture. He walked down to the beach toward her.

For the first time, Morgan felt a twinge of something more than curiosity. His face was solemn and his hands were grasped behind his back, as if he was trying to act casual—or he had a handful of bad news and was trying to hide it. Suddenly she felt a shiver of fear.

Three, four more strides until he was within earshot, and in those moments, a dozen possible catastrophes streaked through her mind, like a movie trailer of worst nightmares. Meredith. Ashton. It couldn't be her kids. They didn't even live here. *My parents had a wreck,* she thought. *My house is on fire. No, it's not on fire, I can see that. No flames. No fire trucks. I've been robbed. Oh please, let it be a robbery.*

"Hey, Bill," she said, holding tight to her voice. If she spoke calmly, the news would be better. "If you're going to arrest me, I confess. I was speeding on the beach."

He didn't crack a smile. Morgan had never seen him so serious.

"You caught the masturbator and you want me to come to a lineup?"

He put his arm around her waist and fell in step.

"Morgan, first I want to tell you that your son is okay."

"Okay? Ashton? What okay? What happened?"

"He's safe and okay. But there's been an accident," Bill Conrad said.

"What, Bill, what?" Morgan was already sobbing.

The moment had come she had dreaded for two dozen years, ever since Ashton first took to the water. So many things could go wrong out there. Getting hit in the head with the surfboard. Being pounded down by the wave that held you under too long. A leash breaking, sending the board flying out of reach. And then one day, out of the blue, she would get the call.

This was the day. And this was the call. Everything went into slow motion, and Bill's voice and her voice sounded like they were talking into big thick pillows. Morgan had just stepped into her worst nightmare; all the feeling was sucked out of her body and arms and legs, and she wanted Bill to shut up. Like when she was little and squeezed shut her eyes and clamped her hands over her ears and screamed out, "I can't hear you, I can't hear you."

"Morgan," he repeated, "he's okay. He's safe."

"Where is he? Why are you here? Bill..."

"We got a call from a sheriff's department in California. They found your name but didn't have your number, and you are unlisted. So they called us. I came right over."

"Where is he? Why couldn't he call?"

Bill pushed her toward the house. "Can we go in and sit down?"

"No. Tell me now." Morgan turned to face him, planted her feet, and whispered, "He was hurt surfing."

"No. Not surfing. He was in an accident. Morgan, can we go inside?"

"No! Tell me for god's sake."

Bill took her arm. "From what they can tell so far, Ashton was mugged."

"Mugged? Where? Is he all right?"

"This morning, early. I don't know many details yet, but he was found near the highway in Half Moon Bay, and he was beat up pretty bad. He's in the hospital and he's going to be okay."

Morgan broke away from Bill's grasp and started to run toward the house. "I've got to call him."

"Wait," he said. "We've got to talk first."

"No, I've got to call my son," she nearly screamed.

"Morgan, wait. You can't. Right now, Ashton is unconscious."

CHAPTER TWO

Sitting on the couch, Morgan clutched the telephone like it was an umbilical cord about to be cut. The St. Bartholomew Hospital hold music was generic soft rock, which was no comfort as the switchboard tried to connect Morgan with the intensive care ward where Ashton lay unconscious.

Omigod, my baby, Morgan thought. Was he wrapped in bandages? Bound to machines and monitors with a tangle of tubes and cords? Was he strapped to the bed, were his arms and legs broken? Was he in pain? She couldn't bear it if he was in pain. She couldn't bear that she wasn't there, that he might wake up and be alone and scared. But there was one thought that consoled her. Faiza. Surely she was there with him.

"How old is he?" Bill asked, pulling a chair over from the table.

"Twenty-five," Morgan said softly, listening for the operator.

"He go to school out there?"

"Yeah. San Francisco State. He's in his last year." The operator came on.

"You're holding for intensive care?" she asked.

"Yes, please," Morgan said. "My son. My son's there."

"Well, they're all with patients right now. Can you call back in ten minutes?"

"Oh, please, I'm calling from Florida and my son's been in an accident," she said. "Can't you find someone?"

"I'm so sorry, sweetie," the operator said. "That's hard. I've got one of my own. What's your boy's name?"

"Ashton Rivers."

"Okay, hold again, hon." And then there was the music again. Why did they play that music? Or any music for that matter. Maybe it was okay for people who were calling to check on their new, healthy baby, or to find out when the hospital benefit is. But otherwise, it did not comfort.

The operator came back. "They still can't talk to you yet, but I checked and he's in critical but stable condition. And don't you worry, hon. He's gonna be okay."

Morgan wanted to hug this woman, whoever she was. How instantly powerful are the bonds we form with the people who take care of our children when we can't be there, she thought. She remembered a doctor in Honolulu once, when Ashton got hit by something unidentifiable in the water. He wasn't sure whether it was a sting or a scrape or a bite, but his leg swelled up as the cut became more and more infected. Nothing seemed to heal it. Morgan called that doctor at least a dozen times, to hear her latest hypothesis, to offer her own. The doctor worked in a small walk-in clinic near the beach that . was, according to Ashton, teeming from morning until late afternoon with a crush of sunburned tourists, moms bouncing coughing babies, old people with the flu. Still, she talked to Morgan unhurried, as if Ashton's cut was the most important case she'd ever had.

"You must be very busy," Morgan said one day, thanking her for the umpteenth time.

The doctor answered: "It must be very hard to be so far away from your son."

Morgan told the switchboard operator she would call back in ten minutes. Then she called Dowd's cellphone. No answer. She called his office in Indianapolis and left word for him to call her immediately.

She turned to Bill Conrad. "Tell me what else you know."

Bill held out his hand for the telephone. Morgan handed it to him. "I've got a guy at the San Mateo sheriff's department, the one who called us. He's standing by." Bill took a square of paper from his shirt pocket and dialed the number on it.

"San Mateo? Where's that?"

"A county south of San Francisco," Bill said. "They found Ashton in Half Moon Bay, a little beach town there." He held up a finger. "Hello, this is Chief Bill Conrad in Florida. I'm calling for Sergeant Jeff Peterson." He waited. "Hey, Sergeant. This is Bill Conrad. I've got Morgan Fay, the boy's mother, here." He handed the phone to Morgan.

"This is Sergeant Peterson with the San Mateo sheriff's department." The voice was formal, but with a softness that was immediately reassuring.

"What happened to him?"

"Well, ma'am, we don't know too much yet." Peterson said. "He is in the hospital with multiple cuts and bruises and a broken leg."

"Broken leg? What on earth happened?"

"We don't know yet, ma'am. Since we can't talk to him." Peterson hesitated. "You know about the concussion?"

"I haven't gotten through to any doctor or nurse yet. But they said he was unconscious. Is he in a coma?"

"I don't know, ma'am. He was unconscious when he was found on the side of Highway 1. At first we though he fell from a car or was thrown out of a car," the sergeant said. "But the officers thought he looked like he had been beaten up, and the paramedics said he had injuries beyond what he would have sustained falling from a car."

"Oh god."

"Ms. Fay?" Peterson asked. "Are you okay?"

Morgan couldn't speak, but nodded, as if he could see.

"Ma'am, we have detectives investigating, and I'm sure we'll know more soon. Unfortunately it was very early in the morning, no one around, and so far no witnesses." Peterson waited a moment and then asked, "Did you know your son was in Half Moon Bay?"

"No," Morgan answered. "But I don't know most of where he goes or what he does. He's in college. And he's a surfer. He goes everywhere to surf."

How hideously ironic this all was, Morgan thought. All these years she had been terrified that Ashton would get hurt surfing, bracing for just such a phone call. And now he goes surfing and gets mugged.

"He was checked into a motel across the street," Peterson said. "With a young woman."

"He has a girlfriend," Morgan said. "She goes to San Francisco State also. She lives somewhere in a dorm. But I think they've actually been living together, sort of unofficially, for a few months."

Morgan gave Peterson the address. Ashton still had a Florida driver's license and used his mother's address as his home. That was how they found her.

"Ma'am, is there anything you can tell me that might help us?" Peterson stalled before asking, "Did your son have any, any, connection with the drug scene?"

"How do you mean?"

"Well, ma'am, does he use drugs?"

"Does he do drugs? Hell no!"

"Sometimes things get, well, out of control, or violent, even during a simple act of buying. Or selling," Peterson ventured.

"My son does not deal drugs," Morgan shouted. "Let alone use drugs. He hates drugs."

"A person doesn't have to be a dealer to buy some, or sell it."

"Give him a blood test. I'll bet my house on it."

"I'm sorry to upset you, ma'am," Peterson said calmly. "Sometimes mothers don't know everything, and these are things I have to ask." He paused, then asked, "What is the girlfriend's full name?" His voice had recovered some of the kinder tone he had used earlier, before he'd accused her of being the mother of a drug lord.

"Her name is Faiza Salah," Morgan said. She spelled it. "It's Arabic, pronounced Fah-ey-sa. Which usually comes out Fie-za. She's from Saudi Arabia."

Peterson seemed interested. "Here on a student visa?"
"Yes."

"Hmm," was Peterson's last comment before they hung up.

*   *   *

Morgan thanked Bill Conrad and insisted it was okay for him to leave. Though she appreciated the smalltown personal service, he wasn't particularly comforting. And she needed to make some more phone calls. Meredith. And then Kate, to tell her that she was on the way to California. Kate lived in Santa Barbara. Then her travel agent. To find the soonest plane.

Meredith wanted to know if Morgan wanted her to come along. The two shared a bit of a checkered history in airplane travel. Ever since an incident a few years before, Morgan had avoided flying alone. Hated it. After a half a lifetime of jetting all over the country and sometimes the world, she now found airplanes to be tubular little claustrophobic death traps. Accompanying her fear of flying was a greater fear that she had become great big chicken shit, a post-menopausal wimp, whose guts and courage had bled out with the last period.

Morgan adored her daughter for offering to go along, because it wasn't easy for her to get time off work on short notice. And Morgan especially loved Meredith for not making her feel like there was something wrong with her.

Unlike Dowd, who managed, in his inscrutable way, to do just that.

"I'll be on the first flight I can get," he said when he called.

"Me too," Morgan said. "Just waiting for the travel agent to call back."

"Morgan, I know this is hard for you. You don't have to go," Dowd said, his tone soft, paternal, dripping with concern.

Dowd's put-downs came in many forms, but the most maddening ones were like this, when he lowered his voice and spoke like a minister delivering the final profound salvo of a sermon on lovingkindness. In between the lines of that gracious offer was the message: You are weak and I am strong, and you would yield to that weakness instead of being there for our son.

"I'm going out there, Dowd," Morgan said. "Ashton's hurt and needs me."

"He needs both of us," Dowd corrected.

"I'm sorry, that's what I should have said. And I'm glad you're coming," she said. It would be some comfort having him there. Dowd was good in emergencies, and his politician personality was ideal for establishing rapport with institutions, like hospitals, and authority figures, like doctors.

"Well, if anything changes for you, if you start feeling anxiety, remember you can always change your mind. Just don't wait too long," he said, with just the barest edge of a tease.

"Not funny, Dowd."

"You and Meredith joke about it all the time," he said.

"I will be there, Dowd," Morgan said, wondering out loud who would arrive first, which of them could get the earlier plane.

"This isn't a contest, Morgan," he said somberly.

"I never said it was."

*   *   *

Morgan spoke with an intensive care nurse named Nancy. Methodically and rather dispassionately, Nancy explained that Ashton was still unconscious but not in a coma. He had suffered head injuries, a concussion, and would hopefully regain consciousness within the next twenty-four hours. He had been treated for cuts and abrasions, including stitches for a gash in his shoulder. His shoulder was dislocated. He needed stitches on one deep cut on his forehead. And his right leg was broken.

Morgan sobbed. "God, what happened? It's like he got hit by a truck."

"He's going to be all right," Nancy said.

All right? How could he be all right? Morgan thought. She

never could bear the thought of either of her kids alone and suffering.

"Has anyone come there for him?" Morgan asked.

"Some detectives were here earlier. But that's all," Nancy said.

"No young woman? He has a girlfriend. I thought she would be there."

"No, no one so far."

Morgan thanked Nancy and hung up, wondering, hoping. Surely Peterson would find Faiza soon.

The travel agent called. Morgan was on a flight that left at 4:40. Still hours to wait. She went into the kitchen to make some coffee. Better do decaf. She was already having heart palpitations. Her stomach hurt. She sat on the living room sofa and drew her knees up to her stomach. She rocked back and forth for a while, then got back up and went into the kitchen to get the coffee. The carafe was empty. She hadn't turned it on.

She put a load of laundry in the washer and without thinking began to make piles of clothes on the bed. Slacks. Tops. Underwear. She went to the refrigerator, stared in the open door for a while, and then began tossing perishables into the trash. She moved some bread and a container of orange juice into the freezer, where it would keep longer. She glanced at her houseplants, realizing she should ask someone to water them while she was gone. How long would she be gone?

Back in the bedroom Morgan began mechanically adding items to her piles. A jacket. A long black skirt, casual but professional—what Meredith called grownup clothes. For meeting doctors and detectives. And ex-husbands.

CHAPTER THREE

Settling into her seat on the American MD-80, Morgan looked up at the video monitor hanging from the ceiling, which was showing a series of soundless panoramas. The camera swooped alongside mountains and over glacier lakes. Alaska, maybe? Then the film circled above a steaming volcanic crater and then over another mountain whose craggy peak was encircled by a doughnut of puffy white clouds.

It wasn't exactly meditative, but it was mildly distracting, and for a moment Morgan forgot to dread the nearly six hours ahead of her in this overstuffed cylinder, breathing recycled air and fighting off the panic that often hung just outside her consciousness.

Pretty soon a flight attendant began demonstrating how to use the oxygen mask, and because they would be flying briefly over the Gulf of Mexico, the drill included how to don the life jackets in case of an emergency over water. She showed how to blow up the life jacket but then instructed, "Do not inflate the life vest until you are outside the plane."

Yeah, right, Morgan thought. The plane has just plunged into the water, everyone's getting ready to slide out the emergency exits into the icy folds of a ten-foot sea, and they're going to *wait* until they're in the water? More likely would be one hundred and ten passengers putting their jackets around their necks and then pulling those cords as fast as their little fingers can find the tabs, vests bursting up and out and people bumping each other and filling the fuselage, like popcorn in a pan.

The plane was moving backward and Morgan wiggled

in her seat, trying to make the stiff cushions yield into a nest. The engines revved deeply as the nose turned right and the plane pulled itself into a taxi. This, she used to think, was the point of no return. When it was too late to turn back. *Well, I sure proved that wrong,* she thought, pushing the memory away and drawing in a deep breath, allowing the air to fill all the way to her belly.

The plane was climbing now, and Morgan could feel the vibration of the landing gear being tucked under the fuselage. Somehow she needed to find a way to absent herself from her own mind. Until she got to that hospital and saw Ashton, there was nothing more she could do.

On the seatback in front of her there was a telephone, with instructions on how to make a call during the flight. She pulled the receiver off and held it in her hand. Did people really use these things? What were her chances of actually getting through to the hospital, let alone someone who could tell her something more than she had learned an hour before when she called from the airport? Ashton was still unconscious and stable. Morgan had almost screamed when she heard that. How could you be stable when you were unconscious? *Wake up, Ash, wake up.*

Ashton was young, barely eight, when he got his first surfboard, and Florida's west coast was a good place for him to learn. Safe. Every morning, when Morgan drove him and Meredith to school, he would plead to stop at the beach and check the waves.

"Oh, come on, Ash," Meredith would complain. "We looked at them yesterday. You rode your bike over here last night. What could have changed?"

"Please, Mom. It'll just take a second."

They'd pull over, and he'd jump out of the car and run to a spot where he could stand and study the horizon, straws of blond hair blowing back off his face. The kid could read wind, currents, ripples on the surface. He could predict the surf by studying wind shifts in the branches of the trees in their yard.

He knew how the movements of entire oceans affected the waves in their little piece of the Florida coastline, and he did every school science report or project on some aspect of the sea's behavior.

So with Meredith sighing and fidgeting impatiently in the car, Ashton would evaluate the day's seas. If the waves were small and weak, he'd be content to go on to school. But if they were big he'd become quiet, sullen, a day of pure torture ahead of him, knowing what he was missing. Every so often, if the waves were especially "rad," she'd let him stay home from school and surf. Meredith was offered equal hooky time, but she hardly ever used it. She loved school and got bored at home.

Eventually Ashton outgrew these waves, and as soon as he finished high school, he moved to California with plans to go to college there. It would be years before he graduated, and the California coast became a base of operations for surf junkets to the monster swells of Mexico, Hawaii, Costa Rica, Australia, Indonesia, and probably dozens of places Morgan never knew about. He'd made a childhood dream come true, to surf with the international pro surfing team. He toured for two years and then dropped out. He didn't like competition.

"I know it sounds crazy, Mom. But when I'm in a contest, the surfing isn't the same. When I'm on the wave, it's still a challenge. And the ride's still great. But it's not, like, fun. The magic goes away."

When he turned twenty-four, Ashton took up college again but stayed in California and surfed every spare moment. Morgan did not think a day went by that she didn't worry about him out on those waves. Wondering if this would be the day she would arrive home and find a message from some makeshift clinic in a third-world country that didn't have a hospital.

"Please stop worrying, Mom," Ashton would insist, sometimes angrily. He believed that fear created an energy field that knew no geographical boundaries, so it could reach him wherever he was.

"Don't you get it, Mom? It makes me less safe when you worry."

"Oh, great," Morgan said. "So now I've got two things to worry about. First, that you'll get hurt, and second, if you do get hurt, that I caused it with my thought waves."

"Something like that," he said.

"No fair," Morgan said. "Moms worry. It's what we do."

"Well, you're going to have to chill," he said, quite serious.

Morgan was glad that Meredith lived nearer, less than a day's drive away. Once, she'd said about her brother, "I kind of envy him. I don't think I ever had something I cared about like that, with such a passion."

"Me neither, kiddo," Morgan replied. "Not for a long time, anyway."

Morgan passed the rest of the flight in the sort of anesthetized disconnection that often settles on one's mind after a shock. She pulled out a paperback, her friend Linnie's third novel, entitled *Tow Away Zone*. Morgan had started reading it a few days before, and after only a few chapters could see where it was going. Linnie's plotlines were all the same. A love affair goes awry, leaving a protagonist in despair but also leading her right into the arms of a soulmate.

Morgan had no intention of really reading. She couldn't possibly concentrate. Maybe she'd never read again. But it kept her neighbor from talking to her, and it was oddly comforting to have a part of Linnie on her lap.

"Please fasten your seatbelts and return your tray tops . . . " Morgan had fallen asleep again. They were getting ready to land in San Francisco. Linnie's novel had dropped off Morgan's lap, and the woman sitting next to her handed it to her with a cordial smile. She tried to smile back, but sighed instead, as a new fear seared through her stomach. Now, the issue of surviving this flight seemed like a narcissistic indulgence compared to what was ahead. She felt so alone.

Most of the passengers were standing, crowding into the aisles and stretching to retrieve bags stowed overhead before the plane stopped moving. Morgan wished there was room to bend over and touch her toes and pull the achy tightness from her shoulders and back. The passengers snaked their way to the exit, and with a sigh of relief she stepped off the airplane.

"Morgan!" a voice shouted.

A hand waved wildly above the clump of people at the terminal. And stepping out of the crowd was the friend Morgan had had longer than anyone else in the world.

"Kate!"

A head shorter than Morgan, Kate stretched out her arms to encircle her. Her dark hair was pulled casually back, with a few strands curling alongside and framing her face. Her appearance was always so beautifully uncontrived. It, and she, just fell into place. "It's been too long," she said.

"You drove all the way up from Santa Barbara?"

"It didn't take all that long," Kate said, her arms still around Morgan's waist as the two old friends fell into step together.

"Oh, I can't believe . . . it's so good to see you."

Friends. The good ones have a knack for showing up just when you think you've used up your last lifeline.

"When did you get here?" Morgan asked.

"I started out right after you called this morning." She stopped and looked up at Morgan. "I've been to the hospital."

Morgan halted and faced her. "You saw Ashton? How is he? What's happening?"

"He's okay. Really. He's still unconscious, but they expect him to wake up within twenty-four hours or so."

"How does he look? What's wrong with him?"

"It's a concussion," Kate said.

"Is he breathing okay? Does he look like he's in pain?"

Morgan had so many questions. Kate took her arm and

pulled Morgan away from some pedestrians she was getting ready to collide with.

"He looks very peaceful," Kate said. "He has an IV and he's on oxygen, and there are some monitors attached to him, but from what I could tell, his heart rate and blood pressure were fine. He's got a broken leg, which is in a cast, and a lot of cuts and bruises. His eyes are swollen."

Morgan was starting to cry. "I want to kill someone," she said.

"I'm telling you everything. So you'll maybe be more prepared," Kate said.

"Is Faiza there?"

"No. But Dowd is there. Talking to lots of people and trying to get some answers, and doing a pretty good job of it."

"Dowd style," Morgan said.

"Yep," Kate said. "Geez, it's been years since I've seen him."

"Does anyone know what happened?" Morgan asked.

"No more than what you already know," Kate said. "Maybe someone will know more by the time we get there. It's about a half hour drive to the hospital."

They drove in silence for a while, comfortable even for two best friends who hadn't seen each other for six months. Morgan reached over and touched Kate's shoulder. She could always tell when Kate was thinking about Jack.

"You okay?"

Kate threaded her fingers through her hair, a habit she had when she was trying to figure out how to say something, or when she needed to get grounded.

"This was the first time I've been in a hospital," she said, adding, "since then."

Morgan mentally calculated the years. Two. Not very long when your whole life has disintegrated. Actually, no amount of time would be enough. Death changes you profoundly and forever, and there's no turning back because of the strange and cruel way death takes the past along with the future.

"Hospitals are so, I don't know, isolating," Kate said. "You step inside and you're out of ordinary time and space and into this other plane of reality. And then when you come back out, it's disorienting. Like you just walked out of being hermetically sealed in a cave. The outside and the sunlight are so much more than they were when you went in—so bright, so shocking. God, hospitals are lonely."

"Thank you so much for being there for Ashton," Morgan said.

"Morgan, listen, I need to tell you something else."

"What?"

"Ashton underwent surgery this morning."

"Surgery? For what?"

"To relieve pressure in his head. Apparently, because of the concussion, fluid built up around the brain and they had to make some holes to drain the fluid."

"Oh my god."

"When you see him," Kate said, "his head is all bandaged up. Like a big white turban. And his eyes are black and blue. Don't be shocked."

"Oh, god, Kate, this is awful."

"I know," she said. "I love that kid so much. Such a sweet spirit. Gentle. How could anyone hurt him?"

CHAPTER FOUR

Morgan caught glimpses of the coastline as Kate drove south toward Half Moon Bay, and the wind splashing in through the open sunroof felt cool and refreshing. But in spite of the bright sunlight, this environment felt strikingly different from the one Morgan had just left, maybe because the California coast was high and craggy and tumultuous, and the west coast of Florida was level and mostly quiet. *In California,* she reflected, *it feels like the storm is yet to come. In Florida, it feels like it's long past.*

The childhood friends had both ended up in places very different from southern Indiana, where they'd grown up. There, the surface of the earth wasn't mountainous, just hilly, and so dark brown and fertile and full of trees that no matter where they went—walking to school, driving to the mall, playing in the backyard—they were circled by green: sun making leaves bright green, backgrounds of dark green, cool green shade in the summer, light always passing through some green gatekeeper or another. Kate called it "rank."

In the fall, when the leaves changed, the color was so intense that it seemed to come in through all the senses, not just sight. Morgan could feel, taste, even hear the colors.

Kate turned into the St. Bartholomew Hospital parking lot and followed a small wooden sign with a red arrow under the word "Visitors." The sign looked hand-painted. Morgan prayed the hospital wasn't a do-it-yourselfer, too. From the outside the building appeared small and old, but clean and white, with nice grass and well-tended grounds. As they approached the main entrance they both started walking faster.

Finally on their own legs and out of traffic, they could move at their own pace.

"Can I help you?" The woman sitting behind the information desk wore a pair of glasses dangling on a string of little beads around her neck and a wide, friendly smile.

"No, thanks," Kate said as they hurried past. "We know our way."

The elevator doors closed, and Morgan didn't even notice which floor Kate pressed. She felt like she was in a tunnel that muffled all the sights and sounds around her.

When Morgan entered the room, and for a long time afterward, she didn't even see Dowd standing by the bed. All she could see was her son, flat, helpless, pale, enveloped in gauze blankets. His right cheek was covered with white tape, his head looked like the Invisible Man, and there were bandages on both his arms.

Morgan was surprised that Ashton's eyes were closed. For some reason, in the hundred times she had imagined this scene in her mind, he had looked up and his eyes showed that he recognized her and reassured her, Mom, I'm okay. But his eyes were closed. Of course.

Morgan reached out tentatively, not sure where it would be safe to touch him. She chose a spot on his chest, just above his heart, to gently lay her hand, just as she used to do when he and Meredith were tiny babies, checking to see if they were still breathing.

"Oh my god." She couldn't hold back the tears.

"Shhhh," came Dowd's voice from the other side of the bed. "The nurses said that even though he's unconscious he may be able to hear us."

She'd been there five minutes, their son was broken into pieces, and Dowd had already found a reason to reprimand her.

"I'm sorry," Morgan whispered.

Through her misted vision, Dowd looked a little older, a little thinner than the last time she'd seen him, and his hair had sprouted more gray. He gazed down at Ashton, his face strained with worry, and Morgan was grateful he was there, grateful he was at least the kind of father who would rush to his son's bedside. Morgan wanted to walk over and fall into him, lean her head on his shoulder, be stroked and comforted. No, she wanted him to be the one to walk around the bed to her side, and gather her up in his arms. But she didn't and he didn't, and the moment passed.

"How is he?" Morgan wasn't sure whom to ask. If Ashton could hear, then should she ask him instead? With Dowd there, she was so afraid of doing the wrong thing.

"No change," Dowd said. "But everything's stable, and he is going to be fine."

"I want to know what happened," Morgan said.

"We can talk later," Dowd said. "I think what's important now, Mom, is that you talk to your son."

"Hey, sweetie," Morgan said to Ashton's expressionless face. "It's Mom. I'm here, and you're going to be fine. I'm here, and I am going to stay right here." She took his hand and threaded her fingers through his limp ones. "It's okay, it's okay."

Morgan was relieved when Dowd left the room. Then she could be with her son in her own way and say whatever she wanted to say, without Dowd as an audience. She told Ashton about her flight and Kate being there and that Meredith sent her love and was thinking about coming out, but she'd told her to wait until he got home. Which would be soon. She laid her forehead on the edge of the bed and cried softly. She didn't know what to do. She pleaded with the Universe to wake up her son.

Where was the doctor? Morgan needed someone to tell her that her that her son wasn't going to die. Or have brain damage. That he would surf again. She imagined him being his old self, laughing, walking. She had always feared the surfing, secretly wishing he would quit and find a sport that was safer. Now, more than anything in the world, she wanted Ashton to open his eyes and grab his board and paddle out and catch the biggest, scariest wave in the ocean.

When Morgan looked up, Dowd was back, but he didn't say anything about her crying. Then he motioned her to come outside the room. With him was a man who appeared to be in his early forties. Of course, when a woman passed fifty, all the men were in their early forties.

"Morgan, this is Sergeant Jeff Peterson," Dowd said.

She shook his hand. "Sure, I talked to you on the telephone."

Bastard, Morgan thought. *You accused my son of being a drug head.*

Sgt. Peterson was light complexioned and appeared to be turning gray gradually and evenly throughout his straightish, shortish hair. His light brown mustache almost matched his sport coat. Morgan thought briefly that the facial hair was a new addition, probably an experiment—partly because he reached up and touched it a lot, and also, he really didn't look that good in a mustache.

"Ms. Fay," he said. "Can I talk to you for a minute?"

Peterson asked if she had remembered anything more about Half Moon Bay—for example, if Ashton had told her why he was going there.

"No," Morgan said. "As I told you, I didn't know he was there." She looked at Dowd. He shrugged agreement.

"What about Faiza?" Morgan asked Dowd. "Has she been here?"

"No," Dowd said. "Nothing from her."

Peterson broke in. "My officers checked out your son's apartment and also located Ms. Salah's dormitory room. We have not found her. We did talk with a young woman in the dorm, a friend of Ms. Salah's, who said she was living with your son but still used the dorm room as, well, sort of headquarters."

"I knew that," Morgan said. Her tone was hostile, and she knew it.

"Ms. Fay," Peterson said. "If I offended you by my questions about the drugs, well, I have to ask those questions."

"I just don't think you believe me," Morgan said. "I know my son and I know what you're thinking. That I'm one of those doting mothers, blind to her son's misdeeds."

"I'm not concluding anything," Peterson said. "We're just trying to find out everything we can, to catch who did this to him. And it will help to figure why he was in Half Moon Bay."

"I told you, probably to go surfing."

"Morgan, calm down," Dowd said. "He's just doing his job."

She clenched her teeth and sucked in a deep breath through her nose. She wanted to jump up and grab Dowd's neck in her jaws, and then jerk it around with her teeth like a mad wolf would do.

"You seemed surprised that Ms. Salah has not come to the hospital," Peterson said, half statement, half question.

"Yeah. They are in love. Inseparable. Probably getting married," Morgan said. "He's hurt; she would be at his side."

"Hmm," Peterson said. "Well, we'll keep asking at the dorm when more of the girls get back from classes."

"You can find me, us, here," Dowd told Peterson. "Or you can call my cellphone." He gave Peterson a business card.

"Mr., uh, Fay?" Peterson asked.

"No, she's Fay. I'm Rivers. Dowd Rivers."

"I'll be in touch Mr. Rivers. Ms. Fay."

CHAPTER FIVE

Morgan returned to her chair on the side of Ashton's bed, and Dowd pulled one up on the other side. Actually, she and Dowd were not supposed to be in Ashton's room except during prescribed visiting periods. But Dowd had talked someone into bending the rules. Still had his ability to talk anyone into anything.

They had met when she was working for a small weekly newspaper in Indianapolis and he was running for city council, his first election. She was assigned to interview him, and was instantly attracted to him. Midwestern guys had a way of being handsome that was just more wholesome than other men—the kind of salt-of-the-earth looks that remind you of the cute boy you sat next to in your favorite grade. In Morgan's case, it was the sixth. To match his good looks, Dowd had personality. Not the kind of celebrity palaver you'd expect from a politician. Dowd seemed real.

Much later she would find out that he was real, but not as she had expected. Dowd was all personality. A big personality that walked. That's all he was. Or all anyone was ever going to know about.

His name was perfect for elected office—the kind of name that you'd vote for just because you like the sound of it. Dowd Rivers. Dowd Rivers. She used to chant his name to herself when she was driving. He didn't call her until after the election. If he'd tried to date her before that, it could have been considered a conflict of interest, and Dowd played strictly by the rules.

The issue came up again a year later, when they got

married. Dowd felt it was detrimental to his political career for Morgan to be a member of the press. After all, he said, objectivity would be impossible for her to maintain, not to mention all the other opportunities for conflict of interest. Anyway, she was going to be the wife of a politician, maybe even a mother one day. What more could she want? This was in the sixties, just a few years after Jackie Kennedy talked to *Meet the Press* about being married to a senator. "If you love your husband," the nation's princess said, "the sacrifices are a joy."

One of the sacrifices, Morgan soon found out, was her name. One evening Dowd and she attended a party fundraiser, along with several dozen candidates for various offices. All of the candidates were men; all of the spouses were women. Everyone wore nametags. The men's gave their names and the office they were seeking. The women were identified by their husbands. Her nametag read: Mrs. Dowd Rivers (Morgan).

"My name is in parentheses!" she told Dowd, in a whispered shout.

"It's just the way they printed them, so people will know you're with me," he said.

Morgan put her face right up to his and put her palms on his cheeks. "Yes, Dowd, but my name is in par-en-the-sees."

He didn't get it. He never got it. He never got that it wasn't just her name. It was a whole self that was being bracketed beneath him. And she never felt the joy in that sacrifice. (Neither, she would bet, did Jackie, who over the years seemed to outgrow all that bullshit.)

Eventually Dowd left office and became a political consultant, but it was too late. Morgan had already spent too long as a secondary appendage, and it would take years to realize how deeply, irreparably angry she was. When Dowd and she were divorced, she dropped the Rivers and took her middle name as her last. It was her first step toward taking herself out of parentheses.

*　　　　　*　　　　　*

Morgan had fallen asleep sitting up in the chair with her

head against Ashton's bandaged shoulder. When she opened her eyes, Dowd was staring at her.

"You look good," he said. "I mean, I know you've been traveling all day and you're tired and all that, but you still look good."

"Thanks," she said. "So do you."

"For an old geezo, huh?"

"I didn't say that."

"Well, I am getting there," he said, patting his paunch and tugging at a hunk of gray hair. Dowd's self-effacing comments were a sort of a preemptory strike. Say it before anyone else thinks it. Also, then he appeared to be humble. Which maybe he was, and maybe he wasn't. No one would ever know.

"What time did the doctor say he'd be back in?" Morgan changed the subject.

"As I told you before, it'll be late this afternoon." Still reminding her when she should have already known something.

There was a muffled ring, and Dowd pulled his cellphone from his pants pocket.

"Dowd Rivers. Oh, hello Sergeant." Dowd listened, glancing over at Morgan as he nodded.

"What?" Morgan said.

"The detectives have found some more information."

"What, Dowd?"

"There's a little beach hotel in Half Moon Bay. It's called the Shore House. Ashton was there for the weekend. He checked in two nights ago. With a young woman."

"Faiza?"

"I'm sure. The description matches," Dowd said. "The detectives are searching the room where they stayed."

"So they spent the weekend there together," Morgan said.

"That's what it looks like. Nothing unusual about that." Dowd nodded, eyeing Morgan. "Yes, Sergeant, she's right here." He handed her the phone.

Sgt. Peterson asked Morgan to tell him everything she

could remember about Faiza.

*   *   *

"I only met Faiza once," Morgan began. "Last Christmas, when Ashton brought her home for a week."

Morgan remembered Ashton standing with his arm encircling Faiza, with the look on his face that he used to get when he stood on the beach, surfboard under his arm, anticipating the plunge into a four-foot swell, the best waves of the year. Clearly her presence in his life took him to that place inside him that was pure joy. And one day, during the week they were visiting, Morgan passed by the kitchen door and caught sight of them standing next to the open refrigerator, gazing into each other's eyes. Faiza reached up and stroked Ashton's cheek, tenderly, seeing him with her fingertips, as if she were touching him for the first time.

Morgan liked Faiza. She was delightful to be around. She had a playful sense of humor, a light, melodious accent, and a thoughtful, unhurried approach when the conversation turned serious. On the outside she projected a quiet, rocksteady independence that seemed older than her twenty-one years. On the inside, Morgan sensed a gentle, unfettered spirit, with a childlike innocence and perhaps also vulnerability.

In the year since Ashton had met her, the two had spent many hours talking about who they each were and where they'd been. Her country mystified him, Ashton told his mom. It was a place where the few rights and privileges women did have were meted out at the whim or the graciousness of the men who controlled the family, and as far as Ashton was concerned, the men who owned the women. Faiza had tried to explain that there were many things he simply didn't understand.

"This is the way I have grown up," she said. "The rules we live by, they are the will of Allah."

He had asked, "But what if you don't agree with the rules? What if you want to live a different way?"

"It is difficult," Faiza said. "Sometimes I feel very torn.

Though I want to honor my faith and my country, inside me there has always been this . . . second person."

When she was growing up, life in the West was a fantasy game she played with her girlfriends. For as long as she could remember, Faiza said, she and her two best friends, quietly secreted in Faiza's room, would pretend to be English or French or American women. They acted out shopping trips in enormous malls, buying sheer blouses and long dangling earrings and tight jeans and tall cowboy boots, and then pretended to dress for dates with handsome young men to big outdoor parties with a band playing loud music. They danced with many other guys too, their long black hair cascading down their back, brushing the see-through blouses and making the young men crazy with desire. Then, maybe, after they tired of dancing, they left behind the party and the men, and jumped into their convertible and sped away, three women scandalously alone.

In Saudi Arabia women could not drive cars, nor could they go out without being accompanied by a male relative. And although women adorned themselves in private—the rich ones had frilly clothes and jewelry—no one besides family members and women friends ever saw anything but black.

When Faiza reached puberty, she could no longer go out in public without covering herself from head to toe. Uncovered women could be beaten or arrested by the religious police. Faiza kept one such abaya in her closet, in case she needed to travel back home, and once, only once, she took it out to show Ashton. Disappearing under the heavy black cloak, she looked like a big black thimble. He could not see her face at all behind the mesh veil, which acted like a two-way mirror. She could see out but no one could see in.

Ashton told his mom that talking to Faiza in her abaya that day was like talking to someone at a Halloween party, but with no eyeholes in the mask. Her soft voice sounded disembodied, coming from somewhere behind the dark curtain. He might have chuckled, but despite her wonderful sense of humor, dressing up in the heavy black cloak wasn't play, and he promised himself he'd never ask her to do it again. He had this odd feeling that asking her to put on the hood and parade around was like asking an American woman to take her clothes off and do the same.

Faiza's games with her best friends easily prepared her for the incredible freedoms accorded women in the U.S. Informal, yet studious, she felt instantly at home in jeans, loose sweaters, and running shoes, which was what she was wearing the day she slid into a seat beside him on the first day of engineering class.

"I'm a lucky one," she said. Her father adored her. After her mother died, when Faiza was just seven, her father found his comfort and joy in his only child. He did not remarry, not even one wife, let alone the many wives he would be entitled to acquire, and indeed was expected to, considering his first did not produce a son.

Lutfi was a very liberal Muslim, increasingly at odds with the country's trend toward radical fundamentalism. He thought that his people were headed back into the Dark Ages and wanted nothing to do with the zealously strict interpretations of the Koran that would only shrink the cultural prison his only daughter was born into. He possessed enough money to share his visions with Faiza. While education was officially encouraged for girls and women, they could only get advanced education if their fathers said yes or, if married, their husbands gave permission.

Lutfi urged Faiza to get as much education as was available to her, and she attended a pricey, private girls' school in Jeddah, where she studied languages mostly, but also took computer classes, science, dressmaking, cooking, and gym—curricula designed to prepare girls for their roles as homemakers and mothers. Only a handful of the universities accepted women, and in the ones that did, female students could not use the library and were taught via closed-circuit television to segregate them from the men. Talks with male professors were done via telephone so the women would not be seen by males who were not family members.

Through her own independent reading, Faiza became fascinated with geology and the environment—two subjects that, if she were a man, she could have studied in preparation for a good job in Saudi Arabia's petroleum industry. But the universities that offered these subjects were closed to women. Faiza applied for a special two-year program of graduate study in environmental engineering at San Francisco State University.

When she was accepted, her father said yes. But the rest of the family and many friends were horrified and furious. How could he send his beloved daughter to the moral and religious wasteland of the United States? Unchaperoned and unveiled in America, Faiza would be ruined, and as ruined goods, Lutfi would never be able to find his daughter a husband when she returned.

Still, he was her father and he could do anything he wanted. And what he wanted, more than anything, was to help Faiza experience her full potential in a fairer place. So he arranged for her to live with the uncle and aunt of a close friend, who had resettled in California many years before but still maintained a Muslim household and the sacred traditions of the faith. Thus, her father created a cover that fended off some of the hostility. He was wise enough to know that when she came back, if she ever did, she could never truly return, that is, live a typical woman's life confined inside a house as some man's shrouded property.

What he was not wise enough to take into account was that he would not be around always to help keep those options open and to protect her.

CHAPTER SIX

The birth of her daughter and son were the happiest days of Morgan's life. She didn't think anything would ever top that. But there was something better, she found out. It was when one was re-born.

Ashton opened his eyes just before daybreak the next morning. Throughout the night, Dowd and Morgan had been taking turns by the bedside while the other napped in the waiting room. Kate had appropriated a stack of the thin, white loose-weave blankets that hospitals use to cover everyone, and they folded them for pillows and curled up on two short, narrow, stiff couches.

What's with hospital waiting rooms? Morgan thought. With the number of people who probably spent the night in those rooms, you'd think it would occur to someone to get softer sofas. She told Kate to go on home, but Kate wouldn't think of it. She said she was staying until Ashton woke up.

Both parents were in the room when Ashton looked up, first at Morgan, then Dowd, as if he was trying to place them, like, I know I've met you before; just give me a minute. His eyes were unexpectedly brilliant and blue, the only part of his body that wasn't wounded.

"Hi, kid," Dowd said.

"It's us," Morgan said. "We're here. You're okay. You're in a hospital. You're okay."

She squeezed his hand and thought she felt his fingers stir slightly. Dowd pushed the call button, and within a few seconds a nurse appeared at the door.

"He's awake," they said in unison.

Ashton still looked confused as the nurse leaned over him, checking the monitors, touching his face and examining his eyes.

"Hey, Rip Van Winkle," the nurse said. "Welcome back." She announced that Ashton was doing fine and the doctor would come by within the hour.

Speaking softly, Morgan gave Ashton the barest of details, avoiding a litany of his injuries. Then she stopped, and they waited. *Say something, please say something.* His lips had dry white patches on them, and Morgan dabbed them with a damp washrag. He took a deep breath and tried weakly to suck moisture from the cloth.

"Faiza," he said. "Where's Faiza?"

Dowd and Morgan looked at each other. They were hoping Ashton would tell them. "It's all going to be okay, son," he said.

"Where is she?"

"Ash, I'm sure she's on her way," Morgan said. That wasn't a lie. As soon as she found out, she would come, of course. "Are you in pain?" she asked.

"Not that I know of," he said, with the tiniest smile.

And then, laughing and sobbing and then laughing again, Morgan whispered thank you thank you thank you over and over again to no one in particular.

*   *   *

Allen Green, MD was probably in his mid-sixties, crisp yet personable, but when he talked to the pair, he only looked at Dowd. Even when Morgan asked the question. For example, she wanted to know what type of surgery was performed on Ashton.

"To relieve the pressure against the brain," he answered, to Dowd. "Concussions can cause fluid to build up between the brain and the cranium. It's called subdural hematoma. Not good. It puts pressure on the brain. In your son's case it was on the right side. We made two, what are called 'burr holes' in the skull."

"Holes? You drilled holes in his head?" Morgan said, shocked.

Dowd shot her a look that said she was being too confrontational. What did it matter if she was confrontational? Morgan thought. The guy wouldn't look at her anyway.

"It's a very normal procedure, not much risk," said Dr. Green. "While we had him in the OR, under anesthetic, the orthopedic surgeon came in and repaired the leg. You'll talk to him, too, of course, but basically it was a fracture of the femur." Green turned to Morgan and added, "That's the big bone above the knee."

"Oh, god, will it heal okay? He's a surfer, Dr. Green," Morgan said.

"I'd say we have a lot more to worry about than whether he can go surfing, Morgan," Dowd said. He turned to the doctor. "What about the concussion? He seems confused."

"That's normal for now," said Green. "There can be a period of amnesia after this kind of trauma. Ordinarily, what's lost is the short-term memory, the hours or days right before the injury. The long-term memory is usually okay. Everything will probably come back within a day or so. However," he added, "sometimes the events immediately preceding the trauma are permanently lost."

"You mean he might not ever remember what happened to him?" asked Morgan.

"That's possible," the doctor told Dowd. "We'll just have to wait and see."

They learned that Ashton had a lot of bruises and cuts that would heal without complication, and that he had no serious internal injuries beyond the fact that everything inside was shaken up, probably from a fall of some kind. There would be a lot of physical rehabilitation ahead, complicated by the fact that he had a dislocated shoulder. The broken leg would require him to walk on crutches for a time, and the dislocated shoulder prevented that. So for a while, Ashton would be in a wheelchair.

"He's going to hate that," Morgan said to Dowd.

"Look, he's alive," Dowd said. "We should be grateful."

Like she wasn't grateful.

*   *   *

Later that morning, Jeff Peterson showed up and wanted to talk with Ashton. By then Ashton was much more coherent, eating ice chips and asking for real food. Every once in a while he would look up toward the ceiling and squint his eyes, concentrating, as if he was trying to pull something out of the air above him.

"Mom, it's like trying to remember a dream," he said slowly, his lips still dry and swollen. "You know how you wake up and you know you've been dreaming and you have these fragments floating around, and you try to grab them but you can't quite get hold of them?"

"I know," Morgan said. "Just relax. Don't try so hard. It will come."

When Ashton found out how long he had been unconscious, his concern for Faiza escalated. He couldn't understand why she wasn't there with him. He insisted on talking with Sgt. Peterson. Because it was a police investigation, and because Ashton was scheduled to be moved out of intensive care into a regular room, the nurses let the detective come in.

"Son, do you remember spending the weekend with Faiza at the Shore House?" Peterson asked. His tone was gentle and unhurried.

"Shore House? The hotel on the beach?"

"Yes, it's white. With yellow trim. In Half Moon Bay," Peterson said.

Ashton placed a bandaged arm on the top of his head, as if to physically press it into service. "I remember making reservations. But that's all. I don't remember going there."

"You were there," Peterson ventured. "With Faiza?"

"If I was with someone, that's who it would be," he said. "God, this is so weird. Trying to guess my own actions."

"Son, did someone beat you up?" Peterson asked.

"Obviously." Ashton grinned. "Maybe they pushed me off a building. Is there a highrise nearby?"

Everyone laughed. That felt good.

Then Ashton's face turned serious, stricken with the thought. "If I was with Faiza, and I've been beat up, then what's happened to her?"

"We don't know, son," the detective said. "We have not been able to locate her."

"Oh god," Ashton said.

"Son, do you have any idea who would want to harm you?"

"No. No way."

"Did you have a lot of money with you?" Peterson asked.

"Hell, I don't even know where I was, let alone what I had," Ashton said.

Peterson fidgeted with his beard. Preparing to ask about the drugs, no doubt, thought Morgan. But he didn't. Morgan found out later that a blood test had showed no drugs or alcohol anywhere near Ashton's body. *Told you so, asshole.*

"Faiza, my god, where are you?" Ashton moaned, his eyes streaked with anguish. He looked up at his mother. "Maybe I'll never remember, Mom. Maybe I'll never know what happened. And if I don't . . . maybe she's hurt. Or in danger. Or . . ."

"They're going to find her," Morgan said. "And your memory is going to come back. It's all going to be okay." Morgan wasn't sure of any of that, but she lied like a mother.

*   *   *

Morgan and Dowd joined Peterson outside the room.

"What else have the police learned?" Dowd asked Peterson.

"Not much. We're questioning people in the area, hoping to find a witness. There were clearly occupants in the hotel room, and two suitcases. I'm sure it's Ashton's and Faiza's stuff but I'd like one of you to identify your son's belongings at some point. Just to verify."

"What about the other stuff?"

"It's definitely hers," Peterson said. "Her name is on the bag. Also, there was a room service cart with untouched breakfast food. And something else I didn't mention yet to your son."

"What?" Dowd and Morgan said in unison.

"A rag, that was dried but clearly had been soaked with some chemical. We're testing it, but from the smell of it, I think it's ether."

"Ether? Like the anesthetic?" Dowd said.

"Yes sir," said Peterson. "I've asked the hospital lab to check Ashton's blood sample. For traces of the same."

"And then what?" Morgan asked.

"I'll ask Ashton about it."

Morgan read something in Peterson's voice. "Wait a minute," she said. "You're thinking they used ether for some kinky drug high or something? Brother, you don't ever quit, do you?"

"You'd better hope I don't quit," Peterson shot back.

"Sorry," Dowd said, apologizing for her.

"Actually, ma'am," Peterson said, regaining a respectful tone, "my theory is more along other lines."

"What lines?"

"Well, from the looks of things," he said, "I think we might be dealing with a kidnapping."

CHAPTER SEVEN

Morgan and Dowd had taken the two chairs and Kate was sitting on the bed when Ashton was moved into his new room. Poles with two IV bags dangled from the gurney, but the monitors were gone. He would be allowed to eat, sensibly, the nurse said. There was still a lot of recovery ahead.

Kate moved aside while the nurse settled Ashton in his new adjustable bed.

"Hi, Aunt Kate," he said with a weak smile.

"Hey, Ash," she said. "I hope you're gonna say something like, 'You should have seen the other guy.'"

"Wish I could," Ashton said. "But I didn't even see the other guy."

"You'll remember. And then I'm organizing a posse," Kate said. "But first I'm taking food orders. Kind of like Meals on Wheels."

Ashton said what he really wanted was some Tom Yum Goong soup. "But I doubt if they have any Thai stuff here."

"The kid's got good taste," Kate said with a wink at Morgan and Dowd. "But I'll find some."

"I'll come with you," Morgan said. She stood to kiss Ashton and surreptitiously feel his forehead, Mom-style. No fever.

"Would you bring some other dishes?" Dowd asked, unfolding his wallet.

"We'll get a feast for four," Kate said, waving away the money.

It felt good to get out of the hospital for a while. Morgan was exhausted and hungry for something, anything, that resembled a fresh food or vegetable. The hospital vending machines contained nothing but candy bars and potato chips, and the food in the cafeteria was either a fried meat or a white carbohydrate. Hadn't these people ever heard of granola? Or green beans? Whole wheat bread?

The nearest Thai restaurant was twenty miles away, so there was plenty time to bring Kate up to date and speculate on what might have happened.

"Kidnapping?" Kate was shocked. "Does she have a rich family or something?"

"Her family is halfway around the world," Morgan said. "Except for this poor little old aunt and uncle."

"What about her parents?" Kate wanted to know.

"Both her parents are dead."

Morgan explained that Faiza's father, Lutfi, had died about six months before. She reported what Ashton had told her at the time:

Lutfi had summoned Faiza back home. He was sick, he told her, and although she was not to worry, it was urgent that he speak with her. She had skipped a week of classes and set out for the grueling trip to Saudi Arabia.

"I may have to stay longer," she told Ashton somberly, as they said goodbye in the San Francisco airport terminal. "What if he is dying?" Tears gathered at the edges of her dark eyes.

Ashton didn't answer, just held her closer. As she made her way in the line crowding toward the gate, he strained to watch her for as long as possible. The very last thing he saw was her bright green L.L. Bean backpack in which she carried her schoolbooks and her abaya, carefully folded and rolled into a small bundle, because she would have to put it on before getting off the plane in Dhahran. A few strands of her long dark hair nested on the top of the backpack.

Ashton waited in the terminal, watching the plane being pushed from the tarmac, listening for the whine of its engines, gazing after it as it taxied and took off. He stayed until the plane became a speck in the sky and then completely disappeared beyond the wispy ceiling of clouds. When he moved to leave, he realized he had been standing with his nose literally pressed against the glass, like he used to do when he was kid. There was a little frost mark where his breath had come out.

The week without Faiza was torture. Most of the time he felt almost lightheaded, he was so disoriented without her. He dove for the phone whenever it rang, knowing she would not be able to call but hoping anyway. One voice inside him would warn, *Get used to this, because she isn't coming back.* Another voice would reassure him, *She'll be back; people you love this much don't go away.*

And then, before the week was barely up, Faiza came back. Her father had insisted that this was her only chance to get out again. Once Lutfi died, Faiza's guardianship would fall to his older brother, Hatim, who in the past ten years had become a raging fundamentalist, joining with those who called for a return to a former time. Hatim disapproved of Faiza's living in America. He thought she should have been married years ago, and he was furious at what he called her father's total defiance of the Koran. He thought Faiza should be punished.

Go, her father told her. Now. She protested. He was going to die without her presence. Go, he said. This is my dying wish and you must obey. It was the first time in her whole life she ever remembered hearing the word obey. Lutfi held her in his arms, and as she wrapped hers around his frail, sick torso, she could feel the outline of his bones.

Moments before Faiza turned to board the plane, her father pressed a small gray box into her hand. Keep this very safe, he said, and use it to comfort yourself and secure your freedom and begin your life with your young man. As soon as the plane leveled off, Faiza got out of her seat and locked herself in a bathroom, where she carefully opened the box.

Inside was a ring with stones bigger than anything she had ever seen, even on the fingers of the richest women. Coiled under the ring was a necklace of brilliant diamonds, and nested in the coil, three stones: one a deep red, one sea blue, one green. Even uncut, they glistened in the dim light of the lavatory. Faiza knew little about jewelry, and while she could see the beauty of these pieces, she couldn't have guessed their value. But she knew her father. And she knew this gift probably represented all the money he had in the world. This was her dowry.

Ashton helped Faiza rent a safe deposit box, but she insisted he be added as a signatory, with a key of his own. She didn't tell her aunt and uncle about the jewelry. When she came to live with them, she had found them to be much older than her father had realized, and they were both quite fragile. Faiza was more often the one with the role of caregiver, shopping and cooking whenever she could.

After one semester, her uncle could no longer drive her the ten miles to school. His driving ability had deteriorated so badly that one day he was stopped for drunken driving. The police officer told him, rather rudely, to give up his license. Faiza moved into a dormitory on campus. At least twice a week she took the bus to their home to check on them and to cook a couple of meals for them to store in the refrigerator. They nibbled like little wrinkled mice, but if left to their own devices they ate nothing but canned soup and toast.

Ashton marveled at Faiza's resourcefulness. It wasn't as though life was a hardship, but it was dramatically different than anything she had known. Yet she met every new change gracefully. From a culture where her future would likely be contained within the walls of her own home, and if she was allowed to participate in the world, it would be shaded by the dark veil, Faiza had walked into the light and almost effortlessly donned her independence.

Once, when Ashton pointed this out, she had laughed and said, "One does not have to learn how to be free."

*   *   *

Morgan's mouth was watering from the pungent smell of curry and ginger, lemongrass and garlic filling Kate's little black Eclipse as they drove back into the hospital parking lot.

"I can't imagine anyone wanting to harm Faiza," Kate said. "Such a sweet, good spirit." Morgan nodded. "All I know is that her relationship with her family in Saudi was not good. Ashton told me she worried about it a lot."

"Worried about what?"

"I don't know exactly," Morgan said. "He just said that she was afraid of them."

CHAPTER EIGHT

"Kate, how long can you stay?" Morgan asked. They were unfolding the futon in Ashton's living room. It smelled dusty, and Morgan wanted to take it outside and shake it. But the hour was too late and they were tired.

The two had left the hospital after Ashton drifted off to sleep. Dowd was planning to stay there for another night, and if Ashton continued to improve, return to Indiana the next day. He was due in a brainstorming session with the governor that afternoon.

The living room was sparsely furnished: a futon, assorted bookcases, television, stereo, speakers, and a desk smothered in books and papers. It looked like a mess, but an Ashton mess. There was a scheme to the piles, and he could tell you exactly where to find every scrap, every receipt, every sticky note.

One corner of the desk, next to the computer, held a snapshot in a plastic frame of Ashton and Faiza on the Golden Gate Bridge, arms around each other, smiling. In the space meant to be a dining area, five surfboards of different lengths and widths were lined up against the wall, their undersides streaked with caked wax. On the pointed tip of one board hung a light yellow sweater, a woman's.

"I'll stay as long as you need me," Kate said, tucking in a green plaid sheet Morgan had found in the closet. On top, they spread another one, different color, different print.

The room got very quiet. Morgan dug into her bag for a candle, lit it, turned out the lights, and they each poured another glass of wine. The candlelight shimmered noiselessly on the dark walls. The room suddenly felt safe, protected somehow from the rest of the world, as if they were wrapped up in a big, soft grandmother-crafted afghan, crocheted from lifelong bonds of friendship.

*   *   *

Since college, whenever Kate, Linnie, and Morgan got together, they always lit candles, making wishes and promises and pledges. Shortly before twelve o'clock on the night before graduation, they had met in Morgan's room. The June moon was full, and its silvery luminousness splayed in, like a waterfall of light through the window.

The three friends sat in a circle on the floor, bathed in the pool of moonlight. Linnie placed a large, rose-colored candle in the center of the circle. She struck a match, then passed the box to Morgan, who struck one and passed the box on to Kate. When all the matches were lit, they joined the three flames and touched them to the candle's wick.

"We light this candle together, signifying our vow to always stay together," Linnie said. "And if we are torn apart, may the candle flame light our way back to each other. So we do vow."

"So we do vow," Kate and Morgan said in unison.

But within a couple of years after graduation, that vow would be usurped by other vows. Vows made to men. Linnie had married Hal that summer, and while he finished law school, she became a nurse. Eventually they settled in Chicago and had one daughter, whom they named Caitlin Fay. Kate moved to California, where her father and mother had retired, and took a job flying charters. She also became a flight instructor and before long was promoted to chief pilot for the charter company. After a few years she was hired to fly corporate jets for a company that manufactured conveyor belts and other maintenance equipment for the airline industry.

One day, on a flight to one of the company's plants in Kansas City, Kate met Adrian, newly elected vice president, and married him two months later. She gave up flying and moved to Kansas City. They were married for ten years, then divorced.

Morgan had taken a job with a weekly newspaper in Indiana and met Dowd when she was covering elections and he was running for the city council. He lost the election, but won her, he liked to say. They married and settled in Indianapolis, and Morgan started having babies.

The three friends stayed in touch, and though their contact was sporadic and unpredictable, they somehow managed to stay abreast of the heart and soul of each others' lives. In college they had shared everything, told each other things they had never told anyone before. In the eyes of the world, they were all at the top of their game. The right sorority, good grades, cute and witty and charming and lots of dates.

The first time Morgan admitted to her friends that she felt something was missing, she was embarrassed. It seemed ungrateful, somehow. She had grown up being told how lucky she was. Why wasn't she feeling that? What was wrong with her? Kate said that the last time she remembered really feeling happy, deep down content, was when she was seven years old.

"I used to love to go to this park. I was allowed to go there alone, because it was next to my house," Kate said. "I'd get on the swings and pump and pump, until I was soaring. And sometimes if I got going real high, my toes would brush the branches of this big droopy willow tree. And as I'd swoop though the air, I'd get this feeling like I was the only person in the world, and it was okay. Like I knew who I was. And what I was, was everything."

"I don't think I've ever felt that way," Linnie said.

"I remember once," Morgan said. "I was four, and I took my little orange wagon and walked all the way around the block. I got in big trouble. I wasn't supposed to leave the yard."

"You soloed a wagon!" Kate laughed. "That was a gutsy thing to do."

"Funny thing," Morgan said. "I wasn't scared."

When, they wondered, did they start feeling the boundaries that would later define their lives? A girl in this world. A young woman in this world. When did they notice it was scary? Dangerous. You are limited. You can't do anything you want.

"When I played doctor with my brothers," Linnie said, "I was always the nurse. They wouldn't ever let me be the doctor. But you know what? I'm not sure I ever asked. And once, when we were having a barbecue, there weren't enough hamburgers to go around. And my brothers got the hamburgers and I got a hot dog. I was so mad, but I didn't say a word. And to my parents and everyone else, it was so logical."

"The boys get the best meat," Kate said.

Such subtle incidents, so easy to pass off as trivial. But if they were meaningless, why did they remember them so vividly? Back when they were in college, women students still had curfews. They had to be in the dorms or sorority houses by 11 p.m. on weekdays and 1 a.m. on Saturdays. The guys could stay out all night if they wanted. Of course the three stayed out later whenever they wanted, by taking turns covering for each other and sneaking each other in through the kitchen entrance. And they thought themselves quite the rebels. But the mindset that deemed them, as females, an underclass, was pervasive and hardly dismantled by a few revolutionary acts.

Of the three, Kate was the one who ventured furthest out of the pattern, by becoming a pilot and penetrating a long-cherished male bastion. Still, the opportunities for her were meager. During the late sixties and early seventies, when Kate began her flying career, there were no more than a dozen women pilots hired by the big commercial carriers. None in the military. Like Kate, most women pilots contented themselves with teaching flying lessons or flying charters.

It would be many years before it was not an anomaly to see a woman in the cockpit of a major airline. The joke among male pilots was that when they heard a woman's voice on the radio, they would turn to each other and groan: "Another empty kitchen."

At their commencement ceremony, the keynote address was given by a portly, balding alum who had shinnied up the corporate ladder to become the CEO of a London bank at the age of forty-two. The theme of his speech was "Follow your dreams," and he would pause dramatically and then repeat the phrase in a kind of poetic cadence, leaning forward and peering into the sleepy, mostly hung-over audience sweltering inside black caps and robes in the searing noonday sun.

Kate was sitting in the row in front of Morgan. She turned back and whispered, "Follow your dream, my ass. The only dream we have at this moment is to not be cooked alive out here. And to have a cold beer."

Maybe Kate knew, at some level, that thirty years later there would be no more than a handful of women CEOs of great big banks. That particular dream was not an option.

Follow your dreams. What were their dreams? Kate's flying was a dream, but it, too, had limits. So as she stepped out into the world she was forced to restructure the dream. Different than following it. Neither Linnie nor Morgan remembered, as children, any particular burning desires, unquellable passions about something they just had to be when they grew up. Except perhaps the desire to get married, and that seemed more like a necessity than a dream.

To Morgan, it seemed that she and Linnie both sort of fell into life as it came along and then adjusted their dreams to fit what they already had. You got the hot dog; so that must be what you wanted. There was a certain truth in that, if one believes that you create your own reality. But that philosophy is an insult in a world of limited options. It was like being told to paint a landscape without any green, and later being asked why it looks so pale, when, after all, you had all the colors in the rainbow.

After she left nursing Linnie published a series of romance novels that were actually

rather successful within that genre. As a reporter, Morgan

thought that was impressive. But

Linnie said her books were "not real writing."

When Jack had died two years ago, Kate got so depressed Morgan worried that she'd never come out of the darkness. The couple had only been together three years, but Morgan guessed they were what are called soulmates, whatever that means. Kate said that the instant she met Jack she had this feeling that something—a search, a longing, a journey—was resolved. It wasn't a rush, she said. It was very quiet, very gentle. "Like I just stepped into a dream."

Being around Kate and Jack, it was as if he had always been there. Morgan remembered having that feeling when Meredith was born. She was placed in her mother's arms, they looked into each other's eyes, and it was as if Morgan had never not had a daughter.

Jack died from pancreatic cancer that moved swiftly and relentlessly. Afterward, Kate rented a small cabin in a woodsy area in northern California, a few hundred miles from where she and Jack had lived. She called it her "one womb cabin." She didn't take a television set, and although there was a telephone, she rarely answered it.

Occasionally Kate called Morgan and they talked, mostly she talked, about Jack. Things Jack did. Things Jack said. Things she did with Jack. Things she never got to do with Jack. And that's what she seemed to need to do. And she'd cry. Sometimes she'd nearly choke, and it sounded as if her sobbing was tearing her insides out. Never once, though, did Morgan hear Kate ask: Why? Morgan was not sure it even occurred to her. Her heart was too broken to ponder existential questions.

In the cabin, Kate read and fixed simple meals and wrote a few short newsy letters to her friends, mostly about what she was cooking or reading. She said she was going to give up flying and sold the Cessna 421 that she and Jack had bought and flown together up and down the California coast, and to

Mexico, Central America, and once to Sao Paulo, Brazil. She transacted the sale through a friend to a buyer she never met.

"But you love flying," Morgan protested when Kate called to tell her. Kate had flown since her ninth birthday, when her father, who flew fighters in World War II, took her up and let her fly his airplane. There had been a time years before when she had considered flying commercial, and she could have made it, easily. Morgan couldn't believe she was giving it up.

"I wouldn't be able to keep a plane in the air," Kate said.

"But that's now. Time will pass."

"I can't imagine flying without Jack," she said.

"But you flew for years before Jack. You don't need Jack to fly."

"I can't imagine the sky without Jack," she said. And then she changed the subject. "I'm learning how to bake bread."

Morgan couldn't help it. She burst out laughing "You? Bread?"

"Oh, Morgan. It's such a challenge. Yesterday I made this enormous loaf with whole-wheat flour and dark molasses and wheat germ. It was so heavy. I figured out how to bake it over the fire, in the fireplace. Like the early settlers."

"Are you going to live there forever?" Morgan asked.

"Nah," she said. "Just until I figure out how to do this bread on the fire. The loaf yesterday was kind of squishy in the middle."

Morgan knew then that Kate was going to be okay. She stayed in the woods a couple more months, and then she moved back to Santa Barbara and started Intrepid Travel.

Kate had a flair for planning trips for other people and an educated knack for finding the best flights. But then she hit some snags, mostly problems with airlines. For instance, it made her furious that airlines would not reserve seats in advance. The airlines expected people to pay for tickets up front, yet refused to guarantee a seat. Kate thought that was unfair. Not to mention, it really makes a difference what seat you have on an airplane, she said. You can get stuck, literally, in the middle seat of the back row where your seat won't recline and you can hardly bend forward to scratch your foot, god forbid you drop something. Kate wouldn't put her clients on such flights and told the airlines so.

Then, she boycotted—girlcotted as she called it—certain airlines that treated her clients with disrespect. She told the airlines what she was doing. They couldn't have cared less.

She did the same with car rental companies that promised one rate to the travel agent, then upped it with add-ons and special conditions when the client arrived at the airport to pick up the car. Now, Kate was down to about two airlines and four car rental companies that she thought were ethical. This limited her options when planning a trip for someone. Intrepid Travel, which had become more of a cause than a company, was diminishing.

*   *   *

Kate pulled back the sheets that they had spread on the futon. She wiggled inside, drew a pillow under her head, and looked over at the surfboards standing like soldiers against the wall.

"Remember in college, Morgan, how you listened to the Beach Boys all the time, day and night? Ever wonder if there was a connection, that you gave birth to a surfer son?"

"You mean, like the egg somehow heard the music or something?"

"Yeah," she said. "You knew 'em all."

"I'll bet I can still remember every word to every Beach Boys song," Morgan said. She blew out the candle and the room settled into darkness.

"Yeah?" Kate challenged. "'Surfin Safari.'"

In a loud whisper, Morgan started to sing. "Let's go surfin' now, everybody's learning how, come on and safari with me . . . "

"Little surfer . . . "

"Little one, makes my heart come all undone. . . "

"Do you love me, do you surfer girl?"

"Ooo waah little surfer girl." Kate howled. "I get around!"

"I'm gettin' bored drivin' up and down the same ole strip, gonna find a new place where the kids are hip . . . "

"My buddies and me we're getting real well known, all the bad guys know us and they leave us alone, I get arou . . ."

Morgan stopped. Suddenly she started to cry.

And then Kate's arms were around her and she slumped into them, her body quaking with sobs.

CHAPTER NINE

Early the next morning Dowd called from the hospital to say that Ashton was beginning to remember.

Morgan and Kate dressed quickly and jumped into the car. They stopped at a fast food drive-in window and bought four egg sandwiches—two extra, just in case Ashton wanted to eat. Dowd wouldn't touch the stuff. They ate on their laps as Kate drove. When they walked into his room, Dowd stood up to greet them.

"Hi, Mom; hi, Aunt Kate," Ashton said. His voice was not perky by any means, but certainly had more energy than the night before. His bed was cranked up into an almost sitting position.

"Are you okay?" Morgan leaned over and kissed his cheek. His face was still pale, but a little weak color was returning to his cheeks.

"Better," he said. "But you know, Mom, there wasn't any place to go but up."

"Don't remind me," Morgan said. "It's so good to have you back. Are you in pain?"

"I feel like I've been run over by a truck," he said. "But they gave me a lot of pain stuff. They really have good dope here."

"Stop it," Morgan said, pretending to pummel his head. "I told that detective that you never touch the stuff."

"He doesn't," Dowd said seriously.

Ashton rolled his eyes. "She was just joking, Dad."

"He said he had some dreams," Dowd told the women. "Memories."

Kate and Morgan pulled chairs closer to the bed.

Ashton began slowly, pausing for shallow breaths. It obviously hurt him to breathe.

"I took Faiza to Half Moon Bay for the weekend," he began. "I'm sure of that. It was, well, a celebration. Of our . . . we got engaged. I asked Faiza to marry me."

"Oh. Wow," Morgan said.

"We were going to call you, both of you," he said. "Later. Maybe even during the weekend. I can't remember."

"Did you go surfing?" Morgan asked.

"Yeah," Ashton said. "I wasn't going to. Really. This was going to be our time, just the two of us. But Faiza insisted. Especially when we saw how good the waves were. Well, when I saw how good the waves were. So I went. Once is all I can remember. She sat on the beach and watched. She said she loved it."

"What else?"

"We went out to dinner down the road to this little Italian restaurant. Real nice. Small. Candles. And then we came back and . . . " Ashton stopped and closed his eyes.

"Can't you remember the rest?" Morgan asked.

"I remember," Ashton said, with a weak smile. "I just don't want to talk about that part. To you guys."

Joking, laughing together again. It was such a relief. Like a kid falling backwards into a pile of autumn leaves when, for that moment, everything in the whole world is perfectly fine.

"Trouble is," Ashton said, "the night is coming back, but I can't remember the next morning. I know Faiza was with me all night. Because, wait, she woke me up once. She was having a nightmare."

"You're sure?" Morgan said.

"Yeah, yeah. Now I remember. She was afraid. Every time we talked about getting married, she'd get really scared. She was afraid of her family. That they would oppose it and try stop us." He nodded sharply. "That's why we were going to sneak off and elope," he went on. "That's why we were going to Half Moon Bay. And then we decided to wait. So we could tell you. Do it the right way. And get your blessing. Faiza really wanted that."

"Maybe you did get married and you forgot that part?" Morgan ventured.

"No," he said. "We decided not to elope, even before we left for the weekend."

"You don't remember anything about getting beaten up?" Dowd asked.

"No, dammit, no. God, I'm so worried about Faiza. If I could just remember."

"Were you maybe injured surfing?" Kate asked.

"He was found on the road, not near the water," Dowd said.

She defended her idea. "The road there goes right along the beach. I thought maybe he might have been hurt and come up to flag down a car."

What if he took Faiza surfing and they both were thrown against rocks? Morgan thought. And he tried to save her, and each time he dove down he was crushed against the rocks, and he dove and dove, wave after crashing wave, gasping and clutching for air, and then she was gone and, bruised and bloodied, he dragged himself up to the road crying *help help help*? Who wouldn't forget that?

Dowd took out his cellphone and dialed Jeff Peterson's number. The detective needed to hear this. Also, Dowd suggested, maybe he could ask some questions that would uncover more fragments of Ashton's shattered memory.

*   *   *

"Do you remember ordering room service?" asked Peterson, who arrived at the hospital a half hour after Dowd's call.

Ashton shook his head.

"Coffee, croissants, a fruit basket, some sweet rolls," Peterson offered, as if the details might trigger some fragments of the past two days.

"Faiza and I like to eat breakfast out—that is, when we

have the money. Anyway, I wouldn't order that," Ashton said. "Especially coffee. Faiza doesn't like American coffee, says it's too weak. And I don't drink it."

"What about the idea that he might have been hurt surfing?" Morgan asked Peterson.

"Nope," Peterson said. "He wasn't wearing bathing trunks. He wasn't even wearing street clothes." Peterson looked down at Ashton, sympathetically, as if he understood how painful it was to have a mystery, and maybe a tragedy, locked up inside you. "Son," he said. "All you were wearing was a pair of jockey shorts."

"Underwear?" Dowd said. "That's it? Whoever beat him up must have stolen his clothes."

"Isn't there anything anyone can do?" Ashton cried out in anguish. "Sergeant, can't they give me some drug or hypnotize me or something, so I can just remember? I just want to remember!"

"There may be more we can do," Peterson said. "It hasn't been that long, and some things have already come back. You need to relax and try to be patient and let the memories return in their own time."

"There isn't time." Ashton shook his head, wincing in pain. "Faiza. She's in danger. I know it. I just can't figure out how I know it. Or what *it* is."

"I have one idea," Peterson said. "But first, Ashton, I need to ask you something. And you have to tell me the truth. No matter how embarrassing, you have to be honest with me. Nothing will come of it."

"I don't understand," he said, "but ask me anything."

"Do you want your parents to leave the room?"

"No, dammit, just ask me!"

"Did you and your girlfriend ever experiment with drugs?" Peterson asked.

"No. No." Ashton said, vehemently.

"Like ether. For a high. Maybe just once."

"What the hell? No."

"There was a rag found on the floor of the room. It had been doused with ether," Peterson said.

"I have no idea," Ashton said.

"Not yours?" asked Peterson.

"Lay off, Sergeant," Morgan said. "He answered you." Dowd narrowed his eyes at Morgan and shook his head, the sign to tell her to hush.

"It's okay. I believe you," Peterson said.

"Geez." Ashton rolled his head to the side.

He is too injured for this, Morgan thought. *Too fragile to be put through the third degree. His insides are bruised and his bones are broken and his head has holes in it, for god's sake.*

Suddenly Morgan felt like a mother lion, teeth clenched, paws digging into the floor, ready to pounce and grab both of those men, the interrogator and the goody-two-shoes ex-husband, by the scruff of their pompous little necks and hurl them out of the den. *Stop it, stop it. Leave him alone.*

"Sorry," Peterson said finally. "But I have an idea that might jog some memory loose."

CHAPTER TEN

Morgan thought the return of Ashton's memory was like reconstructing a letter that had been torn into a hundred pieces. Taking one fragment and then finding one that matched it, and putting those two together to see what they said, and slowly, laboriously, building the whole message.

Peterson returned carrying a shallow metal bowl. In it, a thick square of gauze bandage, wet.

"The doctor said it would be safe for you to have just a quick sniff of this," the detective said. "Just enough to maybe remind you of something. It won't knock you out or anything."

"What's the point?" Morgan said.

"Just a hunch," Peterson said. He walked to the side of the bed. "Son, there is a picture coming together in my mind. I want to see if you can remember anything that might fit into my theory. You game?"

"Anything," Ashton said.

Peterson passed the bowl quickly back and forth under Ashton's nose. "Just a whiff," he cautioned.

"Be careful," Morgan said.

They could all smell the ether, even from where they stood. The pungent, acidic fumes were like genie vapors, snaking out of the bowl and right into their nostrils. Ashton lay back and closed his eyes. His breath became fast and shallow again. He began to cough and gasp for breath.

"That's enough," Morgan said.

"Stop it, stop it," he cried. Morgan grabbed a wet cloth and approached him but he pushed her hand away. "Get it away. Get it off!"

"It's okay," Peterson said. "I've taken the ether away. It's over in the sink."

"Oh my god!" Ashton groaned. "Faiza. Faiza. I can't see. I can't see. Stop!"

"What's going on, son?" Peterson asked.

"I'll tell you what's going on," Morgan said. "This experiment is over. Everyone out. He's had enough."

"Leave him alone, Morgan," Dowd said. "He's remembering something."

Peterson nodded and again approached the bed.

"He can remember later, when he gets his breath," Morgan said. "He's too weak to go through this. This is crazy! Now everyone out."

Dowd shrugged, and he and Sgt. Peterson filed out. Morgan grabbed Kate's arm. "Not you. Please stay."

"Ashton, would you like a drink of water?" Kate asked. He nodded, and Kate poured some ice water from the plastic pitcher on the bed stand. "You've really been through a lot, kid," she said. There were tears in her eyes.

"It was coming," Ashton said. "It was like a nightmare, and I was trying to remember it, but couldn't. Why did you make them go, Mom?"

"Because you need to rest." Morgan crossed her arms over her chest.

"I can rest later. Faiza is in danger. I know it. I've got to get out of here and find her!"

Kate touched the top of Ashton's hand. "It'll come faster if you let go, stop trying so hard," she said. "You're paddling against the current. Just get on the wave and ride it."

He took a deep breath, then grimaced as he exhaled. Kate stroked the back of his hand, speaking softly about oceans and wind and waves, and within minutes Ashton was asleep.

*　　　*　　　*

"For god's sake, Dowd, that's your son!" Morgan almost shouted when she found him in the waiting lounge.

"He was okay," Dowd said.

"Yeah, gasping for breath. He's covered with bandages, Dowd, and he's had surgery on this head, or didn't you notice?"

"Take it easy, Morgan." Dowd spoke in the calm monotone he always used when he was claiming the emotional high ground. "I understand why you're upset."

"No you don't," she said.

"Peterson just wants to find out what happened as soon as possible. Before the trail gets cold."

"Well, the trail can just ice over," Morgan said. "My son is very sick."

"Our son," he said.

"Oh brother, you just don't let up, do you?"

"What are you talking about?" Dowd asked innocently. "I want the same thing you do. For Ashton to feel better and get better. You act like I don't love him as much."

For a second, Morgan mellowed. "I know you love him, Dowd," she said.

"Morgan, would you like some feedback?" Dowd asked gently.

In a moment of softness, she took the bait. She nodded.

"You are too protective of him. He is a man. And you hover over him like he's a little boy still. You've got to let him grow up."

Morgan shook her head and turned to walk out. "Fuck you forever," she said.

*   *   *

One day Morgan came home and found Dowd in the kitchen, jerking the cabinet doors open, slamming them shut, slapping lids onto pans, kicking drawers shut. She had been thinking for several days that he was silently simmering because she had been working late for several nights in a row.

When he saw her at the door, he stopped the tantrum and turned calmly around. She asked him if he was okay. Fine, he said. You're really angry about something, she said. No I'm not, he said, I just couldn't find the top to the big pan. You're angry, she said again. What about? I'm not angry, he said with polite, calm sincerity.

And so Morgan left and went into the bedroom.

Suddenly she was struck by a stabbing pain, like a hard-ball slammed right into her gut. The pain was excruciating and she doubled over, arms clutched around her middle. And there on her knees on the floor of the bedroom, where she shared the perfectly stable marriage with the perfectly composed husband, she realized that her head could try to overlook it, but her body wasn't going to let her ignore it any longer. She was being slowly tortured to death by mixed messages. And nobody was ever going to understand it but her.

*   *   *

While Ashton slept, Morgan went to the coffee shop in the basement of the hospital. Kate offered to stay near Ashton. Eventually Dowd and Peterson joined her, and of course she apologized to Dowd for telling him to go fuck himself. He accepted the apology, because if there is one thing you could say about Dowd, he wanted to look forgiving. In fact, he was whatever he needed to be. Dowd's graciousness came as effortlessly to him as using the correct fork at a dinner party.

Peterson told the two parents his theory. The police had found no traces of Faiza. Her two dormitory girlfriends confirmed that she had plans to go away for the weekend with Ashton. Peterson believed that Faiza had been abducted. What concerned him was the fact that Ashton was so badly beaten. Clearly, whoever had Faiza was rough.

"It's vital that we get a description of whoever came into that room and used ether on him. Maybe he saw faces. Or a car. Right now, we have nothing to go on," he said.

"But why would anyone abduct Faiza? Who?" Morgan asked.

Peterson shook his head and took a sip of coffee, withholding his opinion. They sat there for what seemed like forever at that little Formica table, surrounded by the soft sounds of glasses clinking and voices rising and falling, but eventually the room filled with the aroma of steamed chicken and hot grease and tomato sauce as the kitchen clattered to life for what passed there as dinner.

Morgan's coffee had gotten cold long ago. Didn't Peterson have anything to do besides this case? He said he wanted to be there when Ashton awakened again.

Then Kate appeared in the doorway, waving to them. "He woke up and he's been talking to me," she said, with some urgency. "He remembers what happened to Faiza. He's pretty upset. Hurry."

Ashton's face was red and sweat beaded out onto his forehead from under the bandages that covered his head. His grief and his rage filled the room. He grabbed Peterson's wrist.

"They've got her!" he shouted. "The goddamn bastards, the dirty creeps, they took her! They just took her."

Peterson sat down, pulled his notebook from his pocket, and clicked the top of his pen. "Just start right at the beginning," he said, gently and unhurried.

Ashton lay his head back on the bed, and fragment by chilling fragment, rebuilt the memory of his last few terrifying moments with his beautiful sweet soulmate.

CHAPTER ELEVEN

He wasn't afraid, Ashton told them. It's not that he hadn't been scared before. He had. Plenty of times. Once, when the leash on his surfboard got torn off in a killer wave in Tahiti, he almost drowned, swimming and drifting over a mile offshore. That he took that wave at all, some people might call it downright reckless. But hell, surfing seemed reckless to anyone who didn't do it. Overall, he thought himself pretty cautious and wise. And when he was with Faiza he felt strong and protective. With him, nothing could hurt her.

But that morning three days ago he was neither cautious nor wise, and he damned himself again and again in the harshest courtroom with himself the most unrelenting judge.

She was afraid. And oh, he listened. But he didn't really hear her. He was too absorbed in her loveliness, her light sweet way of being, her broad smile and dark eyes. That morning he awoke first and lay beside her, watching her sleep. The white sheet, so soft and fresh-smelling when they'd slid under it the night before, had slipped off her shoulders and back. He wanted to touch her but didn't, concerned she might wake up, preferring to hold the unbroken stare.

Instead, his palm outstretched about two inches from the surface of her body, he caressed the space that his mother once told him was the aura. The ephemeral outer body was just as much a part of us as the solid part, she said. Some people could actually see auras, she told him, though she had only seen one once, a silver-white, luminescent border around a guy she saw on an airplane.

Ashton squinted and tried to see Faiza's aura. Mom said

that people's auras changed color, depending on how they're feeling. And sometimes their auras gave them away, telling the feelings they were hiding. What color would Faiza's aura be, if he could see it? The previous night it would have been a fear color, whatever that might be. Black? Red? He couldn't recall what his mom had said about specific colors. For him, fear would be hot pink. Day-Glo hot pink. Because fear still held a thrill for him.

He neither understood her fear nor shared it. The gap between them, half a world and several centuries in culture time, was still too huge. It wasn't that he was insensitive. He had held her, soothed her, nodded. But it didn't make sense to him. He didn't get it. In his world, people who loved you were fair, things made sense, mothers protected you, and fathers swallowed their egos and gave you everything you wanted.

In her country, this tender, innocent woman, barely twenty-one, was not just a rebel and an outcast. By some, she was considered dangerous. Evil. But they weren't in her country now. They were in a sweet little beach town in a cozy room with a fireplace and wet bar with granite tops, a CD player, and a balcony practically hanging over the Pacific Ocean. There were four kinds of imported beer in the refrigerator and down pillows on the bed. This was about as safe as America gets, he thought.

He had splurged, stretching his already thin budget to come up with the $205 for this room because, he told Faiza, it was sort of a wedding night. It would have been an actual wedding night, but they'd decided to wait to tell his mom and dad. Ashton really wanted his mother's blessing, not because she would be angry or even hurt to be left out. She wasn't like that. She'd accept whatever he did, even a fait accompli phone call —"Hey, guess what, we're married!" But he wanted her blessing at the actual moment they made their vows.

His mom had this energy about her, this magical presence that somehow, he wasn't sure how, funneled love and protection right into the spot, like when he was little and she kissed his owies. Other mothers did that too, but he could tell they were faking. Her kisses honestly, really, made cuts and bruises stop hurting. If she witnessed their marriage, they'd be blessed. And safe. And Faiza would feel it and stop worrying.

We're in the United States, he told her. You'll be my wife. No one can hurt you. You don't understand, she said, her dark eyes deepening, revealing a place in her that seemed a hundred years old. I've broken laws, she said. I've dishonored my family. My country.

Their night had been wonderful—the romantic dinner, the walk on the beach. As if they were on some fantasy island. Now, ready to go back into reality, he knew they had enough love to conquer anything. They would talk to her family if necessary. Make them understand. How could anyone, no matter how strict his religion, fail to honor true love? How could the universe not protect and support two people who were so clearly meant to be together?

His mother had always promised that everything turns out fine if your heart is in the right place and your intentions are honest and right. Well, his heart was in the right place. And so was Faiza's. He knew, because their hearts had touched and merged.

Faiza rolled halfway over and pulled a handful of sheet up to her chest. She murmured something like, "That feels good," though he had not touched her. God, how beautiful she looked, how serene, and at that moment he had a sudden but gentle sense that everything was exactly where it was supposed to be and happening exactly as it was supposed to happen. The only other time he remembered ever feeling this way was when he was on the top of a wave, getting ready to drop in, the commitment to the wave already made; there was no turning back, and he was suspended in that split second of time. And then came the ride, omigod the ride, roaring, ripping, and he was the wave and the wave was him, and that was all that was ever happening, anywhere, forever.

*   *   *

And then he heard the knock on the door. Several taps, then a pause, then a louder and harder rapping. Maid service? It was so early for that. He got up, reluctantly leaving the bed and especially his reverie on the perfect wave. He pulled on his jockey shorts, and with the chain still hooked he opened the door and saw a short, slender guy standing next to a cart with a linen tablecloth, a fancy basket of fruit, a plate of rolls, and a big silver coffeepot.

"Hey," Ashton said, whispering.

"Complimentary breakfast," said the guy. He spoke with a very thick accent of some kind, and much too loudly. His head looked weighed down with thick, black hair, and it struck Ashton that he looked older and more something, maybe polished, than most room service guys, who were usually young men just getting started or working their way through school.

"We ... I didn't order any," Ashton whispered, putting his finger on his lips to signal the guy to speak softer.

"It is complimentary. With the room," the guy said, not lowering his voice.

"Thanks. Just leave it out there and I'll get it later."

"You must sign," said the man.

"Okay." As Ashton closed the door to unlatch the chain, a flush of panic tore into his gut, like a streak of adrenaline or something, but it was too fast, and so much like the danger feeling he sometimes got at the crest of a wave that he let it go. If he had paused for just a second, he might have noticed that the color of the feeling was not fluorescent pink. Or red. It was black.

Then the door slammed open and powerful arms were around him and his own were pinned to his side. And the "Hey!" he started to shout was blocked by something soft and wet filling his mouth, and the smell, acrid, awful, choked out his breath so quickly he barely struggled, and then he was toppling off the wave and pulled down, down, tons of water swirling and pushing him beyond this world, and he struggled to get to the surface but his arms and legs would not move and the force was too heavy and unyielding, so he surrendered, and in the dark, quiet underside of the wave, he waited.

He never even had a chance to glance at Faiza.

CHAPTER TWELVE

"I didn't do anything. I didn't help her." Ashton pounded his bandaged arms on the mattress.

Morgan wiped tears from the side of her face. Peterson had set his pen aside, as if taking notes was no longer necessary and would only insult the story. He stared compassionately at Ashton.

"Honey, you were knocked out," Morgan said.

"I shouldn't have opened the door. What an idiot. A stupid idiot. What was I—"

Peterson broke in. "Listen, son, what's important now is to try to identify these guys and find them. Did you see more than one man?"

"No, just the one at the door. There had to be more than one, though, right?"

Peterson nodded. "Do you remember who hit you?"

Ashton shook his head in frustration. "I don't remember that at all."

"You're pretty beat up. Did one guy hold you, and another hit you?"

"I don't remember."

"You don't know how you got to the road?" Morgan asked.

"No," he said. "That part's just blank."

"I think you were thrown out of a car," Peterson said. "Do you remember a car?"

Ashton shook his head.

"Maybe they beat him up and then dragged him to a car, and then threw him out when they took off," Morgan ventured.

"I don't think so," Peterson said. "If there were two men, and the one Ashton saw was shorter than him, how could two guys hold onto the girl and also drag an unconscious man around? You're a big guy, son. Too much for one smaller guy to handle."

"Maybe there were more than two?" Ashton said.

"Maybe," Peterson said. "Son, would you work with a sketch artist to make a drawing of the one you remember?"

"Damn right," Ashton said. "Now. Let's do it now."

"I'll have to make a call," Peterson said. "In the meantime, try to keep on remembering. Because we don't have the whole story. There's something more."

*   *   *

Working with a police artist to create the composite sketch gave Ashton something constructive to do, a place to channel his guilt and his rage. Meanwhile, Morgan talked with Peterson in the waiting area.

Now that her son was conscious and out of danger, her concern for Faiza advanced. Until now she had expected Faiza to materialize. Any minute, she'd tell herself, the phone would ring with the news that Faiza was found, safe and sound, the victim of some huge error or mistaken identity. Oops, we kidnapped the wrong woman. We were supposed to grab the one in 203. Sorry. Have a nice day.

Or she'd look up and see Faiza walking down the hospital corridor with some perfectly reasonable explanation for her disappearance. A misunderstanding. She'd been wandering the countryside looking for Ashton. She had amnesia of her own. Something, anything, that would put this horrible nightmare in the past, and everyone could say, okay, okay, it's all been a big mistake and it's over now.

But there was no phone call, no happy reunion in the hospital corridor. Faiza had been abducted, and someone had beaten Ashton to a pulp to get her. She was in trouble. Maybe hurt, or worse. Morgan took those thoughts by their shoulders and shook them like a rebellious child. Fearful that just thinking about them would make them true.

"At least we have something to go on," Peterson told her. "We know for sure she was abducted and we'll have a description."

"But why?" Morgan asked. "They're just two kids staying in a hotel together. Faiza is the sweetest person, a student. Why would anyone do this?"

Peterson's voice lowered. "She is a citizen of Saudi Arabia. And now we know she felt fearful of some members of her family. This is off the record and a bit premature, Ms. Fay, but kidnappings are not unusual in these kinds of situations. It has happened before."

"What kinds of situations do you mean?"

"I mean, sometimes people from these countries want their family member—their daughter or sister or wife—to come back home."

"But Faiza is not a runaway. She is in this country on a student visa, with permission, perfectly legal."

"If someone wanted her back badly enough, that wouldn't matter."

"You mean, they could just . . ."

"They can and do," Peterson said. "They just come over and get them."

*   *   *

Morgan paced like a puppy stuck at the back door. She wanted to talk with someone. Both Dowd and Kate had left town, but Kate said she would come back the following day, when Ashton was scheduled to be moved into the hospital's rehabilitation wing. Morgan tried to call Meredith, but she was out of the office.

The sketch artist from the sheriff's office had arrived, a short woman dressed in jeans and a light blue sweater that hung almost to her knees. She'd brought a laptop computer and a fat tan satchel slung over her other shoulder. After she left, Ashton seemed focused and optimistic.

"Mom, it was amazing. I described the man who came to

the door, and then she punched some keys and the outline of a face came up. And it was pretty close. Then I said, no the eyebrows were thicker and the mouth was different or something like that, and then she'd hit a key and there they'd be. And then she'd move the eyebrows closer together, with the mouse, and then make the nose a little bit thinner."

He went on, angrily. "Then, all of a sudden, there he was. Right on the screen. It was disgusting. That smarmy dirt bag scum. I couldn't believe I was looking in his face. Mom, who did this? Why would anyone do something like this? Who are these creeps? What if they're hurting her?" Ashton's fury melted into guilt. "She told me she was scared. And I didn't listen."

"What was she afraid of?"

"Her family. Especially her uncle. When her father died, her uncle became her guardian. And he hated her being in the United States. He and her father argued about that a lot. That's why Faiza's father virtually ordered her to leave Saudi before his death. Because he knew that if he died while she was still in the country, she would never ever get back out. The night before they took her, Faiza said that if we got married her uncle would want revenge. She was afraid of what he might do."

"What was she afraid he might do?"

"She wouldn't say. Or maybe I never gave her a chance. I kept reassuring her. I promised her nothing bad would ever happen to her. I told her she was in the United States. I promised her she was safe here."

"Ash, we don't know yet what happened. But nothing, nothing is your fault."

"It's not like here, Mom," he said. "She doesn't have any voice in her life. Not really. She has to follow her uncle's wishes. Just getting out of the country to study was a huge step for Faiza. And she was only able to do that because she had a father who was ahead of his time. That's how the Saudi women who do have freedoms and privileges get them. Gifts from their men—fathers, husbands, older brothers. And when that happens, they think of themselves as liberated."

Morgan felt like she was letting Ashton down. A mother should know the answers. A mother fixes things. A mother knows what to do next. Some kick-ass reporter I am, she thought. She was lost.

They sat there in silence for a while. Then he said, "I don't think Peterson is telling me everything. He's holding something back."

Interesting he should say that, Morgan thought. Because she sensed that Ashton had something of his own he was holding back. Mothers know these things. We grew these kids inside, she thought. We knew when they were hungry from day one, and when they were little we snatched them from the jaws of death every single day. When they call with happy news it can change our day, and when they are sad we feel it from a thousand miles away.

Morgan couldn't exactly read Ashton's mind, but she knew he had a secret.

CHAPTER THIRTEEN

"What I don't understand," Kate said, tearing a sheet of paper towel from the roll beside her, "is how somebody can just come into this country and help themselves to whoever they want to snatch up."

The two were sitting on the living room floor in Ashton's apartment. It was late afternoon, and the living room's western exposure trapped every last vestige of the sunset, so bands of amber moved across the floor where they sat cross-legged facing each other. Between them, a carryout pizza was getting limp.

In spite of the police sketch, the investigation had revealed little more about Faiza's abduction. No one in the hotel had seen anything. Presumably the abductors had used the back entrance, not passing the front desk, and the hour was too early for any of the other guests to be wandering about. Peterson was leaning toward the theory that Faiza had been taken by her own family members. If this were true, it would take the case out of the jurisdiction of San Mateo County and become an international matter. And probably one of low priority.

Faiza's belongings haunted the small apartment, especially the bathroom. There was a pink loofa sponge hanging from the showerhead, a bottle of Jean Naté After Bath Splash on the side of the tub, and a pair of earrings, large gold hoops, on the corner of the counter. Her possessions seemed to broadcast that she had vanished. When people died, at least you knew where they were. Or sort of. Disappearance was like a pitch-black room, where you can't see anything. There are no benchmarks, nothing to feel or grab to get your bearings—just infinite darkness.

"We aren't dumb," Morgan said to Kate. "We know what can happen to her."

Faiza was out there somewhere in a part of the world that practiced honor killings, where shamed women were strangled and shot by fathers and brothers to preserve the honor of the family. Where religious police beat women for showing a flash of ankle skin outside their burqa. In Afghanistan, the Taliban forbade women to go to work or to school and ordered windows of their homes to be painted over. They could not even go out and beg. They starved. They ate grass.

In one story, a young Afghan woman was caught trying to flee the country with a man who was not her relative, a capital crime. The woman was stoned to death. Before women were stoned, they were buried up to the waist, to better anchor the body to absorb the impact of the rocks. Had this same fanaticism spread to other Islamic countries, like Saudi Arabia? Hatred toward women could rage like a ceaseless plague, as it had during the three centuries of witch-hunts in Europe.

Morgan shivered. The room was nearly dark now. Kate closed the pizza box on their uneaten dinner, then lit the candle they had burned the first night. A soft glow moved into all the corners, as if the room had taken a deep breath of light.

Morgan remembered once when Ashton was twelve, and his very first love had dumped him. She sat in his room on his bed with his head in her lap while he sobbed and sobbed and told her he didn't want to live anymore. The depth of his grief had frightened her. She thought she had never seen anyone so heartbroken in her life. Then, she could tell him in all honesty that things would get better and the pain would go away before long. That there would be other loves.

"Now, his heart is breaking again, this time for real," Morgan said, "and I can't make any promises."

Later that evening Peterson called. "Can you come down to Half Moon Bay first thing tomorrow?" he asked. "We've got a lead. The first airport we checked, someone identified the sketch. This pretty much confirms that Faiza was kidnapped."

* * *

"We know they went out of this airport," Sgt. Peterson said, after they had ordered coffee. Kate, Peterson, and Morgan were sitting in the Outbound Cafe in the terminal building at Half Moon Bay Airport, a small, one-runway field.

Peterson told them that a guy at Western Aviation, the airport's fixed-base operation, saw the whole thing.

"No one else saw anything," Peterson said. "The cafe opens at seven a.m., but the only other person here was in the kitchen. The guy's name is Rus Styvyson."

Peterson said that Styvyson had come into the hangar about 6:30 a.m., his usual routine. He got a call from Baylor Aviation, a charter company, that one of their charters was coming through between 7:30 and 8:00, and would Styvyson open the parking lot gate so the arriving passengers could get on the plane as quickly as possible? Styvyson opened the gate soon after that and went back to the hangar. He heard the plane come in and went to the door to watch.

"What happened?" Morgan whispered, leaning forward.

Peterson fingered his mustache. He spoke very slowly and, Morgan thought, with great empathy for how his words would fall on their hearts.

"Styvyson said that first a Skybird-5 landed and taxied over near the gate," he began.

"Skybird-5?" Kate turned to Morgan. "Swanky jet, racing Porsche of airplanes. Very fast, one of the fastest, with a long range."

"Yeah," Peterson said. "Styvyson loves that plane, which is why he stuck around. About fifteen minutes or so later, a black Mercdes pulled into the parking lot. Two men got out and then dragged a woman out. Forcibly. They walked her toward the plane."

"What did she look like?" asked Morgan, still hoping for a flaw that would disqualify this story.

"He couldn't tell. She was wrapped in some kind of black cape, he said. As he put it, 'like one of those Arab ladies.' All he could see from the back was that she was probably a little over five feet tall. At first she seemed reluctant, trying to pull away from them, and then she sort of gave in, Styvyson said. Once they boarded the plane, it taxied out and took off immediately. Just left the car in the parking lot. Didn't even close the doors."

"Did Styvyson report it?" Morgan asked.

"He called in the abandoned car. Other than that, there really wasn't anything to report," Peterson said, almost apologetically. "It was a routine charter pickup. Yeah, it seemed a little peculiar to him, the woman in the cape who seemed to protest a bit. But when you meet this guy you'll see. He's seen a lot of peculiar goings-on in his life around airports."

Kate shook her head. "Those bastards."

"How did they get into the country?" Morgan asked, turning to Kate. "Can anyone just fly anywhere they please?"

"Almost anywhere," Kate said. "If you're a legal flight, with flight plans and clearance to land."

"What about people sneaking in? Like drug dealers?"

"That's different," she said. "But in this case, there wouldn't be any reason to sneak in. If someone from Saudi Arabia wanted to come into this country, they could just fly in here with a plane of their own and fly back out."

"No questions asked?" Morgan asked.

"As long as they were inside the regulations," Kate said. "Hell, some of those Saudis have so much money they buy their own 747 and go anywhere they please."

Peterson nodded.

"How do we know for sure it was her?" Morgan said. "That story could be about anybody."

The sergeant eyed her sympathetically. She wondered if he had children of his own. He must, Morgan thought, because he had that knack of bursting bubbles slowly, so instead of exploding, they quietly pop.

"We don't know absolutely," he said. "But we have traced

that Skybird's flight. It went to Bangor, Maine, and from there to Santa Maria in the Azores."

Morgan frowned. "The Azores?"

Kate knew. "It's often a stopover for routes to the Middle East," she said. "Known for look-the-other-way customs, or easy customs if you have a little cash to wave around."

"We're pretty sure those passengers were headed for the Middle East. And there is every reason to believe, considering the timing and the physical descriptions, that the woman with the two men was your friend Faiza."

CHAPTER FOURTEEN

Morgan stood up.

"I'm sorry," Peterson said.

She nodded and walked toward the coffee shop window. Outside, the runway was empty. The airport looked deserted, except for two small planes, maybe four-seaters, tied down on the tarmac, and five or six cars in the parking lot.

"What are you going to do next?" Kate asked.

"We'll officially continue our investigation until we've confirmed that the girl was Faiza," Peterson said. "Which will no doubt happen when we talk with the pilot later today."

"How can they do that? Just waltz in here and pluck her out of Half Moon Bay?" Kate asked. "Isn't kidnapping a crime?"

"In their minds, this is not a kidnapping. She is a citizen of that country and a member of their family. As they see it, they simply are claiming their property." Peterson leaned forward. "You need to realize something. As U.S. citizens, we have strong personal rights, strong protections. Especially as compared to a country like Saudi Arabia. Add to that she's a woman."

"But don't our laws protect foreigners visiting in the U.S.?"

"Sure, and if we could have stopped this, we would have intervened," Peterson said. "But they're long gone, and now it's really out of my jurisdiction."

Morgan turned from the window with her hands on her hips. "Whose jurisdiction is it?"   "We will turn it over to the State Department, but . . . " Peterson shook his head. "The State Department is about matters of state, diplomatic matters. And individuals too, but only if they are our citizens."

"What about the FBI?" Kate asked.

"We could refer this to the Bureau," he said. "But if the abductors have her out of the country and we know it, then it's beyond the FBI. It's an international matter."

"What if we went to the State Department ourselves? And asked for their help."

"If the victim is not a U.S. citizen, or the child of one, then they might be nice, but frankly, they won't give a damn," Peterson said.

"But they attacked Ashton," Morgan said, grasping for a straw.

"What could we do?" Peterson gave a gentle shrug. "Have Interpol track them down for assault? So Interpol gets to the border of Saudi Arabia and says, We want your guy for assault in the United States, and they laugh and say, 'Go 'way, go eat some camel dung.'"

Kate was tracing the checks on the vinyl tablecloth with her fingernail. First a red one, then a white one, then red, white. She looked up and glared at Peterson. "You're saying that once the airplane left the country, we were done."

"Law enforcement is," he said, nodding. And Morgan saw that he was truly sad to have to say that.

"Can we go with you to talk with the pilot?" she asked.

"No, sorry," he said. "You're not part of the official investigation. But I'll give you his name and number."

* * *

After Peterson pulled away, Morgan and Kate walked across a short field to Western Aviation to find Rus Styvyson. The hanger was an old, rectangular tin-sided building. The pitched roof, corroding white, had a huge faded painting of Snoopy sitting on his doghouse wearing his aviator hat and goggles.

They entered a small side door. The inside was lit with fluorescent lights that hung from the ceiling and was dense with the smells of fuel and oil vapors and drippings. Metal shelves lined the walls, piled with tools and cans and airplane parts. In one corner stood an aging stove with a Mr. Coffee and several mugs on top, and a refrigerator mottled with rust. In the opposite corner sat an old car, patiently waiting to be restored. Looked like a '56 or '57, a Chivvy, as they said in Indiana. Overhead, two weathered fuselages were stuck in the rafters.

On the floor in the center sat a pair of two-seater vintage planes. The yellow one gleamed like a brand new toy, every detail finished to a perfect gloss. The other, a white tail-dragger with an arch of red along the bottom half of the fuselage, was equally stunning. They posed there like two proud birds, ready to strut out into the sunlight and then go soaring off to dance and spiral and write "Hello" across the blue sky with puffs of white smoke.

"Relics from the forties—all dressed up and ready to party," Kate told Morgan.

The man who walked toward them was short, gray, and old, as shopworn as the derelict hangar, but he had a big, fresh smile.

"Nice," Kate said, pointing to the yellow plane. "Piper J-3 Cub. And this one's a Champ," she said of the white and red one. "Did you restore these?"

The old man nodded, but didn't say anything. "You fly these?" she asked. Again, he nodded, smiling.

"I'm Kate Shepherd," she said, extending her hand. He shook it. "This is Morgan Fay."

When he shook her hand, Morgan thought his skin felt loose and wrinkled. He then held up one finger in a pantomime to tell them to wait one moment.

He scurried into an office in the back of the hangar and returned holding an appliance that looked like a small microphone. But instead of speaking into it, he held it against his throat, like a singer who's missed the mark, and the next time his lips moved, what came out was not exactly a song. It was a hoarse, whispery growl, like a bear might sound if it could form words.

"Throat cancer," he said, answering the question right off the bat.

"Are you Rus Styvyson?" Kate asked.

"Yeah," he barked.

"These planes are beautiful," Kate said, lovingly stroking a red wing.

"You're a pilot," he said.

"Yes," she said. "Or I used to be."

"No 'used to be,'" Styvyson growled.

"I haven't flown in years."

"Once a pilot, always." Styvyson winked.

"So you flew these?" Kate gestured to the antiques.

"Those and 'bout everything else. Over fifty years all told. Flew the Cub as an instructor in the war," he said. "But it's no fun anymore."

"Too many regs."

He brightened. A cohort. "Teaching's no fun either. San Francisco TRSA. Students never get to fly the plane. All they do is talk on the radio."

Kate nodded empathetically. "Gimme a grass strip and a Pitts any day," she said.   Styvyson hooted hoarsely.

"Mr. Styvyson.," Morgan began.

"Rus," he corrected.

"Rus. We came to talk to you about the Skybird that came through here Monday. The detective said you watched it come and go."

Styvyson walked to the door and pointed out, as if they didn't already know where the runway was. Into his mike, he croaked a shorter version of the story that Peterson had told them.

"Can you remember what the lady in the black robe looked like?"

"Couldn't see her for the cloak," he said. "And her back was to me."

"Was her head covered?" Kate asked.

"Now that you mention it, yes. But . . . "

"But what?"

"Thought I saw long dark hair coming out of the hood-like thing."

"Shoes? Did you see her shoes?" Morgan asked.

"Umm. Running shoes. Like the kids wear. Like Nikes."

"Omigod," Morgan said.

"You know her?"

"Yes."

"She wasn't eager to go flying with those fellas. Tried to jerk away from them."

*   *   *

Before Morgan and Kate left the hangar, Styvyson insisted they visit his office. Tucked back in one corner, the office looked more like a small storage bin, though there was a desk beneath the clutter of papers, books, manuals, and two tall stacks of a yellow magazine called *Trade-A-Plane*. On the office door a plaque read: "Aviation stories and lies told here."

On the wall next to the door, a faded calendar open to June 1962 featured a bikini-clad woman bent over with her hands on her knees. Below it a shelf held a toolbox and what looked like a couple of engine parts. The walls were lined with framed photographs, mostly black and white, of men in dark flight jackets and caps standing next to military planes. Kate circled the room, naming the planes. B25. B17. B24.

"This you?" she said, pointing to one.

Styvyson nodded. "And my crew."

"Where'd you fly?"

"Bombing raids. Over Japan. Right before the end."

Morgan recognized one photograph. "It's the *Spirit of St. Louis*. The real one?" she asked Styvyson.

"No, a replica of the Ryan that Lindbergh flew. That's the one they made for the movie."

"Jimmy Stewart played Lindbergh, right?" said Morgan.

"Yep. I flew all the flight scenes," Styvyson said proudly.

"Did you meet Jimmy Stewart?"

"Never saw him," Styvyson replied. "But I heard that he said I did a good job."

At the door, Styvyson stopped and studied their faces, one at a time. Then he held the microphone back up to his throat. "Good luck," the bear said.

*   *   *

They walked out and across the field. Then Kate turned and looked back toward the hanger. With one hand, she combed her fingers through her hair, pulling it back from her forehead before letting it fall back in place. Morgan had seen that gesture a million times, since they were teenagers. Sometimes she'd do it with both hands—as if she was clearing her head by disentangling her hair.

"I love crusty old guys like that," she said.

"It's like he's part of a bygone era," Morgan said.

"He is the era," Kate said wistfully.

"You miss it, don't you?"

Kate shrugged.

"Come on. Admit it. You love it and you miss it."

Kate shook her head. "It's over for me, Morgan. That all died with Jack. You know that. I'm like Styvyson. It's a bygone era for me too."

Morgan examined her friend, then resumed walking. "Bullshit."

CHAPTER FIFTEEN

The phone in Ashton's apartment rang early the morning after the visit to the airfield. Morgan leaped, expecting it to be Ashton, calling from the rehab center, where the day began shortly after sunrise. Instead, she recognized the voice of Jeff Peterson.

"You have some news?" she interrupted his greeting.

"No, I'm afraid not," Peterson said soberly. "We tracked down the car the kidnappers used. The rental company confirmed it was rented by a guy who fits the description of the one Ashton saw. But he paid cash and used a fake ID, so that's a dead end. The rental company had to send someone out to the airport to pick it up where they kidnappers abandoned it."

"Okay," said Morgan. "So why the early morning phone call?"

"I called to give you the pilot."

Stan Grady was his name, Peterson said. He lived in Pacifica, a beach town south of the city. Morgan thanked Peterson perfunctorily and didn't even set the phone down before dialing the number. It rang four times. She counted.

"Grady here," a groggy voice answered.

What a haughty way to answer the phone. As if he was just too busy or too important for conventional courtesies. Like, I'm answering the phone, but don't take that to mean I'm making any commitment to talking. Before Morgan even said a word, she had already decided that Stan Grady was self-centered and smug.

"Mr. Grady," she began, "this is Morgan Fay. Your name was given to me by Sergeant Peterson of the San Mateo sheriff's department."

"Peterson?"

"You talked with him two days ago, about a flight you commanded. A charter. To Maine."

A long silence. Then Stan Grady said slowly, cautiously, "Yes, I remember."

Cut to the chase, Morgan thought. "I was wondering if I could also talk with you about that flight."

"Are you with the sheriff's department?"

"No, I'm not. I'm a . . . a friend of someone on that flight."

Another pause. "If you're not with the sheriff's department, then what is your interest in that flight?"

"I was hoping maybe we could arrange to get together, to talk in person," Morgan said.

"Our charters are private, Miss . . . Faith."

"It's Fay."

"Fay. I mean, if you're not an official, like with the police or the FAA, then it's really not appropriate for me to say anything about our flights."

Stan Grady's voice was measured, but now a little softer, slightly more accessible than when he answered the phone. Morgan hoped he hadn't read her mind, her hasty nasty thoughts at the beginning. It wasn't that she'd suddenly developed a liking for him. But she did need him to trust her.

He had nothing to gain from talking with her, unless he just happened to be curious. Morgan considered telling him she was a journalist on assignment. Then maybe she would get a foot in the door. But she had a policy. She didn't pose as a reporter unless she was, in fact, working on a story. There were so few ethics in the profession these days, she felt that was the least she could do.

"Mr. Grady. This is really an unusual situation, and I doubt that there is any precedent for it. But there was a woman on your flight. And as Peterson probably told you, we have reason to believe she was there against her will."

"We, the crew, really aren't involved with the passengers," he said. "It's the company's policy. The flight deck is separated from the cabin, and we don't interact with passengers."

"I understand," Morgan said. "I was hoping I could talk with you about . . . whatever you're allowed to talk about."

"Are you a reporter or something?" he asked.

"Yes, actually I am a reporter. But I'm not working on a story here. This is personal. Mr. Grady, we believe the woman on your plane was abducted from an inn at Half Moon Bay early on the morning of the flight. Against her will."

"How do you know that?"

"Because she was with my son when she was taken. He was knocked unconscious and is still in the hospital. They were planning to get married."

Grady asked, "What could I tell you that I didn't already tell the detective?"

"I'm not sure," Morgan said. "Maybe nothing. Maybe it would be helpful to talk with the pilot." She paused. "My son is in agony. And we have reason to believe that the young woman is now being held in Saudi Arabia. Her name is Faiza. My son is only twenty-five, and she's younger. They're just kids. Maybe you could shed some light."

Morgan could hear Stan Grady inhale a deep breath, then exhale with a whistle.

"We could have a cup of coffee," he said. "Hold on while I check my schedule."

They agreed to meet later that morning, which Morgan hoped would allow her enough time to visit Ashton at the hospital after her stop in Pacifica. For now, she didn't want Ashton to know she was doing this. Not yet. Not until she heard what Stan Grady had to say.

Kate wandered out of the bedroom and poured a cup of coffee, raising an eyebrow at Morgan as she finished her conversation with Stan.

"I want you to be there when we meet with him," Morgan told Kate. "Will you go? You know how to talk to pilots."

"Sure," she said. "What's the deal with this guy?"

"What do you mean?"

"You had a funny look on your face. Like you just remembered something you had forgotten," she said.

"I don't know," Morgan said. "The guy sounds real cocky."

"No, there was something else," Kate said. "Like a flash of recognition or something. You know him from somewhere?"

"God, no," Morgan said. "I don't know anyone like this guy, I'm sure of it. I can already tell, he's gonna be a real piece of work."

*   *   *

Morgan, Kate, and Stan Grady settled into a corner table and ordered coffee. Kate engaged the pilot right away in aviation talk, and within seconds they were practically heart-to-heart about inboard engines and FARs and comparing close calls they'd had. Morgan stirred her cup, waiting quietly for the right time to broach the subject of Faiza while she sized up the guy.

Captain Stan Grady. Pilot Grady. Stan the Man Grady. He definitely looked more like a Grady than a Stan. Morgan always thought of Stans as nice but shallow guys, guys who might get by on their good looks or sociable personalities. Not overbearingly charming, but smooth and courteous and comfortable wherever you put them. Grady had a lot of those characteristics, but he seemed to have somewhat rougher edges, perhaps a little more mystery, just enough to make him more interesting than a regular Stan would be.

Also, he was cute. His face had enough wrinkles to suggest he was mid-fifties, and his skin was darkish, less from a suntan than from weathering. For his age, the body was in pretty good shape, firm and not overweight. Morgan doubted that he worked out but he also didn't blob around the house, eat a lot, or spend much time on the couch.

His hair was light brown and cut very short, and although she preferred long hair on men, his hairstyle fit his face and his solid, rectangular masculine head. There were either gray flecks or blond flecks in his hair, she couldn't tell which. His eyes were blue.

It's a good thing people can't read each other's minds, Morgan thought. On the drive down to Pacifica, she'd had a flash that he might get together with Kate. That is, if he didn't turn out to be too much of an asshole. She didn't tell Kate this, but it occurred to her that they might be a match. Two pilots. Not exactly a replacement for Jack, but someone to get Kate back into the air.

Kate nudged Morgan, who had clearly been daydreaming. "Grady just told me he flew C-130s," she said. "Those are those humongous cargo carriers. They're so big, they can roll a bunch of army tanks right in the back and still have room to spare."

"Did you fly military?" Morgan asked him.

"Not officially." Grady looked away and took a sip of his coffee, a gesture that made his answer most inscrutable. There was something very annoying about him. He postured with a kind of understated confidence, like a man of few words. A mask for conceit, Morgan was sure of it.

"Who did you fly for?" she asked.

"USA Transport, a big cargo carrier that is no longer in business," he said. "I was a freight dog." He pronounced the word "dawg." In its heyday, he said, USAT flew a lot of relief efforts, like food and wheat into the Sudan and to Ethiopia. "It was the most expensive food in the world, especially if we dropped it. We once figured out it cost ten bucks a pound for wheat."

"Dropped it?"

"Sometimes," he said. "Because we were taking it into places surrounded by rebel forces." Grady made it sound simple and cut-and-dried.

"What happened to USA Transport?" Morgan asked.

"Went out of business in 1998."

"What happened?"

"Peace broke out. And famine is no longer the big news," he said, rather sarcastically.

"Do you miss it?" she asked.

"I've pumped enough adrenaline for one lifetime." Grady grinned at Morgan, a grin that felt like a put-down. "People don't get it," he added. "The liberals want to go in and fix it all. We might be these great powerful Americans, but you ain't gonna go out in the world and change a thing. War, hunger. I've seen it. You can't make a dent."

"But you took food in to starving people," Morgan said. "That's a dent, isn't it?"

Her question was met with a shrug just short of an eye-roll.

Morgan paused for a moment, then asked, "Stan, could you tell us anything about the day you flew Faiza out of Half Moon Bay?"

"Everyone calls me Grady," he said.

"Okay, Grady."

"Look," he said. "I didn't fly her out. Doesn't work like that."

"Didn't you notice that she was being practically dragged onto the plane?" Kate asked.

"You've gotta understand charters," he said. "That's what they are. Charters. I'm the captain of the plane, period. Not responsible for the people who hire us."

Grady put his hand on Morgan's arm. The gesture made her shiver, just under the surface of her skin, where she hoped no one could see.

"Look, babe. I know you must feel awful about what happened. But we have a policy. Interacting with the passengers is verboten unless it's drastic, like an emergency, or if someone is killing someone. It's their charter, their business, and we're not even supposed to think about it."

"But didn't it occur to you, or your crew, that this might be a kidnapping?" Morgan asked.

Grady hesitated. Then he doled out the next words with

meticulous care. Morgan knew he was lying.

"I was really pretty focused on the preflight and on getting the plane in the air. I will tell you it was a quick pickup. Our instructions were to wait on the ramp with the engines running, and as soon as our passengers arrived, we were to take off. Which is what we did. They got out of a car and hurried right onto the plane. Then we flew them nonstop to Bangor."

"What happened then?"

"Our relief crew took over, and we flew deadhead home."

"Where did the Bangor flight go?" Kate asked.

"To Santa Maria in the Azores and then to Saudi Arabia," Grady said perfunctorily, knowing that Morgan and Kate already knew.

"Where in Saudi?"

"A city called Dhahran. On the eastern coast. On the Persian Gulf."

"Faiza's home is near Dhahran," Morgan said.

"In Bangor, did you see anyone?" Kate asked.

"Nope. They didn't get out of the plane, and we changed crews without going aft. My flight attendant told me the woman never moved from her seat and was not allowed to eat."

"Did you ever see her?" Morgan pressed.

"Babe, she was covered from head to toe. In black."

CHAPTER SIXTEEN

The three walked out to the parking lot. Morgan exchanged a glance with Kate that said, *All in all, this meeting was a big waste of time.* Morgan checked to see if there was any spark between the two pilots. Nothing detectable. When Morgan said, "See you later," Grady answered "Not if I see you first." Which was pathetically silly. Corn on the cob, her father used to say.

They might have exchanged a brief, courteous goodbye, except Morgan inadvertently opened the conversation again. Stan Grady was like a party popper, one of those little nondescript-looking tubes that, when you pull on the ends, erupts with handfuls of confetti and ribbons, a lot more that you'd ever think could be stuffed in the tube.

"You know that part of the world," Morgan asked him. "Is there any way we could make contact with her?"

"Babe, it's gonna be next to impossible. If she's being held somewhere, even in the home, she's being watched all the time. A woman can't go out alone. So it's not like she can whip down to the 7-Eleven and use the pay phone."

Grady leaned back against his car, a black Cherokee, older model but shiny and well kept. He took off his mirrored sunglasses and fingered them while he readied himself to talk.

"This is religion we're talking about. And more people have been killed in the name of religion than anything else. Like the Muslims, and what they do to women. To us, it's great injustice. To them, it's the will of Allah."

Grady tipped his sunglasses toward them. "There's stuff happening all over the world. Thirty or forty years ago we didn't give a shit about it. Not because we wouldn't have cared, but because we didn't know it was going on. If you wanted to go someplace over there, it might take two months on steamers and trains and camels. Now, you could go out to the San Francisco airport, get on a plane, and be in Jeddah in twenty-four hours. So now we want to go in and change it all."

Grady stuck his glasses in his shirt pocket and brought out a pack of Marlboros. Not lights, but the undiluted kind. He lit one with a blue pocket lighter and sucked in a big drag.

"People just don't get it. Take a place like the Sudan. Life means nothing. People will become slave traders and sell their own kids. They can always have more. When I was over there, one priest took us to a refugee camp. Everyone got one bowl of bulgur wheat, made into a paste with water. That was all the food in a day. I saw this woman sitting with a baby on one tit and she's got to be seven months pregnant. Explain that to me." Grady laughed. "I know this is crass and it's politically incorrect, but it's the truth."

Morgan didn't interrupt while he blew a quick series of smoke rings.

"And the Arabs," he went on. "They're the worst. Big hypocrites. You walk into a shopping mall and there the guys are, all decked out in Western gear—Dockers, jeans, sport coats, loafers. Then here comes little mama traipsing behind in a black robe with her head all covered up.

"A couple months ago I was in Tysons Corner, Virginia, right outside Washington, D.C. They have Arabs all over the place. And they have this TV station, channel 22, and it's all Muslims. I mean, we can't go into their country, but they can come over here and have a goddam TV station. I was in a cab there, and the driver, he was probably drivin' a camel two weeks ago."

"Guess you don't like them much," Kate observed.

"You're wrong," he said. "I just see them for what they are. Saudi has oil. We need oil. We are an oil-based society. Just try to go out and start your car without it. The rest, it's a cultural thing. Not a personal thing. Your kid's girlfriend might as well be from the moon, as similar as her background is to yours."

His racism took Morgan's breath away.

"It's not that simple," she protested. "Faiza had been in this country for three years. And she wanted to stay here, with Ashton, for life. To get married and have . . . to be free."

Morgan realized she had tears in her eyes. Grady softened.

"Religion just happens to be a matter of birth," he said. "And freedom is relative. It's a great ideal, but it's our ideal. If you are born into a cattle-herding nomadic family in the Sudan, you're probably going to grow up to be a cattle-herding nomad in the Sudan."

"So you're saying Faiza hasn't got a chance?"

"No, babe. I'm saying that what happened is the nature of their culture, that's all. If the girl's been grabbed by her family and taken back home, then she offended someone—her family, not to mention Allah—and she's in deep doo-doo. And if you try to interfere, you're going to get way over your head fast."

Grady climbed into his car and replaced his sunglasses, shielding his eyes from view.

"What would you do if she were your girlfriend?" Kate asked.

Grady closed the door and rolled down the window, blowing out a long column of smoke

"I don't know, babe. If I were as young as he is, and as much in love, I'd probably grab the first plane in sight, a couple 'a M-16s, and go get her the fuck out of there."

CHAPTER SEVENTEEN

Ashton had been in the rehab center for two weeks. When his wounds had healed sufficiently, he was taught how to operate a wheelchair, his locomotion until the dislocated shoulder healed enough to allow the use of crutches. His progress was dogged, fueled by anger and urgency to get home where, he believed, he could do something, anything. He wanted to go somewhere, anywhere, and threatened to roll his wheelchair right up the wall and along the ceiling, like a crazed spider.

The good news was that the physical therapist promised he could go home in a couple of days. The bruises had receded, and most of his cuts and abrasions had reduced themselves to scabs or rough red patches. The doctors were just waiting for the broken leg to mend a bit more before they sent him off in a wheelchair to fend for himself.

His upper body was incredibly strong and muscular, from thousands of hours of paddling through waves, so he could maneuver himself well, though not without effort, in and out of the chair. During the quiet times, when he wasn't working with a physical therapist or practicing chair maneuvers in the corridor, he simmered with pure rage. There was nothing anyone could say to console him. He needed some glimmer of hope, but there were no straws even to grasp at.

Ashton persuaded Morgan to buy a cellphone with call forwarding from his apartment, in case Faiza tried to get word to him. It rested on a charger on the bed stand, when he wasn't holding and staring at it, coaxing it to ring. But it lay there mute, like an abandoned boxcar. They both seemed to know that there would be no phone call from Faiza.

On top of his grief and rage, Ashton beat himself up relentlessly. I should have protected her. I should have been able to stop them. I shouldn't have opened the door. I told her she was safe. I didn't believe anyone would hurt her. I should have listened. I should have should have should have.

Peterson called to say there was no more progress as yet. He was probably already onto another case, Morgan thought, and Faiza's was in a file someplace, slowing sinking to the bottom of someone's pile.

Dowd called every day and offered to fly back out when Ashton was released from the rehab center. Morgan declined. Kate said she would be there, and they could handle it. Morgan told Dowd about their meeting with the pilot.

"Don't get Ashton's hopes up," Dowd said.

"What do you mean?" she asked, knowing.

"I know what you're thinking," Dowd said. "That you can jump in this thing and miraculously do what law enforcement can't do."

"That wouldn't be so hard," she said wryly.

"You know what I mean, Morgan," Dowd said sternly. "I've made a lot of calls, talked to a lot of people in government. High places. If they've taken her out of the country, there's nothing anyone can do."

"Or will do," she said.

"It's not that people don't care," Dowd argued. "They do. And for god's sake, I do. But this is simply out of our hands."

"Bullshit. The president could help. If he wanted to."

"There you go again, Morgan," Dowd said. "You have these grandiose ideas of your power. And you lead Ashton to believe you can do some kind of magic." His voice lowered and softened a bit. "Look, I didn't talk to the president, but I got pretty close, to real higher-ups in the State Department. Their hands are tied."

"Screw hands tied," Morgan said. "That's political bullshit."

"It's reality," said Dowd. And he should know. He was the voice of it—while Morgan was the voice of unreality, of hyperbole, of unreasonable expectations.

Morgan stewed in angry silence, and Dowd waited. At last he said, "Morgan, you may not be able to fix this one."

There it was. The bottom line. Mom trying to make everything fine. Chasing all the hurts away. Kissing the owies and making them all better. Always scrambling to resurface the kids' roads to level out the rough spots. This was what Dowd thought of her. That she was overprotective, overindulgent, and forever stepping in to rescue.

She knew that when he said she might not be able to "fix" this one, he wasn't only talking about Faiza's abduction. Morgan could hear it in his voice. He believed Morgan was being driven by guilt. That she was trying to make up for abandoning the marriage and the family and being the one who smashed them into this fractured casualty of divorce. As usual, it didn't matter what subject Dowd and she conversed about, or whatever the lines in the script. There was always another subtext. The marriage. They were always talking about the marriage. Divorce messes with your head forever.

"Just don't promise what you can't deliver," Dowd said.

"Look, Dowd, that kid is hurt bad. And the only thing that keeps him going, the reason he gets up in the morning and into that wheelchair, is so he can get the hell out of there and go find Faiza and get her back."

"As much as we all want that, it doesn't look good," Dowd said. "In fact, it's probably going to take a miracle."

"Well, then," Morgan said, "we'll just have to make a miracle."

And even over the telephone line, she could hear him rolling his eyes.

CHAPTER EIGHTEEN

Back when Morgan was working at the *Dispatch*, the editors loved her fighting spirit, as long as she colored inside their lines. So for a while she got along fine, swirling in the momentousness and drama of breaking stories and tight deadlines. Every moment was of consequence, every story an opportunity to expose a bad guy or cast the spotlight on injustice or rattle somebody's cage. Oh, they were all so important.

Morgan was on a mission then, a mission made possible because she had the power of the daily press behind her. With words and ink, she chased after flawed people and systems, exposed injustice and corruption in sheriffs' departments and council chambers. She championed victims of corporate greed or institutional perversity. A family who couldn't get medical care for their baby because they were too poor. An elderly couple bilked out of thousands of dollars on bogus insurance policies. The owner of a small flower shop, now bankrupt and closed, who was harassed by the county tax collector for a measly $50 in back taxes.

When Morgan wrote a story about how the city's animal shelter had an unwritten policy of putting ugly dogs to death before cute ones, she earned the title of Underdog Reporter. Once, she returned to her desk and found a red cape on the back of her chair, with the gold letters "UR" sewn on the back. Under the letters was a black paw print.

Morgan won awards and civic accommodations. She was on a roll.

And then one day she met Hazel Presley.

She had gone to court on a tip. The hearing was to determine whether Hazel could continue to live in her own home, or should she be committed as mentally incompetent. Hazel was in her late eighties and had lived alone in the same small bungalow for as long as any of her neighbors could recall. On a pittance from Social Security, she managed to feed herself and a couple dozen cats in the midst of towers of trash, old magazines and newspapers, and years of accumulated dust and filth. Every year on Christmas Eve, Hazel cooked two chicken potpies in the grimy oven of her two-burner stove.

This particular Christmas Eve, Hazel fell asleep while the potpies were baking and awakened to a house full of smoke. Neighbors called the fire department, and the firefighters who came inside to extinguish the pies were probably the first people to enter the house for decades. Luckily, none of the old newspapers caught fire.

No one knew who actually reported Hazel, but late that night the police arrived and took her to a psych ward for observation. When a staff psychiatrist examined Hazel, probably the hundredth such patient he'd seen in the past week, she was tired, hungry, and terrified. He pronounced her "confused, mentally incompetent" and recommended she be sent to a nursing home.

To Morgan, Hazel didn't look crazy. Sitting alongside her public defender in the hearing, she followed the proceedings intently, her gray-brown eyes squinted in concentration. But she sure looked scared. Her white hair was tied back with a rubber band and her tiny bony hands trembled as she patted into place a few thin wisps that had slipped loose.

The hearing was routine and perfunctory. The lawyers made brief, dispassionate opening presentations, the psychiatrist gave his opinion, the lawyers talked some more, the judge asked some questions, and so on. Morgan was jotting down some notes when she thought she felt someone tap her on the shoulder. She looked up but there was no one there. Then, she could have sworn she heard a voice whisper, "Look."

Look at what?

"Look."

Morgan scanned the courtroom, and then it hit her. Besides her, Hazel was the only woman in the room. And she might as well not have been there, because when the men talked about her, they didn't look at her, they gestured toward her. If she had been an antique vase up for auction, they would have been more personal. How could they decide whether she was mentally competent if they didn't even look her in the eyes?

From the tone and content of the proceedings, Morgan could tell that Hazel didn't have a chance. The decision was made before anyone even came into the courtroom, and none of the men saw anything to salvage in the life of an eighty-nine-year-old woman who lived alone in a filthy house. And they didn't ask her what she might want to save. At the close of the hearing, before he stripped her of all her rights, the judge asked Hazel to come forward for a few questions.

Standing next to the huge polished bench, Hazel had seemed to shrink even smaller, and the judge had to lean forward to get a good view of her. She was trembling. The judge nodded paternally and cocked his head to one side.

"Mrs. Presley." The judge grinned. "Are you related to Elvis?"

Everyone in the courtroom burst out laughing. Tears filled Morgan's eyes, and her throat tightened as if there was a lump burning in it.

But it wasn't a lump. It was her career, and she was choking on it.

Morgan's editor thought she was spending too much time on the story about Hazel. She wanted her to move on to something "more people could relate to."

"People aren't interested in old ladies," the editor said, in the high-pitched voice she used when she addressed anyone she outranked. She saved a deeper, richer tone for those further up on the ladder she was climbing. When she talked to reporters, it sounded as though she was squeezing her voice through a hole that was too small.

"You can have one more week," she whined.

Morgan worked day and night. She interviewed neighbors and psychiatrists and reviewed court records. She found a psychiatrist who was willing to reexamine Hazel. He not only found her "as sane as you or me," but also pronounced her "delightful."

Because Hazel was a ward of the state, the nursing home could forbid visitors, which in Morgan's case, they did. She finally sneaked in one Sunday afternoon and sat with Hazel on her little bed in a room she shared with a woman in a coma. By now, Hazel really was confused. She didn't understand what had happened, or why. Also, she was being given nightly sleeping medications, which were dulling her senses all day and stealing what life force was left in her frail body.

"When can I go home?" she asked Morgan, her speech fuzzy.

"Soon, I hope," Morgan lied.

Even if her story aroused extraordinary public outrage and by some miracle the court reconsidered its decision, Morgan could see that Hazel was already into the downward spiral of nursing home confinement. The hopelessness, the drugs, the monotony, and the sheer betrayal were killing her spirit.

She was weeping when Morgan left.

"My cats. My cats. Will you look after my cats?" Hazel begged.

Morgan nodded.

It turned out that people did care about eighty-nine-year-old women, and the story sparked extraordinary public outrage. However, the same weekend it was published, Hazel died. Morgan's editor interpreted the outcome as validation of her original point of view.

"Just because a story's well-written doesn't mean it wasn't a huge waste of time," she griped.

After Hazel, Morgan couldn't get interested in anything except stories about women. She went on a binge. She wrote about women who had been raped. She wrote about women whose bosses had fondled their breasts and then threatened to fire them if they spoke out. She wrote about a woman firefighter, the first female on the force, who had to fish dead rats out of her boots before every fire.

Morgan told the stories of women who, as children, had been sexually assaulted by fathers, uncles, older brothers. She wrote about women who were beaten up by their husbands, and she did a whole series about women who were in prison for killing the men who had beaten them up. One of these women, who shot her husband after he raped her with a shovel handle, was serving a life sentence. Her trial had lasted three days.

Morgan attended workshops on employment discrimination, childcare, and welfare, and over the next year, acquired a vast network of experts, advocates, and activists working on behalf of women and their children. She received dozens of letters a week, mostly from women.

She wrote more stories that year than the three previous years put together. And then one day she was summoned into the office of the managing editor, Richard Frasier. Frasier had always liked Morgan's work, because he knew that even when readers disagreed with her, she pushed their buttons. Controversy sells papers, and disgruntled readers keep the pot stirred. Frasier was slick and smooth, but to the point.

"You've developed some tunnel vision, here, I think," he said.

Morgan blinked. "Tunnel vision?"

He had a computer printout listing all of her stories in front of him.

"For the past year, all of your stories have been about women, mostly downtrodden ones. I think it's time for you to diversify."

"Diversify?" His key words were like tennis balls, and all Morgan could think of to do was lob them back.

"I'd like to see you do stories about a variety of people, in many different walks of life."

"But my stories *are* about people in many walks of life."

"No. They're only about women," he said.

"But don't we have a lot of other specific beats? We have the police beat, the business beat, the environmental beat, the Washington beat. Why not a women's beat?"

"Women aren't the same as politics or the environment. Those are issues."

This man had a short fuse. Morgan realized she had to tread very cautiously.

"Um, I think my stories have all been about issues."

"But only one group's issues," Frasier said. He was starting to get annoyed. Morgan had about forty-five more seconds on this fuse.

"What do you want me to do?" she asked in her most respectful tone of voice.

"I want you to write more of those blockbuster stories you used to write. I want you to go after bad guys again. Find some more corruption. Expose some more political sleaze-bags."

Frasier leaned forward. "Look, Morgan, people are starting to talk. They're calling you a feminist vigilante and say that you're using this newspaper to advance some sort of personal agenda. You still have a good future here. I want the old you back."

Morgan told Frasier she would think about it, shook his hand, and left his office. She didn't even try to explain to him that the old her was long gone. The old Morgan had died that day in the courtroom with Hazel.

Every evening for the next two weeks, Morgan quietly and systematically packed her files and belongings and took them out of the newsroom one box at a time. Everyone thought she was cleaning up her notoriously messy desk.

When all but a couple of boxes were gone, she walked into Frasier's office and resigned. He didn't put up even a hint of a fuss. He was so arrogant, so accustomed to squandering talent, that it probably didn't occur to him that she might be missed. That afternoon she walked out of the *Dispatch* for the last time, hugging her remaining two boxes.

She paused in the parking lot near her car, looked up at the five-story building where she had spent the past ten years, and said out loud: "Morgan, what the hell was that all about?"

CHAPTER NINETEEN

The morning after her uninspired conversation with Dowd, when Morgan arrived at the rehab center, she found Ashton in a frustrated fury. He spun his wheelchair in a frenzied whirl and announced that he thought they should go to the press.

"Maybe," Morgan said.

"You must have some friends at the *Examiner*," he urged.

"Yeah." She was hedging and not sure why.

"So let's do it," he said, slapping his fist into a cupped palm. "Expose those creeps."

"We need to think it through to the end. Because if the goal is to cause a big public outcry—"

"Damn right," he interrupted. "To get them to find her and give her back. What else?"

"Who's our target?"

"Well, first the public," he said. "Then, I guess, the CIA and the State Department."

"Peterson has already explained why they wouldn't be interested."

"What if we get so much national outrage that they have to listen? Mom, you do this all the time. You can write stories that practically incite people to riot. They storm the Bastille after they read your stuff."

"Honey, even if we made it to the primetime news shows with this story, there isn't much our government can do. They're not going to start a war to get Faiza back. She isn't even a citizen. If you two were married, maybe; but even then I think it's a long shot that we could get anyone to help, even though we might get lots of sympathy."

Morgan could feel Ashton getting angry, but she was surprised when he shouted at her.

"Why won't you at least try? Why are you trying to weasel out of writing a story? You've gone out on limbs before, lots of times."

"I'm not trying to weasel out of anything," Morgan said. "I'm trying to figure out what would be in Faiza's best interest."

"You sound like Dad."

His accusation stung. Ashton's voice choked and he glared at her, then looked at Kate. "My mom's losing her edge," he snapped, whipped the wheelchair into a 180-degree turn, and tore down the corridor.

Kate put an arm around Morgan's shoulder. "You're trying to fix it for him, but you don't have any control, really. And he feels like a first class wimp."

"But maybe he's right," Morgan said. "Maybe I am losing my edge."

Kate laughed. "Morgan, you couldn't possibly lose your edge."

"Oh, Kate. I've been losing it all along. For years. I haven't made an impact on anything for so long. And now, when there's a chance to do something, I'm hedging."

"You're not hedging," she argued. "You're gathering information as fast as you can. You can't help it if Peterson's sitting on his butt. And I, for one, trust your instinct about the newspaper."

"How do you mean?"

"Well," she answered, "for some reason you don't want this out in the news."

"Dowd says I'm getting Ashton's hopes up. And now Ashton says I sound like Dowd."

She smiled. "You know, girl, Dowd never was very good for your self-esteem."

"That's an understatement," Morgan said. "But I keep thinking about what that pilot said. About going over and getting her."

"And?" Kate said.

"Maybe, for now, it's better if they think they got away with it."

Kate nodded.

"And if what Grady said was even remotely possible, we still don't have a clue where she is."

"I've got an idea about that," Kate said. "It's wild, but you know, I've been in California for a long time."

"What?"

"I'll tell you later," she said. "When I set it up."

Morgan would have pressed her further but she was watching Ashton roll around a corner and out of sight.

"Ashton's holding something back," Morgan said.

"Well, yeah, the amnesia," said Kate.

"No, more than that. Something else."

"Any idea what it might be?"

"No. Maybe a problem with Faiza's visa, or something else about her family."

Morgan couldn't explain it, but it was a hit she often got as a reporter, that a piece of a story was missing. That someone wasn't telling the whole truth. Sometimes she knew what had tipped her off, like a verbal slip, or a person's body language, or a look in their eyes. But usually it was more of an intuition. And she was rarely ever wrong. Especially about her own son.

"I can feel it, Kate. There's something he's not telling us."

* * *

That evening Morgan sat down at Ashton's desk and turned on his computer. When the screen sprang to life, she signed on and called up Amnesty International's home page. She knew of Amnesty's worldwide mission against civil rights abuses and their campaign to free political prisoners, but what she didn't know was that in 2000, Amnesty had taken on Saudi Arabia.

In an international campaign called "The Secret State of Suffering," the organization condemned human rights violations in Saudi Arabia, particularly the execution and torture of prisoners, vicious floggings, foot and hand amputations, and electric shock to force confessions. A special report about women stated that women were especially persecuted because of sexual identity; for example, subjected to rape and sexual torture when they are in custody of the police or government. Morgan sent an email asking for information.

"It's chilling to think what might be happening to her," she confessed to Meredith later on the phone. "And it's tearing Ashton apart, to have absolutely no contact."

"That's why he got so mad at you, Mom," she said. "There isn't anyone else to strike out against right now."

Meredith and Morgan had been calling each other every day. Meredith's life was fairly crisis-free at the moment. She was finishing her master's degree and getting ready to start a job in the marketing department of a magazine publisher in Atlanta.

Morgan could tell her daughter was poised to come out to California if things got worse or if they got some terrible, unspeakable news. But for now she was continuing as mission control, doling out shreds of very noncommittal information to try to keep Dowd and Morgan's sister, Grace, believing they were fully informed. Morgan didn't want to worry them, and Meredith had the tact of an ambassador.

"I feel like I've been put in a pitch black room with a dart in my hand, and I'm supposed to hit the bull's eye," Morgan said.

"It's okay, Mom," Meredith told her. "You're gathering facts, building the story."

Meredith offered to get on the internet and try to find women's groups or advocacy groups who could help.

"I don't think Saudi Arabia has women's liberation organizations," Morgan told her.

"Probably not big public ones, but as you told me once, Mom, there are feminists everywhere women are getting put down."

"But women there are very restricted. They can't even walk down the street without a male escort. They sure as hell can't go out and form chapters of NOW."

"Think of it, Mom," Meredith said. "All it takes is a computer. You don't have to go outside or attend any meetings or even talk on the phone to anyone. And you can be anonymous. The internet is the perfect place for an underground."

"I wouldn't know where to start."

"I do. I'll call you later."

"Okay. I love you, kiddo."

"Love you, too, Mom."

Morgan sat back down at the computer. There was mail. She clicked on it, and found the following message:

> Hello, Morgan. My name is Larry Edwards. I am the Saudi Arabia coordinator for Amnesty International, and I understand you would like to talk to us about an issue there. Please let me know what would be a good time for us to talk, and I will call you, or you can call me.

He'd added his telephone number at the end of the message. Morgan picked up the phone, and dialed.

"This is Larry Edwards."

"Hi, Larry, this is Morgan Fay. I just got your email. Is this a good time to talk?"

CHAPTER TWENTY

Larry Edwards had a young, friendly voice. Morgan immediately liked him. He taught Middle Eastern studies at the University of Illinois and worked as a volunteer for Amnesty International, which he referred to as AI. He explained that although the U.S. headquarters was in Washington, D.C., there were volunteers located throughout the country. The world headquarters for AI was in London.

"How can I help you?" he asked.

As Morgan told him everything that had happened, he listened intently, murmuring a nod now and then. He understood easily, and when he interrupted and asked for clarification on some detail of the story, his tone was curious, not skeptical. When she was finished, she asked Larry, "Do you think our theory is right? That she was abducted by her family members?"

"Most probably," Larry said. "There's a lot of religious diversity, even in one family in Saudi. What you've described, the father being more liberal and the brother quite fundamentalist, is a common scenario."

"So the brother is a religious zealot who wants Faiza punished?"

"That would be the surface reason," Larry said. "But a lot of what passes for religion over there is really about power and control."

Morgan sighed. "There and everyplace else." She asked Larry if AI would be able to help.

"I can't really say at this point," he said. "But I can't be very encouraging. The focus of AI is on political groups, opposition groups, and the victims of governments. The young woman is not any of those. Unfortunately, this probably falls into the category of a family dispute. It's not that we don't care or don't think there are injustices. It's simply not within our mandate."

"Can you help us find out where she is?" Morgan asked.

"Saudi is a very tightly controlled country," he responded. "It's governed by a royal family with no particular interest in exchanging information with the outside world."

"They're happy to exchange oil with us," she offered.

"Oh, sure," he said. "But the rest of their business is nobody's business."

Larry explained that Saudi Arabia was a monarchy without elected representatives or political parties. At the time, the country was ruled by King Fahd bin Abdulaziz, a son of the king who had unified the country in the early twentieth century. The government declared the holy books of Islam —the Koran and the Sunnah of the Prophet Muhammad—to be the country's constitution. There was no concept there of the separation of church and state, and the government suppressed opposition views, as well as much information and communication from the outside world.

"Of all the Arab countries, we know the least about Saudi Arabia," Larry said. "The U.S. has an embassy there, and our military personnel are there, but it is difficult for individuals from the U.S. to travel there unless they are invited for business reasons, and all foreign media is forbidden.

"Being in trouble there is a lot different from being in trouble here," he went on. "Especially if you have violated Islamic law, because it is also the law of the land—Islamic law as interpreted by the rulers, that is. And the Saudis are deeply conservative Sunni Muslims."

Larry explained that an organization called the al-Mutawa'een, or religious police, was known as the Committee to Prevent Vice and Promote Virtue. Its job was to monitor public behavior.

"It's the Mutawa'een who might club a woman in the street if she is caught without her head and body covered," he said. "Or without a man. Women can't leave the house unless they are in the company of a male relative or an employee. They can't board a bus alone, or travel outside the country. They can't drive cars.

"The Mutawa'een can arrest, intimidate, abuse anyone they want. And they do. Arrests are often arbitrary, and people, especially foreigners, are detained for long periods of time. In a more conservative city, like Riyadh, the Mutawa'een might break up a gathering of women, not because any law is being broken, but just because they don't like it."

In court, a woman's testimony did not carry the same weight as that of a man, Larry continued. One man equaled two women. "In criminal cases, you need two witnesses, or four in the case of adultery. Unless there is a confession. So there is considerable incentive to try to get confessions, through coercion or torture."

He paused to exhale a deep breath. "I must tell you, there is very little anyone can do for Faiza. Especially since you don't know for sure where she is, or even if she is imprisoned. Most likely she's being held in a home."

"Why do you say that?"

"Because in Saudi, the family is sacrosanct. And the family takes care of its own problems. Or actually, the male head of household does."

"But she's in a lot of trouble," Morgan ventured.

"Oh, yes, I would think so," Larry said. "She has been involved with a non-Saudi man and a non-Muslim to boot. She has violated religious law, which is tantamount to violating state law."

"Does Amnesty take a lot of action in Saudi Arabia?" Morgan asked.

"No. We don't do zip there," Larry said. "The government won't let us in, and frankly my dear, they don't give a damn what we say. They control everything, including internet access, and Amnesty International's web page is locked out. Direct pressure from the U.S. government is the only thing they might respond to."

"So if you decided to take Faiza's case, what would you do?"

"Well, first you have to find her. Then we'd exhaust all the routine channels, such as contacting the Saudi government and writing letters and so forth. And at the same time all those things are not working, we'd try to get the State Department involved."

Larry did not offer much hope for State Department involvement. But he did give Morgan the name of someone she could contact there. He also gave her the number of a woman in San Francisco named Vicki Saba, whose daughter had been abducted to Saudi Arabia several years before.

"There's something you need to understand," Larry said. "This country is, in a way, very new. Up until only recently, Saudi Arabia was an agricultural, pastoral, desert, tribal society. The oil industry changed it into a rapidly urbanizing one with a ton of money. There has been sudden wealth, sudden technology. Even if your friend was not in the royal family, hers could be very well off, and it's quite feasible that they could charter a plane and come over here to get her."

He paused. "You know, I see this country as sort of schizophrenic. Modern technology being used to perpetuate a medieval lifestyle."

"Larry," Morgan ventured. "In your literature, AI calls for giving political asylum to women who are persecuted because of their sexual identity. Consider that Faiza was abducted because she is a woman. So in that sense, isn't she a political prisoner of sorts?"

"Not really a political prisoner," he said. "But if she were to escape, we might help her get asylum in a safe country."

"Here in the U.S.?"

"Maybe," he said. "It would depend on how much clout her family has in Saudi. You see, our government and the Saudi government are very cozy."

"This is so unfair," Morgan said, not to attack Larry, but in frustration about the whole picture. "Everything is so damned political."

"I'm sorry I can't be more encouraging," Larry said. "But I will talk to the London office about it. A lot will depend on whether this case would fall within our mandate, and also what resources are available right now. Her capture is a gray area. She is an adult, and she is not allowed to travel freely, so her human rights are being violated. But it's a judgment call. In the meantime, we would need some proof that she is imprisoned and wants to get out."

"Could she be at risk of an honor killing?"

"We don't think there are a lot of honor killings in Saudi Arabia," Larry said. "It seems to be more prevalent in other countries, such as Jordan. But it's possible. We know so little about what goes on inside those borders." He paused. "However, it is against the law for Saudi women to marry foreigners or non-Muslims. And even though she wasn't married, she consorted with your son. And adultery is a crime."

"So you're saying that . . ."

"There is ample reason to believe that her life is in danger."

CHAPTER TWENTY-ONE

This was Kate's wildass idea: To contact a psychic.

"Granted, we're in California," Morgan said, actually laughing. "And I'm no stranger to metaphysics. But still . . . "

"No shit," she said. "You were the one having séances when the rest of us were out in the backyard tying clover necklaces."

When Morgan was in grade school she'd been fascinated by the supernatural and devoured stories about haunted houses and ghosts. She and her older sister, Grace, put on séances in the basement of their house, where, with the help of lots of string, they made tables rock back and forth and spooky knocking sounds on the wall. They dressed in their mom's old silky nightgowns, shawls made from scraps of netting, and handfuls of chains with pendants they found in a jewelry box that belonged to their grandma (amulets, Grace called them).

Once, they took a white bedsheet and wrapped the middle around wadded up newspaper in the shape of a head, and then made the sheet (visitor from the spirit world, Grace called it) fly across the basement. They weren't allowed to burn candles, which would have created the perfect ghostly ambiance, so they covered flashlights with red and purple silk scarves. Even though the strings were painted with black ink, the room had to be pretty dark to conceal them and fool their devotees, who were younger kids whom they further distracted by holding their flashlights under their chins and closing their eyes and chanting: "Oh spirits, be present for these nonbelievers."

It was very effective. Their coup came when Skipper Bailey, the neighborhood bully, saw the sheet-spirit come sailing across the room. Skipper had a crewcut that stuck straight up, making his head look like an upside-down pear with grass on the top, and his complexion was pale, which made the ruddy smears on his cheeks stand out, accentuating his nasty temper and petty cruelty.

For a delicious moment, they had him spooked with the flashlight capers and the chants and, perhaps, the power they claimed back in their little basement coven. When a corner of the ghost sheet brushed across his head, he screamed and ran howling up the basement stairs.

Later they cheered, and Grace said they had been vindicated, and when Morgan asked her what that meant, Grace said it was like revenge where the spirits help.

Grace predicted that Skipper would never put another wriggling half-squashed stinkbug down Morgan's shorts. And he never did.

*   *   *

Morgan and Kate helped Ashton unpack and get settled in the living room in his wheelchair. Morgan chatted about how the doctor had said he would probably be out of the chair and onto crutches in a couple of weeks. He smiled weakly. He had been aloof and distant ever since he'd yelled at her that day in the hospital for not going to the press.

Sometimes she wanted to grab him by his huffy, cold shoulders and remind him how much she had done for him during the past few weeks, few years, life. And then she'd remember that it wasn't personal, that he was angry not at her, but at some pokerfaced, anonymous computer-sketched thug that no one could apparently identify or touch. And, most of all, he felt impotent—not even a failed rescuer, but worse, he saw himself as a non-rescuer, a guy who didn't even try to fight back, and he was fist-pounding, wall-kicking angry at himself.

Morgan let Kate break the news about the psychic. "Desperate times call for desperate measures," she said, a little too brightly. He was noncommittal. He'd seen his mom do plenty of unconventional things, but this was right on the edge.

Morgan nodded. "It isn't as if we have a lot of options at this point," she said. "Anyway, it's not like astrology is avant garde anymore, now that Republicans do it. Hell, Nancy Reagan had an astrologer on call in the White House. We still don't know how much of Reagan's policies in those days were influenced by that."

"Probably some of the better ones," Kate said.

"So go along with us, okay?" said Morgan.

Ashton grimaced. "Don't I usually?"

"Oops. Too late," Kate said, glancing out the window. "She's here."

When Autumn Spiritwind stepped out of her dark blue Saturn, Morgan could tell right away that she wasn't going to be any garden-variety, 900-number psychic. The instant her foot touched the pavement, it seemed to be grounded, as if there were magnets in her Birkenstocks, riveting her to the earth and drawing in energy from somewhere deep in its core. A bumper sticker on her car said: The Goddess is alive and magic is afoot.

She wore a long skirt, indigo splashed with purple and rose flowers, the style of skirt Morgan always wished she could wear but when she put one on, she looked like a Halloween-costume gypsy. Autumn Spiritwind probably never looked like anyone but herself. An orchid shirt hung loosely over the skirt. The shirt, Morgan observed later, was actually jersey, but it fell around Autumn like silk. She wore one long strand of crystals, small pastel chips of fluorite, and then another silver chain with an enormous chunk of rutilated quartz that looked like it might have broken off a meteor. Her hair was a gorgeous dark blonde, loose and thick like in shampoo commercials. Morgan felt a twinge of envy. Autumn probably lost more hair in a day in the tub drain than Morgan had grown for her whole life.

She guessed Autumn was also in her early forties, but her hazel eyes, soft but catlike, burned with the warmth and knowing of a much older person. She carried a large, fringed burlap bag, straight out of the sixties. Kate walked out to greet her, and when Autumn saw her, her wonderful smile opened even wider.

The instant Autumn Spiritwind walked in the door to Ashton's apartment, Morgan felt the energy of a woman who walked her talk. Ruthlessly honest, unequivocally confident. And who demanded the same from everyone around her. Morgan silently wondered what color her aura would be. Orange, maybe. Mixed with red and circled by white. Power colors surrounded by wisdom.

There were no preliminaries. Autumn went right to work. Gently, she asked the group to sit in a circle. "Grab pillows or whatever makes you comfortable," she said. They arranged themselves next to Ashton's wheelchair.

Autumn knelt and dug into her burlap bag, removing various props. She unfolded a silk scarf with a whirlwind design of purples, golds, greens, and yellows, and spread it out in front of her. On the scarf she set out two white and three green candles, an incense holder, a small ceramic bowl, a deck of tarot cards, and a bundle of dried sage. From a small red silk pouch, she drew an assortment of crystals, among them amethyst, quartz, moonstone, fluorite, and obsidian, and slowly, thoughtfully arranged them in a grouping, as though she was setting up a display at a flea market. Morgan found it rather hypnotic, watching her.

Next, Autumn reached into her bag and brought out a pack of matches. With a grin and a wink, she held them up for them to see. On the cover was a photo of the early Elvis on one side, the older Elvis on the other.

"Got these at Graceland last year," she said. "Aren't they a hoot?" Kate laughed, but Ashton and Morgan held theirs back. "Hey, it's okay to laugh," Autumn said. "You don't have to be heavy and solemn. The guides like it better when you lighten up."

Autumn lit the candles and held the dried sage over a flame. The sage bundle ignited, flamed briefly, and then smoldered like a big cigar. Smoked curled out from the end, smelling a little like marijuana, only sweeter, less pungent. She passed the bundle around her body, and with her hands, gently wafted the smoke toward her face. Then she passed the sage to Kate, who followed the same motions, and passed the bundle to Morgan, who smudged herself and then wafted the smoke toward Ashton. He looked embarrassed at first, then shrugged and took the stick.

Autumn sat back, closed her eyes, and began to breathe deeply and evenly. "Let your eyes close and breathe with me," she told them.

Omigod, Morgan thought, *if only Grace could be here.* Oh great spirits, be present for these nonbelievers. They could have Skipper Bailey's balls with this scene. Several minutes passed. Morgan could feel them all relaxing into the mood. Maybe nothing would happen; maybe the so-called guides wouldn't talk to Autumn Spiritwind. But for sure they weren't calling Ashton on the silent cellphone.

"We are here about one who has been taken from us. We thank the guides and ask for information to be channeled through me, so that we may learn of her whereabouts and her state of well-being."

Autumn opened her eyes and turned to Ashton. "The guides want me to hold an object, something that belongs to her."

He nodded toward the yellow sweater on the tip of the surfboard, and Morgan got up and handed it to Autumn. She folded the sweater on her lap and stroked it, like she was cuddling a kitten. Then she was silent.

They sat that way for a long time, long enough for Morgan to notice sounds that would have ordinarily been white noise: the faucet in the kitchen dripping into a cup of water, cars moving outside in the street, the hum of the refrigerator motor.

Finally Autumn spoke.

"The guides are sending me sensations from her. It is the energy of fear. Fear and anger. But, as we know, anger is the face of fear. It is that kind of anger, and another kind as well. There is self-righteous anger. She has been grievously wronged. There are those who would try to confuse her. Try to persuade her that she deserves a bad fate. That she is the one who has transgressed. There is a confusion of guilt and shame and blame around her, and . . . and . . . "

Ashton drew in his breath and exhaled with a deep sigh, a sigh that asked, What, for god's sake, *what*?

"Meanness," Autumn said. "Mean-spiritedness."

They waited. Finally, Ashton whispered. "Where is she?"

"I am getting a message," Autumn intoned. "But I'm having trouble decoding it. You see, the guides speak to me through images, not language. Language is a human construction and not a medium of expression between this world and the unseen world. There, they use pictures to speak to us. So the process is like recapturing a dream from fragments and partial images."

"What are you seeing exactly?" Kate asked.

"That's the trouble. It's all dark. No images. No pictures, or shapes, or outlines, or anything that would give me a clue. Only black. Pitch darkness. No light."

"Oh God," Ashton said. "That means she's . . ."

Autumn grasped Ashton's hand. "Oh no, dear. I know what you are thinking. No. One thing is certain. The guides tell me it is not a death I am perceiving. They say, Her life force has not left your world. She is alive."

They all nearly collapsed with relief, as though they had just gotten the call with the reprieve from the governor. Here, in a few minutes in a smoky circle around a bunch of candles and rocks, they were already one hundred percent believing this woman, who was plucking answers out of the cosmos somewhere. From a source Morgan couldn't verify.

What would Peterson think about this? Or Dowd? Dowd pooh-poohed anything that couldn't be proven by a laboratory test. He would say, statistically, she has a fifty-fifty chance of being right.

But, Morgan reasoned, even if she was wrong, in this moment they needed her to be right. And maybe that's why it was okay, for now, to go along. To let herself believe this woman. To let herself feel relief. Oh great spirits, be present for these nonbelievers.

Autumn picked up the tarot cards and began dealing them out in front of her.

"The Emperor," she began. "She is in the hands of authoritarian figures. Males. Males who rule with an iron fist." Autumn laid out more cards. "There is a religious theme to her plight. It is about religion. The men are acting out religious law. She is the victim of a harsh patriarchy, of dogma, rigid rules."

Autumn dealt another card. On it was the picture of a woman, clothed in red and black like streaks of light, with an eerie smoky background. The figure had a chain on its neck.

"The Devil card," Autumn pronounced. She paused, regarding it, and nodded sadly.

"Now I understand the darkness," she said. "And the absence of light."

"Oh God, what?" breathed Morgan.

"She is in a prison. A prison with no lights."

CHAPTER
TWENTY-TWO

After Autumn's pronouncement, they sat in horrified silence for a long time. If this were true, Faiza must have been arrested.

Morgan remembered the Amnesty International report about the medieval prison conditions in Saudi Arabia. It told of people being held for months without being allowed to make contact with anyone, let alone a legal representative. Of trials that lasted less than an hour. Of confessions forced by torture and summary executions without warning. Floggings. Rapes. Beheadings.

"Can you tell us more about the prison?" Morgan asked.

"I must go very deep into my meditation," Autumn said. "I will need some time. And help. Everyone, I want you to concentrate all your energy on this woman. Don't try to see her in any certain way, or ask for anything. Only think about whatever aspect of her comes to mind. And stay with that image."

In pagan times, Autumn explained, covens of witches would make contact with one of theirs who was being beaten, tortured, and raped by the Inquisitors. The witches would concentrate their energy and send it to the captive, to comfort her, to surround her with support and love. Sometimes they would help the woman leave her body so she could escape the pain, or they would take some of the pain away from her and distribute it among the group. The stupid, arrogant tormentors had no idea this was going on, no clue they were raping an empty vessel, a woman dead to them.

Autumn's breathing was at first deep, then changed to shallow and soundless. Morgan's legs had gone to sleep, so she stretched them out in front of her, massaging her tingling thighs while still maintaining the image of Faiza.

Morgan had trouble picturing Faiza's face, because it had been a while since she'd seen her, but she could recall how the young woman smiled, wide and uninhibited, her lips holding nothing back, her dark eyes sparkling with a touch of mischief. As if she never lost awareness, not even for a moment, of the deliciousness of freedom. If Faiza were an animal, Morgan thought, she'd be a lynx, loup cervier, lithe but hardy and frisky, with keen eyesight.

"This is not a trance," Autumn said. "I am not a medium. I am fully conscious, connecting with the universal flow, with the All That Is, and in that flow I am open to messages from the guides and from sensations about beings and events, because we are all one. We are not really connecting with another separate being, but rather with the oneness that is us all. In this space there is no distance among us, there is no separation of time and place."

"My image," Ashton said quietly, "was of Faiza curled up on my lap, my arms around her. Then I wrapped a soft, thick blanket around us both, hiding her, comforting her." Under the blanket, he said, he stroked her long black hair, as smooth and glassy as the back of a wave.

"I felt her. I really did," he said. "I think she got it. Felt me there."

Autumn reached out to pick up one of the lighted candles and turned it slowly in her fingers.

"I'm confused," she said. "The guides are sending me sensations of a place that is not as—not as hard as a conventional prison. It is dark, very dark, but not like a prison in other ways." Autumn paused, then sighed and nodded, like a news anchor getting cues from the control room through an earphone.

"The woman is confined, held against her will, and she is terrified by the darkness. It is not a prison. It is another type of building. I think maybe she is in a house. Locked in a room."

"It's her uncle," Ashton said.

"Can you reach this household?" Autumn asked.

"No," Ashton said. "I never knew his name. I only knew her father's name, and he has died. But wait . . . Faiza has two relatives who live here. They were her chaperones, sort of, although she is the one who watches over them. They're really old."

"Do you know where they live?"

"Yes," Ashton said. "I went there sometimes with her. To take them food."

"Call them," they all said together.

"No," Ashton said. "They are too old and frail, and their English is not very good."

"Go see them," Autumn directed.

"We'll all go," Kate said.

Autumn rose and stood over Ashton's chair. "Close your eyes," she directed. He obeyed, and she placed his hand in hers.

"You must let go of the guilt," she said gently. "You did your best."

Ashton shook his head vehemently. "No, I did nothing."

Autumn looked confused. "Don't you remember?"

"Remember what?" he asked.

"You must remember," she said.

Ashton dropped his face into his palms, and Autumn gently pressed her hand on his head. They remained that way for a long time.

"Omigod," he finally groaned.

"You remember," she stated.

He looked up from his hands, his eyes wide as a struck dog and his color pale as an oyster.

"I remember," he whispered.

*   *   *

As Autumn knelt and collected her props and tucked

them back into her bag, they all chatted quietly. The mood was still very ethereal. "Keep the candles burning," Autumn said. She rose to leave, but then sat back down again. "There's one thing that's confusing me still."

"What?"

"When I was connecting with the energy in the dark room, at first I felt that she was alone. And then I also felt the presence of another being."

"Someone is in there with her?"

"It's unclear," Autumn said. "The feeling was of two life forces. The image was like two candles side by side in the dark. Only one was a much bigger and brighter flame than the other. The second was like a tiny little light. Does that make any sense to anyone?"

Kate and Morgan shook their heads. Ashton's eyes looked wide and startled.

"What is it?" Autumn asked him.

He looked away. "Nothing."

"Something flashed across your face. What were you thinking?"

"Nothing," Ashton repeated, rather vehemently. "I'm mad as hell. Isn't that enough?" He clenched his fists and pounded them into the vinyl armrests. "Those bastards! Those goddamn bastards!"

Autumn turned again to Ashton and spoke sternly but with kindness, like a schoolteacher you might both love and fear.

"You fought for her once," she said. "And you will fight for her again."

CHAPTER TWENTY-THREE

After Autumn Spiritwind left, Morgan searched Ashton's eyes. "You fought for her once," she said. "What did Autumn mean?" Then she and Kate listened in grieved shock as Ashton's missing memory came pouring out.

That morning on Half Moon Bay, at first his eyes wouldn't open, he told them. He had pulled at his eyelids from inside, trying to pry them open with his thoughts, his will. His mouth tasted like someone had poured Novocain down his nostrils into his throat—full, acidy, numb. Something was pushing on his forehead from inside, and he wondered if his brain was exploding.

Maybe he had been hit by his surfboard. Maybe he was drowning and his head was filled with water. Maybe he was at the bottom of the ocean and the pressure was collapsing his skull. *Faiza!* he shouted, making no sound. Of course, he was shouting into water. His mouth must be filled with it. And then he remembered that he hadn't been on a wave. He had been standing at a doorway. And now he was on the floor, clawing at dry, institutional carpet and trying to see, to get up.

Faiza! Where was she? He had to get his eyes open. And on his feet. Whoever had done this to him, the man who had grabbed him, he must have Faiza now. *Faiza!* he screamed soundlessly again. The room was quiet, except for a rustle somewhere in another dimension, coming from where his ears and head were.

Someone was in the room, moving quietly and quickly toward the door. He saw legs and some black, the bottom of a dress maybe, but it was all blurred. He rose to his knees, squinting like someone with bad vision who had just lost his inch-thick spectacles.

And then the awful acrid smell rose up from his chest, or it could have been from his throat, and he toppled back onto the floor. Just as he realized he had been poisoned, he heard the door shut soundly, and he knew they had taken Faiza.

Later, maybe seconds, maybe minutes, he drifted back into the hazy altered state that passed for consciousness, but this time he was slightly more cognizant. He surveyed the room, the bed, the open bathroom door, and came to the conclusion, with the elemental reasoning of a drunk, that Faiza was really gone.

Ashton stumbled to the door, opened it, and paused to figure out which way led out. Right. No, left. Left was longer. He remembered the room was at the end of the hall. Left. He set his legs in motion to run, but it was probably more like a careen, his legs limp as wet socks. He lifted and set them down in front of him, as fast as he could manage. He lurched onward as if in a horrible nightmare, but at least his legs were moving.

Ashton crashed into the glass double doors and thrust his body against the lever. They opened with a thwock, and the morning sun stabbed at his eyes like hot razor tips. He covered his gaze, searching the parking lot.

And that's when he saw the two men, pushing Faiza into a black Mercedes. They had her arms and she was twisting, trying to yank herself free. The black cloak they had wrapped around her fell halfway off her shoulders in the struggle, releasing her muffled cries.

Faiza! he shouted weakly, hoarsely. It looked as if she turned slightly, toward his voice, but the men grabbed her head and pushed her further into the car. Faiza! he screamed again. *Faiza!*

He loped toward the Mercedes as the door shut and the

car began to move forward. And then he was in the air, leaping, flying toward the back of the car, like a bodyguard who's heard gunshots fired at a motorcade. The driver accelerated, and Ashton gripped his fingers into the rim of the back window in order to stay on the trunk.

The windows were tinted too dark to see inside, but he imagined Faiza craning to see him, her mouth open in fear and shock and her lovely dark brown eyes reaching out, pleading, *help me, help me.* He clung on for dear life, sprawled on the slick metal, miraculously keeping hold as the vehicle careened out onto the road. He beat on the window, shouting, Let her go! Let her go!

The car began to swerve, first left, then right, its tires squealing as the driver jerked the steering wheel, slammed the brakes, sped up, like a bucking bronco trying to expel its rider. When the automobile reached a speed of probably fifty miles an hour, a sharp cut to the left tore away Ashton's grip and hurled him dozens of feet into the air, flinging him onto the pavement, where his body bounced and twirled like a discarded soda can before rolling to a stop in the weeds on the shoulder of the road.

CHAPTER TWENTY-FOUR

When Morgan was growing up, she was fascinated by teeter-totters. First you were on the downside, and then you were on the upside and your partner was on the downside. Up and down, back and forth. The speed and rhythm of the rocking seemed to depend on the weight of the two riders, but there had to be an exact instant somewhere in the middle of each cycle when the shift actually occurred. A subtle point in time when the bulk of the weight on one side yielded to the other.

So, as Ashton told the story of what happened that morning, Morgan felt a shift inside her, like a teeter-totter, a microsecond when the balance flipped and something inside her crossed over. Maybe it was the absolute knowledge that Faiza had indeed been abducted against her will, now indisputable because there was an eyewitness. Or the chilling picture of her being pushed into that car. Or the ghastly image of Ashton hurtling down the side of Highway 1.

She wasn't sure what did it. But during that unidentifiable nanosecond, Morgan went from anger to rage, from insult to hatred, from passive to active. She wanted to get Faiza back more than anything in the world. She wanted to kill those bastards who attacked her son. She suddenly despised Faiza's country for its misogyny and her own country for its indifference.

She longed to get her hands around Grady's little pilot neck and throttle him and his don't-ask-don't-tell smugness.

He could have stopped it and he didn't do a damn thing. And she was mad at Dowd for telling her to leave it to the higher-ups, for implying that she was powerless.

And she was furious with herself—for what? For not stopping it somehow. For not protecting her child. For not being able to kiss the owies and make them better. For not being able to wave a magic wand and make Faiza reappear. For not doing the impossible.

And sometime during that moment, Morgan vowed that she would do whatever it took to get Faiza back. It was her against them now.

She wanted revenge. She wanted justice.

*   *   *

"You drive," Morgan told Kate, as they piled into Ashton's Saturn wagon. "You know the city."

Ashton handed Kate the keys and maneuvered into the back, where he stretched his broken leg out on the seat. They folded his wheelchair and slid it into the rear compartment where the surfboards usually rode.

"How you doing, kid?" asked Kate, squeezing Ashton's good leg. He smiled and shrugged. She started the car, took a moment to acquaint herself with the dashboard, and then peeled away from the curb as though this little green car was an old friend. She zipped around two corners and swiftly merged into the traffic on the parkway.

Following Ashton's directions, Kate maneuvered the slender streets and precipitous hills with their almost perpendicular drop-offs like the aerobatic pilot she was. Kate was as good a driver as she was a pilot. Though she drove fast and boldly, she was provident in her moves, and even when she was talking her attention stayed on the car, the road, the horizon.

Of Morgan's two best friends, Kate and Linnie, Kate was the one with her feet most on the ground, Morgan thought. How ironic. The pilot, the flyer, was the grounded one. Maybe it was the navigational skills, or maybe a certain temperament, but she always seemed to know where she was.

Linnie was good at particulars and always had stuff in her purse that other people needed but forgot, like aspirin and lip balm and a Swiss Army knife with a corkscrew. She would never find herself out of cigarettes at midnight. But Linnie also had a wild side. She was the one who came up with crazy ideas of places to run off to and pranks to pull. In college, for instance, it had been her idea to sneak into the psychology lab in the middle of the night and free all the white rats from their little Skinner boxes.

And Morgan? She was not sure what she contributed. Linnie said she wouldn't have thought of freeing the rats if it hadn't been for Morgan, who had been so upset when she learned one day in class that the rats were denied water before the experiments. No wonder the poor dehydrated creatures learned so quickly to press the little levers to get water.

Before they opened the lab window and the rats, with some urging, scurried out of the cages and over the windowsill and into the tops of the hedge, they let them all drink from a huge bowl of water. That was Linnie's idea. Kate thought they should leave the cages with the doors ajar, suggesting a scenario of one rat getting free and going around letting all the others out.

Linnie and Kate said Morgan inspired them. So, say, if they robbed a bank, Linnie would draw the map and pack the ropes and things, and Kate would drive the getaway car. And it would have been all Morgan's idea.

When Ashton was hurt and Morgan called Linnie from the hospital, Linnie had offered to come out and help. Morgan replied that everything was under control but perhaps they would need her help later. It was comforting that she was a nurse, and Morgan called her often to ask questions about Ashton's leg or one of his other injuries, questions that may have seemed menial to the doctor, but that Linnie answered quite thoughtfully and sympathetically.

Who in her life gets even one friend like this, someone

who would drop everything and be at your side? And Morgan had two. *That's just plain lucky,* she thought.

*   *   *

Baasim and Yasmeen Salah lived in a duplex on a narrow side street. The house was old and small, but very tidy. The steps looked newly painted gray, with strips of green synthetic turf on the center of each step. On each side of the top step stood two clay pots of pink impatiens. The soil looked dry, and fallen blossoms littered the area around the base of the pots. The stems of the plants were beginning to curl and wither.

There was no way to get a wheelchair onto the porch, so Ashton waited while Kate and Morgan walked up and tapped gently on the door. When there was no response, Kate knocked again. They waited, and still no answer.

"Let's try the back," he suggested. But on the way they were hailed by a woman waving from the doorway of the second apartment. She was probably in her early eighties, wearing a vanilla shirtwaist and clutching a dark blue sweater around her shoulders.

"She probably won't hear you," the woman said, shaking her head. She had a distinct middle European accent, German or Polish maybe.

Ashton smiled up at her and extended his hand. "We're friends," he said. "Do you know if the Salahs are in?"

"As I said, she won't hear you."

"Is she all right?" Ashton asked. "I'm a friend of theirs, and this is my mother and her friend."

The woman shook her head sadly and pursed her lips. "It's so sad. I've known them for twelve years. We take care of each other, you know? And now there is nothing I can do if she don't hear me."

"What happened?"

"You don't know," she said, part question, part statement of fact. "Very sudden, bless his heart. Sitting in his chair in the living room. Last Thursday."

"Baasim died?"

"No one phoned you?"

"No. My girlfriend is their niece, and she has been. . . " Ashton stumbled.

"Out of town," Morgan finished.

The woman nodded. "Oh yes. The sweet young woman who came to visit. Too bad. Yasmeen won't talk, she won't even look at me. I don't know if she hears or not. I take food over, maybe soup and toast and some cheese, but she don't eat. Sometimes when I go back, some of the food is gone. But only little bites."

"Is there any other family?" Morgan asked.

"No one," said the woman. "Only neighbors and me."

"Do you think it would be okay if we went in and paid our respects?" Kate asked.

"The door is open," she said. "You know, if they find out, they will come and get her. The neighbors are pitching in, but don't you go reporting her. She don't need no more trouble."

"We won't do anything that could hurt her," Ashton assured her.

The woman nodded, instantly willing to trust him. Ashton was so gracious, and so gently authentic. Morgan thought she'd burst with the awareness that he was no longer a child, hadn't been one for some time—but what a fine man he'd become.

Morgan turned the knob and the door yielded. The living room was dusky dark, and it smelled like the inside of a neglected closet. Yasmeen was sitting in an overstuffed olive green chair, her hands dangling over thick, wide armrests. Her body looked almost like it had been posed, but her eyes stared vacantly ahead, as if indifferent to whatever the body was choosing to do.

The room was furnished simply but neatly, with furniture styles that looked like an arrangement in a middle-grade consignment shop. The hardwood floor was dulled but clean, like an old school library. The green chair had a mate, a smaller version separated from the larger one by a round pedestal-lamp table. Morgan wondered if the chair Yasmeen was sitting in was the one in which her husband had died. A small sideboard held a display of a half dozen photographs in an eclectic assortment of frames. Among them was a black and white snapshot of Faiza, smiling broadly, a white scarf wrapped around her head.

Yasmeen did not acknowledge their entrance. Kate walked over and knelt beside the chair. She greeted the woman in a soft voice, and when she didn't respond, Kate lightly touched her arm. Still nothing. They all remained in silence for a few moments; then Kate tried again. Yasmeen stared ahead.

Morgan picked up the photo of Faiza from the sideboard and knelt down on the other side of the chair. Kate looked up at her and shook her head. Morgan knew what she was thinking. They could not tell this woman the truth about Faiza. They could not deepen her grief any more.

"My son visited here with Faiza," Morgan said, speaking slowly and deliberately. "He is waiting outside. Do you remember?"

Yasmeen turned her head slowly, looking first at the photo and then into Morgan's face, her stare still blank and lifeless.

"I'm sorry about your husband," Morgan said. "This is my friend, and we came to see if you have heard from Faiza recently." Morgan sounded as if she'd just run into her at the vegetable counter in the grocery store.

Yasmeen looked back at the picture.   "Gone," she said.

Kate and Morgan exchanged glances. Was she talking about Faiza or her husband?

"Yes," Kate said, noncommittally. "I'm sorry."

"Gone." Yasmeen began to moan softly, in a voice slightly louder than a whisper. Tears filled her eyes, and she covered her face with one hand.

"Have you heard from Faiza?" Morgan tried again. Yasmeen moaned into her palm.

Morgan felt so sorry for this woman. And apologetic for their intrusion. How many times had she, as a reporter, tried to coax information out of someone whose heart was breaking with grief? You can be as gentle and respectful as possible, but you still want what you want, and what they want is to be left alone. So you try to convince a mother who has just lost her baby, or the sister of a woman who's been beaten and killed by her own husband, that what they share with you will somehow enlighten others and therefore help make the world a better place to live. Which, in the case of news, was usually not what happened. Of course the one you're really trying to convince is yourself—that you have a higher purpose there. But what you're really after is a good story. And you'll say whatever you have to say to get it.

"Who is gone?" Morgan said.

"All, gone," Yasmeen mumbled. She took the photograph and wrapped her bony arms around it. Then she rocked from side to side, weeping louder now.

"Where is she?" Kate asked.

Suddenly, Yasmeen seemed to be awake to her visitors' questions, and their concern. She spoke with a heavy but rich accent, all in present tense.

"She is taken back. She is punished. We cannot speak. Haatim call my husband and say she is gone to us. His heart is break."

"Can you tell us where she is? Do you know an address? A telephone number?"

Yasmeen shook her head. "Noooo. I never know that. The men only talk. My husband know but I do not."

"Is there an address book? Or a place where the numbers are written?"

"My husband know but I do not," Yasmeen repeated. "When my husband gets back, he know."

Kate touched Yasmeen's hand and rose. Morgan started to follow, but Kate waved at her to stay put. Why prolong their stay? Even if there was a way to get the uncle's telephone number, what good would it do for them to call? "Hello, this is the young man your niece defied the will of Allah with. Could I speak with her please? We haven't talked in such a long time, and how are things over there, anyway? Hot?" It seemed like a dark comedic monologue.

Kate walked nonchalantly across the room to the sideboard and, not taking her eyes off Yasmeen, floated into the small desk chair. Part of the sideboard was a small pull-down secretary, closed, with a tarnished gold key in the lock. Kate nodded to Morgan, with an expression that instructed her to keep talking to Yasmeen. Morgan followed her command and continued a one-sided chat with Yasmeen about her house, her furniture, the flowers outside. She told her how sorry she felt for her loss. Yasmeen did not respond. But she also didn't notice Kate, who had opened the secretary and was slipping her hands into the desk drawer.

"What were you doing?" Morgan whispered later, when they got back outside.

"Look, there had to be an address book or an index card with a telephone number and address for Faiza's uncle in Saudi Arabia," Kate said.

"But this poor woman. You rifled through her drawers?"

"Not drawers. Drawer. One. And we need that address," Kate said. She handed Ashton a small book. The cover was old, cracked brown leather, and the little alphabet tabs on the pages were worn or missing altogether. "We can return it later," she said.

"Oh, geez," said Morgan.

Kate shrugged. "Look, we need that address. Now we've got it."

Morgan started to smile, and then out of the corner of her eye saw a form in the doorway. It was Yasmeen, barely balancing, her shoulders bent forward and her frail hands clutching the doorframe. She looked out at the three of them, and then directly into Ashton's eyes.

Yasmeen's eyes were no longer glazed, but dark brown,

and as wide and penetrating as an owl's.

"You help her," she said, in the tone of not a question, but a demand.

Ashton turned back toward her. "Yes, ma'am, we will," he said, as steady and sure as when he planted his feet on his surfboard and cut into the face of a wave.

"We will help her."

CHAPTER TWENTY-FIVE

Morgan spread the blanket out on the beach. She took the precious cellphone from her backpack to make sure it was turned on, then tucked it back in, safe from the gusty wind and the wet sand, as if it was a brand new baby and she was the nurse.

It was hopeless, of course. It had been almost two months and they all knew Faiza wasn't going to call, but whenever the phone did ring, she felt a small part of her stir that she reserved for the improbable. Hello, this is Faiza, the breathless voice would say. It's all been a big mistake. I'm in London. Or Amsterdam. Or Toronto. I'll be there on the next plane.

Kate left two days after their visit to Yasmeen's, to go back to Santa Barbara for a while. Before she left, she went to the university campus and easily found a professor of Arab and Muslim studies to translate the purloined address book, which was in Arabic. She was able to get the address of Faiza's family in Dhahran.

In the meantime, Ashton and Morgan had spent most of their time stationed at the computer, taking turns on the keyboard. They got up to eat meals or to go outside for a walk —a roll, as Ashton called it. His shoulder was healing quickly, and the doctor said he could try the crutches in another week. It would be months before the leg healed, but the prospect of getting out of the wheelchair was lifting his spirits. This day, he had asked Morgan to help him maneuver over to the beach.

She settled onto the blanket as Ashton gazed out at the

water, studying the horizon.

"Good waves?" she asked.

"Yeah," he said, a little sad but mostly matter-of-fact. "It's good."

Here they were, just like when he was growing up: Morgan sitting on the beach, squinting into the sun, trying to identify Ashton in the dozens of faraway silhouettes as they plunged down and across the face of the waves, or bobbed in the white froth, or stretched across a board, arms circling like paddlewheels, pitching the point of the board headlong into the exploding whitewater, under and over and back out to sea to catch another and another wave. Only today, of course, he wasn't out there, but sitting right next to her.

Morgan still had difficulty spotting him when he was out amidst the pack, even though she memorized the design on his board and the color of his wetsuit and knew by heart his own special style as he dropped in on a wave, his way of pushing and leaning from his left-handed stance with his head tilted slightly, as he zigzagged across the face or bent into the tube, his arms out like wings.

When he was on his board, he was completely in the moment, drawing strength and self-reliance from his very truest nature. It was that style, and that inner power, that had made him a top surfer, put him on the international pro tour, where he had surfed for two years and become a champion. Now he surfed for fun, but even in California, where the competition was fierce, he always attracted attention wherever he surfed, not for his movements as much as for his energy.

From the day he'd started surfing, Ashton had found himself out there—found his truth in a sea of metaphors. Even when he was very young, he could stay out in the water for three, four hours, sitting on his board, watching the horizon, waiting for the next set, patiently holding out for the best of the best wave. Sometimes he'd let dozens go by before he whipped his board around toward shore, his choice made, paddling furiously, committed to that wave over all the others.

He'd surf every drop of water out of it, and when it broke, it was as if he'd pulled it down with him. He said he read it and moved with it. That the wave ruled.

Morgan thought, How could she sit on the beach on a sunny California coastline, plenty of food in her stomach and no real fears, while at the same time, on the same planet, within a day's airplane ride, other women, women she regarded as sisters, were living in terror, being raped, starved, having their clitorises razored off, being imprisoned or shot or stoned for their sex? Morgan hadn't the barest understanding of that kind of terror. Grady had a point. Years ago, without the communication we have now, we didn't know all this was happening. Now that we did know, the reality of these women's plight was overwhelming. And, she thought, imperative that we not ignore it. That we act.

Sometimes she really missed the days when she had the power of the press behind her. The ability to inform— to effect change in the world—was intoxicating. The trouble came when the press forgot that the power was simply a result of having a monopoly on information exchange. The press controlled the subjects of debate, the debates themselves, and how the debates were resolved. Frustrated readers were free to disagree, to call in, to write letters. But the final rebuttal belonged to the paper. They always got the last word. Their story was truth. Everyone else's was opinion.

Inside the newsroom, journalists shared a certain arrogance that rarely went challenged. For Morgan, that arrogance extended to her whole view of herself. She confused the press's power with her own. The two became entangled, blended, and finally fused.

In the years since she'd resigned, when she could no longer piggyback on that magnanimous illusion, she often felt powerless, lost. Without the huge audience, the dramatic public impact, her work seemed of no consequence. What was the meaning of our lives? It seemed as if the big, visible acts carried more importance than the smaller, less public ones.

Kate disagreed. She believed that any action, when done consciously, was a great act of power. "The simple act of watering one houseplant, if you are fully aware and in the moment, can have the whole universe in it," she said.

Morgan squinted, confused. "I don't think I understand."

"In that precise moment, giving water to the plant is the only thing that is happening. So it is also the most important thing happening. It's a perfect act, and because it's perfect, it contains incredible power, all the power there is. And the ripples of that act spread out everywhere."

"But watering that plant doesn't quench the thirst of the millions of people in the world without water," Morgan argued. "Whereas, if I wrote a major story about a village without water, I could probably get a well dug."

"Some believe that the smallest act of pure love and right intention can cause huge shifts," Kate said.

Kate told Morgan that she had had such feelings when she was living in her one womb cabin, baking bread.

"When I was kneading the dough, really focusing on kneading the dough, I would sometimes get this feeling of completeness. And it felt wonderful. Here I was, I'd just lost everything in the world I cared about, and I was having this feeling that I had exactly what I needed and that nothing was missing. In a weird way, it was almost euphoric."

"So what's the point of anything?" Morgan wondered. "Why don't we all simply go to cabins in the woods and water plants and bake bread? Why did you come back?"

"I'm not sure," Kate said. "It seemed like the right next thing to do."

"Do you still have that feeling when you bake bread?" Morgan asked.

"I haven't baked a loaf of bread since I left the cabin."

*   *   *

"Ashton." Morgan touched his arm and he looked down at her. His face was so somber, so hollow, so full of adult pain.

"One day, when you were about ten years old, I remember I'd been sitting out on the beach watching you surf nonstop for about three hours. You came out of the water and were standing there dripping into a towel, and I asked you, 'What do you think about when you're sitting out there all that time, waiting?' And you know what you answered?"

"What?"

"You said: 'I'm thinkin' about the next wave.'"

He smiled. "You know, Mom, I'm not mad at you. I never was," he said.

"I know."

"I took it out on you. Everything. It's not your fault. I'm sorry."

"It's okay, kiddo," Morgan said.

"I'm going to surf again, Mom," he said.

"I know."

"How does it happen, Mom?" He gazed out to the waves. "That everything can suddenly be so, so...gone? Faiza. Our plans. Even my legs."

They sat silent for a while. Then he continued.

"I was thinking that I'd make a deal. That I would give this all up, never surf again, if I could have Faiza back. But that's a joke. There's no trade there. Even if I gave my legs. If there was a god, which I don't think there is, he'd laugh at that. Me thinking anything on my body could be worth even a fraction of her."

"I don't have an answer," Morgan said.

"So what am I supposed to do?" he asked. "What am I supposed to think?"

"Think about the next wave, kiddo."

CHAPTER TWENTY-SIX

Morgan and Ashton pored over the internet. The more they read, they more they realized this was far from a simple black-white, good guy-bad guy situation.

It would have been easier to blame Islam and consider Faiza a victim of religious persecution. But the truth was more complicated than that. Morgan was fast learning that Islam was a religion founded on principles of peace, mercy, and forgiveness. The word "Islam" meant submission—submission to the word of God, or Allah, in Arabic.

Morgan realized that Islam does not, in and of itself, call for egregious acts of violence against women. It seemed to her that, like any other religion, the practice of Islam depended on who was doing the interpreting of God's word. Heaven knew, just in the U.S. people interpreted and practiced Christianity in many ways. And who was it who said that in human history, more people have been killed and tortured in the name of Jesus Christ than any other religion?

The women's holocaust—the killing of perhaps five million "witches" in central Europe in the Middle Ages—was perpetrated by guess who? The church. And very recently, news of terrible atrocities by the Taliban in Afghanistan was reaching U.S. ears. No one sect had the corner on cruelty to women.

One scholar pointed out that the Qur'an, also spelled Koran, calls for spiritual equity between the genders. Everyone is equal when they get to Heaven. The Qur'an says that man is responsible for the family, but that does not mean he is superior and that the woman is subservient. Muslim women can own property, keep their maiden names, and are entitled to financial support from their husbands.

The fact that there were not any women prophets was due to the physical challenges of that role, such as prayer prostrations, considered unfeminine, not because women are spiritually inferior, the scholar said.

The man inherits twice as much as a woman, but this is balanced by the fact that she gets supported. Marriage is for love and peace, and a woman can refuse a marriage proposal. Before the Qur'an, there was female infanticide. The Qur'an ended that practice. The text urges husbands to be kind to their wives, even if they don't like them.

However, there did seem to be room for a little spanky-spank once in a while. The scholar quoted this passage:

> Men are the protectors and maintainers of women because Allah has given the one more (strength) than the other and because they support them from their means. Therefore the righteous women are devoutly obedient and guard in (the husband's) absence what Allah would have them guard. As to those women on whose part you fear disloyalty and all conduct, admonish them (first), (next) refuse to share their beds and (last) beat them lightly.

In another reference, it was written that a man could beat his wife as long as he didn't leave a mark.

Under old English law, men were entitled to hit their wives as long as they hit with a stick no wider than a thumb; thus the phrase "rule of thumb." This law persisted in America for many years.

In one reference to the Islamic version, a light beating was defined as what one might do with a "miswak" (a small toothbrush). The rule of miswak, Morgan presumed.

Polygamy was okay for men, but not for women, because that would make it too hard to determine the lineage of offspring. Polygamy was recommended in wartime, when many men have been killed, to take care of the surplus women and the widows.

The Saudis, however, practiced a rigidly fundamentalist version of Islam that disregarded many of the protections the Koran afforded women; not so different from the way fundamentalist Christians would pick and choose among Bible verses and the teachings of Jesus.

Morgan turned to Ashton, who was sitting beside her at the computer, reading along as she scrolled through articles and postings. They both shook their heads, thinking the same thing. Saudi Arabia was not a good place to be captured in, if you were female. Islam may have been founded on peace and very good intentions, but the Saudi version was riddled with potential hazards for women.

The phone rang. It was Meredith, calling with some discoveries of her own. Morgan handed Ash the living room phone and headed for the extension in the bedroom.

"Mom and Ash, I found a group called Sisters Islam Society (SIS). It's a support group for Muslim women, to talk about stuff they aren't comfortable discussing with their husbands. I've been reading their posts for hours. Long debates about the wearing of hijab, the veils that women wear. Some think it is oppressive and should be eliminated. Others argue that covering from head to toe actually makes women freer. They are not being judged for their bodies and are less likely to be attacked or raped."

Ashton broke in. "Faiza thought the West had been too quick to judge that practice, without trying to understand it. She said a lot of women prefer to wear the veil."

"What about her?" Meredith asked.

Ashton chuckled. "She liked her Gap jeans. But she did get perturbed at American feminists."

Ashton explained that Faiza thought that many feminists, in their zeal to liberate the female world, stereotyped all Arab women as pitifully oppressed and needing to be rescued by their bold American sisters. This denied Arab women their very real strength and failed to acknowledge the progress they were making themselves in their countries.

Meredith said, "I don't even know Faiza, but I am beginning to feel very protective of her. She is up against a centuries-old establishment, where her life is determined by others. How did she ever find the courage to come to the States?"

"Her father," Ashton said. "He was a real planetary thinker. He believed that the world was changing and that before long all religions would be things of the past. Replaced by a new truth. Faiza said it would be like 'Hahmpty Dahmpty," he said, imitating her accent. "People would take all the pieces and form them together into something altogether new."

"He was an anomaly?" Meredith asked.

"Not as uncommon as you might think," Ashton answered. "Faiza said there are lots of Saudis—men and women—questioning the severe rules of the country. Piercing the veil, so to speak. It has a lot to do with contact with the West. And the internet. And maybe, her father thought, the evolution of humans. Like we were going to actually become kinder and gentler."

"Obviously her uncle is not one of the evolving ones," Meredith said.

"No, that's why her father wanted her to get out of the country before he died."

"It must have been hard for her," Meredith said. "To leave her family, her friends, her home, everything she knew."

"She has unbelievable resilience," he said. "She would get scared, or sad. Sometimes she'd cry. But then there would be this part of her, this look she would get in her eyes that seemed to come from somewhere deep inside her, to comfort her. And in those moments it would be like she was a hundred years older than me and just faking me out in this great young body."

The three fell silent for a long time. And then Ashton said angrily, "Dammit. I can't stand this! We're sitting around on our butts, staring at the goddam computer, and Faiza is . . .

who knows where?"

CHAPTER TWENTY-SEVEN

Morgan's heart came close to breaking every time she had to face Ashton's rage, grief, and frustration. She felt she could do little; but this time Meredith stepped in.

"We're not just staring at the computer," Meredith said. "And if you'll keep your pants on for a minute, little brother, I'll tell you what I found out."

"I'm all ears," Ashton told her.

"This organization, SIS, has members all over the world," Meredith said. "A couple hundred."

"Anyone in Saudi?"

"I'm not sure yet. I send an email to the contact name for SIS, who turned out to be a woman in London. After a few messages back and forth, she said she would pass my message on to the rest of the group."

"What did you say?" Morgan asked.

"I said I was a student, which is almost the truth, and that I was interested in Arab women, particularly women in Saudi Arabia. Which is the truth for sure. And I asked if they had any members there who would correspond with me.

"The next day I got a message from a woman named Naheed. She said she got my request and was happy to talk with me, but she was in Kuwait. I thought, well, that's close. So we did some online chatting for a while. I planned to kind of ease into specific questions. Didn't want to scare her off."

Meredith and Naheed talked about their lives, work,

ages, where they lived. Meredith learned that Naheed was a devout Muslim who worked at home, writing pamphlets about Islam for distribution in non-Arab countries.

Eventually Meredith broached the subject, indirectly, saying she was trying to find a woman in Saudi Arabia who had once lived in the United States.

Naheed wrote: Who is this woman?

Meredith: Her name is Faiza Salah. She lives in Dhahran. I have her address.

Naheed: If you have her address, why not write her or call her?

Meredith: Her family does not wish for her to have any phone calls.

Naheed did not respond for several hours. Meredith was sure she had lost her. So she signed off.

Later that day, when Meredith signed back on again, she found a new message.

Naheed: I cannot help you. There is a woman in Riyadh who sells the kind of   clothing you are looking for. Her email is: Sheena@rasa.com

Meredith did not answer the last message. Whatever scared Naheed away, maybe an angry husband, Meredith did not want to get her into trouble.

She contacted the address Naheed had given her. Sheena turned out to be a woman with a mail order business selling abayas, the robes and headpieces Saudi and other Muslim women are required to wear. Meredith checked out her online catalog.

"She creates designs that make the robes more stylish," Meredith said. "I told her it was great-looking stuff. The name of her company, translated, means 'It's Cool to Cover,' a pitch to appeal to younger women."

"Why did Naheed give you Sheena's name?" Ashton asked.

"Well, that's just it," Meredith said. "I think she might be connected in some way to an underground. Everything was very cryptic, but here's how it went."

Meredith: I want to get some clothes, something special, for a friend in Dhahran. I   have her family's address, but do not know where she is.

Sheena: Is she with her family?

Meredith: I am not sure. I have not heard from her. But it is important that I know.   I want to surprise her with the clothes. She is sad and needs the clothes very much.

Sheena: If you buy the clothes from me, I can perhaps help you. Do you wish to   place an order?

Meredith: Yes, please. You select what I buy.

Meredith told her the name and Dhahran address. Then, out of the blue, came a puzzling question.

Sheena: Do you know of the Woman's Room?

Meredith: No.

Sheena: I might need to look in the Woman's Room for the styles you desire. That   will take some time but I will reply to you later.

At first Meredith thought they might still be talking about fashion—until she researched a bit more. She found references to the Woman's Room in reviews of a book about Saudi Arabia entitled *Princess* by Jean Sasson, published a few years before. The book caused quite a stir, and in one article, Muslim critics panned the book, claiming it was filled with lies and misconceptions.

"For example," Meredith told them, "the critics said that the use of the Woman's Room is outdated, a part of the country's barbaric past and no longer used as a method of punishment."

"Punishment?" Ashton said.

"I got the book and read it last night," Meredith said. "It's about a woman member of the Saudi royal family. Oh, the stuff she says they do to women! Honor killings and beatings and even, in one case, stoning a young woman for having a baby out of wedlock."

Meredith went on, her voice breaking as she spoke.

"In the book, a seventeen-year-old girl gets locked up in a completely pitch dark room—no windows, soundproofed walls. Her family actually created the room in their mansion for this punishment. And she is sentenced to stay there for the rest of her life. They pass food through a little opening in the door and take out waste through a hole in the floor. No one is allowed near her or to make any contact with her. Forever. And no one in the household can hear her cries."

She paused. "That is the Woman's Room."

Morgan remembered Autumn's reading, and her skin stung with fear. She could hear Ashton's breathing, amplified by the shared phone line.

"Why was this girl put in the room?" he almost whispered.

"For having an affair with a boy who was not Muslim."

The phone slammed down so hard it reverberated in Morgan's head like a stereo, one ear hearing it from the receiver, and the other from the living room.

"Poor guy," Meredith said. "I wish I were there."

"Me too," Morgan said. "I'd better get off now. Thank you for the research. Love you."

"Love you, too, Mom."

*   *   *

"Ashton, it's all speculation," Morgan said as she walked back into the living room. "We have no evidence that practice even really goes on there. Let alone how it might pertain to Faiza."

"Get real, Mom. Remember what Autumn said? About the darkness? That it was black and alone like a prison, but not exactly a prison? What if it's true?"

"Then we'll deal with it," Morgan said.

"Mom, I've got to do something."

"I know. And we will."

Morgan stroked his head. He had been sweating, and his soft blond hair was slightly damp, like when he was little and came running in from the backyard on a summer afternoon, hot and flushed and smelling that wonderful wet kid smell.

If only they could go there, she thought. Back into that kitchen, where at a certain time every morning sunbeams would actually dance in through the window and splash all over the yellow and white vinyl flooring, like the special effects in a movie. And even if he was running in with a nasty bruise or a bloody cut on his hand or a fresh bee sting, and he'd cry and wail, Morgan would know what to do. Get a first aid kit, sit him up on the sink, wash the wound, and dab it with Betadine because that doesn't sting. His cheeks would have streaks, little rivulets of tears and dirt, and she would wipe those off with a cool rag.

Then it would be over. And he would be okay. She would have fixed the owie. God, how easy it was then to fix it.

*   *   *

Neither of them spoke for a long while. But Morgan sensed there was something unsaid. It hung between them like an apparition waiting to be noticed.

"Ashton, there's something boiling inside of you," Morgan said finally.

He didn't move.

"You've got to get a grip. These outbursts. They aren't helping anybody."

"Leave me alone," he said, without conviction.

"Not until you tell me what's going on." Morgan sat down facing him square. "This is not another piece of lost memory. This is something you are holding back."

He shook his head, not in refusal, but in resignation. "You're right. There's something I haven't told you."

Morgan sat still, restraining her breath, trying not to disturb the air between them.

"Remember," Ashton said, "when Autumn said, I don't remember the exact words, that she was confused, because she felt the presence of another in the dark prison?"

"Uh-huh."

"Faiza. . . thought she was. No, she knew. We knew. She was late—two months late. And then, that weekend in Half Moon Bay, we bought one of those do-it-yourself pregnancy tests."

Morgan met Ashton's eyes and waited.

"It was positive, Mom. Faiza is pregnant."

CHAPTER TWENTY-EIGHT

The next day, after the stunning revelation about Faiza's pregnancy, Morgan called Larry, the man she had talked to at Amnesty International.

"This is Larry Edwards."

"Hi, Larry. This is Morgan Fay. Do you have a minute?"

"Sure. In fact, I was going to call you later."

"You were?"

"I had a chance to talk to central office, in London, about your situation. Though there was some interest and certainly much sympathy, I don't hold out much hope that AI can help. Because she's a Saudi national, and she is presumably with her family . . . "

"Only presumably," Morgan said. "For all we know, she could be in the hands of international terrorists, or thugs from another country."

"True, but I think you and I both know what has happened. And frankly, it would be a stretch for AI to be effective here. Even if we organized a big letter-writing campaign, it wouldn't faze those guys. Saudi stonewalls any efforts from the outside. There's a wall around that kingdom, even in cyberspace."

"What about your civil rights campaign?"

"Well, there have been some ripples from that," Larry said. "The king appointed a group to look at legal reform, and they invited a United Nations rep into the country. That's more than they've done in the past. At least they are acknowledging that there is such a thing as civil rights."

Larry paused. "You know, Morgan, there are a lot of people in Saudi who want change. People who are fed up with dictators. Lawyers, for example, who would speak out if it was safe to do so. Change will come, eventually," he said.

"But we need it to come fast," Morgan said.

"I don't think there's much hope of that. Our government isn't all that hot on change either. Haven't you noticed? The U.S. doesn't like to annoy its friendly neighborhood dictators. Saudi Arabia is the most influential country in the Middle East, and the royal family is deeply entrenched. And if you think our government moves slowly, it's a jackrabbit compared with Saudi. By the way, did you get a chance to contact Vicki Saba?"

"Not yet. But I read a web page that mentioned her, and others."

"Then you know how nearly impossible it is to get the Saudis to budge on these things. I mean, Vicki had legal custody of her daughter, and in ten years of nearly constant pressure on anyone and everyone inside and outside the government, she's barely gotten to first base."

"I noticed that our State Department doesn't exactly flex its mighty muscles," Morgan said. "They wrote her all these letters about how sorry they were and how difficult it was to intervene in Saudi family matters. Blah, blah, blah. Geez, if it were some of our servicemen who'd been kidnapped, or some senator's kid, we'd be all over them like a sweat."

"Morgan, there's a lot more to this, as you well know. Off the record? Our government maintains a very light touch when it comes to Saudi. Why? Three words. Oil. Oil. And weapons deals. I guess that's four words."

"I feel so helpless."

"I'm sorry."

"Larry, I have to tell you something. Last night my son told me that Faiza is pregnant."

"Oh, god. Are you sure?"

"Yes. Would that make any difference in getting some help?"

Larry paused for a moment. "I don't doubt you, Morgan, but honestly, even if it made a difference, there is no proof that she is pregnant. I believe you, but others might think it's fabricated to arouse more sympathy."

"Do you think I should contact the State Department?"

"I already did. Talked with my closest contact there. Unofficially. Frankly, this situation won't even make a tiny ripple there. Think of it. The State Department hedges on getting back children who are full-fledged American citizens when their mothers have legal custody. Politically, your girl is nobody."

"Even pregnant with an American citizen's baby?"

"I'm afraid so. In her country she is the property of her family, and so will the child be. And legally, in that country, it is strictly a family matter."

"So this doesn't add anything to our chances of getting help?"

"No. And, I have to tell you, it puts her in even more danger," Larry said. "Being unmarried and pregnant with the child of a non-Muslim, she has seriously violated the law."

"What if we got stories in the papers, and on *20/20* and *60 Minutes* and CNN?"

"You could try that," Larry said dubiously. "But when it's all over and done, I doubt if it would make a snowball's difference. The Saudis couldn't care less what's on our television. Unless they live here and have a station."

"Yeah, I heard," Morgan said.

"And if you cause a big hubbub about it, you attract a lot of attention to yourselves."

"That's the point, isn't it?" she asked.

Larry was silent for a moment. Then he said, "Umm, unless you don't, for some reason, want to be in the spotlight."

"What do you mean, Larry?"

"Did you know Vicki hired mercenaries to go in and steal her daughter back out? Talk to her about that."

There was silence.

"Larry, do you think we could so something like that?"

"I can't really advise you about anything like that," he said quietly. "That would be much too dangerous."

"Let's just say, hypothetically, that we could. Barrel into that country and grab Faiza. Would Amnesty help us then?"

"Hypothetically, just hypothetically, if someone was escaping a country where that someone were being held against her will, and if her life would be in danger if she returned, then that someone would be eligible for asylum in the United States," he said. "And Amnesty does help such persons get asylum."

"And the baby?"

"If the baby is born on American soil, it's an American."

"Thanks, Larry. I've got some ideas now."

"Well," he said. "You didn't get them from me."

CHAPTER
TWENTY-NINE

"I want nothing more to do with the man, especially his name," Vicki Saba said to Morgan, breaking a tortilla chip and dipping one half into a small dish of guacamole. They were sharing a plate of nachos at a window booth in a small Mexican grill. She was one of those people you can share food with right away.

Vicki was medium height, slightly plump, with an efficient smile that welcomed but didn't try to light up the room. Her light brown shoulder-length hair fell straight and unstyled, but shined with highlights, as though she brushed it often. She was the kind of woman who groomed herself out of habit and custom, but had long ago turned her attention to other matters.

"My unmarried name was Matthews," she said. "But I keep the Saba because that is my daughter's. When I get her back, I'm changing both of our names."

Twelve years before, Vicki had met a man from Saudi Arabia. He was an engineer, working for a construction company in Houston with interests in the Middle East. Hamzah, her husband, developed designs for housing projects in Saudi Arabia. He was dark and swarthy and exotic and doted on Vicki, sweeping her away with lavish romantic evenings and constant attention. Nothing to portend what was to come.

"The Saudi men come here and they act very liberal," Vicki said. "They dress nicely and they have great manners, and it's like you're dating Lawrence of Arabia. And then you marry them and everything changes."

When she went with Hamzah back to his country, she found herself in a barren, harsh, and dangerous world. Assigned to the household under the eyes of her Saudi mother-in-law, Vicki lost all of the privileges she had in the United States. Her husband controlled her passport, and she couldn't drive or leave the house without his permission.

"You have no power over there," Vicki said. "And your own government can't help you. It's terrifying when you realize what you've lost. I lived under lock and key."

"How did you get out?" Morgan asked.

"My daughter Sarina was two when we went to Saudi. She was an American citizen. When I wanted to come back here to visit my family, Hamzah permitted it. As soon as I got back to Houston, I got a lawyer and filed for divorce. That's when the real trouble started. Hamzah came over and wouldn't leave me alone. He called me and followed me and really scared me."

"Was he abusive?" Morgan asked.

"Not in a physical way," Vicki said. "Although he was a tyrant when we were in Saudi. He would have beaten me up if I'd provoked him, and nobody would have done a thing to stop him." Her tone softened.

"He wasn't a monster. He had some real kindness inside him. But he was also a complete product of his culture. It infuriates these guys when we stand up for ourselves. It dishonors them in front of their family. And because they have a whole different idea about women, they don't understand a woman having freedom. It's not a concept that computes in their heads. The Koran is the law of the land—and they interpret it to mean that women should submit to the will of men. They see it as 'protecting' women."

Morgan told Vicki that they believed Faiza was imprisoned in her uncle's home.

"That would be the best of all possible alternatives,"

Vicki said. "But she is at risk for an honor killing. And don't let anyone tell you it doesn't happen anymore there. It happens a lot. These men deny everything. But it's true. They kill their daughters all the time."

Vicki got a divorce and was awarded full custody of her daughter. After a few months, Hamzah seemed to give up. A year went by and she didn't hear a word from him, but to be on the safe side she moved to San Francisco, where she had friends. She enrolled her daughter in a church preschool.

One ordinary day, she picked up her Sarina at school. They walked out to the street where the car was parked, one of Sarina's tiny hands clutching her Little Mermaid lunchbox, the other hand wrapped tightly in her mother's. Vicki took no notice of the white van that had pulled up alongside her car.

As she opened the door to the backseat where Sarina's car seat was, she let go of her daughter for a second. In that instant, two huge hands descended on her daughter and they snatched her so fast it looked like her little body literally disappeared into thin air. Vicki screamed and tore down the street after the van, and even got a part of the license plate, but the police were never able to find it again, or her daughter.

"That was ten years ago," Vicki said, and now she was sobbing. Morgan guessed that she hadn't told this story even one time without breaking down.

"There isn't a day that's gone by that I haven't done something—made a phone call, written a letter. I've written thousands of letters. I've been to the State Department a dozen times and I've gotten on a first-name basis with two ambassadors to Saudi Arabia," Vicki said. The tears had stopped now and she had regained her anger. "Nobody has done what I've done, politically or diplomatically. Most parents don't even get past the front door with the State Department."

"Are there a lot of children like Sarina?" Morgan asked.

"Thousands, who have been internationally abducted," she said. "There is an organization called Parents International, trying to get foreign countries to help get these children back. Because these kids are United States citizens."

"The State Department doesn't help?"

"They only posture. At first I was referred to the Saudi Arabia desk. They described Saudis as 'clients.' How much help do you think I got there? In 1987, because of pressure from parents who had lost children, the government created a children's issues division at State. But that office has just become a place to keep the files."

"Have you ever tried a rescue?" Morgan asked.

"Twice," Vicki said. "Both failed. The first one, they almost got her, but then there was shooting and they had to back off."

"They?"

"There are a lot of these paramilitary groups coming out of the woodwork. Because there's a growing demand for their services. But you have to be careful. Some of them are experienced and honest, but a lot are out for the money. They'll dump you in a heartbeat. It's really hard to find people you can trust."

"What about the second attempt?"

"They didn't even try. They just took the money," Vicki said. "My family has helped, but we've used every penny we all have."

Morgan didn't know what to say. She thought about what she would do if this were Meredith, and the thought was terrifying.

"What are you going to do next?" she asked.

"What I do every day. Go to work and then plan the next action."

"Will you try another rescue?"

"Oh, yes," Vicki said.

Lunch was over, and they stood up to leave. Vicki put her hand on Morgan's shoulder, which Morgan took to be her version of a hug. There were tears again in her eyes.

"You know, Morgan, it's all about money. Hamzah paid somebody to come and kidnap Sarina. And now I have to come up with a fortune to get her back. Whoever has the most money wins. If you've got the money you can get your kids home, and if you don't, you can't. It's so unjust. We literally have to buy our kids back."

*   *   *

Morgan saved her tears for the drive away. She couldn't imagine being in Vicki's shoes. Since Meredith was born, she doubted that a day went by that wasn't in some way predicated on keeping her children from being lost or hurt or stolen. No matter what you're doing, that instinct is never very far from the surface. When you become a mother, you are suddenly able to do two things at once. You can read and listen for their cries, you can drive a car or go to work or watch a movie or cook or play or party—and one eye is always on the lookout for any threat of harm; one arm is always mobilized to reach out and snatch them from danger. It's a constant and personal battle, keeping all the evils of the world at bay.

We're like the mother duck herding her ducklings across the street, Morgan thought, *only the street's gotten a whole lot busier.*

What if you slipped up? Or worse, what if you fell victim to some force beyond your control, the irrational capricious Universe, random acts of violence? These were the nightmares of motherhood. Morgan couldn't imagine anything more horrible in all of life than losing a child. And Vicki's was snatched right out from under her nose in broad daylight.

One thing was certain. Through the chill and the rage that hung over her after hearing Vicki's story, a surge of determination popped out, like the sun breaking over the horizon in a cloudy morning sunrise. Vicki had done everything in her power to do and had still not given up. She would give her life to save her daughter.

Morgan realized they had to come up with something else. They didn't have ten years. If Faiza was pregnant, she was at close to four months along. That gave them less than six months to get her, and the baby, Morgan's grandchild, out of that country.

CHAPTER THIRTY

When Morgan got back to the apartment after her lunch with Vicki Saba, she found a note from Ashton.

"Wish me luck on first day of crutches. Went to meteorology class to talk to prof. about the whole thing. Love, A."

Grabbing the chance for some privacy, Morgan dialed Stan Grady. He answered on the second ring. "Grady, here."

"Hi, Stan. I mean Grady."

"Why, hi there, Morgan."

The sound of him recognizing her voice gave Morgan a jolt, but kind of a pleasant one. It was that shimmery feeling inside her gut, like maybe her stomach and her uterus had, just for fun, switched places. Damn.

"I was wondering, if you had a minute . . . do you have a minute? I mean, do you have to go do a flight or anything?" She sounded seventeen years old. No, fourteen.

"No. I mean, yes, I have a minute; and no, I'm not flying until tomorrow." He sounded older. Like eighteen.

There was an awkward pause. Then he asked, "What's up?"

"Could we meet somewhere?" she asked. "I need to talk with you in person."

"Hmm. Sure."

He gave her directions to a place about two blocks from where they had met before. An outdoor cafe, he said. Right on the beach.

"Think you can find it?" he asked. Morgan said yes. His directions were flawless, detailed. She was a little surprised he would so readily agree to meet her. Surely he could tell that she wanted something from him. Something she was pretty sure he would refuse to give.

When Morgan got to the Cliffside Cafe, Grady was already seated at a small round table in the corner of the sundeck. He had a cup of coffee and was sucking on one of his Marlboros. There was a typical Pacific breeze, hefty and constant, and the seawater below churned with waves that frothed and arched back against the walls of the bluffs, as if they were trying to beat their way out of confinement. As if they didn't have enough room in this whole enormous ocean.

Grady smiled as she sat down, and her inner organs did that switch-around thing again. She tried to remind herself of all the stuff she really didn't like about him. His haughty attitude. His refusal to get involved with the world's problems. His self-centeredness. His stupid cigarettes, which she wanted to bum.

"Thanks for coming," Morgan said, hoping her sincerity would overrule her contempt.

"Sure," Grady said. "Your call surprised me."

"It did?"

"Yeah. Look, I know you don't like me very much. Why would you? I'm the guy who flew the plane."

"You were just doing your job," Morgan offered.

"Sure. But you're not the kind of person who does a job if you don't agree with it. I bet you never followed directions you didn't agree with. Or if you thought you were hurting someone. You'd make a lousy Marine."

"No shit." She actually laughed. "But I've done my time under someone else's thumb."

"But no more," he said. "And face it. I've got this hunch we don't exactly have the same politics."

Morgan nodded and looked down, pretending to be watching her hand stir her coffee. But instead she was peeking at his hand stirring his. The back of his hand was wide and strong-looking, with a light brown patch of soft hair. She imagined the hand doing various things, like shifting gears and opening a door, or pushing in a throttle or holding a yoke. Or holding another person's hand. Or gently touching that person.

Morgan looked up and directly into his eyes. "Politics or not, I need your help."

"Want something to eat?" he asked.

"No thanks, I just ate lunch," Morgan said, confused. Was this a diversionary question, or did he really give a damn that she ate? What an inscrutable, annoying man.

Trying another approach, she asked, "That company that you flew for, that you were telling us about . . . did you enjoy that work?"

"Well, as I told you, I pumped enough adrenaline for a lifetime."

"How did you get into it?"

Grady lit another cig and leaned back in his chair.

"The company, USA Transport, was a cargo carrier. So for years I flew freight in the C-382, the civilian version of the C-130. The Herc. But there was also this other part. There was this captain I'd been flying with for a long time. Gordo. He had more hours turning short final than most pilots have their whole lives."

"Short final?"

"That's the final leg of the flight's final approach. You're really close to the runway. Like a quarter mile. And really low."

Morgan nodded.

"So one day we were sitting in the commissary at the base airport," Grady continued, "and I was updating my log book. I was so proud, talking about how I had ten thousand hours. Gordo's sitting there, and he pulls the pipe out of his mouth and tells me he's got thirteen thousand hours just in the Herc. Christ.

"Gordo recruited me. One day he asks me, would I like to do some stuff that was different than the normal stuff. He said, 'The one thing about it—you don't know nothing.' I flew as his copilot and then eventually was upgraded to captain. So then Gordo and I were the two captains, and we had a couple of other crews doing what we all called the 'super-secret shit.' I was in the right place at the right time."

"Did you swear to some kind of oath?"

"Nah," Grady said. "It wasn't spoken, no oaths or anything. It was just understood. You knew that if you fucked up, you'd be like in *Top Gun,* flying rubber dogshit out of Hong Kong. For my crews I picked older guys, guys fifty-five and up. They had been in the military and they knew how to keep their mouths shut."

"How come you can talk about it now?" Morgan asked.

"There's a lot I still wouldn't talk about," Grady said. "But the company's out of business, and that brand of rodeo is a thing of the past." He grinned. "Like I am, I guess."

"Did you ever go to the Middle East?"

"Shit, babe, you name it, I've been there."

"Doing food drops mostly?"

"A lot more. Like, we took the Delta Force all over the place. You know, the longhaired boys with no names. There were eight to twelve guys on a team. Always dressed in civilian clothes. They usually had dirt bikes or four-wheeled vehicles. Once we went into Boston Logan, and we pulled up and shut down the inboard engines and opened the rear hatch, and they just disappeared through the fence."

Grady went on to explain that because USA Transport was a private company on contract with the government, the missions were technically not official military operations. This allowed the government to operate conveniently and secretly outside what was politically correct.

"I made two trips to Panama to get Noriega," Grady said. "Both failed attempts. Eventually the regular army got him. And remember the riot a few years back in the federal prison in Atlanta? I took two groups in there.

"Half the time you didn't know where you were going. You'd go in and somebody would hand you a package and a flight plan, and you'd take off and go. We flew without flight plans lots of times. There were times when we'd land out in the middle of nowhere. There are lots of airports that are not on charts."

Morgan angled her head questioningly.

"So people didn't know where we were. Or what we were carrying. Once, during the Iran-Contra thing, I went into El Salvador with a paper that said I was carrying forty thousand pounds of fire extinguishers."

"And you never looked?"

"Hell no. You kidding? I didn't need to know, didn't want to know. Sometimes we covered the USA Transport insignia on the tail and changed the N-number on the plane. We'd go in one place with one N-number and leave with another one."

The server filled their cups. "Sure you don't want anything to eat?" Grady asked.

"No. But you go ahead."

Grady ordered a hamburger, with cole slaw.

"You probably don't eat meat either," he said. Morgan shook her head. He laughed. "Thought so."

She leaned back and folded her arms. "You're sort of like a spy."

"No, I just flew 'em. I didn't know nothin'. Hell, inside the company most people didn't know what was going on. One day we picked up the longhaired boys at Pope Air Force Base in North Carolina. We had a special pallet for the back of the plane that had fourteen seats in it, and we put that in, plus two vehicles. We were supposed to take them to the Nevada desert and drop them off and then come back and pick them up a week later.

"So we pull up on the ramp and there's this female airman, a little two-striper, directing us in there. These two civilian vans come up and pick up these guys and take them off. And the female gets real upset. She says, 'Who are you people?' She won't give us fuel—says we're not authorized to be there. And I say, 'We need some fuel and we'll be on our way.' And she says again, 'Who are you people?' and storms off in her jeep. So we casually mosey inside to wait.

"In about five minutes, this Air Force staff car comes tearing up and stops, and out gets this full-bird colonel. The guy with him is a Hispanic. We never knew his name, but he was around a lot, and we called him Taco. And the colonel says, 'The problem has been taken care of.'

"So then the female comes up to me and she is actually shaking. She salutes, which you're never supposed to do to a civilian. And she says, 'Sir, is there anything I can do for you?' I tell her, 'You can get me twenty-five thousand pounds of fuel.' And she snaps to attention and says 'YES SIR.'

"After that we flew to a maintenance base USAT had at McClellan Air Force Base in California, and we pull up and get out. We're wearing our black windbreakers and black pants— we never wore uniforms—and this mechanic looks in the back and sees the pallet and says, 'What the hell is this pallet doing here? We don't transport passengers. Who *are* you guys?'"

Grady took a big chomp from his burger. "What about you?" His question was muffled by the mouthful.

Suddenly Morgan's life seemed dull and adventureless. Still, he peered at her over his burger, blue eyes bearing down on her, eating and listening with equal gusto, while she offered a synopsis of her past few years of what must have sounded like a terminally ordinary life. When he finished eating, she segued back to his favorite topic, himself.

"Tell me more about the longhaired boys," she said.

He grinned. "We came in to Eglin Air Force Base one day to pick up the Rapid Deployment Group, which was sort of like the Delta Force. Only these are the kind of guys that when you look into their eyes, they're glazed over. Trained killers. If they ever get out, you'll have to take them someplace and detox their nervous systems before you can put them back into society."

She laughed.

"So we're coming into Eglin and we radioed clearance control. But they said we weren't cleared, so if we landed we would be in violation of FARs, federal regulations. So we radioed the tower that we were coming in to land, and the tower said if you want to land, you land at your own discretion. We did, and then ground control told us, 'USA Transport, turn right and pull up on the pad.' And we thought, hmm, the way to the ramp is to the left. So we turned right anyway, and as we pulled up a fire truck and two squad cars, all with lights going around, pulled in front of us. We stopped and shut down the engines and then just sat there. We didn't budge. Five minutes later, guess who shows up but our friend Taco. He waved everybody off. And we went on our way."

Morgan must have been a good audience, because Grady showed no sign of stopping his narrative. And she didn't particularly want him to.

Out of the blue, he said, "You're a good listener."

"Easy. You've got great stories," she said.

"Ahh, I'm nothin' but an old has-been cowboy," he said, shaking his head. "You wouldn't want your daughter to marry one; you wouldn't want your son to grow up to be one. But if you ever had a chance to do what these guys did, most people'd do it in a heartbeat."

"Are you done?" she asked.

"Talking? Hell no." He laughed.

"No, not talking. Are you done rescuing people?"

"I already told you. Been there, done that, bought the T-shirt, and I don't even wear the T-shirt anymore."

"I don't believe you," Morgan ventured.

"You don't want to believe me," Stan Grady said.

CHAPTER THIRTY-ONE

Grady leaned forward and rested his chin on a fist. He looked at Morgan, and with his eyes asked, What do you want? She shifted in her chair and recrossed her legs.

"Faiza. My son's girlfriend. We have good reason to believe she is being held prisoner by her family. And yesterday, my son told me she is pregnant."

"Holy shit," Grady said.

"Grady," Morgan said. "We have to get her out."

He shook his head.

"What? You think we shouldn't? Couldn't?"

"I didn't say anything."

"You shook your head," Morgan said.

"I was just thinking what a mess you got yourself in. It's a fucking pickup truck stuck in a mudslide in the rain."

"*We* got us in? You flew the goddam airplane!"

"Look, don't lay this on me. I already explained about charters."

"Can you help us?"

"How?" he asked. His tone was hedging.

"Backing up." Morgan took a deep breath. "Let's say, hypothetically, that someone wanted to get another someone out of Saudi Arabia. Hypothetically, could it be done? Are there people who do this sort of thing?"

"Babe, there's people who will do anything, anywhere. You only need one thing."

"What?" Morgan asked.

"Money. Moolah. Cash. Green stuff. That's all it takes."

"You mean I could find someone to go over and bring Faiza back?"

"For the right price."

"Like what?" she asked. "What would your price be?"

"I wouldn't have one. Because I wouldn't do it. I'm retired, remember?"

"Are we talking hundreds? Thousands?"

"Probably hundreds of thousands," Grady said.

"What would be your price?"

"I said, no price. I wouldn't do it."

"Fifty thousand? Hundred thousand?" Like she had this kind of money.

"Nothing!" He was getting a little steamed, which Morgan rather enjoyed. He was so cocksure. She liked ruffling his plume.

"Okay, okay," Morgan said. "But you are saying that this could be done. By someone."

"Yep. It could be done."

"How long would it take?"

"To put together that kind of thing? Months. Maybe a year."

Morgan said, "Hypothetically, if it were you, how would you start?"

"I'd start by making some phone calls," Grady said. "Listen, you want to take a walk? I'm stiffening up, sitting here."

Grady glanced at the check, slapped a ten and a couple of ones on it, and scooted his chair back. He took Morgan's hand, led her toward a brick fence that enclosed the sides of the patio, and boosted himself up and over the fence. Then he reached back to lift her over. When he gripped her waist with his hands, she felt the sensation of his touch on every inch of her body. Damn. When her feet were on the ground, she quickly broke away from him.

They walked along the edge of the bluffs, in silence for

a while. Since he had interrupted the conversation, Morgan decided to let him start it up again. Eventually he did.

"Look, Morgan, what you are thinking about is very high risk. This isn't some reporter with a tape recorder and a camera going someplace chasing a hot story. You're going to need some hired guns. And people to drive cars and fly airplanes. You don't know what you're going to come up against when you get there. And it's going to take a shitload of money."

"How much?"

"Oh, to do something like this, you're gonna pay for the knowledge, the experience. It's not only getting the people, it's getting the right people. And for them to risk bodily harm, you're probably going to pay twenty to thirty thousand a person."

Morgan nodded, as if she had the slightest clue where that amount of money would come from. Grady sat down on a flat boulder and she joined him.

"You have that kind of money?" he asked.

"No," she said. "But I believe that if you really need something, and your intent is for good, that what you need will come to you."

"Oh, yeah. Miss—excuse me, *Ms.*—positive thinker idealist."

The patronizing asshole. "When did you get your cynic badge?"

"Listen, babe, I earned it fair and square." He held out a lit Marlboro. "Want a drag?"

"Sure." She took the cigarette and inhaled a long drag. Strong, hot, familiar. She suppressed a cough.

"Lemme tell you a story," Grady said. As he talked, they passed the cig back and forth, like two teenagers sneaking a smoke behind the gymnasium.

"This was back in the eighties," he began. "We were on a relief mission, taking food from Nairobi to Juba in the Sudan. It was the week before Christmas. I was walking into the weather office, if you could call it an office, out in the middle of nowhere. It was one of the old crummy buildings, you know, where the wiring goes on the outside of the walls.

"This one guy who worked in there came up to me and says, 'Capitan, could you please favor me?' He reached in his pocket and pulled out an old, crumpled U.S. five-dollar bill. He wanted me to buy him, in Nairobi, a bar of Omo soap, which is like the Lever bar there, two pounds of sugar, and a pair of size thirty-two shoes. I told him it would be two days before I could get back. And he said that was okay.

"So when we got to Nairobi I went shopping and bought the stuff, and I also saw this shirt, so I got that too. I think I spent close to twenty bucks, but that was okay. When I got back and gave him the shirt, I told him it was a present from me to him, and he started crying. Because I'd given him a shirt. Because when you only have one change of clothes and you wear those clothes all the time, every single day, and somebody gives you another one, you're darn right you're gonna cry."

Grady shook his head and exhaled a stream of smoke. "It's so poor there. One egg costs a dollar, and a dollar is a month's wages. The guy couldn't thank me enough, and he walked around and showed everybody the shirt and his new shoes.

"Two days later this lieutenant colonel comes tooling up to the plane in a brand new Isuzu trooper. He says, 'Welcome to my airport.' He was military, the commander of the entire area. And he says, 'Capitan, can you do something for me?' And what he wants is two bottles of Johnny Walker red and two bottles of vodka, and he hands me a hundred dollars. And I said, 'Colonel, we're not supposed to do this kind of shit.' I told him, 'We're here for Caritas, and we're not supposed to have booze on the plane.' He laughs. He says, 'Capitan, you might want to consider problems you could have with your airplane if you don't do this.' So I said, 'Give me the goddam list.'

"I got the booze. When we landed, here comes the big fat fart in his Isuzu to pick up his booze, and he says, 'You have helped the people of Sudan. Tonight we will toast you.' And I thought, 'Fuck you and the Isuzu trooper you rode in on.'"

Grady mashed the butt into the ground with his shoe. "So, you know, when some do-gooder rings my doorbell and says, 'Would you like to donate some money to the African relief effort?' I say, 'Why don't you come in and we'll have a little chat.'"

"I've got to get going," Morgan said, standing up. She felt a little dizzy, probably from the first cigarette she'd had in a couple decades; or maybe from something else.

Grady stood up too. He made her nervous, standing so close. She couldn't look at him, and instead stared out at the water. He reached over and with one arm gave her a little squeeze. She put one arm around his waist, meant as a light, friendly, so-long gesture. But they both hesitated, holding the hug an instant too long.

Then his other arm was gently pulling her shoulder around toward him, and she couldn't avoid looking at him. He leaned forward and kissed her. It was a perfect first kiss. Lips soft enough to yield to hers, firm enough to hold their own. When she didn't resist, he caressed her lips with his, like he was licking honey off rose petals. He put his hand on the back of her neck, his fingers buried into her hair, and she literally melted into his arms. The next kiss was deep and determined, touching her deep inside, as if he was filling her whole body. It had been ages since anyone had kissed her like that. Maybe never.

"God, you're beautiful," he said, a little out of breath.

They turned and walked arm in arm back along the bluffs to the parking lot, all the while Morgan thinking, why did she always have the best chemistry with the wrong men? And wasn't he designated for Kate? What happened to that scheme?

When they got to her car, he didn't try to kiss her again, but instead put his hands on her shoulders and held her an arm's length away.

"I'm sorry," he said.

"Sorry?"

"I'm sorry I can't help you, babe."

Morgan got in her car and pulled away. When she thought about his kiss, a surge went through her belly. Damn. She looked in the rearview mirror and saw him getting into his Cherokee.

She said out loud: "You self-absorbed, cocky, arrogant coward. You'll never see my ass in bed."

CHAPTER THIRTY-TWO

What was she thinking? Sitting across the table from some man she barely knew, talking about hiring mercenary soldiers? Morgan wasn't even sure exactly what a mercenary was.

She envisioned a bunch of half-crazed, revenge-driven thugs, tough as chains, with tattooed arms and torn-rag sweatbands around their heads. She'd never even met anybody like that. Well, no wonder. They were playing hide-and-go-seek in unmarked planes with guys like Grady spiriting them from place to place. These guys definitely did not have functional childhoods.

After hearing Grady's tales and being drawn into his covert world of intrigue and testosterone, the idea of getting some "hired guns," as he called them, actually sounded reasonable. Now, back in her own ordinary little car, no longer brain dead from post-kiss euphoria, it all sounded crazy. True, she had been fantasizing for some time about a brazen rescue of Faiza from the clutches of her evil uncle. But translating that into a real plan, a real mission, and very real danger, was a different story. Not to mention the big bucks. Where on earth would the money come from?

Morgan needed to think. It would be premature to talk to Ashton. Why get his hopes up? So she stopped the car on a pullover and found another rocky perch overlooking the Pacific. The air was getting cool, and the skin on her arms felt moist and clammy. She wished she had brought a jacket.

Just because Grady was out of the picture didn't mean an end to the idea. There had to be other Gradys around. She was an investigative reporter, a trained tracker. She could find anyone. Maybe she could locate that guy named Taco. Hello, Air Force? Do you have a Hispanic who used to run interference for secret pseudo-military airplanes?

What could be riskier than hiring operatives off the street? Their motive would be money, pure and simple. Morgan wanted someone who would care about the stakes. Who would be doing this not for greed, but for the greater good. Sounded like fiction; no, fantasy.

The sun was beginning to change to white-gold as the sunset began. Suddenly Morgan was thinking of Faiza. Was there even a sliver of light able to penetrate her prison, the pitch black so-called Woman's Room? How viciously cruel, that punishment. The thought of it made Morgan want to scream at the freedom of the sky dimming above her, the grand ocean before her, the indifference of the trail of cars swishing by on the highway behind her.

This was not an execution of religious law; it was an act of revenge and power and pure hatred of women. How long could a human survive in pure darkness, utter silence? How long could one hold onto one's sanity? Morgan had read accounts by prisoners of war imprisoned for years in excruciating conditions. And of course the Holocaust survivors. Some force much greater than the power of the tormentors kept those people alive and allowed them to preserve that part of them that was sane, good, hopeful.

Morgan silently prayed that such a force would surround Faiza. Would it work to send her light, via prayer waves, like the witches did in the Middle Ages? Autumn thought so. It was worth a try. So Morgan imagined that she could borrow the band of golden sparkles that stretched out across the Pacific in front of her and send them somewhere else. She cut an imaginary window in Faiza's prison and rerouted the light in through the opening, as if she were God playing with mirrors. In the image, she saw Faiza embraced by sunlight. That felt good.

But what they really needed coming in that window were a couple of soldiers who had a helicopter on the roof.

When Morgan got back to the apartment, Ashton was sitting on the couch, his crutches propped next to him, and on the floor sat four young women. They were a darling bunch, two white and two Black, dressed in a mix of jeans, hip-hugger khakis, halter-tops, and loose denim shirts.

"Mom, this is Ellie, Jennifer, Mavin, and Courtney. They are friends of Faiza."

"This is awful," said Courtney, who was wearing a light green baseball cap with a curly light brown ponytail scrunched through the opening in the back. "We can't believe they haven't found her yet."

"We want to help," said Mavin. She had tears in her eyes.

Ashton said, "Mom, while you were gone, Sergeant Peterson called and said they were, well, not exactly closing the investigation—it will remain officially open—but they won't be actively looking for the perpetrators anymore. Blah blah blah."

"We expected that," Morgan said.

"Why won't the police do anything?" asked Courtney. "Or the government? She's a student here. A person. Why don't they care?"

"Hello, remember poli-sci class?" Mavin said. "We don't muscle around in countries like Saudi. Oil, sister, oil."

Courtney just shook her head. "God, it's awful. Faiza is, like, the sweetest person in the world."

"And funny, too," Mavin said. "She cracks me up, the observations she makes about things here. Like, one day, I was saying how this guy in our class was such a geek, and how it would be so creepy to go out with him. And she says, 'Creepy, I'll tell you creepy.' Which she pronounced so cute, kind of like 'crehppy.' And she says, 'Creepy is when you have to marry him.

And you don't even find out until afterwards that he's a geek. Thaht's crehppy.'"

They all fell silent. Jennifer broke it. "Ashton said you all were thinking about rescuing her." Jennifer was slightly built, and her skin was deeply dark, clear, and gleaming, as if it was almost brand new. She had a room next to Faiza's in the dorm. The other three lived in an apartment off campus.

Morgan sat down on the floor with them and leaned against the sofa.

"We're asking ourselves if that is a possibility." She sounded like a frigging spin-doctor. "What I mean to say is, I know it's possible. But stuff like that costs money. Big bucks."

"We could do a fundraiser on campus," Ellie said.

"What kind of big bucks?" asked Jennifer.

"Beyond carwash or bake sale big," Morgan said. "Hundreds of thousands big."

Ashton picked up his crutches and hobbled out to the kitchen. They heard the water running. He came back and sat down again, as if he'd made a decision along the way.

"I can get the money," he said.

Morgan eyed him, stricken by his naïve determination. "Oh, honey—" she started.

He interrupted her. "I can get the money." Then he swore them all to secrecy and told them about the safe deposit box containing the gemstones that Faiza's father had given her.

"What kind of stones?" Courtney asked.

"I'm not sure," he said. "One big diamond. And some other stuff I didn't recognize."

"How many?" Courtney asked.

"A handful."

"A handful could be a lot, or jack shit," said Courtney, whose father, it turned out, was a jeweler whom she worked for in the summers.

"I think one might be a ruby," Ashton said.

Courtney gave a little shrug. "It could be a good ruby or

a crappola one. Same with diamonds. They're all worth something, but if you want a hundred thousand, it'd better be good stuff. Do you want me to call him?" she asked. "My dad, I mean."

"Could you ask him how to get stones appraised without actually telling him why?" Morgan asked her.

"It's okay. You can trust my dad," Courtney said.

"I'm sure we can," Morgan said gently. "But I just have this strong feeling, girls, that for some reason we need to keep this whole thing secret for a while."

The others nodded conspiratorially.

What a script, she thought. And who was the angel who sent these four sweet young women and a daddy who's a jeweler?

CHAPTER THIRTY-THREE

After the girls left, Morgan told Ashton that she'd decided to go back home to Florida for a while. He was briefly resistant, but not surprised.

It had been nearly two months since she got that terrifying phone call—and already way too long for Faiza to be imprisoned.

"I need to take care of a few housekeeping things," Morgan said. "And I'm at a loss here. I don't know anyone. I can do a lot better on my own turf, where I have a lot more contacts—friends, reporters, government people. It's only for a short while. Then we'll reconvene."

Gripping his crutches, Ashton loped over to the window and stood looking out. Morgan studied his profile. It had the lines of his dad's; classic lifeguard looks. As she stared at him, she saw two faces, the adult face blending into an image of the child's face, like a video cross-fade. There was Ashton as a towheaded three-year-old, tearing out across the yard to investigate the morning's big mystery, a limb that had fallen out of a huge elm tree the windless night before. He pulled at it and climbed on it and dragged it out in the open, and after speculating all day on this enigma, announced there was a big crack in the limb that had finally given way. Mystery solved.

"Mom," Ashton said. "There's something I want to tell you."

Morgan sat down on the couch and pulled her feet up,

sitting cross-legged. Ashton's news flashes had been rather dramatic of late.

"Remember the surf trip I took last year to Tahiti?"

"Sure."

"Well, something happened there, and I want to tell you about it."

She nodded, and he leaned against the wall opposite her.

"You know, Tahiti is an island of mountains made from a volcano," he said. "It's surrounded by coral reefs with lagoons in between the island and the reefs. The seawater pours in and out of the lagoons through channels. That's where we surf— just outside the channels.

"It's really wild stuff. The waves are enormous. The swells that get to Tahiti travel all the way from Antarctica. They have so much distance to travel, and they spend so much time lining themselves up, that the smaller ones get taken over by the bigger ones, and they create these huge, massive long swells that are basically consistent in direction the whole year round. And the bigger the swell, the more current you've got going in the passes."

Ashton came alive when he talked about surfing. Year upon year, endless wave upon wave, he had acquired a true mastery of the motion and behavior of entire oceans. In a language a person could only learn lying on his belly on a board, waiting and watching, sailing on the crest or tumbling and sputtering headlong into the froth, he had learned how to read that water. And, Morgan suddenly realized at this moment, he had done it all by himself, without her or anyone else's tutelage. And without her protection.

The surface of her skin was already chilling. Ashton's stories about surfing always held her spellbound, but to tell the truth, she rarely allowed the pictures to penetrate the reaches of her mind where she might actually contemplate the extent of the danger he often put himself in. Those doors were secured by mommy-locks, a special kind of denial that permitted her to hear without having to believe that any of it really happened.

Today, however, she sensed that Ashton's story would break open those locks forever, and the truth and the terror would come rushing in like a tsunami.

"That day we got our boards and we started paddling out," he told her. "There was Pete, the guy I'd come with, and our friend Danny, he was a local. Danny had never surfed there, and Pete, he was a little nervous.

"It was going crazy out there. You could tell it was big. 'Cause when you see a wave breaking and it takes two seconds from when you see the wave breaking—like one, two—to hit, you realize that if you jumped off something and it took two seconds to hit the ground, it'd be a pretty high jump. And it was breaking slow. When waves break slow, it's big. Big, slow-moving giants. So I started getting that feeling, that *whoooo*, that *yeah!* feeling, when you yell to your friends, Yeah, this is killer! And try to get everybody going.

"We got out there and noticed straight off that there was a current pulling us basically out to sea, out this pass. Plus we were surfing right on the corner of where the barrier reef ended. About fifty yards to our left, the waves were sucking up real tubular and going sheee-*boooom* on dry reef. That's like the death zone. And it's kind of pulling us over to it, so we're always paddling in."

Ashton paused, gathering himself. "From there, Tahiti looked so far away. You couldn't see the houses on the beach. Only their roofs. You couldn't see the white of the beach. We'd been there for about an hour. I was having fun. I dropped in on a huge wave, my first wave, and Pete said, 'Man, that was the gnarliest thing I've ever seen.' I wasn't really scared. I had some adrenaline running, but that's normal anytime the waves are big enough that they hold you down long enough to make you come up gasping. Your heart's pumping more when you're in that situation.

"We were catching a lot of waves, and Danny went in on a long one and went further into the pass. So we couldn't see him. And then Pete looked up and said, 'Man, there's a big one.' And I said, 'Yeah, man.' I paddled a little bit deeper than I was, so my ride would be a little longer. At that point I thought it was a normal wave; I was paddling like crazy to catch it.

"And then, as soon as it got close—a hundred yards—it was like, omigod. You could see the whole bottom of the ocean. Mom, this was not a wave. It was something else.

"What had happened was, so much water had piled up on this wave and there wasn't enough water in front of it for it to break and move forward. So it just sat there, not moving. And I knew right then we weren't going to be able to get through this wave. Because it wasn't a wave."

"Was it like a tidal wave?" Morgan asked, breathless, trying to picture it.

"Yeah, basically. But even tidal waves, they suck all the water out first, so they can move forward. This one just sat there, like it was stalled. A huge-ass stalled wave. And I'm yelling, 'Paddle, Pete!' Because Pete really doesn't have a lot of experience out there. And we're paddling, paddling.

"But we're paddling downhill.

"All the water's rushing down into this thing, so fast, maybe five knots. You could see the topography under us, and even though the water's rushing down, it's still so so deep, ten to fifteen feet deep. And the wave is sitting there, growing. It was twenty feet. I'd never seen a wave that big before, and never since either.

"Pete yells 'Omigod!' and I'm yelling, 'Paddle, Pete! Paddle!'

Ashton leaned forward, resting against his crutches. He propped his broken leg on the floor, though did not put any weight on it.

"When we first saw this wave, it looked like it was going to come over and do what a normal huge-ass wave does. Usually waves give you ground because you meet them halfway. And you can get under them. But this one didn't, it just stayed there. We're paddling so fast and it's not giving us any ground.

It didn't look like it was ever going to break.

"Then, when it started breaking, it wasn't like waves break. Usually when waves break, you see blue water breaking and then a tube at the top, crashing down. But this one was like it was breaking from the bottom up, the white was going up it, a rush of water coming up. It didn't tube. It became froth. It imploded. As if finally the water behind it said, we can't wait up, and pushed it over.

"All the while it made this horrendous grinding sound, like *cwwrrrrrrr*! It looked like a giant waterfall, moving backwards. It was the most frightening thing I've ever seen in my entire life."

Ashton paused, his eyes faraway and wide with fear.

"What did you do?" Morgan whispered.

"I swam all the way to the bottom, until my ears were popping, and got down there, and I could feel it going over, *bwwwwwwahhh*, like a jumbo jet's right over your head. And I thought, Oh my god.

"I didn't feel anything on my ankle. I didn't feel the tug of my leash. Usually it feels like a ton of weight pulling on your leg. But nothing was pulling. And I knew then that I was in big trouble.

"When the thing passed over, I started swimming up. The crazy thing was, when I swam down, it took me maybe four strokes to get to the bottom. But when I swam back up, I was swimming and swimming and swimming, and it was all clear water. Because what had happened was, there was a discrepancy of about twenty feet. The wave sucked out all that water from the reef, and when it filled back in, it was so so deep.

"I had already started blowing out my air, and it was still forever before I would get to the surface. When I came up, I was already panicky because I knew my board was gone.

"As soon as I got up, I started yelling. I don't even know what I was yelling. I was so scared. Pete wasn't anywhere, and I couldn't even see his board bobbing. I wanted eye contact with somebody. Something. To let Pete know—I'm here! But he was gone. I looked around to make sure there wasn't a bigger wave coming, because the first one of the set is never the biggest wave. When this kind of thing happens, you don't want another one on you. I knew if there was another wave like that, I'd be dead. And there was another wave, but I had been pulled so far out, it went right under me.

"I was out in the middle of the ocean now. Because we'd paddled so far out to that monster wave, and it had sucked us further out, and I'd gone under, so I was now way, way out, where the currents were harder. I'm swimming, and I can look down and see how deep it is. Maybe thirty feet deep, and I'm swimming and swimming and my board's gone, and I know that I've gotta swim in."

Ashton moved his arms in swimming motions, and huffed, demonstrating and reliving the fatigue, the breathless panic.

"So I'm thinking, swimming, looking around, swimming, thinking, swimming, trying to think bearings, trying to figure out what the hell I'm going to do. I'm trying to figure out options. This had never happened to me before. So I'm thinking, okay, the current's going out, I'm not making any progress, I'll swim harder. Umm, if I swim across the channel over there —no, I'll end up in a bigger channel, the huge one that runs in between the islands, not where you want to get caught. So I'm swimming straight in towards shore. I do it for a little bit, probably a minute, even though I know I'm not making any progress, because that's my last option.

"I knew that even if somebody came out with their board, it wouldn't do me any good. Two people couldn't get on one board, because you have to paddle too fast to make any progress at all. The only way in without a board was to swim."

Ashton took a deep breath. "That's when I realized, they can't save me. I was out there by myself. And I didn't know if Danny or Pete was even still alive. Because as far as I was concerned, that wave took over the whole damn place.

"I was really panicking now. I was like three breaths behind, 'cause I was so scared. And I was thinking, man, I'm going to drown out here in the middle of the ocean because I'm swimming and swimming and not making any progress. I'm getting sucked back out.

"Every minute I didn't make a decision, it was getting worse and worse for me. I got to the point where I was right on the tip of the reef, the place where the waves were breaking on dry reef. That place will tear you apart if you get slammed into it."

Ashton came over to where Morgan was sitting. She had slid off the couch and was sitting on the floor, leaning against it. He lowered himself slowly onto the couch.

"Mom, all I could think about was staying on top of the water and getting the next breath. It was hard to keep myself up, because I'm so damn tired I can't swim very well anymore. And I'm breathing in water. Air, water, swim.

"Then all of a sudden I thought about Faiza. It was like she just popped into my mind. Not seeing her face or hearing her or anything like that. More like her essence. Like she was cheering me on.

"And right then, I looked over that dry reef and saw it a whole different way. The waves that usually looked so huge and menacing, crashing in on dry reef, looked like my saviors. It was nothing but dry reef with gnarly waves breaking on it, what normally I would see as unrideable surf, and it was the sweetest thing I've ever seen.

"So I swam right for it. I thought, I'm gonna ride one of these waves in on my belly, catch it and bodysurf the damn thing in. And all this time I feel Faiza, not her voice but her energy. C'mon, Ash. You can make it. Go, go, go.

"I thought, If I'm going to die, I'm going to die trying. So I started swimming and swimming and swimming, as fast as I could—it was a real sprint. I was up on top of the water, crazy, really losing my breath. But I knew the other side of the reef was lagoon, and if I could get inside the breaking waves without dying, they'd push me in. And I'm swimming and swimming, and I had the feeling there were big waves. I was lucky. I saw one coming and I said, You've gotta catch this wave. Gotta, gotta, gotta.

"And I get the wave! I suck in a good breath, and I'm on my belly. I was just . . . all that panic turned into complete joy. I knew I'd be okay. I caught that wave, and it pushed me and pushed me and pushed me. I rode that wave to a piece of dry reef where the water was maybe one foot deep.

"I stood up. I looked around for Pete and Danny, but there was no sign of them. I had this weird feeling that I would see Faiza, because she was there all along, yelling, 'C'mon! You can make it.' It was that kind of feeling—a feeling that everyone was watching. But I didn't see anyone. I stood up and I was yelling, YEEAAAH! YEEAAAH!

"I can't even breathe now, and I hunch over and I start puking. I puked everything I had. And then I look over and I see my board, floating in the lagoon about four hundred yards away. I jumped off that reef and did freestyle across.

"In the lagoon the water is calm. Some parts of the reef are really shallow, so I'm swimming and pulling myself over coral heads and jumping into the next deep part. I got to my board, and I lay on it, huffing and puffing for maybe half an hour. And then I see them both, paddling up the channel, looking for me.

"Pete said, 'Dude, when I saw your board in there, and I didn't see you for about forty-five minutes, I thought you were dead.'"

Morgan was trembling. She wanted to wrap her arms around him, but didn't, afraid she might break down. Ashton looked straight at her.

"You can get in real trouble out there, Mom."

"I don't want you to get in big trouble out there." Morgan said softly.

"What? You want me to sit around here and die of old age?"

"No," Morgan said. "But I do want you to die of old age."

Ashton said, "Mom, it was Faiza's spirit that pulled me out of that mess. I know it. And now she needs me to pull her out of one. I don't know exactly what's going on, but I know she wants me to do something. I don't know exactly what or how, but I'm going to do something."

*   *   *

Two days later Morgan flew back to Florida. The telephone was ringing as she walked into her house, and she picked it up before she even set down her bag.

"Morgan? Grady here."

"Oh, hi. I just walked in the door from the airport."

"I figured," Grady said. "Your son gave me your number and told me you were on the way home."

"Can I call you back in a little bit?" Morgan said.

"Oh, sure. Take your time. I just wanted to tell you something."

"Uh-huh."

"I've been thinking. And, well, I could make a couple of phone calls."

CHAPTER THIRTY-FOUR

The man known as Taco listened without saying a word as Grady outlined the predicament. Morgan stayed silent. The three were cloistered in a small office adjoining a cavernous hangar in Florida. The setting reminded her of Rus Syvyson's digs at Half Moon Bay, except this one was newer.

The smell of fuel and oily tools wafted in the door but didn't linger in a stale film as it had at Rus's; instead it was carried on a breeze through the open window. The desk and shelves held the same clutter of aviation paraphernalia, only less musty, and the photo gallery hanging on the walls looked the same, except it was Taco standing next to the warplanes or amid a pod of smiling guys dressed in flight jackets.

"We might not be asking you to do anything at this point," Grady said, matching Taco's inscrutableness. "Maybe we just need to know what you think. Hypothetically. Is it possible?"

Taco never told them his real name, though Grady eventually told Morgan his first name was Enrique. But, he said, just call me Taco. Maybe he'd gotten used to it. Or maybe in the military you accepted that kind of thing, even if it meant being nicknamed after fast food.

Taco sat with one foot resting on the open bottom drawer of his desk. He was rather cute, and younger-looking than Morgan had expected. Retired from the military, he had to be in his fifties, she guessed, but not a strand of gray hair.

He wasn't even Mexican. He was of Spanish origin, grew up in Cuba, and fled to the United States with his parents shortly before Fidel Castro overthrew the Batista regime in 1959.

Earlier, Grady had told Morgan that Taco became a citizen when he was eighteen and the next day joined the Army. Once, in a rare moment of openness, he had told Grady that he never wanted another day to go by that he couldn't defend his family. So he'd joined the Army to get the training and the firearms to do that. In the bargain, he got to pay back the U.S. for taking his family in. He figured that all his years in the Army equaled admission for three.

"Anything's possible with enough money," Taco said.

"Could you help us? Put us in contact with the right people?"

Taco shrugged. "I suppose I could."

"How do you think it might go?" Grady asked.

Taco leaned back in his chair and kicked the drawer shut with his foot. "You need to stay away from the mercenaries," he said. "They do what they do for money. So if someone comes along with more money, they will dump you and go with them. They are good fighters, yes. But they don't care who they are rescuing. Your lady friend or a camel—it doesn't matter. What you're paying for is their expertise, their risking their lives, and that's all you're getting. But you cannot pay for loyalty. Loyalty can't be bought."

"Are there such people?" Morgan asked. "People who do this and who care?"

Taco jerked his chin at Grady and grinned. "This caballero used to care. Though he will tell you different."

"Look, Taco, I'm done with all that. But what about some of the other guys?"

"Maybe." Taco opened the drawer again and propped his other foot on it. "First of all, you don't know what you're going to go up against when you go into this place to get the lady. Are there going to be five guards? Two guards?"

"It's a private home," Morgan interjected.

"That doesn't make any difference in Saudi," he said. "If the people are rich, they have guards. And because something like this has happened, this abduction, there will probably be more guards. It's going to take two vehicles, maybe three. A dozen people to do it right."

*   *   *

A lot had happened in the three weeks since Morgan left California. Courtney, Faiza's school friend, had driven Ashton to the bank, where they retrieved the jewels from the safe deposit box and then immediately delivered them to her jeweler father for appraisal. In the safe deposit box, Ashton also found Faiza's passport and visa. This was very good news. They weren't worried about needing a passport to get her out of Saudi; after all, they weren't exactly asking permission. Her passport would not contain the necessary authorization stamps, but it could serve as proof that she had been in this country legally.

After the day Grady had called and offered to help, more than a week went by before Morgan heard from him again. He told her that there would be few phone calls. They would do their planning in person. The next week he called and said that he would be piloting a charter to Atlanta and wanted Morgan to meet him in Orlando that weekend. That was it. He gave her directions, but did not reveal whose house it was.

The directions led her to a subdivision near Kissimmee named Sky Grove, a conclave of pilots and aviation enthusiasts. The houses looked like ordinary ranch homes, aligned in nice neighborly rows, except each house had a hangar next to it, and the street also served as a taxiway to a small airstrip at the end of the block.

Grady answered the door, introduced Morgan to Taco, and they walked over to the hangar where she guessed Taco spent most of his waking, and probably many sleeping, hours. There were two planes inside: a sleek, white newish-looking four-seater, and a chubby little tail-dragger, old and ready for polish, with the cowling off and two enormous red toolboxes open on the floor beside it.

*   *   *

Taco was asking Grady, "How are you getting the plane in?"

"I'm not getting anything in," Grady said. "They are. I figure they could come right into Dhahran."

"You can't take all of them in at one time," Taco said, adding, "whoever they are."

"I know. But the escape plane could go in under the pretext of an airplane being brought in as a demo," Grady said. "That's legitimate. Remember Larry Wolfe?"

"The Wolfman." Taco smiled. Morgan wondered if he was jealous of this much cooler nickname.

"He's an airplane broker in Houston now," Grady said. "He told me the other day that he's representing a corporate 727 that's for sale in Saudi Arabia. Some sheik has this plane and he wants to replace it with something bigger, one of those Boeing business jets, the 737-800."

Taco nodded. "There's always shit like that happening. But you need something smaller and faster."

"The S-5," Grady said.

Taco nodded. "Good. So you'd come in under the guise of bringing in the S-5 to demo it to a customer. That's how you're going to get your flight crew in. And when you do that, you look legitimate to the surrounding people there at the airport. The authorities see this limo drive up, and Sheik Khalib gets out to go look at your airplane. You would look very stupid if you pull up with an airplane that you say you are going to demo and you sit there for twenty-four hours and no one shows up. Somebody would start to smell a rat."

"How do we get the rest of the guys in?"

"By sea," Taco said. "Maybe through Bahrain." He stood up, walked to a bookcase, and rifled through a stack of maps. Almost immediately he found what he was looking for, then spread out a map of Saudi Arabia and surrounding countries on the desk.

"Here's Dhahran," he said. "And here's Bahrain." Taco explained to Morgan that this island in the Persian Gulf, adjacent to the coast where Dhahran was located, was like the French Riviera for Saudis, and they had even built a bridge from Bahrain to Dhahran.

"Why not have them come in the plane?" she asked.

"Too many. Too conspicuous. In the plane we only have the flight crew—two pilots and a mechanic, and two attendants," Taco said. "And you'll need vehicles. Land Rovers."

"Land Rovers?"

"That's Land Rover country. There's thousands of them. White, usually. We have 'em and we'll blend right in."

Morgan noticed that Taco had switched from "they" to "we." Was he in? She dared not ask.

"Doesn't the S-5 have a head in the back?" Taco asked Grady.

"Yeah. There's a bathroom and a little living area."

"The dividing walls that separate that area from the cabin. There's space in there, right?"

Morgan was lost, but Grady understood exactly what Taco meant. "Yeah. We can hide the weapons there," he said.

She looked at Grady. Guns? He shook his head slightly, enough to tell her to not say whatever it was she was thinking. She shut up, but suddenly realized for the first time that this whole thing was real. Up to this point she'd been an actor in some melodrama of rescue and revenge. They were going on a bloodless, easy re-kidnapping. They'd hop on their hot plane with their gang of daring bubbas and have Faiza home in a jiffy. Guns?

To Morgan, guns were like spiders or snakes. For most of her life she was so scared of them she couldn't even touch one. Once, for a story, she had attended a gun class taught by a retired sheriff who had to practically hypnotize her to get her to pick up the gun, or "acquire your weapon" as he called it, and when it was her turn to fire he'd grasped her shoulders and said, "Squeeze, squeeze" over and over again until she pulled the trigger.

Morgan had screamed when the gun exploded. After the blast she shook so hard she had to put the gun down. She hated guns. What they did, what they stood for. At least spiders and snakes had a function in the environment and on the food chain. Violence begets violence, as they say, and Morgan did not believe the path to peace was through the barrel of a gun.

Grady and Taco were leaned over the map, heads together. This was going to be a problem.

"So we come into Dhahran with the S-5 and we demo it to a couple of customers," Taco said. "Can Wolfman set that up?"

"Probably. Or someone he knows."

"We're gonna need a couple of days, to hang around there and let the airport mucky-mucks get real accustomed to our comings and goings."

"Can the flight crew leave the airport?" Morgan asked, beginning to see the pieces of this plan come together.

"Oh, sure," Taco said.

"What about women?"

"Well, if there were women they'd be more restricted. They'll have to travel with men, and cover up."

"With an abaya?"

"It's best. Why tick off the locals by flaunting the customs? That only raises more doubts and questions. And we don't want that." Taco paused and thought for a minute. "Why would there be women?"

"Why not?" Morgan said.

Grady cleared his throat and reached in his pocket for a Marlboro. She noticed he had switched to lights. "Want one?" he said to them both.

"No thanks."

"I finally quit," Taco said. "But yeah, sure. No ashtrays, though."

He leaned forward into Grady's lighter, took a deep drag, and blew the smoke up toward the ceiling. Then, remembering something, he handed the cig to Morgan and stood up. He opened one file drawer after another, rummaging through the folders, slamming them shut and moving on. Finally he pulled a sheet out of a file. The tab was labeled "Intl.—Misc."

"Off the internet the other day," Taco said, handing it to them. It read:

APPROVAL GIVEN FOR PRIVATE AIRLINE COMPANY
SOURCE: SPA News Agency, Riyadh

The director-general of the Saudi airline Saudia, Khalid Bin Abdullah Bin Bakr, announced that approval has been given for the establishment of a new, private airline company in conjunction with two U.S. firms. Bakr said that the national company for air services would develop the private air transport sector to meet the needs of businessmen, corporations, and senior officials, and would be transformed into a joint stock company within two years of its establishment.

He said that an agreement has been reached between the new company and the U.S. company Atlantic Aeronautical, which builds the Skybird jet, to implement a program that will include partial or total ownership of private jets, as well as the leasing of private jets. The company will be based in Jeddah.

"The Saudis are going to be buying fucking Skybirds," Grady said.

Taco grinned. "Maybe they'd like to see ours."

Before they left Taco's hangar-house, the two of them agreed to rendezvous back there in about three weeks. Grady planned to maneuver his schedule to bring him back to the southeast, and Taco said he would call and invite Grady and Morgan to a party.

"That is all we say on the phone," Taco said firmly.

Time was passing so fast. If Faiza was still pregnant, they didn't have any to waste. Taco saw Morgan's dismay when he said three weeks.

"These things take time," he told her. "I know you are feeling urgent, but it might take months to put this together. There is a lot of planning to do. Much we have to know about. And people to find."

Months? "But it's possible?" she ventured.

"As I said before, anything's possible with enough money," Taco said.

"How much money?"

Taco hesitated briefly. "Maybe twenty thousand per man."

"And we need ten men?" she asked, as if she was in Wal-Mart trying to figure out how many gallons of paint it would take to do the living room.

"Would you do this?" she asked, bargaining with money she didn't even have yet. "If I could give you the twenty thousand?"

"I'd need a lot more than that," Taco said. "If you want me to put it together."

"How much more?"

"Fifty thousand," he said, "if I decide to do it at all."

From the corner of her eye, Morgan could see Grady cringing. He had obviously hoped they'd get away from this first meeting without talking about money. She decided that covert operations must be like swanky hotels. If you have to ask the price, you probably can't afford it.

"Taco," Morgan said. "Please help us. This young woman will be killed if we don't get her out."

"I'll call Grady," he said. "And remember, no questions on the phone. It's simply a party."

"Can I ask you what to bring?"

Taco smiled at her. "Sure. And maybe I'll tell you not to bring a thing. I'll say everything's taken care of."

CHAPTER THIRTY-FIVE

Grady walked Morgan to her car and she lingered, about to burst with questions. He opened her door.

"We don't hang around out here talking," he said, rather curtly. "I have a room not too far from here. Follow me there. Go ahead and pull out, and I'll catch up and pass you."

Grady was driving a seafoam green Taurus, a rental car, Morgan assumed. Through the rear window she could see the back of his head and neck. When she first met him, she remembered noticing the way his hairline curved along the back of his neck. He had clean cut hair, but the neckline was a little ragged. For some reason, she found that sexy.

Still, the man annoyed her terribly; only because they were working on a common goal would she allow the slight bond forming between them. Right now they needed him, and she could certainly put up with his apathetic attitude and his refusal to get involved with anything that didn't concern him or that risked his safe little job and his fixed-rate life.

"From now on," Grady said, holding the motel room door open for her, "we have to assume we are being followed. Even today, though we probably aren't."

"Who would follow us?"

"Taco has a past. He might be retired now, but if old buddies from that past start showing up, someone might get suspicious."

"Who would get suspicious?"

"You don't get it, Morgan. This is the real world. Taco probably has more enemies that he doesn't even know about than you and I have casual associates. Not to mention the government. Taco may be retired, but he has skills that give him power and make him an object of concern. Taco's what they call 'out in the cold,' and if he stays there, he can live peacefully and work on his little airplanes and go to air shows and die of old age. That's the unspoken deal."

Why did she always feel like Grady was talking down to her? Maybe because he was.

"Want a drink?" Grady said. Then he laughed. "I've got water and one Coke and two beers from last night in the ice bucket. Not a great selection."

"Beer sounds good," Morgan said. He opened one.

"I can't drink today," he said. "I'm flying out later tonight. FAA regs. Eight hours from bottle to throttle." He opened the Coke.

The motel, called Sunset Beach, wasn't anywhere near the ocean or even a small lake. It was an old-Florida-style, one-story row of rooms with an office at the end. Each room had a small horizontal casement window next to the door. There were two double beds with mattresses so flat and squared off they looked like boxes of typing paper. They were covered with napkin-thin bedspreads in a dark red and green floral design. The place looked like the room in the movies where the kidnappers take the kid.

"Nice room," she lied, suddenly uncomfortable.

"No, it's not," he said. "But it was just for the night, and close to Taco's."

"Why didn't you stay with him? Oh, right, I get it."

They sipped their drinks. Grady was sitting on one bed and Morgan on the other. She wondered if he was thinking about kissing her again, and if so, how he was planning to get into it. Because she wasn't going to help him one bit. He could figure out his own moves. She hoped he didn't. Then she hoped he did. So what if he did? It was fun, it would be fun again, and there was nothing else to it. On the other hand, it could be pretty dangerous, kissing on beds. Beds have a way of pulling you into their force field. Even these hard-ass cheapo motel beds had a certain magnetism.

"Grady, tell me about the guns," Morgan said.

"It's like American Express, babe," he said. "You don't leave home without 'em."

"I never thought about there being violence. I abhor violence. I hate guns."

"You can hate guns all you want. But this is the real world." He knit his brows. "How did you think we were going to get her out?" he added. "Stroll up to the door and say politely, 'Hey Khalib, we think it only fair that you give us your pregnant niece'? And then Khalib, he says, 'And I think it only fair that you spend some time in our lovely Dhahran jail.'"

"I don't hate these people," Morgan said. "I hate what has happened to Faiza."

"Spare me the psychobabble," Grady said. "Who do you think created the mess your friend is in? If they didn't think women were pieces of property over there, she'd be out of that room and in Target buying maternity tops."

"Does that justify going in and blowing people away? It's like Vietnam. Or Yugoslavia. Where we decide what's right and barge in and mete out our own justice."

"This isn't like that," Grady said.

"What's the difference between a whole Army and a handful of hired guns?" Morgan asked.

"Maybe no difference. But you do what you have to do," Grady answered. "There'll be no rescue mission if there are no guns."

"But Grady, can't we just use cunning—like on *Mission Impossible*?"

He rolled his eyes. "Morgan, this is not a movie script. This is reality. You can go out and find the best men in the business. If you tell them where you're going, and that you want them to go in without weapons, they'll say, 'You can kiss my ass and the horse I rode in on,' and they'll turn right around and walk off."

"What about nonlethal weapons?" she suggested. "Like those little stun bags that can knock people down."

"You don't give up, do you?" He smiled. "You could use some of that. Mace. Or zappers. But you're gonna have to have some guys toting metal. I'm sorry."

For a second, Morgan felt that Grady really understood and that he was truly sorry. His voice softened.

"I'm not saying they're going to have to use the weapons. Or that it's going to be a big gunfight and a run. But the Saudi guards are gonna be armed too. You ain't gonna find the people you want to go in and do this, if they can only carry a Bible and wear a peace sign on their chest."

Morgan took a sip of beer. Before the bottle left her lips, Grady moved over to her bed and took it out of her hand. He reached over and set it on the nightstand, and by that time his other arm was around her, pulling her closer to him. His lips caressed hers with little gentle nibbles, and then, when he felt her relax into his arms, he pressed his kiss deep into hers. He put his hand behind her head and lowered her back protectively, as though he was expecting her head to hit concrete.

For the moment she yielded to him. He moved his body against hers and kissed her neck and her shoulders and the side of her head. The more she surrendered into him, the deeper and longer his kisses.

"I could kiss you for hours," he said.

"Me too," she said. "But . . . " She could feel him inside her even though he wasn't even near there. And according to the earlier vow she had made to herself, he never would be.

"But?"

"I need to leave now," she said.

Grady pulled back and looked her in the eyes. "Are you thinking that I'm expecting something, because I'm helping you? Because I'm not."

He took a long breath in and exhaled with a deep sigh.

"You're right," he said, even though she hadn't said anything. "We need to stick to what we're here for. And besides, I never mess around before a flight."

"Hm?"

"FAA regs. Eight hours from body to throttle."

Oh, brother. What a jerk.

*   *   *

During the two-hour drive home, Morgan rehashed the issue of the guns. Grady was right. She was in la-la land. What was she thinking, that they could conduct a pacifist mission in an armed world? *Mission Impossible* was fiction. And they weren't exactly going over the border into Connecticut.

The whole thing suddenly seemed very impetuous. That's what Dowd would say. That she was, as usual, leaping onto a moving train without really thinking about where it was going. And then, long after it had roared out of the station, trying to figure out where she was and realizing that she'd left everybody else back there standing on the platform.

Morgan found an oldies station on the radio, turned the volume all the way up, and sang along, nearly shouting the songs, pumping her head with the music, beating the rhythms on the steering wheel.

"If you believe in forever, then life is just a one-night sta-a-a-nd. If there's a rock and roll hea-a-a-ven, well you know they're gonna ha-a-ave a band band BA-A-A-AND!" The music was clearing, cleansing, like being flushed out with a garden hose. "Hey, hey Paula, I wanna marry you. Hey Paul, I wanna mah-rrrry yooou too" always took her right back. She was there. She could feel high school.

Today, the music made her think of Grady. She'd known his type in high school. Cute, cocky, masculine. He was the kind of guy she fell for every time. And then outgrew. But damn, what a kisser.

Morgan thought of Faiza in that dark room, her own little private death row. It didn't matter what country she was in. She could be across the street or across the globe. It didn't matter if it was a religion or a state that held her. And it didn't matter whose cultural system they crossed over to get her. All that was irrelevant. Like a bird, Faiza knew the difference between a cage and freedom. That instinct is inborn; it was neither dependent on a society nor could it be quashed by one. Freedom transcends belief systems, Morgan thought. In a universe of total relativity, freedom may be one of the only real truths.

Still, Morgan wanted to get her out without violence. And she had to believe that could be done. They needed Taco's help, and the help of his brand of guy. But maybe there was room for compromise. For cunning and ingenuity.

"Whole world over, so easy to see. People everywhere just GOT TO BE FREE . . . "

Morgan turned off the radio, and although her head was still buzzing, it felt clear.

When she arrived home, she went directly to the phone and dialed.

"Linnie?"

"Morgan! It's good to hear your voice. What's happened? Is there anything I can do?"

"Listen, Linnie. I think there is. Could you, by any chance, come to Florida? Like, soon?"

"How soon?"

"Maybe within a week. I'm going to call Kate, too, so we'll have to coordinate."

"I think I probably can."

"I need your help," Morgan said.

"I'm sure I can, then," Linnie said. "What's going on?"

"I shouldn't talk about it on the phone. And I can't explain why."

"Oookay," Linnie said. "Hint?"

"We need to have a meeting of MCC."

Linnie thought for a second. "Oh!"

"We need to reactivate the group," Morgan said.

"Mujeres?"

"Yes," Morgan said.
"You're kidding."
"I'm dead serious."
"Okay, then," Linnie said. "I'm there."

CHAPTER THIRTY-SIX

Kate and Morgan grew up in a small Midwestern town that probably didn't even unpack the Democratic ballots at the primary election polls. Linnie's town, though in southern Illinois, was also tucked away in the Corn Belt, and thus very similar.

Their three histories were like the sycamores entrenched forever in their backyards, gripping deep into the rich soil, shedding their leaves in the autumn, growing and leafing each spring, season after season, getting bigger and fuller and shadier with each predictable year. It was safe, but with an insulation that often comes with safety.

The world news was reported in a daily afternoon paper, but it rarely invaded cheerleading practice or pep rallies or prom night. Because no matter what the newspaper said, the big issue of the afternoon was more likely what team the Bulldogs were facing Friday night or whether the temperature was cold enough to freeze the ice in the skating rink.

These were towns where farm boys were allowed to miss school during planting in the spring and harvest in autumn. Towns where you could take skirts and sweaters home from stores to try out, with no receipts, no charges. Bring it back if you don't like it, and pay later.

None of them recalled ever locking the doors to their houses during the day, or even at night. "If we hadn't taken vacations," Linnie once said, "I wouldn't have known we had locks." There were no "bad" sections of town. They didn't fear crime, kids could go where they wanted, and although some were probably being molested in their own homes, it didn't happen on the streets.

The biggest scare in Kate and Morgan's town was when Leslie Ivey, a killer known as the "Mad Dog," escaped from prison in Indianapolis and was rumored to be at large in the area. Mad Dog Ivey got his nickname because he shot people execution-style. The whole town mobilized, terrified, and they locked their doors for the first time.

Ivey was eventually captured and no harm came to anyone in town, although one dentist, Dr. Callahan, was sure that a scruffy stranger who had come into his office wanting a tooth fixed was Mad Dog himself. He sure looked like the photo in the newspaper, Dr. Callahan said. And he sure was in a hurry. The whole town speculated about that for weeks, shuddering at the prospect that Mad Dog might have penetrated their safe, sunny little ball of cotton. But after a while they unlocked their doors, and life went on.

In the early days of the Vietnam War, any guy who wanted a deferment could get one. The draft board knew every boy, and there were no favorites because they were all favorites. As for the civil rights movement, it was like a war that was going on in some other country.

Years later, Morgan would brag that there were no racial problems in the town where she grew up, but the truth was that they didn't have racial problems because they didn't have diverse races. In a town of 18,000, there were only two Black families. Everyone knew their names, but not so they could call them up and invite them over. They were good families, everyone told themselves, though they never got close enough to find out. In high school, the integration ratio was three Blacks per twelve hundred students.

As Kate, Linnie, and Morgan moved through college, the world expanded somewhat, and they did, at times, look up and around them. But the Midwestern university they attended was also a cloister, what someone in the sixties called "the seat of campus rest." Whatever seeds of activism or revolt they did inadvertently sow fluttered to the ground like wispy maple pods and were absorbed on a thick cushion of soft soil, where they could germinate peacefully and safely in their own sweet time.

Meanwhile, they sunned themselves on the roof of the sorority house and talked about their lives and their classes and their boyfriends, and the only soldiers they worried about were the fraternity guys who were riding in the Little 500 bicycle race. They weren't purposefully shallow. They just hadn't been shown the whole picture yet.

"Let's promise we'll always stay together," Linnie said one day. The three were sitting in her room. Morgan was sprawled on the bed, Linnie was hunched back in her desk chair with her feet on Morgan's lap, and Kate was scrunched in the corner, hugging a pillow to her stomach with one arm, and with the other hand twirled a strand of hair around her middle finger.

They had all let their hair grow out long and straight, to look like Mary Travers, of Peter, Paul and Mary. This was their bold statement of independence, rebellion against convention. Linnie's light brown hair was naturally wavy, so hers grew out rather stylishly, in spite of attempts to brush it into compliance with the hippie look they desired. Kate's dark brown hair was rich and full, and the longer it got, the more luscious it looked.

Morgan's, thin and fine with wispy bangs, was the only hair that came out with the requisite look, flat on her head and breaking at her shoulders into stringy little sections. But she didn't look like Mary. She looked like she needed a perm and a cut. Or a guitar.

During their junior year, Trap, the fiancé of one of their sorority sisters, dropped out of school and immediately was nabbed by the draft and sent to Vietnam. That was the closest they came to the war.

When Trap returned from an eighteen-month tour, he was dark and despondent and desperately needing to talk to someone about it. But Maggie, his fiancée, didn't want him to speak about it at all. She was tired of having a long distance relationship, tired of writing letters when everyone else was getting dressed for dates, and she was tired of worrying that he was going to get shot when everyone else was worrying about getting pinned. She wanted her boyfriend back the way he used to be, and why couldn't he put the whole thing behind him?

Late one balmy spring night, after Maggie went in to bed, Trap and Morgan sat outside on the trunk of his car in the sorority parking lot. They polished off nearly a whole six-pack of Black Label, and Morgan listened to him for hours and hours. He wasn't her boyfriend, so it was easier for her to hear him talk about the killing and the having to shoot men you didn't even know and the slogging through the jungle mud, dragging torn-up bodies, and the men screaming for morphine. And never knowing where the enemy was or who the enemy was, but knowing he could jump out and blow your face off at any moment.

Trap sobbed, and Morgan felt deeply sad for him. No wonder he stayed awake at night. Inside him was a nightmare waiting to be dreamt.

Morgan lost track of Maggie after graduation. She never knew what happened to them, whether they got married, whether they stayed married. And it would be another thirty-five years before she understood what she had heard that night on the trunk of Trap's car.

Dowd and she rarely talked about Vietnam. He was older than Morgan and already beyond the draft age when the war was shifted into full gear and began sucking away the men by the dozens. When the two were married, the social and business world in which they moved was virtually void of veterans.

Then, for some reason, after their divorce, when Morgan started dating again, it seemed as if every man she met was a Vietnam vet. Though their wounds were now scars, they were deep and scary, and the pain was like Trap's. Some would still sob if they talked about it, and all of them carried so much guilt and shame and remorse.

After lovemaking one night, a Marine she was dating asked Morgan if it bothered her that he had killed people. She didn't know how to answer. But she knew that what plagued him was not that he had done it, but that when he did it, he'd believed in it. Morgan couldn't find fault with that. Not now, anyway. When he was in the jungle, fighting somebody else's stupid, immoral power game, she'd been over here, not speaking up about it, not really caring about it. She should have asked him if it bothered him that she didn't try to stop the war.

The spring of their junior year, Kate, Linnie, and Morgan flew out to California to see what was going on. The antiwar movement in full swing, they arrived at Golden Gate Park dressed like flower children in bright pink and yellow T-shirts and jeans, with batik vests, because they didn't have any flowered skirts.

They were hanging out when they met three guys. One had a ponytail. His name was Brew. The other two had scraggly beards and greasy hair down to their shoulders. The guys drove a Volkswagen bus that was full sixties. The inside was lined with turquoise carpet squares, some of them peeling off. There were shoes and wadded up shirts, and it reeked of pot.

There was a problem with the steering on the bus; it could only turn left. The guys joked that it was political. If they wanted to go somewhere on the right, they would have to drive beyond the spot and then make a series of left turns to come back to it. The bus went tearing up steep inclines, like a movie car chase, and then drove up a one-way street the wrong way, and when they leaped over the peak of that hill, Morgan was sure they were going to crash head-on into some huge truck.

The guys started smoking marijuana, and they were getting pretty high. Brew would sway with the turns, crooning things like, "That's far-fucking-out, man." Kate, Linnie, and Morgan looked at each other. Now they were getting nervous. They all had been drinking beer, but the wild ride in this decaying old VW bus was sobering.

Brew and the other guys were starting to grab at them. Brew pulled Morgan up to him and nuzzled his hairy face into her neck. She almost threw up. When she wriggled away from him, he made a growling sound and said something about how she wasn't going to be able to avoid him forever. He was a big guy. If it had been just him and her, she wasn't sure how she would defend herself.

And then Morgan began, somewhat gradually at first, to lose consciousness. She felt woozy and sleepy.

She was vaguely aware that, after multiple left-hand turns, the bus was tearing onto the Golden Gate Bridge. The bridge lights overhead moved across her vision in fuzzy streaks, like a time-exposure photograph.

She tried to hold up her head but it kept falling back, as though someone had a big concrete hand on her forehead.

*   *   *

Some time later, Morgan was aware that the VW bus was stopped in a dark, wooded area, and the rear door was open. A cool fresh breeze wafted in, diluting the smoky stench of the inside of the bus. She could hear crickets, chirping slowly, like a 78 record played on 33. She shivered and began to come to, but not enough to move or to speak.

It was like one of those dreams where your throat tries to scream but no sound will come out. She could see Linnie on the other side of the bus, and she looked asleep. She couldn't see Kate. Her mouth was dry, and she felt like she was grabbing for oxygen. Big smelly arms on both sides of her were dragging her out of the bus, and she couldn't do anything but yield.

The big smelly arms propped her up against something, probably a tree, and let her go. Her head hit something hard. Through the haze, she watched two big hairy silhouettes stumble back toward the bus.

Morgan still couldn't move; her arms seemed stuck to the ground. The next minutes felt like hours, but her awareness was beginning to gradually return, and she reached up and felt that her bra had been unfastened and her shirt was pulled up over her breasts. She gagged.

She couldn't see Linnie, but they were dragging Kate out of the bus and laying her down about twenty feet from where Morgan was propped. Her shirt was up over her bare breasts, and they were leaning over her and unfastening her jeans. Morgan screamed, Stop it! but no sound came out. *I've got to stop them. I've got to stop them.* They pulled Kate's jeans down over her hips, and Morgan saw one of them unzipping his own. She heaved in deep breaths, and the feeling in her arms began to return.

Just then, she heard Linnie's voice.

"Get your fucking hands off of her or I'll blow your brains out!"

In the shadows, Morgan could see Linnie's outline. She stood with her feet planted slightly apart and her arms stretched out in front of her, hands clasped together on a pistol pointed straight ahead.

"Whaa--a--a?" The guys looked up, and one stumbled back into a tree. One grabbed at his open fly, and the other stood up and held his hands up in the air.

Linnie growled, "I said get away from her, you dirty fucking bastards. God, I'd love to blow your butts off!"

The three guys backed away from where Kate lay, waking up now.

"Don't move," Linnie shouted, brandishing her weapon.

The guys complied and stood quaking in a huddle a few feet from Kate. Where the hell had she found a gun?

"Kate, Morgan," Linnie said, still aiming her arms toward the guys. "Get in the van. Go. Go." Morgan pushed herself up and walked tentatively over to Kate, helping her to her feet. She felt nauseated and hangover tired, and her head was splitting.

"Get in the van and start it up," Linnie ordered. "The keys are in the ignition."

While Kate and Morgan did as she told them, Linnie stood facing the three guys, repositioning her warrior stance whenever they made the slightest move. Morgan heard a scraping click, like a gun being cocked, and one of the guys slurred, "Please, lady, for god's sake, don't shoot."

When Kate and Morgan were inside the van and its engine was chugging, Linnie backed toward it and got in, her weapon still pointed toward the guys. Kate was in the driver's seat.

As it turned out, they were about two hundred yards from a two-lane road, on a dirt pull-off. Kate backed the van so she could make a left-hand turn onto the road. Linnie was still shouting at the guys to stay where they were or she'd fire, and they never moved while they watched the dust and gravel splatter from the tires as Kate spun up onto the road and peeled away.

Linnie leaned out of the window and kept her weapon pointed at them until the bus was far from the turnoff, and then, red-faced and as angry as Morgan had ever seen her in her whole life, she drew back from the window and hurled her gun, which was nothing but a big crooked stick, out into the night.

The ride back that night was unforgettable. Every time Kate turned, the steering column on the VW bus creaked, and the inside smelled like a salvage yard. They were terrified that they would get pulled over and busted for probably a ton of drugs hidden behind the carpet squares. Or they could get arrested for stealing a car, although they were pretty sure that their toked-out rapists wouldn't want to interact with any cops.

Kate found the bridge, and after they crossed it, Linnie remembered some landmarks from the circuitous ride, so she navigated them through another labyrinth of left hand turns until they spotted the entrance to Golden Gate Park. They drove to the spot where they'd parked their car and ditched the van.

The next day they took the ferry to Sausalito, where they sat outside and ate lunch at a trendy little cafe on the water. They were scared and sickened and mostly embarrassed that they had let that happen. Morgan thought it was all their fault.

"They drugged us," Linnie said. "Only mine wore off first."

"We never should have gotten in that van," Morgan said.

"Geez, Linnie. Packing wood," said Kate. They laughed. "How did you cock the trigger? It sounded so real."

"Zippo lighter," Linnie said. "Found it on the seat. When the lid snaps down, it sounds just like a gun cocking."

"When the chips are down, we're a formidable team," Kate said.

"We've got brains and guts," Linnie said. "We could be operatives. Have adventures and rescue women. Rid the world of dirtbags."

They all forced a cheer and pledged their forever loyalty to their threesome, which they named "AP," the Asshole Patrol.

"We need a battle cry," Kate said.

"How about, Down with dirtbags!" Morgan offered.

"No, something more chic, like the Marines have Semper Fi."

"Puhleeze. Marines are not chic."

"You know what I mean. Something Latin, or French."

"What's Latin for 'We stand up for ourselves'?" Linnie asked.

"Vini, vidi, vici?"

"Forget it. How about Spanish?" Morgan said. *"Mujeres con cojones."*

"Women who don't back down?"

"Sort of," Morgan said.

"Mujeres con cajones?" Linnie said.

"No," Morgan laughed. "Cajones are drawers. Cojones are male genitalia."

"Oh! Women with balls!"

They clinked beer bottles.

"To the MCC! Mujeres con cojones!"

CHAPTER THIRTY-SEVEN

"So I got to thinking," Morgan said to Kate. "Maybe there is a compromise between *Mission Impossible* and *Gunfight at the O.K. Corral*. Maybe there's a way to get Faiza out of that house without blowing everyone away. After all, it worked for us in San Francisco, when the bastards who inspired the MCC just *thought* Linnie had a gun."

She told Kate about Grady's idea of bringing in a demo airplane and posing as its crew. "But he and Taco just assumed the whole group would be men. And when I asked 'Why only men?' they looked at me like I was from Mars—er, well, Venus."

The two were sitting in a small open bar on a concourse at the Tampa International Airport, waiting for Linnie's plane, due in about thirty minutes. Kate had coordinated her flight from California with Linnie and had arrived an hour before. Kate's new assistant in the agency was working out well, giving Kate the freedom to take some time away. She carried a cellphone in the outside pocket of a large shoulder bag, to troubleshoot whenever necessary, but so far it hadn't made a peep. They ordered two glasses of water and one light beer to share, but each drank her half beer so quickly, they ordered another one right away.

"I think you're on to something," Kate said, drawing a folded page out of her bag. "I brought you this from *Travel Weekly*, a magazine for travel agents."

Morgan perused the article, about Saudi Arabia beginning to open the country to foreign tourism. Recently, the article said, two university alumni groups had been permitted to travel extensively throughout the country for the express purpose of sightseeing. Over the years, only select religious pilgrims and business travelers had been allowed into this closely guarded culture. The change, according to the writer, could be attributed to the Saudis' wish to be better understood by the rest of the world—an attitude perhaps tweaked by a plunge in oil prices. Choosing tourists from educational institutions was intended to ensure that the visitors would be sophisticated and educated and, the article stated, "well-behaved."

In most provinces, women tourists were expected to wear scarves and abayas, but could often shed the wraps once inside the hotels. The article also warned that the religious police, though they didn't usually harass foreign women, would yell at a tourist to put on her scarf or button up her robe. Many places were closed to women, such as health clubs and men-only sections of restaurants. Such restrictions and blatant segregation often raised the hackles of a Western woman, the writer said, adding this advice: "Stifle it. This is a take-it-or-leave-it situation, and it's far more productive to learn from the experience."

Kate slammed her hand down on the clipping when Morgan returned it. "Stifle it? What kind of Archie Bunker advice is that? I wrote the magazine and said that it was unforgivable to write about the inhumane conditions of women in Saudi as if it's okay because it's part of the 'culture.' I said that the term 'culture' is used worldwide to hide the hatred and oppression of women. I said that travel agents should refuse to send clients Saudi Arabia and to any other country that enslaves women."

"Between defending women and taking on the airlines, you're going to have about two clients left," Morgan said, loving this woman.

"I know. But I'm done with shutting up." Kate stuffed the article back in her purse.

"You know, there's an upside to all of this," Morgan said. "If the country is becoming more accustomed to seeing foreign women . . . "

"And if we have to cover up . . . "

"The oppression, in a way, gives us freedom. In veils, we can move about like quiet little nuns. Not bothering a soul. We sure would be less conspicuous than a bunch of long-haired white guys with big bulges in their jackets."

"Your attention please."

For some reason, the voice over the loudspeaker, which usually squawked unnoticeably like a television blaring in another room, caught Morgan's attention. She raised a finger and Kate stopped talking.

"Would Mrs. Mujeres Cojones please pick up the nearest page telephone?" The voice pronounced the "j" as in English.

"Mrs. Moo-jerries Koe-joe-knees, please pick up the nearest page telephone."

CHAPTER THIRTY-EIGHT

Morgan and Kate screamed like teenagers when they saw Linnie at the baggage claim. She was trying to drag an enormous violet-gray suitcase off the luggage bay. It was so heavy she had to walk alongside the moving belt, inching a little off at a time, until the bag toppled onto the floor with a thud.

"Don't worry," Linnie said. "It's got huge rollers."

Kate laughed. "Did you have to pay extra for that?"

"Nope. It's sixty-nine pounds. Just under the max," Linnie said.

"What's in there?" Morgan asked, hoisting the behemoth upright and onto its rollers. As she got it rolling, it almost knocked her over. "It's a body bag!"

It was as if the three had been together last week instead of nearly two years before. They picked up the conversation as though were in a restaurant and had stopped talking just long enough to place an order.

"You know, I like to have my own hair dryer and hot curlers and stuff," Linnie said, as she and Kate wrestled the monster suitcase into the trunk of Morgan's car.

Linnie's hair did look good. Shorter than before, but almost shoulder length and falling into soft waves, like a child's careless, natural curl. Linnie always worked hours on her hair to make it look like she hadn't done a thing but get out of the shower, step into the sunlight, and shake her head like a puppy.

"And I had to bring a manuscript I'm working on, and

my laptop and a bunch of books," Linnie said. "Hal thinks I'm meeting my agent at a publishing conference in Tampa."

"Are you?"

"Nope." Linnie slammed the trunk lid shut.

"Does he know you're meeting us?" Kate asked.

"He knows I'll probably see Morgan. But no, not you too, for a reunion."

"What? He wouldn't let you?" Morgan laughed, knowing how absurd that question was. With Linnie and Hal there was no "letting." She did as she pleased, or so it seemed.

"It's not that," Linnie said. "It's that he's such a pain in the butt sometimes. You know, he's always made really good money, but he hates to let it go. He's so . . . lawyer-y."

When Hal got angry it wasn't yell-and-shout furious angry. It was withdrawal angry. After twenty-nine years of marriage, Linnie said, Hal didn't need to verbalize. He didn't even need to use body language. His disapproval just registered, as quiet as a thought, and hung there in the threadbare psychic space they shared.

"There always has to be a reason for everything," Linnie continued. "He's as generous as a cow if the money is going to some purpose. But ask him to blow money on something wacky, and the wallet slams shut like a frightened clam. He's not, well, frivolous."

"But you're earning lots of money on your books, aren't you?" Morgan asked.

"Not lots, no. Shit, my books are all in paperback and I get eleven cents a copy. But it's enough to take care of myself." She shrugged. "Besides, it doesn't matter to Hal whose pocket it's coming out of. It's still the same principle to him. And . . . he thinks you guys are completely crazy."

"None of us is *completely* crazy," Kate said. "We each have a slice of crazy, and when we get together, the slices make a whole pie, which kind of puts us over the edge."

Linnie's eyes gleamed. Morgan recognized the mischievous look Linnie got when she paged herself in airports, simply to hear how her name sounded on the loudspeaker. It was the look she probably got when she asked the dispatcher to help find Mrs. Cojones. It was the look she got when she pulled a newborn kitten out of a pouch tied around her waist underneath her gown at Baccalaureate and stroked its tiny head with two fingers. When in the middle of a silent prayer it mewed, she tucked it under her arm, but let it peek out through the folds of the sleeve.

It was the look she got once when she told them about the comatose male patient with the gargantuan penis. It happened back when she was an intensive care nurse, and the man needed regular catheter care. As head nurse for that floor, she put a sign-up sheet at the foot of the bed, because the other nurses were arguing about whose turn it was to change the catheter.

Her gesture was not meant to be disrespectful. Linnie regarded life as so sacred she'd nurse a moth back to health if it bumped into a lightbulb. But she thought that the man might regain consciousness if he got a sense of how much his anatomy was appreciated. He actually did come to, about two weeks later, and eventually Linnie would base one of her romance novel characters on him. Length and breadth, Linnie said, grinning.

After retiring from nursing when she was forty, Linnie had started reading romance novels. She read hundreds, sometimes one a day. Her version of a midlife crisis, she said, unapologetically. After about a year she bought a computer and sat down to write a romance novel of her own.

She titled the novel *Tow Away Zones*. It was the story of a nurse who finally finds her soulmate, tragically, in a dying patient. The nurse and the patient only have two weeks together before he dies, but she manages to spend many hours and most nights in his hospital room, with the curtains wrapped around the bed. Because of his condition, they can't have real sex, but in her mind she imagines these incredibly steamy scenes with him sleeping in her arms, and she sobs because she's finally found her true love, only to lose him. After the man dies his twin brother shows up, and the nurse realizes that it's the twin brother who is really her soulmate. The dying man was sort of a transition guy, the bridge relationship. And it didn't have the slightest thing to do with tow away zones.

The book bombed; Linnie could not find a publisher. But in the process, she discovered she had a latent and nearly genius talent for programming computers. And from this, she began creating computerized love stories. She devised a way to program a plotline, so that basically all she had to do was plug in certain names, information, and scenes, and voila, another book. After the first two, Linnie figured that for each new book, she only had to generate what amounted to fifty pages of new material.

Linnie's book titles were all taken from street signs and only vaguely related to the plot, if at all. After *Tow Away Zones* came *Men Working*, and then *Curves Ahead*, *Dangerous Intersection*, *Speed Controlled by Radar*, and so on. The most recent was called *Slippery When Wet*. Like her first book, the story revolved around a woman finding one man, thinking he was the one, then coincidentally through him, meeting the real one.

Once, Linnie was on an airplane to New York and was stuck in a particularly minuscule center seat in one of the back rows of a Boeing 727. Clearly, too many seats had been crammed into the cabin just to squeeze a little more profit out of the flying public, and this annoyed Linnie to no end. Using the telephone mounted on the seat back in front of her, Linnie called information and got the number of TWA's headquarters in St. Louis. Then she placed a call to the CEO of the company.

When the CEO's secretary answered, Linnie explained that she was calling from one of his airplanes and that this was not an emergency, but urgent. No doubt pressing some panic pedal under her desk, the secretary calmly told Linnie the CEO was not in his office, but she would transfer her to someone who might be able to help. The call was routed to the director of marketing and public relations, who answered promptly.

"Hello, this is Lynn Prather," Linnie said in a friendly but firm professional voice. "I'm on your flight 616 to New York City, and my seat sucks!"

As they drove toward her house, Morgan asked Linnie, "Why don't you get things out in the open with Hal?"

Linnie responded that no relationship was perfect. To Morgan, having this lie hanging between them seemed too great an imperfection to overlook. She still believed that there could exist a relationship that was completely authentic, with neither big lies nor little white ones. But then, Linnie was still married and she wasn't. That was an argument for something. Linnie did love Hal, and he was a good man, an honest lawyer, and as kind as he was smart.

"He's my soulmate," Linnie said. "I'm sure of that. But not the kind of soulmate I write about in my books. The couples in my books are soulmates and they have passionate love connections, too. They get to have it all."

"You don't think you can have it all in real life?" Morgan asked.

"Not entirely," Linnie said. "I have Hal, and the rest I make up."

CHAPTER THIRTY-NINE

"Your plan is outrageous," Linnie said.

The three friends were sitting on Morgan's lanai, looking out at the Gulf of Mexico, which was robin's egg blue and calm, waves rippling softly along the shore.

"A covert operation is crazy enough, and then you're planning to go along?" Linnie swayed forward and back in the cane rocker, the only one on the porch. Morgan loved to rock and always intended to add a couple more rockers, but never had. Throughout the weekend at her house, the three alternated curling up in the rocker, like little girls taking turns sitting on grandma's lap.

"On the other hand," Linnie said, "sitting here with the two of you in this incredible setting, anything seems possible."

Linnie and Kate loved Morgan's house. It was very simple, a wood frame three-bedroom beach house on stilts. Morgan had built it on a lot she and Dowd had bought decades before, when the price of Gulf-front property was still within the reach of an ordinary mortal. The only reason she could afford to own it now was because she already did.

This was the first time in Morgan's life she'd ever had a home with everything exactly where she wanted it. When you buy a home configured by someone else, you're always accommodating to someone else's taste and lifestyle. In this house she accommodated no one but herself.

It had a beamed ceiling and hardwood floors, and windows precisely where she wanted them. The kitchen was open to the living room, exactly where she wanted it, and each closet was designed just for her. Even the bathroom faucets had the style of knobs she preferred. And the ceiling-high ragged flagstone fireplace and hearth came straight out of a particular childhood fantasy in which she was a good but very mysterious witch living at the edge of a rainforest that spilled out onto a beautiful beach.

On the three sides of the house that did not face the Gulf, she allowed trees and bushes and palms to grow to their hearts' content, and they seemed to thrive on the freedom. Oleanders with pink and white blossoms rose past the windows as high as the roof, and there were two schefflera as big and full as maple trees.

Inside, she decorated minimally. Because the view from every window was like a painting, the house seemed not to need pictures on the walls. Those she did have were mostly watercolors done by local women artists, photos of Meredith and Ashton, and some goddess prints by Susan Seddon Boulet. On the floor and shelves, in no particular arrangement, she'd put shells and feathers she'd found on the beach, and a variety of pottery, mostly from local art fairs. She loved light blue earthy glazes.

Morgan understood what Linnie meant. The more she talked with her two friends about the idea, the more possible it sounded. Being with Linnie and Kate made Morgan feel like she could do anything. It was as if their three separate energies combined into something wilder, bolder, than any one of them was individually.

"Why do you want to go along?" Linnie asked. "Why not just pay the guys to do it?"

"First of all," Morgan said, "we may not have enough money. Ashton is having the gemstones appraised, but we don't know their value yet, or whether we can sell them."

"If it's money you need," Linnie said, "I can help. I just got another advance. And in the airport, waiting for you two,

I got an idea for another book." Linnie sketched the plot. The soulmates meet somehow when their luggage gets mixed up. The title would be *Many Bags Look Alike*. They all laughed.

"Don't you always use road signs?" Kate asked.

Linnie grimaced. "I'm sort of out of signs."

"Linnie, you are so sweet to offer," Morgan said. "But there's more to it. I want this rescue to be non-violent. If I could have such a plan in place before I met with Grady and Taco again, there's a chance they might agree."

The three friends sat up most of the night, trading places in the rocker like musical chairs, drinking wine first, then coffee, then decaffeinated coffee, and finally herbal teas. They planned and replanned, wrote notes on a legal pad, and then wadded the paper and started over. Sometimes, whoever wasn't in the rocker stood up and paced.

About three a.m. they walked onto the beach and decided to take a swim. The water, brightly lit by a fat crescent moon, was friendly and flat as a lake. They tore their clothes off and waded out, hopping up and down in a circle until they got used to the coolness. Then they relaxed, arms out and heads resting back on the surface of the water.

"I feel like I know Faiza," Linnie said. "Like she's a little sister or something."

"Me too," Kate said. She had no children of her own, and had always been an honorary aunt to Ashton and Meredith. "We've sort of adopted her."

There was silence, except for the quiet trickles as they moved their arms back and forth through the dark water.

"You know, Morgan," Linnie said. "What you're planning is terribly dangerous."

"I try not think about that too much," Morgan said. "Because the alternative—leaving her there in that room? I couldn't live with that. I couldn't live not knowing what happened to the baby, my grandchild. And Ashton. Every day it's like another piece of him joins her in the darkness. If she dies, I'm afraid a part of him will die too."

"Have you talked to Dowd about this?" Kate asked.

"Grady said not to talk to anyone who's not involved. No exceptions."

Then it was quiet. Bits of moonlight sparkled on the surface of the water, as though someone was stirring the sea with a big spoon, trying to mix the light in.

Linnie said softly, "You know, Morgan, I can't go with you."

Morgan didn't say anything.

"I could never put this one past Hal. It's not like a getaway weekend. Or a fake conference in Orlando. I can't exactly say, 'Bye bye, honey, I'm off to meet my agent in Riyadh.' But I want to help in other ways."

"I understand," Morgan said, halfheartedly. What did she expect? Her friends to drop their lives and get on a plane with her to go risk being arrested in a country that hates women? To tell the truth, she hadn't actually heard Kate say whether or not she was coming, and she was afraid to ask her outright. Linnie saved her the trouble.

"What about you, Kate?" Linnie asked.

They were shuffling along in the water toward the beach. Once on dry sand, Kate drew a towel around her, and, still thin enough to have leftover towel, rubbed at her hair with the corner. She pulled on her T-shirt and shorts, folded the towel once, and sat down on it. Linnie and Morgan did the same, and no one spoke for a while.

Then Linnie asked, "If you could do one thing different in your life, what would it be?"

"I hate that game," Morgan said. "I never can think of only one thing. I have lots."

"Okay," she said. "Not the one thing, but *a* thing."

"Umm, okay," Morgan said. "I'd protest the Vietnam War."

"I would have become a doctor, rather than a nurse," Linnie said.

"Really?" Morgan turned to her. "I've never heard you

say that."

"I never realized it until recently," she said. "What about you, Kate?"

Kate leaned back on her hands and gazed out at the water. "Well, what I'm thinking about is not a big thing, like what you two said, but all evening it's been on my mind. It's something that happened several years ago, with Jack. We had taken our plane to the Florida Keys for a diving trip. We stayed at a lodge called Hawk's Cay, near the middle of the Keys, and this place was famous for its pet dolphins.

"They had this lagoon, and in the lagoon there were three bottlenose dolphins in a fenced-off area about the size of a swimming pool. Maybe a little bigger. And every evening they'd do a show, with someone from the lodge feeding the dolphins and making them jump for fish. All the guests would gather around and get all excited about being so close to these dolphins. Their names were Lenny, Max, and Shipwreck.

"I hated it. The spectacle. The dolphins penned in like that. I mean, I really hated it. Jack was surprised at my reaction, it was so intense. So he asked a man who worked for the lodge, and the man said that the dolphins weren't really in captivity. He said they could come and go as they pleased, because the fence was at the low water line, so at high tide they could jump over. That was a bunch of bullshit. Jack and I checked it out. There was no way those dolphins could get out, unless maybe there was a huge storm surge or a tidal wave or something.

"So I was talking with Jack about it in the bar one evening, and this guy approached us. He's a small-built man, but wiry-looking. Maybe early thirties, with a scruffy beard. His name was Dick. He had a wild, sort of gutsy sparkle in his eyes, but he was polite and well-spoken. He asked if we were there diving, and we said yes, and then we talked a while about the dolphins, and pretty soon he asked if we would help him with something.

"Dick wanted to set the dolphins free. His plan was to wait until late at night, put on our diving gear, and enter the bay about five hundred yards north of the pen, where there was a wooded area. Then we'd swim underwater with only one single light to the dolphin pen and cut the fence wide open. Voila! Lenny, Max, and Shipwreck, free at last."

"You've never told us about this," Morgan said.

"I know. Because I was so embarrassed. Jack and I talked about it and considered helping him. But then we got to worrying about getting caught. If we got arrested, those goofy Keystone cops there might impound our plane and all that. So we told Dick we couldn't help. So there I was, indignant and self-righteous about the plight of these dolphins, but when I was given the chance to actually do something about it, I chickened out."

"What happened?"

"Dick tried to do it alone," Kate said. "But he needed more help. He had to surface near the pens to get his bearings, and the lodge security guard saw him and busted him. It was only a misdemeanor, because he'd only made a couple of cuts so far in the fence. He was in jail one night, and then some friends bailed him out."

Kate sighed. "And you know what? It turned out there were these dolphin parks all over the Keys, keeping dolphins in pens, like zoos, and pretending the dolphins could come and go at will. Bullshit. Some of these places even let people get in the water and swim with them. And because the dolphins go along with it and have these grins on their snouts, everybody thinks they're happy to be there. Dick told us that these places practically starve the dolphins before training them to do these jump and splash tricks. They're so hungry they'll do anything.

"A couple years later I saw Dick's picture in the paper," Kate said. "He was in California, trying to stop an aquarium from acquiring two new dolphins for their dolphin tank. It turns out that Dick was a famous activist for dolphin freedom. He's written a book and he's started programs to help captive dolphins reacclimate once they're returned to the wild. This guy wasn't afraid of getting arrested. That was the last thing on his mind. He was so passionate about what he believed. I had the passion, but it stopped with words."

Morgan realized that her life, too, had always been about words. She saw herself as this premier activist, churning out stories that exposed bad guys and defended the underdogs, on her little personal mission to right wrongs and speak out for fairness and justice. But in a way, she was always one step away from where the action was. She was always the observer, never the doer. Protected by a screen of newsprint, a shield of words, she'd never had to cross into enemy territory with her very own feet. All she had to do was write the stories about the people who did.

What they were facing now, this was different. This was not a story about reality, but reality.

"Morgan, I'm in," Kate said, "There's a dolphin inside me that wants to get free."

CHAPTER FORTY

Two weeks went by without a word from Grady. Had he forgotten? Was this whole thing just a big game with those guys, two burned-out, washed-up fakes, beating their aging chests and talking secret agent talk to impress the girls?

Morgan pelted Grady's answering machine with messages, which maybe wasn't too smart, since he and Taco had been very adamant about not using the telephone to make plans. But she kept her messages cheery and superficial, disguising her deep concerns in bubbly timbre, sounding like she was an old girlfriend trying to charm him into returning her calls.

Ashton called at least once a day, impatient. Once, briefly, Morgan thanked the crutches. They kept him from running off and taking things into his own hands, at least for now.

The weekend after Kate and Linnie had visited, Meredith came. Morgan was relieved to have the company, and she and her daughter tried to distract themselves with shopping and eating out. But the subject of Faiza and Ashton was never more than a whiff away from the surface, and they found little at this point with which to console themselves.

Meredith was still corresponding on the internet with Sheena, the woman with the hijab mail-order business. Through an exchange of cryptic emails with Meredith, Sheena confirmed what they feared. There were rumors of a woman being held in the Woman's Room at the address they knew to be Faiza's uncle's. How Sheena got this information they would never know, but Morgan assumed there was some kind of underground, made more possible, Meredith said, by the recent expansion of the internet into Saudi Arabia.

On the pretense that Meredith wanted to buy some clothes to give as a surprise, Sheena wrote that she would try to find someone inside the house who could "get measurements" for the clothing without telling anyone. But this would take time. Meredith must be patient, Sheena said. There may not be anyone who could help. There was no way to know at this point.

Time. Patience. Wait. There were stalls at every turn. And meanwhile, Faiza was languishing in the dark while her pregnancy, assuming it was still viable, was growing every day. Though the news from Sheena was heartbreaking, Morgan also felt strangely relieved. If Faiza was the woman in the room, then at least they hadn't killed her.

One day Morgan called Larry at Amnesty International, to tell him the latest. In his opinion, the family head would wait until the baby was born before meting out any punishment to Faiza. If the baby was a boy, it would be especially precious, but in any case Larry thought the baby would be taken in by the family, which typically blessed and honored children who shared the same blood. It was the outcast mother who would be judged and sentenced.

For Morgan, the times between visits from her friends and her daughter were empty and scary. She awakened every morning filled with anxiety, as if she'd had a bad dream that she couldn't remember. She was getting heart palpitations, something she hadn't had for a couple of years, since menopause. Menopause. Now there was an experience. It had been like riding on Disney's Space Mountain for about two years, spiraling down and down into the pitch blackness, the capsule jerking and squealing and ripping away any sense of orientation or direction, lost and plummeting in a runaway body in the dark.

What if this anxiety escalated into panic? That was what had happened when Morgan forced the plane to turn around on the tarmac. It took her almost a year to be able to fly again—and then, only with the help of about sixty different mantras and Linnie's tranquilizers. And now she was making plans to fly halfway around the world in a plane that was too fast not to be claustrophobic, for how long? The longest flight she had been on since the panic attack was four hours. It must take dozens of hours to get to Saudi Arabia. What was she thinking?

Morgan wished she had someone to talk to about this.

One thing for sure was that she had Grady on the brain. If she permitted herself, she could drift right back into his kiss, the feel of his body over hers on the motel bed, heavy but not crushing, like being enveloped under a stack of rough, thick blankets on a cold night.

The chemistry mystified her. She didn't really like the guy. Well, maybe she liked him a little. But she didn't respect him. He was self-centered, self-serving, and clung to his cynical version of the world like his life depended on it.

Would it kill him to soften a little? To give up the bravado and the jaded I've-seen-it-all attitude? What was he going to do with the rest of his life, now that he'd decided there was no reason ever to reach out to help another person? Was he going to spend the next twenty years flying his stupid little airplanes and smoking?

Morgan corrected herself. He had helped her. Even though Grady was very clear that his participation stopped there, and he was not going on any missions, he did make the contact with Taco. *Cut the guy some slack, Morgan. He did reach out, if only as a gesture.*

So, Morgan thought, what was she so angry about? Maybe she wished he had refused to fly the plane to begin with and helped Faiza get away. He knew what was going on. He could have walked off his stupid little pilot job and done what was right for a change. How could he stand by and let it happen? He did worse than let it happen. He made it happen. He flew the airplane. How could she be so physically attracted to someone she held in such low regard? Rhetorical question.

Who was he, anyway, but a man with no backbone? A man with no ethics. A man who wouldn't stand up for anything.

A man who made her want to take off her clothes.

Over the years, Morgan had given up trying to understand the mechanism that created attractions and pairings. She'd learned that she could not make herself fall in love, or fall out of love. That place deep inside where we hold the sensation we call love can't be observed by the naked eye, or analyzed by even the most curious mind. It can't be broken down into elements, like in a lab; it can't be diagrammed like a sentence in English class. It was either there or was not there. It was that feeling, when you were with someone, that you didn't want the time to end. And you couldn't make it be there when it's not, and you couldn't get rid of it if it's there and you don't want it.

She remembered when her daughter was in high school, she'd fallen hopelessly in love with Daniel, a boy in her class, and they saw each other every day for months. They couldn't get enough of each other. Morgan began to wonder if they were going to start looking alike and trading clothes. Then the passion began to wane a bit; there were suspicious spaces between their contact. Some days he wasn't waiting outside her last period class, that sort of thing. Pretty soon Meredith discovered Daniel was secretly seeing another girl at a neighboring high school.

Meredith had been heartbroken, but her anger and outrage at his betrayal fueled and propelled her into a speedy new life without him. Pissed off beyond imagining, she started dating someone new. One day, four or five months later, Daniel called. And then dropped by. And before long, behold, they were madly in love again.

One day Morgan asked Meredith what was going on.

And Meredith said, "You know, Mom, it doesn't matter who you're with. You love who you love."

CHAPTER FORTY-ONE

Every day Morgan felt something different. She went through emotional states like a jogger goes through socks. One moment she'd feel strong and purposeful, infused with belief in her extraordinary power, like the mom who lifts up the two-ton truck that's crushing her kid. Then she'd tell herself, hell, that's an urban myth. Nobody ever really did that. Women don't lift trucks, and faith does not move mountains. And ordinary people don't get on airplanes and invade other countries.

She took long walks on the beach and contemplated how normal her life was. Oh, sure, she had been a lot of unusual places and witnessed her share of weird people and uncommon events. She had fought battles with her stories and put herself on the line. But always within respectable parameters. And reasonably safe ones.

As she passed people on the beach, dressed in their bathing suits and leaving wispy trails of suntan lotion scent, it seemed so outrageous to be planning a covert rescue mission to the Middle East. Who would believe it? This life she led and the people who circulated in it were so ordinary. Beach walkers on the west coast of Florida.

Once, Morgan remembered talking to her sister about a guy Morgan was dating, and she was trying to decide whether to continue the relationship. She felt this incredibly strong attraction to him, but at the same time, she was troubled by something. Not sure what it was, and not trusting it, she asked Grace.

Her sister told her, "Just follow your heart."

"I'm trying, but my heart is confused," Morgan told her.

And Grace shook her head and said, "Your heart is never confused."

*   *   *

Screw the cryptic phone conversations. If the spies got her number, then tough shit. Morgan desperately needed to talk to Larry Edwards about this, and so she called him. Being as circumspect as possible, she let him in on what they were planning. At first, he didn't say a word.

"Bad idea, right Larry? You think it's a bad idea."

"I really can't give you an opinion," he said cautiously. "As I told you before, we would never advise anyone to put himself in that kind of danger."

"Okay, be specific," Morgan said. "What happens if we get caught?"

"Well, you probably won't be executed," he said.

"Oh, great."

"It is some comfort to know you won't be dragged into the center of town and have your head chopped off, don't you think?"

"But we are U.S. citizens," Morgan said.

"Which would make it an international incident. And the Saudis could say, quite defensibly, that you came into their country and broke their laws and they have a right to punish you."

"And how would they do that?"

"Throw you in jail," Larry said.

Morgan shuddered, remembering the Amnesty report about abuses and torture of Saudi prisoners.

"Couldn't someone from the U.S. get us out of there?" she asked, thinking of Dowd and his political connections.

"Maybe, if they let you make a phone call," he said. "Which they probably wouldn't."

"But, eventually..."

"Eventually, probably," Larry said. "And you would be deported. But Morgan, you're talking about prison like it would be a temporary inconvenience. Think about it. You don't want to spend even a day in a Saudi jail."

Morgan didn't reply.

"And here's something else to consider," Larry went on. "Maybe the girl's family is well-connected to the governor of that province, or maybe even to the royal family. Then you're really in big trouble. Because once they've got you in prison, they could easily trump up a charge. Put some drugs in your plane and say you were smuggling, for example. And the punishment for drug smuggling is death."

"How could they do that, with the rest of the world watching?" she asked.

Larry gave a bitter snort. "Remember the American kid they were going to cane in China? The world was watching that, but half the people in the United States thought they ought to beat that kid to a pulp. Because he broke the law there and deserved what he got. If you were arrested for drugs over there, you would not be guaranteed the sympathy of the American people. Half of them would think you got what you deserved. Plus the Saudis have their own PR companies in the U.S. You were in the media. See if you could track down and untangle that lie. You'd better have another plan."

Larry paused, then spoke very slowly and forcefully. "You *must* understand how incredibly dangerous this is."

To Morgan, his point was finally beginning to soak in. The phone receiver slipped, and she switched hands to wipe the wet one on her shorts. Her bravado, her militant heroics were all oozing out through the pores in her palms. Was she brave enough to face a Saudi prison cell? Arab interrogators? Shit, no. Who would be?

"Larry, you're scaring me."

"I intend to," he said.

"You think I should give this up?"

"I didn't say that," he said. "But have a plan. A signal. Someone who would know if you disappeared, and who would know where you were and where you were taken."

"Then that person would go to the State Department?"

"That's the idea," he said. "But of course, you have another problem there. What are you going to tell the State Department? The truth? They're not gonna like that much. You got caught kidnapping a woman from a country we're buddy-buddy with?"

"The media?"

"Only if you know someone who can make it into a big story. A really big story. Otherwise, what's the story? 'My friends went to Saudi and didn't come back.' Four lines. Bottom of page twenty."

"I know someone who would help us there," Morgan said.

"It's got to be someone who can take it all the way to the top," Larry said.

From the day nearly four months ago, when Morgan had returned from the beach to find out that Ashton was hurt, there had been no firm footing. Maybe it was always going to feel this way, a sort of dreamlike state, as if she was floating just a few feet off her normal reality. She was skeptical and she was scared. And every day drew her a little further out of her comfort zone.

Like the sand crab. First it sticks one claw out of its little hole and feels around, tentatively. Then it ventures a bit further. A leg. Half a body. Pretty soon it slips all the way out and tiptoes sideways along the beach. But it keeps the hole in sight, and at the slightest disturbance on the surface—the shadow of a bird's wing or the rumble of a human foot—it scurries sideways and drops back down into the hole, so fast it looks like it's being sucked in.

Should she venture out or should she jump back into the hole? Would she ever be sure? Would she ever know the right thing to do?

Morgan thanked Larry for the information he was sharing with her and asked him once more what he thought she should do. And once more, he was noncommittal.

"If it were you, what would you do?" she pressed.

"You don't need to know what I would do, only what you would do," he said.

"Oh, I know. Follow my heart."

"But tie your camel," he said. They laughed, but it was flimsy.

Before hanging up, Larry added, "Morgan, it's like this. If it works, do it. If it doesn't work, don't do it."

CHAPTER FORTY-TWO

Grady called Morgan from Atlanta. He had been traveling almost constantly for the past two weeks, he said, spending layovers in New York, Milwaukee, Houston, and Toronto. He apologized for not being in touch, but he wanted to call from some other location than his home.

"Our host is planning the party," Grady said.

"Does he have some ideas about who to invite?" Morgan asked. A part of her wanted to roll her eyes and mutter, Oh, brother! at the cryptics. But another part, in her heart, started to pound, and a wave of anxiety rose up and wrapped around her stomach.

"There will be three guests," Grady said.

"When?"

"Maybe within a couple of weeks," he said. A couple of weeks? Everything was taking so much time.

"Who are you bringing?" Grady asked.

"Well, there's me and Kate. That's all so far."

Grady didn't say anything. Finally he spoke. "You're going to need pilots, babe. For the Skybird."

"I was hoping . . . you . . . "

"Didn't we have this conversation?" Grady asked, a reprimand in his voice.

"Well, yes, but. . . "

Intimidated by the scolding, Morgan couldn't finish her sentence. He wasn't going to do this, he said. Period. End of story. He launched into one of his soliloquies about how he'd been there, done that, all over the globe.

And then a startling thing happened. Grady made her laugh. About Saudi Arabia he said: "The one thing about flying to that part of the world? You know when you get there. Because there's a big enema bag hanging in the sky over it."

Morgan cracked up until her belly hurt.

When she stopped laughing, Grady asked, "What about Kate? How good is she?"

"She's the best. But she gave up flying a couple of years ago."

"I know. She told me that day at Half Moon. But she didn't lose her ticket."

"No, she lost something else," Morgan said.

She told Grady about what happened with Kate and Jack. As she talked, she could feel the atmosphere between them beginning to soften. Morgan wasn't sure what she said, but she could feel that something touched him. His next comment came from the warm, cozy place in him that she had felt in his arms.

"You don't just give up flying," he said. "Not if it's in you. Which it usually is."

"I tried to talk her out of selling her plane," Morgan said. "And many times since, I've tried to persuade her to fly again. You should see how she comes alive when she talks about it. Even that day we met you at the airport. She glowed."

"A pilot with her experience wouldn't take that long to get rated for the S-5," Grady said. "Month or two, maybe."

Morgan told Grady she would talk with Kate. And then he surprised her again. He offered to drive down and talk with Kate in person. Pilot to pilot, Morgan supposed.

For a guy hell bent on staying out of this, he kept reaching his hand in more and more. And for an instant the thought blipped by her head, that Grady and Kate would find each other attractive. That was, after all, Morgan's initial scheme, to get the two of them together. Before she met him, that is.

Well, if that happened, so be it. Trouble was, she suddenly didn't think so much of the idea; in fact, to be honest, she was feeling a tiny bit jealous.

*   *   *

Morgan's intention was to ask for asylum for Faiza, on the grounds that her life would be in danger from reprisals if she returned to her own country. That asylum was not assured, however. The U.S. Immigration and Naturalization Service was a wild card. They could deport Faiza in a heartbeat. At the very least, they could take her into custody. Wouldn't it be hideously ironic if they got Faiza out of her prison in Saudi Arabia, only to have the INS throw her in jail here?

Morgan had talked with INS, anonymously, and learned that the only way Faiza could stay in the U.S. permanently was to apply for resident status. To do that she needed to be sponsored by a U.S. citizen. The most expedient way through this red tape was to marry one.

"We'll get married right away," Ashton said in the next phone conversation.

"Ashton," Morgan said carefully. "I have to ask you. Do you have any doubts, any doubts at all, that this is what Faiza would want?"

"Mom, what are you talking about?"

"Think about it," she said, then cringed. She sounded like Dowd.

"My god, Mom, that's crazy! She's locked in a dark room and she's pregnant, and who knows what terrible thing they'll do to her, maybe leave her in there forever, to wither away alone in the dark. Who wouldn't want out of that?"

"You know her better than anyone," Morgan said. "But consider this for a minute. I know that Faiza wants to be rescued. But when we take her out of Saudi Arabia, she can never go back. It is the country of her birth and childhood, a homeland she must love very much. It will be lost to her forever. We would be taking her whole heritage from her. And once she's here, she would, in effect, belong to you. She couldn't stay here without your help. So there it is again. A man pulling the strings. Her safety and future at the mercy of the generosity of a man."

Ashton listened, but disagreed with most of what his mother said.

"I know she wants to be here, and she wants to be with me," he said. "That's what she was telling me, that night in Half Moon Bay, before she was kidnapped. She felt this coming; it was like a foreboding, and she was terrified of her uncle. She wanted to be with me forever. She said she felt safe with me, and I said I would protect her. And . . . the very first time something happened, I couldn't even do that.

"Mom, you've got to trust me. You can have your doubts, but please don't give up. I think about her all the time, and I know she's thinking about me and calling out to me to help her. Every single minute of every single day, I fight back the urge to yell and yell and yell. I feel like I'm going to explode. And now you come up with all these reasons not to get her out."

"I just want to be sure," Morgan said.

"Mom, you can't be sure of anything. But you know what you know," Ashton said. Then he told her a story about one day when he took Faiza surfing. As he reminisced, his voice became calmer and lighter.

"She wanted me to teach her. So I took her out a few times, when the waves were real small, and I'd get her on the board and then when a wave came, I'd push it, to catch the wave. She loved the ride, but she never could even get to her knees, and she never got any control over the board. And she'd roll off the board, laughing, and say. 'Oh, Ashton, thees ees soh much fun. Like flying. So free.'

"So one day I got one of my long boards, big enough for two, and also on the long board the ride is smoother and more stable. I took her out, with her sitting in front of me, and we paddled around. Then I waited for the perfect wave. Pretty soon here it came, and I caught it. And as I stood up, I wrapped my arm around her—she's so light and has the tiniest middle—and pulled her up against me.

"She let me hold her, and I kept her right there. I'd never surfed like that before, and it was so cool. The ride was long and smooth, and I turned a couple of times, but mostly just kept it straight in. It wouldn't have worked so well if she'd been tense, or if she'd tried to move herself. But she totally let go into me. It was like we were dancing. Only there was only one of us."

"Ashton," Morgan said. "Don't worry. I'm not changing my mind. We're going to go get Faiza."

After she hung up the phone, she decided that from now on she would banish her doubts when possible, and when not, she would keep them to herself. Hesitancy would only erode their chances of success. For now, they needed commitment and the confidence of a laser beam.

But silently, without ever discussing it with anyone, she made another vow. Faiza's real freedom would come later, and Morgan would help her. She promised herself that she would support Faiza in becoming truly free, whatever that meant, even if someday it meant leaving her son.

*   *   *

Four days later, Ashton called with news about the jewels. He said the value was substantial, but his tone was gray and methodical.

The necklace was made with a bucketful of colorless, brilliant-cut diamonds, the most highly prized, mounted unevenly in two rows, in platinum, like a cluster of shimmering stars. Ashton said that spread out, the necklace looked like the path to Heaven. Courtney's father said it was one of the most beautiful pieces he'd ever seen and was worth around a hundred thousand dollars. The other piece, a ring mounted with rubies and emeralds, and the loose stones, a ruby, an emerald and a sapphire, were all similarly valuable, easily worth another fifty thousand.

"So how long will it take?" Morgan asked.

"It can't be done," Ashton said. "Not now, anyway."

"Why not?"

"We don't own them," Ashton said.

"You mean he can't sell them?"

"Not on a legitimate market," he answered. "Not without Faiza to authorize it."

"Omigod," Morgan said.

"How soon do these guys need to be paid?"

"All in advance," she said. "That's what Grady told me."

They had a problem.

It took Morgan hours to get to sleep. Sometime after midnight the phone rang. She had just fallen asleep, and the conversation was so short that in the morning she wondered if she had dreamed it.

The voice said, "Do you want to come to a party?"

"Yes I do," Morgan said, still groggy and hoping she was saying the right thing.

He told her the date, one week from now, and the time, five p.m. She recognized the voice as Taco's.

"Can I bring anything?" she remembered to ask.

"No," he said, before the phone abruptly clicked. "Don't bring a thing. Everything's taken care of."

CHAPTER FORTY-THREE

The door into Taco's hangar was glossy, burnished metal, and Grady held it open for Morgan to enter. From far back in the hangar, she could hear men laughing, big husky guy laughs that wrapped around the high walls in the space above their heads.

They walked through the hanger, past the two little planes, which looked the same except the cowling had been replaced on the red taildragger. Outside the office, against the wall, was a long folding table, like the kind used for church pot-luck dinners. Spread out on it were giant maps. One looked like an ordinary road map and the others bore mysterious hiero-glyphs, like nothing Morgan had ever seen at AAA.

She would later learn that these were called sectionals, the maps of aviation, with markings about air space and air routes and airport landing codes and interpretations of the ground as perceived from the sky. As Morgan and Grady approached, the laughing stopped, dissipating into a faint echo that hung for a few seconds in the new silence.

Taco was tipped back in his office chair, his feet hooked on the curve of the table base. A man sat in another chair at the end of the table, and a third was leaning against the wall, his foot propped on the tabletop. The one sitting down had a thin face, medium-length graying hair, and looked like he might be on the short side. The other guy was larger and hulky, his hair darker brown than the other, but he definitely had also been visited by the gray fairy.

They both stared at Morgan, but not in a way that made her uncomfortable. Their eye contact was unprobing and their handshakes perfunctory, something to get out of the way so everyone could get on with business.

Taco introduced them as Soho and The Bear. Morgan figured Soho was the littler one.

"Soho and Bear," she said, extending her hand to the smaller one.

"It's *The* Bear," Soho said.

"Oh, I say the *the*?"

He nodded, and Taco burst out laughing.

The other two didn't smile. It wasn't that they frowned. It was that their mouths, like their eyes, simply fell into a position of neutrality. Pleasant, non-committal, without emotion, or at least any that Morgan could read.

The Bear pulled a chair around for her and then went off to get more for himself and Grady. She sat down and folded her elbows on the table, trying to act relaxed. Like, yawn, I meet with covert operators every day. One thing was sure. This was about the furthest from the *Mission Impossible* force as they could get.

Later, Grady would tell her that Soho and Bear, *The* Bear, were both retired from Special Ops, the U.S. military's expert soldiers, trained for the most dangerous missions. This group, who were mostly from the Army and Air Force, operated outside the mainstream military channels, in a world of its own. It was so secret, Grady said, that a lot of the time the people in it didn't know what they were doing or why.

Grady greeted both guys with recognition. He seemed to know Soho the best, because they chucked each other on the shoulder when they shook hands. Morgan felt terribly out of place, up to her neck in testosterone, like she was the little sister hanging with her big brother's buddies from the high school football team.

On the drive over, she had asked Grady what would motivate these men to want to help them.

"Money, babe," he said. "These guys have retired, and they've got the good life. They're done pumping adrenaline. The only thing they want to pump is into their bank accounts."

"Will they think it's too scary to go into Saudi?"

Grady laughed. "Babe, these guys don't get all that scared. And for the right amount of money, and if you've got the right people, there is no place in the world that's too scary to go into."

"Was it always about money?" Morgan asked.

Grady thought for a moment. "It varied. A lot of these guys, it was a job. Other guys, it was exciting. And a lot of them, you couldn't tell. You look at them and there ain't nothing in their eyes. And you figure, for what they do, there must be something going on in there, but you can't see it."

"What about you, Grady?" When she said his name out loud, she felt a kind of electric squiggle go through her. *Damn.*

"Look, don't make it all so mysterious," he said. "You bleeding heart women have to have all this meaning in everything. With guys it's a lot more simple. It's adventure."

"But isn't adventure about taking risks, taking action, living on the edge?"

Grady smiled, patronizingly. God, he pissed her off.

"And to take action, don't you have to take a stand?" she added.

"Make it what you want," he said. "To these guys, it doesn't matter if they're bringing back your kid's girlfriend or a nice piece of driftwood from the Arab Sea."

As it turned out, Grady was wrong, at least about The Bear. During the first half hour around Taco's table, in a soft but very deep voice, The Bear asked questions about Faiza—who she was, why they wanted her out. When Morgan told him and the others about her abduction and their recently confirmed knowledge that she was being locked in a dark, soundless room, Soho's expression remained inscrutable, but The Bear looked down and shook his head and muttered something Morgan couldn't understand.

Directing her next comment to Taco, she said they needed to talk about money. So she would know what they needed. She didn't say where the money was coming from. She wasn't sure herself.

Taco answered. "Fifty grand, for me, to direct the whole thing." When Morgan looked shocked, he added, "That includes supplies, the plane, getting vehicles, all that."

"Oh," she said.

Was that a bargain or not? The last big thing she'd bought was a used Mazda MX3, and negotiating that was a nightmare. As for this band of has-been international ruffians, Morgan only knew one of four of their real names. They came from a world that a few months ago she didn't even know existed. But for some reason, maybe reporter's instinct, maybe dire necessity, she trusted these guys.

"Twenty g's per man," Taco said to Soho and The Bear. They both nodded. These guys were so hard to read. Did that mean yes, they heard him, or yes, they agreed, or yes, he was full of shit?

Taco stood up and pulled the topographical map to the top of the pile. The map showed all of Saudi Arabia, plus the countries that border it, Yemen, Oman, United Arab Emirates, Kuwait, Jordan, the southeastern portion of Iraq, and the seas, the Persian Gulf and the Red Sea. He pointed to Dhahran, on the Persian Gulf.

"She's here, somewhere. We'll be bringing the plane into Dhahran International to demo. We'll show the plane to a couple of sheiks for a couple of days. We won't overstay our welcome, but we also won't try to get in and out too fast. It's business, it's legit. We'll be there just long enough that they get used to seeing us. We'll stay at Dammam Sheraton, about five miles from the airport. We'll make reservations for a week, like we're not sure how long this deal might take."

"So what if al-Sheiko really wants the plane?" The Bear asked.

"We sell it to him. We'll be long gone before we have to

make the deal," Taco answered.

"Sorry," The Bear said. Apparently, it was not cool to interrupt with logistical questions at this point. Too bad, because Morgan had hundreds.

Later, she would learn that it was Taco's job to figure out all the details, such as contacts and times and places and props and clothing and weapons. Everyone else simply showed up and did what he was assigned to do. God, these guys really trusted each other. They must have taken one of those ropes courses together.

Taco continued. "So, we're established at the airport. And you guys come in through Bahrain." He tapped a finger on the island in the Persian Gulf, right off the coast, near Dhahran. "You okay with that?" The pair nodded.

"Who else you got in mind?" Soho asked.

"Buck and maybe Crater," Taco said. "Four. For the land group."

Morgan wondered if Crater was the guy's last name or another nickname. He was so big he made craters when he sat down. He jumped out of an airplane over Turkey without a parachute. He could throw a punch like a meteor. Who knew?

"In the plane, it'll be two pilots, a mechanic—that's me —and two more flight crew. I ain't got pilots yet," Taco said. Almost pointedly, Morgan thought, he didn't look up at Grady.

"We meet at the house. The land group is in pairs. Three go in, one stays out. Backup only. The three who go in hold the staff and whoever might be home, while me and my group, we go in and get the girl. We bring her out and into our car and drive to the airport, like touristos out for a cruise.

"We've got the plane waiting, a flight plan filed, and we stroll onto the plane and wave bye-bye and get the hell out of Dodge. You guys are on your own. You go out the way you came in, or however you want to. If it all goes smooth, you'll practically be fucking spectators."

He looked at Morgan. "Any questions?"

"How will we decide when to go in?" she asked.

"One possibility, we find an informant inside the house. We don't know yet how big the staff is, but I guarantee it'll be mostly Indians or Filipinos. They might bribe, they might not. And even if they do, there's always the chance of double-cross. I'm gonna have to work on that."

Morgan told Taco about Meredith's contact on the internet. They decided to push Sheena for all the information they could get. They needed a diagram of the house, and lots of information about the residents, their habits, and particularly when they might be out of town.

"Okay, that's your assignment," Taco said to Morgan. "If that doesn't work, then we'll send Soho over to hang around the military base for a while." The U.S. has a military base at Dhahran airport, he explained, and through his old contacts, they could get one of the rescue group in the country with few questions asked.

"And here's your other assignment," Taco said to Morgan. "We can't just fly into Saudi. To get into the country legit, we need business visas for the whole crew. Call the Saudi embassy and get applications." She made a note. "To get a visa, you need a letter of invitation from whoever you're doing business with."

"I can take care of the visa part," she said. "But where would I find the potential customer for the plane?"

"Grady," Taco said. "I know you're not in, bud, but you've got the contacts. Would you call the Wolfman? See if he can set something up for us." Larry Wolfe was the airplane broker Grady knew who was representing a corporate 727 for sale in Saudi. "Somebody there is looking for a Skybird."

Grady had just sucked a big drag from a cigarette and was rolling the ashes off into a small metal ashtray that was so crusted with soot it looked like the bottom of an old Weber kettle. Throughout the briefing he hadn't said a word. Morgan got the feeling he was thinking about something, but when he looked up at Taco, his expression was empty, like he was waiting for the bell to ring so he could go home.

"Sure, I'll give him a call," Grady said flatly. "Is this a private sale, or want to set up a dummy company? Never mind," he said. "I'll decide."

"What about pilots?" Taco asked, ignoring Grady's coolness. "Any ideas?"

"Fuck, man, you know the same guys I do," Grady said. "And you're the one getting the big bucks."

What was up with Grady? Maybe he felt left out. The guys were going out hunting and not taking him along. Well, he'd had his chance and made his choice. He'd made that choice when he took off with a kidnapped woman in the back of his plane. Now he could stay in his safe little house and smoke while his friends cleaned up the mess he'd made.

"Questions?" Taco asked.

"Who's the rest of the flight crew?" Soho wanted to know.

Taco gestured toward Morgan. "She will be going. And one other?"

"Yeah," Morgan said. "Another woman. We'll pose as the flight attendants."

The Bear and Soho looked at each other and gave her the Dreaded Eye-Roll. Head back, eyes rolled up, groan—the basic put-down expression from men that says, *Oh, you women. There you go again. Give us a break.* With these guys, it meant, *Women? You gotta be kidding.*

"Listen," Soho said. "I know she's your friend. But what we're doing here, we need professionals."

"I understand," Morgan said. "I'm a reporter. Which means I've got some tracking skills. The rest? I'm a fast learner."

Soho shook his head. "Do you understand, we're committing a crime here. And it's against a Saudi citizen. They won't take kindly to this."

"There's no crime I see," she said. "She is a prisoner of war, a victim of religious persecution."

"No, she's a victim of stupidity," Soho said, sounding like

Grady. "Let's get this straight at the get-go. This is not political. If anything, it's religious, but it's on the far side of religion. It's a way of life. You can't make her a prisoner because she's not a prisoner. If they don't like what she's doing, they can take her out and fucking stone her."

Soho tilted his chair back against the wall, his foot on the table.

"And you too," he said. "That is not a place for women."

CHAPTER FORTY-FOUR

Morgan looked at Grady. He was running his thumbnail along his bottom teeth.

"I've been thinking," he said. "This other woman, Shepherd, is a pilot. Good one. She can fly the S-5 like driving a fucking Maserati."

"Wait a minute," Soho said. "First she's on the plane at all, which is a stupid idea, and now she's fucking flying it?"

"Hold on, Soho," said The Bear. "They're used to seeing American woman over there. Since the Gulf War, they been crawling all over the place."

The Bear turned to Morgan. "Soho's forgot it's almost the twenty-first century."

She smiled and looked at Grady questioningly. This was news to her, about Kate. When did he see her fly? He gave her a look that suggested she wait until later for the details.

"I don't know," Soho said. "I don't like this. It's always been men. We've never had women along."

The Bear folded his arms and nodded agreement. Morgan wondered if they were thinking, What if they're having their periods?

"Look," she said. "If this is going to be an insurmountable problem, then let's decide right now. Nice to meet you guys, but I have to move on. Because I'm going. First of all, I can't afford eight guys at twenty thou apiece. I can pay Taco and you guys and two more. And I still need pilots. Second,

I'm smart and conniving, and in a couple of months I can learn whatever I need to know to pose as a flight attendant. Third, my friend Kate is a crack-ass pilot with about a trillion hours . . . "

"Twenty thousand," Grady said. "More than me."

"Right. And fourth, we're both post-menopausal so you don't have to worry about PMS."

Morgan thought Grady was going to flip. Soho jerked forward and the back of his chair careened against the wall. The Bear started laughing. Taco reeled back and slammed his palm on the maps.

"One more thing you need to know," Morgan said. "No lethal weapons in the house."

"What?" The Bear almost shouted. "You talking about guns?"

"I don't want anyone to get hurt," she said.

"You gotta be kidding," Taco said.

"Jeesus, lady," The Bear said. "You want us to go over to fucking Saudi Arabia to kidnap a woman? And you want us to do it without guns? You gotta be nuts."

Taco jumped in. "Really, kid, this is ridiculous. At the airport alone, there'll be military police. Jeeps, with fifty-caliber machine guns. Ever seen them? They're the kind of guys who shoot first and ask questions later. Especially at Dhahran. They had a terrorist bombing there a few years back and they're real sensitive. And that's just the airport. There will also be local police."

"I understand," Morgan said. "But you need to understand. I believe that violence begets violence, and that war and anger and hatred are at the root of why this woman is in prison."

On that, she got another Dreaded Eye-Roll. But they didn't walk away. Not yet, anyway. Taco had said they needed to avoid mercenaries, because they wouldn't give a shit about why they were doing this. But these guys were old cronies of Taco and Grady, hand-picked by Taco because they were different.

"How so?" Soho asked.

"Faiza was abducted with violence," Morgan said. "She's being held against her will, in a place where the men would probably get away with shooting her if they wanted to. But if we go storming in, shooting a bunch of people to get her back, then we're no better than them. And nothing will change."

"If we don't," Soho said, "we're fucking dead."

"Yeah, fuck, dead," said The Bear.

Taco turned to face her. "Look, kid, nobody says there's going to be any shooting. But there has to be protection for contingencies."

"You mean, if someone gets caught?" she said.

"No, we don't plan for anyone to get caught. We don't talk about it, we don't plan for it," Taco said abruptly. His tone was stern, a clear message telling Morgan not to mention the subject of capture again. She wondered if that was superstition, like actors saying "Break a leg" instead of "Good luck."

"But we may have to shoot our way out," he went on. "We don't know that. And if we do, we're not going to go to a gunfight armed with a knife or a slingshot. You don't go into a country like that unarmed. You have to protect yourself at all costs."

Morgan glanced at Grady, but he was picking at something on his boot and did not look up.

"I don't know what to do," she said. "I need to think about this."

The Bear spoke softly. Morgan noticed for the first time that he had a Southern accent. "Due respect, ma'am, but you ain't gonna find anyone else. Anybody you ask, just gonna say, 'You want me to do what? And do it how? And I ain't got nothing to protect myself with? You can't pay me enough.'"

"Does anyone here understand what I'm talking about?" she asked, exasperated. They all shook their heads.

No one spoke for what seemed like a very long time. Taco leaned forward and studied the maps. Morgan looked at the map of Saudi Arabia. It seemed strange to be seeing a country so distant, so alien, on an ordinary map, like one you might pick up at a gas station and stuff in your glovebox. And it probably wasn't all that different in appearance. When they got there, would it look like Nevada, with palm trees like in Florida? If she got there. Which was seeming doubtful.

What if she hired these guys, told them where to go, and stayed at home like a good girl? That's what they were all thinking. And why not? Let the boys go over and shoot their little hearts out, literally. Bring Faiza back and I won't ask how you did it. Grady was right. She was Miss Goody Two Shoes, living in a fantasy, trying to have a real life Mission Impossible. Which was, as it turned out, impossible.

Grady heaved a big sigh that puffed out his cheeks. "Maybe there's a compromise here," he said. "Maybe you could use nonlethal stuff to overpower the house staff. Like gas or pepper spray or sting balls. That possible?"

"Military's been using some of that stuff," Taco said. The others nodded.

"Soft kill," Soho said, with an amused grin. "Shit, the Marines took sting ball grenades and foam and a bunch of that shit into Somalia in '94, to get the U.N. boys out," he added.

"Those people pray five or six times a day," Taco said. "And they gather the whole household in to do that. I was figuring to go in during prayer time, the one at sunset. So if there's only a couple of guards not at prayers, we were gonna have to take them down quietly anyway."

"How long do prayers last?" Grady asked.

"Fifteen minutes, half hour tops," Taco said. "We'll find out for sure from our informant. But either way, we're gonna plan on getting in and out in fifteen."

"Then we make a run for it?" Soho asked.

"Hopefully it'll take them a while to figure out what's happened. They'll think it's a robbery. But not for long. We're gonna have to haul ass," Taco said.

"That could be done without guns," Soho said. "As long

as they don't start shooting."

The Bear nodded. "But we carry our weapons, right?"

"Have to," Taco said, turning to Morgan. "That okay with you?"

Morgan realized that to get Faiza home, she would have to make these concessions. This was the way the game was played, and she didn't make the rules. And if she stuck to her guns, which was no guns, they'd probably get caught or shot themselves and never get Faiza out.

Morgan pictured herself face to face with a bunch of raging Arab men after they'd barged into their house to steal their property from them. And they tried to defend themselves, and their house, or maybe sent police after them. Could she face the prospect of a crazy car chase, a street gun battle, machine gun pellets shattering the side of their car? And them with a couple of spray cans and some pellet guns?

Still, this was rationalization. Violence does beget violence, and what she was doing would not break that cycle. What would Martin Luther King or Gandhi say about this? Was there any way to justify compromising principles of nonviolence under certain circumstances? If there was a way, she had no idea where in her mind or her heart to find it.

Maybe this was why these guys didn't talk about failure. Worrying about something going wrong and someone getting hurt stopped you in your tracks. To go forward, she must assume that they would go in as planned, take Faiza out peacefully, and maybe even with some love, or at least forgiveness, in their hearts.

Plus, she had another idea up her sleeve to help them get into and out of the house. But it could wait. These guys had had enough of her suggestions for one day.

One at a time, Morgan looked in the face of each of these men, meeting their eyes, coveting their uncomplicated bravery.

And she said, "So, do we have a deal, or what?"

CHAPTER FORTY-FIVE

The sky was darkening as they walked out to Grady's rental car, and Morgan could hear muffled rumblings of thunder in clouds far off on the western horizon. The air felt cool, a little moist, and she wondered if it ever rained in Saudi Arabia, and if it was really as scorching hot as people reported. Grady opened the door on her side and waited for her to get in. He shut the door gently and walked around to the driver's side. His expression was thoughtful, almost moody.

"Are you in a hurry to get back?" he asked. They had met earlier at a Denny's restaurant and left her car in the parking lot, to appear as a couple arriving at Taco's alleged party.

"Why?"

"There's something I want you to see," Grady said. "If you can spare a couple of hours."

Morgan said she could, and Grady pulled out onto the street. His energy was rather stony and businesslike, precluding the idea that what he wanted her to see was the inside of his motel room. That was a relief. And, she had to admit, a tiny bit disappointing.

They drove to the Orlando airport, which was about forty-five minutes from Taco's hangar house. As it turned out, Grady had flown a charter to Orlando, which coordinated nicely with the meeting. He said he would be flying out later that evening, whenever his passengers, a bunch of Disney execs, decided to show up. He had three or four hours before he needed to be at the airport to file his flight plan and get the plane ready to go. His copilot, Rich Cramer, was off somewhere killing time.

After they had driven about ten minutes in silence, Grady said, "I thought you might like to see the plane."

"Sure," Morgan said, a little confused as to why he would go out of his way to show her an airplane. He read her hesitation.

"This is like the plane you'll be taking. Probably," Grady said.

He pulled into a small parking lot next to a building comprised of a hangar and another smaller section, which was the terminal. The name, Executive Airways, spanned the top of the hangar in bronze letters and was stenciled above the door to the office and waiting area. Just beyond and slightly behind the hangar, Morgan could see the tail section of an airplane. From her vantage point by the car, she couldn't imagine what kind of front could be attached to this incredible empennage.

The vertical stabilizer looked like something from *Star Wars,* angling steeply up from the tail. The horizontal stabilizers were mounted at the peak in a V-shape, as though they had been blown back by the sheer force of the wind. The jet engines mounted on the tail were big and sleek, tapered slightly toward the tail.

As they walked around the building, the whole plane came into view, and even on this cloudy day it gleamed as if it had its own private source of sunlight. It looked like it was sculpted out of white glass. Along the fuselage were thin stripes in soft gold and a huge Roman numeral V, which reflected onto the wing as if it was a mirror. The plane was long and pencil-thin, and the wings slanted back with the wingtips turned upward, so it seemed to be streaking forward even when it was standing still.

Grady was enjoying her reaction. "Cool, huh, babe?" he said. "And this is the outside. Wait'll you see the inside."

As they walked toward the plane, Grady pulled a clicker out of his jacket pocket and aimed it toward the plane, to disarm the alarm system. Then he opened a panel on the side, flipping two switches. With this, the hatch door opened and stairs hummed down.

As they climbed the steps, Grady told her that the Sky-bird V had been designed about five years before. At a cost of about $20 to $30 million, only about a dozen were made each year at Atlantic Aeronautical Corporation in Savannah. When they stepped into the plane, he turned left into the cockpit to turn on the auxiliary power system. All at once the interior lights illuminated and the air conditioner purred gently.

"This puppy will go sixty-five hundred nautical miles without a pit stop," Grady said. "It cruises at Mach eight-seven."

The cabin was one of the plushest domains Morgan had ever seen. Tall, cushy bone-colored leather reclining seats, soft sea-blue carpet, sleek wood and leather paneling, with side tables and television monitors and little holes for drinks everywhere. The lighting, from some embedded source, created sepia tones and an aura of diplomats and royalty. The windows were big round portholes with gold-handled shades. This cabin screamed for someone to have sex in it.

Morgan fell back into a chair and raised the footrest.

"You really fly this?" she said.

Grady had the grin of a high school kid showing off his new Corvette. He grabbed her hand and led her into the cockpit. The overhead lights were off, and the digits on the instrument panel glowed blue. Grady climbed into the seat on the left and pointed for Morgan to sit in the other. The seat was deep and low in the cockpit, enveloped by gauges and numbers and levers and switches. It was the way she had always imagined the inside of a space capsule would look.

"This cockpit has it all. The newest, the greatest, all the bells and whistles," Grady said. "It'll fucking talk to you."

"Talk?"

"Like, ground proximity," Grady said. "It'll say 'pull up, pull up' if you need to. It's sex, babe. Pure sex."

Morgan put her hands on the control wheel, gently, because this plane seemed ready to detonate, and with the barest touch it might lurch forward and take off. She wondered how it would feel to have the skill to fly something like this. Kate said that climbing into a cockpit and starting a plane was no different than getting in a car and driving off. Morgan couldn't imagine. But then, she was a writer and knew lots of people who would freeze trying to put together the first line of a letter. To them, her ease with writing was equally mystifying, she supposed.

Still, there was a particular kind of magic around flying and the accoutrements of that art, like this exquisite little cockpit with its secret language and its power to free humans from the limits of gravity.

"So, what do you think, babe?" Grady said. "Feel any better about the trip?"

"I made a 737 turn around on the tarmac," Morgan said.

"Ah," said Grady. "So that's what's been bugging you."

"You knew?"

"Sure," he said. "You're not the first. Lots of people get scared."

Morgan shook her head. "This wasn't just scared. It was like there were corks in my feet and someone had unplugged them and all my insides had gushed down and out through the holes."

And then it all came tumbling out, this secret no one knew. She told Grady how all her connection with reality had vanished. As if she no longer existed in that time and space and she was hanging somewhere outside, as though she had exited this world for another dimension. She was utterly terrified.

"Yeah, I know," he said. "It starts with mild claustrophobia, and then if you don't relax, the feelings get stronger and stronger until you're in full-scale panic. It's like a spiral."

"The flight attendant announced that they were returning to the terminal for someone to deplane. And they took my luggage off and everything. It was so humiliating. I never want to go through that again."

"I understand," he said.

"This plane's like a canister," Morgan went on. "The

thought of being cooped up in it makes me feel like a beetle at the bottom of a jar, lunging in crazed circles, slipping on the sides of the glass."

"Whoa," Grady said.

"What if we get halfway around the world and I panic? What if I go crazy with fear? And then the mission would be ruined, because there would be this deranged woman to contend with. Maybe they'd have to turn back. Maybe my madness would get us all arrested . . . "

"You could stay behind," Grady said. "Let the others do it."

"No," she said. "I want to go. It's my idea, and we're going to need women."

"You're a brave lady."

Morgan listened for patronizing, but there wasn't a hint. She didn't know why, but with Grady she was always poised to be offended. And when instead he was straightforward or warm or caring, it took her by surprise.

She really wanted to keep on disliking this man. He was immature and unconscious. He may be dressed in a flying suit, with a gorgeous, torrid airplane, but he was still a man full of himself, out for himself, and if he got too close, capable of inflicting great pain. Who was he? Sometimes Morgan thought he didn't have two scruples to rub together. Other times, he touched her at the center of her heart.

"Thanks for bringing me over," Morgan said. "Talking about it helps."

"You don't sound convinced," he said.

"It's such a long flight."

He was staring at her, but she couldn't look back at him. She gazed out the front window and imagined what it would be like to be above the clouds, scanning the whole expanse of the sky. Pilots definitely got the choice view in an airplane.

"I took Kate up in the plane," Grady said.

"You did? When?"

"Day before yesterday. Baylor Aviation just bought this

plane, and I had to fly out to Savannah to take delivery. So I brought her along."

"You two flew to Savannah and back?"

"I told you I'd call her," Grady said.

The day before, Kate had left several messages for Morgan, and she had called her back. But they kept missing each other. Kate had said she had something to tell her. So this was it.

"Let her tell you about it," Grady said. "But lemme say one thing. That woman is a damn good pilot. One of the best I've ever seen. She could learn to fly this Skybird a in a heartbeat. She'll fly it like singin' a song."

Kate, flying again. Now that Morgan had sat in this cockpit, she could imagine her there. She'd settle into that seat and know the meaning of all those codes and numbers, and the knobs and instruments would be instantly familiar and welcoming, like a letter from an old friend you've missed dearly. And she would know what to turn and what to pull to get that plane to leave the ground.

"There's something else I want you to know," Grady said.

"What's that?"

"My opinion? She could take your mission to Saudi Arabia."

Grady stood and took Morgan's hand to help her climb out of the cockpit. He kept hold as they walked back into the cabin, and she didn't try to pull away. But this time, as she scanned the lush cabin, she remembered that this was the plane that had taken Faiza away, and Morgan pictured her frozen in one of those executive chairs, her terror and fury concealed by the robe and veil. She wondered if they ever let her recline and go to sleep, or if rest was also forbidden to women who had offended the men.

So when Grady pulled her against him and lowered his face to kiss her, she was angry at the men who stole Faiza, angry at the family that possessed her, angry at the country that allowed them to torture her. She stiffened.

"What's wrong?" Grady said.

"I can't," Morgan said.

"This wasn't the plane we used," he said.

"What?" she said.

He repeated. "This wasn't the plane that we used to fly her to Saudi. We have two. This one's similar, but not the same plane."

Morgan felt her throat getting thick and she knew she couldn't hold back the tears. She started to sob, and Grady repositioned his arms to hold her closer.

"It's okay, babe," he said, with a tenderness that stunned her.

"No, it's not okay," she said. "I'm so scared. It's so crazy."

"You'll do fine on the flight." He grinned. "Shit, you can watch television all the way if you want to."

There was a smear of mascara on Grady's shirt. Morgan dabbed at it with her finger. The stigmata of women. She hated that she wasn't brave, that her courage was nothing but a role she played. The empress had no clothes. Why was she doing this?

"It's not only the flight," she said.

"I know," he said, and this time when he kissed her they both dropped slowly toward the floor, ending up on their knees, squeezing their bodies tightly together, until it seemed that every square inch of their thighs and torsos was touching. His one hand was pressing on her back, the other cradled her neck. The way he kissed was the way she had always imagined it would feel when she fell in love. What a mean trick of the universe, to deliver it in a package she couldn't possibly open, or keep.

Grady leaned forward like a dance partner leading her into a back bend, and they sunk into the thick carpet, Morgan on her back and Grady over her. On his neck was the faintest fragrance, a musky sandalwood, and his body covered her, yet without heavy weight. She wanted to be naked. She wanted him to make love to her.

Then, with the small scrap of left brain that remained, she asked herself: Then what? They say that before you die, your whole life passes before your eyes. For women, the same thing happens before high-risk sex. A parade of former Mr. Wrongs passes before your eyes.

In Morgan's version, they were the ones with whom she'd had instant, savage chemistry. She'd jumped into bed, ignoring the objections from her wee inner voice. And for all that sweet and delicious passion of the moment, one paid forever. It was like an emotional Exxon Valdez disaster. The cleanup seems to never end.

"Hey, Grady!" The voice came from outside the door. Grady lifted back onto his knees and stood up, extending his hand to help Morgan up. His movements were brisk but not hasty, and he gazed at her with regret. By the time they were standing side by side, no longer holding hands, Rich Cramer's head was peeking in the hatchway. Grady introduced them.

"You've got her fired up," Cramer said.

It took Morgan a beat to realize the copilot was referring to the plane.

"Am I late?" he asked.

"No, we're not leaving for a couple hours," Grady said. "I was showing her the plane."

Cramer grinned. "Like it?"

"It's beautiful," Morgan said. Turning to Grady, she said, "I really need to be getting back."

"Hey, kids," Cramer said. "I'm not staying. I'll be back later. Sorry I interrupted."

"No problem," Morgan said. "I really do need to get going. Long drive."

Cramer backed out the hatchway, waving a quick good-bye. When he was gone, Grady put his arm around her again and drew her toward him. But she pulled away, and he let go.

As they walked toward the exit, Morgan wondered when she might see him again. There was no reason for him to come to any more meetings with Taco. He'd agreed to help make some contacts, but he could arrange that over the telephone.

She also wondered if he was thinking the same thing. But neither of them asked. It was amazing how much they didn't say to each other.

CHAPTER FORTY-SIX

Following her tour of the airplane and close encounter with Grady, Morgan was able to reach Kate. She told Morgan that two days before, Grady had called and invited her to tag along on the flight to Savannah. She just couldn't pass up seeing a brand new Skybird up close, she said. And anyway, it was a chance to check out the plane they were planning to use for the rescue.

What happened after that was unexpected, as she explained.

*   *   *

There was no time for Kate to make the drive to San Francisco, so Grady told her they would pick her up at the airport near her home. The captains were two other pilots from Baylor Aviation, taking a charter on to Washington, D.C. Grady, Cramer, and Kate tagged along as passengers to Savannah, where they would take delivery on the new Skybird that Baylor had just purchased. The five other passengers were an entourage of politicians—two U.S. Reps, a couple of aides, and one lobbyist, who may or may not have been connected to each other but who were getting a cut rate for the flight because of the stop in Georgia and the unscheduled one in Santa Barbara.

They left California shortly after dawn and were in Savannah by late morning. While Grady and Cramer completed the paperwork and the protocol involved in buying an airplane, Kate entertained herself exploring the production facility. By the end of the day, she knew every inch of the Skybird's exterior and a lot about its cutting-edge aerodynamics.

Late that afternoon Grady and Cramer climbed into the

cockpit, and Kate, alone in the cabin, submerged herself in a leather recliner. The pilots had left the cockpit door open.

They took off hot, and Kate guessed that they were climbing at the plane's maximum speed. It was like high school, only instead of a souped-up Chevy peeling off from the stoplight, she was in the back seat of a multi-million-dollar airplane. Zero to sixty in seven seconds was now 4,000 feet per minute. No real difference, except the boys were men now, and the toys were bigger and more expensive. But they loved to make the tires squeal, and the most important thing was how fast you could take off from somewhere.

Kate couldn't hear the radio transmissions from her seat, but she had a pretty good idea what was going on up front. After leaving Savannah, the pilots would be instructed to switch the frequency to Jacksonville center, which would give them instructions west. All instrument flights are constantly under the direction of a communications center. As the plane moves along, each center hands off to the next along the route, like a bucket brigade, so the plane's location is always identifiable and its path always under someone's control. After Jacksonville, they would be handed off to Atlanta center, and so on.

Kate had flown cross-country hundreds of times, but nearly always up front. She felt left out back there. A stranger to this part of the airplane. The view from the cabin porthole was limited, admitting less than half of what was out there, like a bird who can only see out of one eye.

They'd been in the air about forty-five minutes when Cramer walked back into the cabin.

"Want to go up front?" he asked.

Kate hesitated. "Really?"

"It's Grady's idea," Cramer said. "But I'm gonna love the nap. And you're gonna love the view."

Grady turned and waved her in, and as she slid into the cockpit's right seat, she picked up the headset and drew it over her ears. Suddenly embarrassed, she looked at Grady. He had invited her up, but he hadn't offered Cramer's headset.

Cockpits are little absolute monarchies. They belong to the pilot. He, or she, tells you what to do, and what stuff you can touch and cannot touch. It doesn't matter how nice the pilot is, you don't take anything for granted. Kate had picked up the headset out of instinct. She should have asked. Grady smiled, as if he didn't notice.

Kate scanned the panel. Though the placement of some equipment was different than she'd seen before, the instruments and gauges were distinctly familiar, like old friends. The last time she'd been in a cockpit, she was in the left seat and Jack was in the right. She could feel him there, his quiet confidence and skill, the way his broad hands and thick fingers dwarfed the controls. The memory might have made her cry, if it hadn't been for her conditioning. She never broken down about anything when she was behind the controls of a flying airplane.

"We're cleared to flight level four-one-o," Grady said. "Here's the autopilot. We're doing Mach eight-one," he said.

* * *

Kate paused in her story to explain to Morgan what that meant. Once a plane gets above 25,000 feet, because the air is so thin, the airspeed is expressed in Mach numbers, rather than miles per hour. Mach is the relationship of the airplane to the speed of sound. At Mach .81, they were cruising about 550 miles per hour.

"We were on flight path J-2, which is a jet route in the sky," she continued. The plane was on autopilot, giving Grady the freedom to explain the finer points of flying the Skybird.

* * *

This was the swankiest cockpit Kate had ever seen, and Grady was bursting to show it off. The navigation and communication equipment was in a row above the instrument panel, like an eyebrow. Grady pointed to the dual heads.

"We've been switched from Atlanta to Memphis center," he said.

The navigational system would hold two radio frequencies at a time, Kate knew, the current center and the upcoming one. When the copilot switches to the next center, the former center's frequency goes into standby mode, so he can flip-flop back to it if needed.

As they cruised, Kate studied Grady. She knew about the kiss and about Morgan's schizophrenic attraction and revulsion. Kate could understand the confusion. The guy was cocky, and he really had some bad verbal habits when it came to women. On the other hand, he was an excellent pilot—steady, cautious, no showoff stunts. And he was a good teacher. He didn't over-explain or patronize.

"It's obvious you know your ass from a hole in the ground in an airplane," he said to Kate.

*　　　　*　　　　*

That part annoyed Morgan, the consummate feminist. Would it kill him to cut out the bubba jargon?

"I know, but can I finish telling you what happened?" Kate asked. "The radio came through my headset."

*　　　　*　　　　*

"Skybird Three-Two-Nine Delta Mike, contact the Houston center, one-three-two-six-five."

Kate recognized the plane number and the instruction from Memphis to switch to the next frequency. Without even glancing at Grady, she pushed the microphone switch and answered, "Okay, one-three-two-six-five for Three-Two-Nine Delta Mike."

She looked at Grady. Out of pure instinct, she had crossed the line again. And that startled her. Whether she liked it or not, flying was inside of her. Part of her. And she couldn't push it away. After all these years, it was still there, and it would stay there, probably forever.

Grady grinned. "Go ahead," he said, teasing. "You've taken over anyway."

Kate tuned into 132.65, pushed the transfer button, and the numbers switched, putting Memphis in standby.

"Houston center, Skybird Three-Two-Nine Delta Mike is with you, flight level four-one-zero," she said.

"Cleared Direct Junction," the voice answered. "J-2 flight plan route."

Kate handled the radio from that point on. The plane practically flew itself. It was equipped with INS, Inertial Navigation System, so when the center told them to go to Direct Junction, all Grady had to do was punch in the code for that location, hit GO, and the autopilot steered the plane toward the correct headings. Push-button flying, Grady called it. From Direct Junction they headed toward Palm Springs and then the Los Angeles area, where they were stopping to pick up two clients.

The flight was beautiful. Because they were headed west, they chased the sunset. Behind them, they could see a dark line across the horizon, the edge of the descending nighttime, dividing the sky into yesterday and tomorrow. The darkness followed them, coming down slowly after them like a curtain. Out the sides of the window, they could literally watch the night fall. Then, in front of them, as the rim of the earth tipped up to cover the last of the sun, there was a bright green flash and a rose-blue afterglow silently exploded in the sky.

Grady started their descent. He turned to Kate and said, "Why don't you disconnect the autopilot and fly it?"

She took hold of the control wheel and disconnected the autopilot.

"It's your airplane," he said.

Right away Kate could tell that the Skybird was easy to handle. At higher speeds, it was bit heavier on the controls than she expected, especially on the ailerons and the elevators, but once they got down to 10,000 feet and 250 miles per hour, the airplane flew like a dream. The engine's whir was no louder than a home air conditioner. Grady took over the radio now, to get the vectors for their approach into Los Angeles.

"LA approach, Skybird Three-Two-Nine Delta Mike with you, one-five thousand."

"Skybird Three-Two-Nine Delta Mike, turn right heading three-one-zero, intercept the ILS two-five left, cleared for the civet one profile arrival."

Kate followed the instructions precisely. You never forget how to fly, her father used to tell her.

The night was clear and dark when they passed over Palm Springs, and off in the distance they could see a white glow shimmering on the horizon, almost like there had been another sunset. As they crossed the border of hills and rugged mountain ridges that encircle the Los Angeles basin, it was as if someone had suddenly plugged in the world. As far as the eye could see, for fifty or sixty miles, the land was nothing but a blanket of lights, millions and millions of lights. And in the sky above those lights were others, the beacons from dozens of other planes approaching and circling the airports around Los Angeles, like lightning bugs clustering over a summer field.

She came in on runway 25 left and brought the plane down as if the runway was made of priceless silk and she didn't want to tear it. As she slowed the engines and turned the plane onto the taxiway, Grady gave her a thumbs-up.

Kate felt how deeply she missed Jack. And she knew it was really her own self that she missed. In those few minutes, she remembered who she was, and why she flew.

CHAPTER FORTY-SEVEN

Meredith lost Sheena in cyberspace. The last she heard, Sheena had promised to find out more information about Faiza, to confirm she was indeed being held in her uncle's house. But then the email messages Meredith sent to Sheena were returned, no such address.

Using the ruse that she wanted to order clothing, Meredith tried every internet channel she could think of and even contacted an old friend who was a computer hacker in college. The search was looking fruitless.

Then one day, out of the blue, Meredith received a message.

Sheena explained that she had changed the email and website addresses, and that she was back in business after a temporary hiatus, which she didn't explain. Their exchange was brief, and in it, Meredith tried to ascertain how Faiza was doing:

Sheena: I have confirmed that the address you gave me is correct.

Meredith: Thank you. Is it still possible to send the clothing?

Sheena: Yes. You wish this to be a surprise, is that correct?

Meredith: Yes. I hope the sizes will be right. I have not seen my friend in a while.

Sheena: I am sure she is the same.

Then Meredith tried something very bold: Is there anyone inside the home who can help us with the surprise?

Meredith stayed on line waiting for the answer, but there was no response from Sheena. Two days later an email arrived from another sender, whose identification was a series of numbers. The writer did not identify herself or himself, but from the tone, Meredith wondered if it was Sheena using another address:

1674321: You must erase this message immediately. Do not make copies. Otherwise, our efforts to help you will fail.

Meredith: I promise.

1674321: This is an organization to serve women; it is illegal and there is much danger. The woman is locked in the Woman's Room. There is a maid in that household who contacted our organization many months ago, seeking help for herself. We are attempting to make contact with her. Do not send us any messages. Wait for our contact.

As promised, Meredith destroyed the message and then called Morgan and reported it from memory.

"I don't know what's going on, Mom, but I don't want to cheat even a little bit," Meredith said. "I erased the message right away."

"Who do you think these people are?" Morgan asked.

"Obviously some kind of underground," she said. "My guess is they are trying to infiltrate the house. I've never said what our intentions are, but they must have figured we want to get her out."

Another week went by. Morgan spent most of the time near the telephone. To be on the safe side, when they wanted to talk about the rescue, they discussed "ordering the clothes." Maybe this cloak-and-dagger secrecy was overkill, but the anonymous contact within Saudi Arabia looked like their only chance to get the information Taco wanted, and the connection seemed very fragile.

Finally, Meredith called with news that she had received a message.

1674321: Are you still interested?

Meredith: Yes, please.

1674321: There is a housemaid. She is Filipina and her passport has been taken from her. She wishes to leave. She also feels sad about another thing. She will help if you will help her.

Meredith was not sure how to respond. What could she promise? She answered, "I will tell you shortly," and called Morgan. They concluded that Faiza was the "thing" that the housemaid was sad about. Morgan called Grady.

"I know you're out of this. And I know we're not supposed to talk much," Morgan said. "But I need an answer quickly. And I didn't think I should call Taco." She told Grady, as succinctly as possible, about Meredith's contact with 1674321.

"That's great," Grady said.

"Do you think we can trust it?"

"Maybe. There are lots of Filipino and East Indian house servants in Saudi. They come there with the promise of riches and high positions. Dumbasses. Sometimes after they arrive, their so-called employers take away their passports so they are not free to leave. They are virtually slaves. It's particularly tough on women because they're confined at home and it's harder for them to get away."

"What should we tell this maid?" Morgan asked.

"You may have already told her too much," he said.

Both Meredith and Morgan understood that this woman was hoping they could help her escape.

"If she wants to leave with you, that's a problem. It would compromise the mission too much. You could promise that, but you'd have to double-cross her at the end."

"No way," Morgan said.

"I didn't think so," Grady said. "Let me think for a minute and get back to you."

He called back about a half hour later.

"Taco says to keep the explanation to a minimum," Grady said. "Say nothing about who or where we are. Offer to get her a passport and two thousand dollars U.S. In exchange, she helps us get in the house and shows us the room. While we're there, uh, you're there, you slip her the passport and the money. Then we tie her up, maybe gas her, to cover her involvement."

"What if she gets caught with that stuff?"

"That's her problem, babe."

"How do we get the passport?" Morgan asked.

"If you can get her name and a contact in the Philippines, like a family member, we could actually get a legal one. Well, almost legal. If not, then you'll need a full description and a photo or sketch. Bring it all to the next meeting. This is Soho's specialty."

Morgan couldn't help but notice that Grady kept slipping and using the word "we." *Huh. He's so cocky, it's probably his version of the Royal We.*

"Thanks, Grady," she said.

"Welcome," he said. "And babe?"

"What?"

"Tell your daughter: Nice work."

* * *

Over four months had passed since Faiza's abduction. Ashton was still on crutches, but the leg was nearly healed. Another week or so, the doctor said. He managed to make it to his classes, however numbly. He wore his portable phone on his belt, like a sheriff with his six-shooter, and carried extra batteries like spare bullets, so if the phone ran out of power he could reload in seconds.

Ashton never gave up the hope that Faiza would call. He believed it possible, even when Meredith told him the news from Sheena that Faiza was indeed in the Woman's Room.

Willing himself to get up every morning, Ashton attended all of his exams, and although his grades were barely passing, he managed to finish the quarter. "Someday you'll be glad you did," Morgan reminded him like a good mother, but he wasn't convinced. She thought that his perseverance, however lackluster, proved that when he looked into the future, he had more hope than despair.

Ashton missed Faiza so acutely that most of the time his personality was flat, like someone who'd stayed up all night and was trying to stay awake through breakfast. He asked her if he could come to Florida to her house after he got off the crutches.

Morgan was glad Ashton was coming. There was something she needed to tell him, and she wanted to do it in person.

She needed to tell him that he couldn't go with them on the rescue.

CHAPTER FORTY-EIGHT

"What?" Ashton shouted. "How could you say that?"

"I've been thinking about this for a long time," Morgan said. "It's too dangerous."

Ashton had just come up from a swim in the Gulf and joined Morgan on the lanai. He was still hobbling a bit, but the scar on his leg was beginning to heal and recede behind his suntan. He rubbed his hair with a towel, then flung it on the rocking chair and sat down.

"That's crazy, Mom. You're going. It's not too dangerous for you. And Kate."

"That's different," she said.

"How is it different?"

"Well, first of all, we need women for the rescue." Morgan told Ashton that she had a plan, which she was going to present to Taco and the guys at the next meeting.

"You need men, too," Ashton shot back.

"And we've got them. We have enough people."

Ashton stood up and walked behind the rocking chair. He gripped the back of the chair and shoved it back and forth in jerks, as if to pound his trembling into obedience.

"No way, Mom. You can't do this."

"I'm in charge," Morgan said. "And I don't want anything to happen to you. If it did, I'd never forgive myself."

"Nothing is going to happen," he said. "You said it yourself. You quoted Susan B. Anthony. Failure is impossible."

"We need someone, you, to handle things back here.

What if we got caught? We'd need someone to intervene and get help to us."

"Meredith can do that," he said. "Or Dad."

"Don't you dare tell Dad."

"Why not?" he asked.

"He would never approve. He'd probably try to stop us."

Ashton didn't promise. Morgan let it go for now.

"Ash, please. We can do it without you. You need to stay back, be waiting for her. You need to be where it's safe."

"Look, Mom. I've got the jewels. I can go to the black market with them and go out and hire my own frigging mission. There's plenty of these guys around."

"I don't want you there," Morgan said.

Ashton took his hands off the chair and sat down again. He leaned toward her. His voice resonated with a sudden calmness and depth, and for the first time Morgan saw in his eyes the father he was going to be.

"Faiza is going to be my wife," he said. "She has my baby in her. I've got to be there to help get her out."

"We'll talk about it tomorrow," Morgan said.

He protested, but she stood up and pulled open the sliding glass door. "I'm going to bed."

She hated walking away from him like that, but she needed some time to think. She knew she was right. What they were planning might be crazy, but it was her own crazy. To take him along was irresponsible and dangerous. She always protected her children. She would not deliberately march him right smack dab into harm's way.

*   *   *

Kate sided with Ashton. When Morgan told her what had happened, Kate was surprised.

"You think I misled him?" Morgan asked her.

"Well, to be honest, all along I thought he was going," she said.

"It's too dangerous. It's a hair-brained scheme, and I can't let him risk his life."

"You're risking your life," she said. "And mine."

"Yes, but that's me risking my own life. And to tell you the truth, I think it might be wrong to let you risk yours."

Kate's eyebrows shot upward. "You're having doubts?"

"Of course, I've had doubts all along. They come and they go. But I can never get to a point where I feel totally comfortable with this."

"You think you ever will? Morgan, you can't take the risk out of everything."

"But this is off the charts," Morgan protested. "And now you're involved, and we're all playing way outside the safety zone."

"I know," Kate said soberly.

"You fly airplanes. You know about taking risks. I've always been more of a wimp. You're up in the sky, I'm sitting on the ground," Morgan said.

"You're one of the bravest people I know."

"How so?" Morgan said in disbelief.

"You had the courage to have children," she said.

"I never thought about that as requiring courage."

"You had the courage to have them, and to stand beside them," Kate said.

"Tell me honestly. Do you think this is too dangerous?" Morgan decided that if she heard the slightest hesitation in Kate's voice, she would phone Grady and call the whole thing off.

"Listen, Morgan. Say you saw a wrecked car and it was engulfed in flames, and you knew someone was trapped in that car. And the fire is out of control, and maybe going to explode any second. Would you try to help, or would you stand away, where it was safe?"

"Oh, god," Morgan moaned.

"Well, what would you do?" she repeated.

"I don't know," Morgan said. "But I hope that I would have the guts to help, to try to get them out. I couldn't live with myself later if I didn't try."

"Doesn't that tell you something?" she asked.

"The way I see it, you and I can risk our lives if we want to. I'm my own person, you're your own person. We've had full lives already. It's different with a son. It's wrong for me to risk his life."

"He risks his life all the time when he goes out in the ocean to surf," Kate said.

"I know, but that's his choice and I can't stop him," Morgan said. "And I'm not sponsoring him."

"Sure you are. You bought him his first surfboard when he was eight."

"Yeah, and if he'd gotten hurt, I'd feel responsible."

"So it really comes down to who gets the guilt if he gets hurt," Kate said. "And you don't want it."

"Kate, this is about a lot more than guilt."

"You sure?" she said.

"I'm sure. I don't want to lose him."

Kate didn't have children. How could she know the terror of losing a child? On the other hand, Morgan sensed that her questions were coming not from a place of misunderstanding, but rather a place of deeper understanding. Kate saw Ashton as a man, maybe a rather new one, but a man nevertheless. She loved him with all her heart, but she also could allow him to be his own person and act on his own behalf.

Later, Ashton approached Morgan while she was sitting at her computer.

"Mom, you busy?"

She had to smile. When he and Meredith were small, she would explain to them that she needed to work and they should not interrupt her when she was sitting at the typewriter. So they would tiptoe up to her and put their soft little hands on the arm of the chair and lean toward her, in voices so quiet they were like little puffs of breath in her ear: "Mom. Mom." They thought that if they whispered, it didn't count as an interruption.

"It's okay, sweetie," she said, turning to face him. He sat

down on the edge of the bed.

"I've been thinking. We're a team, and we have to stick together. It's not going to help Faiza if I storm off and try to do this on my own. I am grateful for all the work you've done on this. Nobody could have a greater mom. And I don't want you to take this wrong, but I think you need to take a look at your reasoning. Because it's flawed."

"Well, you're not alone," Morgan said. "That's what Kate says."

"Look at the things you write about, Mom. Your ideas. They're about women being put down. You get so mad when men treat women like they can't take care of themselves. You say it's demeaning. Why is that?"

"Because it's condescending," she said. "And if you are condescending to someone, then you are assuming your superiority. The basis of inequality is the belief that women are lesser than men. That attitude reinforces that belief."

"Mom, your protectiveness of me is the same attitude, only in reverse. Don't you see? You're condescending to me. You say that you are equipped to go on this mission, but I'm not. It's okay for you to take the risk, but I have to be kept safe. It's not fair, Mom, and you know it."

"It's what mothers do," Morgan said. "We worry. And want to protect you."

She gave him a hug, and agreed that he could come to the next meeting at Taco's, and they would decide from there. She was stalling, and Ashton refused to acquiesce.

"Mom," he said, "you are hurting me much more by treating me like this than I could possibly get hurt on a hundred missions."

CHAPTER FORTY-NINE

The first meeting in Taco's hangar was odd; the second was surreal. Bunched around the table, leaning in to study the maps, the group was the most unlikely of compatriots, like a team selected at random from a hundred thousand names scrawled on little scraps of paper and thrown into a huge hat.

Maybe the otherworldly aura was due to the addition of Buck and Crater, which definitely tipped the balance in favor of people with fake names. Kate, Ashton, and Morgan were the only ones there under their own recognizance.

The five men were strangers whom Morgan couldn't even identify by ordinary means, yet they were all getting ready to knot their ropes to each other and head up a rockface together.

Who were these guys? The line of trust that connected her to them was thin. And the source of it all was Grady, a stranger until a few months ago, who was not even present to tie together his creation.

The big surprise of the evening was Buck. Morgan had expected a guy with that name to be a sort of John Wayne type—husky, squared off, speaking in an unhurried drawl, like a cowboy at a rodeo. Where this Buck got his name was anyone's guess.

He was on the short side, slightly paunchy in the gut, with dark hair and an olive complexion that showed creases of aging around the eyes but was still smooth and clear along the cheekbones. His dark eyebrows were so bushy and heavy, they seemed to actually weigh down his eye sockets. He had a long muscular nose, and when he wasn't smiling, his upper lip sneered up, as though he had just gotten a whiff of some nasty smell.

Grady had told Morgan that Buck had flown for Air America in Vietnam and then spent six years flying for Emery Air Service in the United Arab Emirates. From what she could gather, Emery was the name painted on the outside of the airplanes, but the missions belonged to a secret someone else. Morgan also learned that when you asked these guys questions like, "What kind of flying did you do there?" the answer was, "We just flew." And if you asked something stupid like, "Did you do any covert operations?" they pretended they never heard you—as if you were a kid asking your folks if they ever had oral sex.

Buck was an Arab. His parents were from Morocco and were killed in an automobile accident when he was a year old. His much-older sister, who was married to an American, had brought him to the U.S. and adopted him, making him an American citizen. Though his ties to Morocco had diminished by the time he reached adulthood, he knew how to speak Arabic. And he looked like it. As soon as she met Buck, Morgan realized that the final piece of her plan had just fallen into place.

Crater was medium tall and lanky, balding on top, with a ponytail tied with a rubber band at the back of his neck. The hair in the ponytail looked scraggly but lustrous, as if it would smell freshly shampooed. Crater's eyes didn't appear to be looking at anything, depthless, as though the eyeball was painted on. Morgan got the feeling that the only emotion that would awaken those eyes would be anger. And she guessed that didn't happen very often, if at all. Of all the four no-names, Crater seemed the most neutralized, with a cool self-assurance and a natural efficiency. A Taurus, with Taurus rising.

Crater's story was by far the wildest. In the early eighties, while he was flying for USA Transport, he lived in Galveston, Texas, and in his off hours he gave flying lessons in a Cessna 172 that he owned with two other pilot buddies. One day Crater gave a flying lesson to a woman named Tally, who operated a community food service program for Mexican and Guatemalan refugees. He fell in love with her, not because of the food kitchen, but because he fell in love with her. And because he was in love with her, he volunteered at her food program in his spare time.

Guatemala's history is a story of violence and civil war, murder and disappearances. As Crater heard the stories of these atrocities from Tally and the refugees in the food kitchen, he became angry. His flights into Guatemala began as rescues of family members and friends of those he met in the food kitchen. Later, he and a partner brought out other refugees, making dozens of secret flights in and out of the country. Often they went in at night, landing an old DC-3 cargo plane on grass airstrips cut out in the middle of the jungle and lit by rows of homemade lanterns. Although they could take two dozen people at a time, that was still a tiny fraction of the victims left behind.

One night they lifted off out of the jungle near Quetzaltenango with four families, two men, and two orphaned children, one an infant. The passengers sat on pallets of canvas mounted along the sides of the cargo compartment. About ten minutes out, Crater's copilot got a radio transmission from their contact in Guatemala. He was breaking their radio silence to tell Crater that one of his passengers, a man, was not a refugee, but instead a drug smuggler on his way to Texas with a pants-load of cocaine.

Crater was furious, but said nothing until they were halfway home. Then he gave the controls to his copilot, got a .44 caliber pistol out of the cockpit storage compartment, and stormed into the back. He grabbed the man by the back of his jacket and shook him, digging the barrel of the gun into his forehead. As the man protested in a garble of hysterical Spanish, Crater dug into the man's pants and extracted the packages of dope.

Crater pulled a heavy canvas bag out of a storage box on the floor and at gunpoint, ordered the man to strap on the parachute. When he was sure the laces were correct and tight, he yelled to his copilot, who slowed the plane down to about one hundred knots and lowered the flaps. The passengers watched in horror, holding their breath and clutching their children, as Crater pried the rear cargo door open. The wind screamed and sucked at Crater and the smuggler, their hair matted against their heads and their jacket bottoms flapping on their legs.

Crater took the man's index finger and stabbed it against the parachute front, threading it into a metal ring.

"Pull. Pull. This. Pull!" Crater shouted over the cyclone tearing in the opening. Then, in a series of shoves and kicks, he thrust the terrorized man out the opening. The man's leg was last to go, a booted foot that stuck for an instant on the rim of the door before disappearing with a pop. Crater tossed the dope packets after him, pulled the cargo door shut, and the plane seemed to tremble before the engines droned into smooth flight.

Crater forced a smile at the passengers as he backed toward the cockpit.

"Sorry. It's okay. *Lo siento. No problema. Lo siento, mi amigos.*"

And these were the guys who were going to escort them all through the streets of Dhahran.

CHAPTER FIFTY

"Let's get started," Taco said, and they all found chairs and drew them up to the table. Buck perched on a wooden stool, which made him taller than the rest. Soho and The Bear both smiled at Morgan, and gratefully she felt the mood relax from the formality of their first meeting. The two new men had evidently been briefed before Morgan, Kate, and Ashton arrived, because Taco skipped preliminaries.

"Here's the base plan," he said. "We'll go back over it later and clean up details. The plane comes into Dhahran with two pilots, the two women, and me, as mechanic. I can also be a relief pilot. I fly the Skybird."

The guys chuckled at some inside joke. Apparently Taco could fly anything.

"We are there to demo the plane," he went on, "which we will do on the first full day. We'll stay at the Dammam Sheraton, here." He pointed to the map. "We'll have reservations for a week, but we'll be out of there before that. We won't move until we think the locals are comfortable with us and used to seeing us around. We'll come and go to the airplane, make some friends with guards, and when we're part of the woodwork, then we go.

"You guys come in through Bahrain. We don't see you until we go, but you'll know where to find us. We'll make minimum radio contact. We'll set the time in advance and proceed with three signals: Go, no-go, and abort. Okay so far?"

They all nodded. "What does 'No go' mean?" Morgan asked.

"Delay. If there's a problem at the house and we have to

make another time," he said.

"And 'Abort'?"

"Only in case of a big problem. Where we have to scrap the whole thing and get the hell out." Taco's response clipped the end of Morgan's question, which told her not ask him to speculate on such a problem.

"We'll come from the hotel in the car we've used all week, probably a Land Rover or a limo. Not sure yet. Whatever the locals are used to seeing us in. You guys come in two vehicles. You can be armed. But we're going for non-lethal weaponry. If the house staff and family is small, we will hold them and tie them up. We'll use gas if we need to overcome them. We fire only if fired on. You guys cool with that?"

Soho, The Bear, and Buck nodded agreement. Crater shrugged, with a look that said: I don't get it, but we do whatever the little lady wants. She's paying.

"So, you're waiting outside and we get the girl and bring her to you?" said Soho, who Morgan realized was captain of their team.

"Right," Taco answered. "We haven't seen the house yet. If it's on a busy road, that might be too conspicuous. Then we go to plan B."

"Which is?"

"I don't know yet," Taco said. "Have to wait till we get there."

"I don't like that," said Buck.

"How 'bout this?" Soho said. "When my men get there, we scope out the house right away, and if there's a problem, we decide what to do and leave a message for you in the hotel. We'll code it."

"I don't want you guys around us at all," Taco said. "One little thing that alerts someone that we're not who we say we are, and we're dead."

"Any chance of getting a layout of the house?" Crater asked.

Taco looked at Morgan.

"Maybe," she said. "We have a housemaid who's helping us. We need to get papers for her. We have asked, through the underground, for a diagram."

"Do you have the stuff for Soho?" Taco asked.

Morgan dug in her satchel and handed Soho an envelope. Meredith, bless her, had managed to get the name and address of the housemaid's grandparents in the Philippines. Then, Meredith simply picked up the telephone and called information. She found them on the second try. Although their English was very fractured, Meredith was able to communicate her intention to help their granddaughter. While the woman cried oh, oh, oh, and sobbed, the man left the phone and returned with a neighbor whose English was much better, and he translated her request.

A week later a very weathered manila envelope arrived, plastered with stamps, containing a small color snapshot of a young woman with a round face and straight dark hair, and one sheet of notepaper listing her height and weight and birth data. She was the same age as Faiza.

Soho glanced at the contents of the envelope. "Fine," he said. "Fine."

Morgan was dying to ask how they were going to do all this—get fake passports, sneak into countries through the back door, materialize in Land Rovers on the streets of Saudi Arabia. But there was some kind of spell in the air with these guys, a taboo on such questions. She kept her mouth shut, and when Ashton seemed about to ask, she shot him "the look" that told him to stay quiet.

"I still don't like the setup at the house," Buck said, after Taco pointed out the checkpoints on a land map of the area. "Depending on traffic, we could be thirty minutes from the airport. This whole thing, where we go in and bring her out, is too conspicuous. It's a setup for a chase. And we don't want to end up making a run for it to the plane."

"Yeah," Crater said. "If we have to shoot it out and run for it, they'll be all over us like sweat on sweat."

"Couldn't we go in at night?" asked The Bear.

"It'll be close to dusk, probably dark by the time we leave the country," Taco said. "But we have to go into the house during the prayers, when the family's all in one place. We'll go at the last prayers of the day."

"House is probably alarmed," Soho added.

Morgan shifted in her chair and caught Taco's eye.

"I have a suggestion," she said.

They all stopped talking and turned toward her. For a second her confidence drained right through her and out onto the hangar floor. Then she felt Kate's smile, reminding her that it was a good idea.

"Taco, Kate, and I leave from the airport. Kate and I are veiled, covered from head to toe. We're expected to dress like that when we go out anyway. So nobody's going to question that. We walk up to the door like friends making a house call."

Morgan paused. "With Buck, an Arab, the plan is even better."

No eyerolls so far. At least she had captured their interest.

"There will be a wall around the house, I'm sure of it. So the three of us meet you guys—Buck, The Bear and Crater —inside the wall. You guys go in and do your thing. Kate and I go with you to the room where they're holding Faiza. We are carrying an extra abaya. So when we leave the house and get into the car, Buck goes with us. We now have two men and three women. Because of the hoods and cloaks, no one can see who the women are.

"We leave that house like we're going out for a drive. When we get back to the airplane, Buck is posing as a wealthy Arab businessman who is looking at the plane. He chums up to the airport guards in Arabic. If necessary, he explains why he has brought along his wife. When we get to the plane, the woman in the Arab couple is veiled. We take off, presumably taking the Arab man for a demonstration flight."

"Then Buck goes home with you?" Taco asked.

"Yes. He'll have to."

Taco patted his chin with the tips of his fingers. A few quiet minutes passed. Morgan made fists to stop her hands from trembling. Her palms were clammy.

Finally he announced, "This is good. But what about the flight out? If we're staging a demo, we'd have to file a flight plan."

Kate was ready with the answer. "We file like we're going on a demo flight. But we don't follow it. We file a second flight plan with Universal and take right on off out of the country."

Universal Flight Service was an international flight planning service, Kate told Morgan and Ashton. By filing with them, they would be following international regulations for leaving the country. But they would not tell Dhahran air traffic control about that second flight plan.

"So you're still making a run for it?" asked Buck.

"Yeah," Kate answered. "But we're in an airplane that can do Mach ninety, not a pantywaist Land Rover on a dusty single-lane highway."

"I like this woman," said The Bear, with a smile so wide you could see way inside his mouth. He opened his jaws to let out a big bear laugh.

"What about him?" Crater asked, jerking his chin toward Ashton.

"He's not going," Morgan said.

"He's not? Then what's he doing here?" Crater said.

Before Morgan could answer, Kate put her hand on Morgan's arm.

"Morgan, I didn't tell you this before. I'm sorry," Kate said. "But there's been a little change of plans here. And, well, we're going to need Ashton."

Just then the door to the hangar slammed shut. Grady walked in.

CHAPTER FIFTY-ONE

When Morgan saw Grady, she got that funny little double heartbeat, like a hiccup deep in her chest. He looked strong and purposeful as he strode across the hangar toward them. Grady always walked like a conqueror claiming the ground under him for some distant monarch.

The guys "hey'd" and "yo'd" like they'd been expecting him all along, and Taco raised his hand in a kind of salute wave. Kate smiled at him, and he gave her hand a brief squeeze as he walked up to the table. The gesture made Morgan's little heartbeat happen again, and this time she identified the feeling as a pang of jealousy.

Was there something going on between Kate and Grady? They'd been flying across the country together in that airborne sex chamber. Maybe he'd kissed her too. And maybe it was a lot nicer to kiss someone who didn't hate your guts. Kate didn't have the same irritation with Grady as Morgan felt. She thought he was a good pilot, and that counted for a lot in her book, outweighing some of his other, less endearing qualities.

It serves me right, Morgan thought. The ugly thoughts she'd had about Grady would push anyone away. And anyway, wasn't this her scheme from the beginning? To pair Kate and Grady, to get her back into the air? She believed what they say: Be careful what you ask for; you might get it.

But Kate would have told her if there was anything going on with Grady. When it came to men, Kate and Linnie and Morgan had a vow, a lifelong covenant they'd made in college. Males did not come between them. Once, they had conducted a ritual in which they promised that at the barest hint of a triangle, the man must be sacrificed. That night, they had lit candles and declared the sisterhood sacred, and they burned dried leaves in a small clay pot to create smoke that would carry the intention heavenward. By sacrificed, they didn't mean that they would hurt him. They just meant that they'd dump him.

"I've been thinking about who we could get to fly this," Grady said. He glanced around the table at all the guys, but then his gaze stopped when he got to Morgan. "And, well, if we're gonna lease from Baylor, and it's my plane, I know it; I oughtta fly it."

He kept his gaze on Morgan until she looked away. After a second's respite, she looked back at him. At that moment, she could have walked right into his arms and never turned back.

"You're going to fly us?" she said.

He nodded. "And so's she," he said, gesturing toward Kate.

"I'm sorry to spring this on you, Morgan," Kate said. "But it wasn't for sure until now." What was this, some kind of grand entrance?

"Can you fly the Skybird?" Morgan asked her.

"She can fly anything she puts her mind to," Grady said proudly, as if he was her damned coach or something.

"After this meeting, I'm heading up to Savannah," Kate said.

"Savannah?"

"To Flight Safety. That's where I train for the Skybird," she said.

"How long?"

"Probably a month."

Kate told Morgan that she'd wanted to surprise her. And she had. To get her type rating for the Skybird, she expected to attend ground school for two weeks and then practice in the simulator for two more weeks after that, logging about twenty-five hours there. When she finished the training, she would have to pass a test and a check ride in the airplane.

In the meantime, Grady had arranged an interview for Kate with Jim Baylor. He saw no problem getting Kate hired with Baylor Aviation. As for getting her on the crew for the Saudi trip, Morgan would simply request her and Grady as the pilots.

"So you see, Morgan," Kate said. "Since I'm moving up front, we need another person on board. We really need Ashton now."

Before Morgan could protest, Kate lifted the pile of maps on the table and drew out two enormous charts. She pulled Ashton up closer to the table. "Want to plan the route?"

Taco stood back; the flight plan was the pilot's job.

The chart that would take them across the North Atlantic was written in an exclusive language of lines and numbers and peculiar symbols. It looked like someone had tried to save paper by squeezing in ten times as much information as the space would allow. But it all made sense to Kate, and Morgan thought this must be what babies feel like when adults read books to them.

For a second, Morgan envied her dear friend. She and Grady could communicate in this secret tongue. They could get into the private backyard clubhouse that Morgan was barred from entering because she didn't know the passwords. But as Kate leaned over the charts, it was with an energy Morgan had not seen in her for a long time—as if she suddenly took up more space, expanding and fully occupying the part of her that had been empty since Jack died.

Morgan realized that the envy she felt had nothing to do with Grady. What she envied was seeing Kate step back into her life, reclaim her knowledge and her power, and with it, finally answer her own calling.

"These are NAT tracks," Kate was saying to Ashton. "When you cross the Atlantic, you fly on them. They're like highways. They are changed every day."

"Because of wind and weather changes?" Ashton asked.

"Right. On these tracks you're assigned an altitude, and

everybody goes the same airspeed, eighty-two mach. So we all move at the same speed. Planes are spaced at least fifty miles apart. No one deviates from these rules. We all know there's a lot of traffic out there."

Kate explained that once a plane gets about two hundred fifty miles offshore, it is out of radar range. At that point the pilots switch to high-frequency communication, which is controlled through Aeronautical Radio Incorporated, called ARINC. Using HF frequencies, pilots report their positions and navigate using flight control centers along the way.

"Okay, we'll take off out of Kissimmee," Kate went on. She had her arm around Ashton, like a big sister. Morgan knew that Kate was showing him, at long last, the actual road that would take him to Faiza.

"To cross the ocean we follow intersections, which are basically points of latitude and longitude," Kate said. "They all have names. So, for example, we're going to trout intersection," she tapped her finger on a point on the chart, "then glibs, manna, priss, bermuda, hench. And then from there to fifty west, thirty-five north. When we get to that point, we head over to Santa Maria in the Azores."

"That's the same place you landed with Faiza the first time," Ashton said to Grady.

Morgan thought she saw Grady flinch. But he quickly recovered, ignoring Ashton's question with a comment of his own.

"In this plane, we could make it all the way without refueling. But here's what we're thinking. We stop in Santa Maria and fuel up to the gills. Then we go into Saudi with enough fuel to get us back out without refueling again."

"We can't get fuel there?" Ashton asked.

"We probably can," Grady answered. "But sometimes those guys get quirky and give you trouble about getting fuel. If that happened, we'd still have enough to get us out of the country."

"If we can fuel in Saudi, we can make it all the way home

nonstop," Kate said.

"Good plan," Taco said. "What about the return?"

"Like I said, we file an ordinary flight plan to Riyadh, but once we're in the air, we get the hell out of Dodge," Kate answered. "It's only a few miles and we're out over the Gulf."

"Hold it," The Bear said, and burst out laughing, a deep mellow laugh right from the gut. "You think that's safe and you're home free? Look here. You got Iran to the north and Iran to the east; right next to that, you got Iraq. Those are fucking no-fly zones, and if you could get through them without Saddam's guys shooting you down, then the next stop is Syria." The Bear pronounced Saddam Hussein's name like George Bush used to, rhymed with Madam.

Kate's eyes widened. "They'd shoot at us?"

"You damn betcha they would," said The Bear, still laughing.

Soho and Crater joined the fray. Easy for them to yuk it up. They were getting out by boat, or maybe by dematerializing, or whatever those guys did to get away from places.

"Shit," Grady said.

"Damn," Taco said.

"Look," said Buck. "We get above fourteen thousand, and we're out of range of the SA 7s and the SA 9s." To Morgan, he explained that these were heat-seeking missiles that were fired from the ground using handheld launchers. "But if they come after us with SAMs, we can't outrun that," he went on. "Those are surface-to-air missiles, and they can catch up with just about anything."

"You're right. North and east are out," Taco said.

"West?" Kate asked.

Taco put his boot on the table and pushed his chair back. "Yup. When we get off the ground, if the pilot's got enough guts," he winked at Grady, "we make a straight beeline across Saudi. To Egypt. That's the only way."

"Are we safe over Egypt?" Kate asked, looking at the map.

"You'll be at a high altitude," Soho said. "They won't come after you unless it's real, real important. Like if what you did would cause an international incident or something. Unless you've just made off with King Fahd's daughter, you'll be too small shit for them to chase."

"What about Israel?" she said.

"Nope," Soho said. "If they don't know you, they'll put a couple of fighters out there to escort your ass in. Egypt's better."

Standing in silence for a while, they all absorbed the plan. Morgan looked over at Ashton. His fists were clenched. He was ready to go. No one, including him, seemed to notice that they had just concocted the most blatantly outrageous scheme anyone could ever dream up.

To these guys, it was all in a day's work. Or play. To Morgan, it seemed otherworldly, standing there talking in normal tones of voice about outrunning the armies of major Middle Eastern countries. They might as well have been kidnapping the Pope.

Taco broke the silence. "It's all the more important that we leave the country peacefully, calmly, without arousing any suspicions. Soho, we've got to get that girl out of the house and not have anybody chasing us. We've got to cruise into the airport and get our butts on that plane without making a ripple. Grady, Kate, we need to make a lazy ass taxi, and mosey off like we're out for a fucking Sunday drive."

Then Taco turned to Morgan. "Your plan, about walking out with the girl and posing as Buck's wife, that's pretty smart."

Morgan smiled. Ashton reached over and squeezed her hand. "Thanks, Mom," he mouthed.

"Okay," Grady said. "We file a flight plan to Riyadh, and when they tell us to descend, we simply go on. At that point we're a third across the country. With about four hundred miles to go."

"Less than an hour," Taco said. "We head straight for

Egypt, then hang a right across the Mediterranean, before you get to Libya for chrissake. If we need fuel, we stop in Greece. Then straight for Madrid and across the pond. Or we take a right and head up toward Europe and get in between the jetliners."

"Hauling ass," Grady said.

Kate and Morgan slapped their palms together in a high five. Under her breath, in a voice that only Morgan could hear, Kate said: "Mucho grande cojones."

"Yeehaah!" Buck yelled. "Ride 'em cowboy!"

CHAPTER FIFTY-TWO

Time advanced mercilessly. It had been over five months since Faiza was abducted, and they were still weeks away from actually climbing aboard the plane that would take them around the globe to get her back.

Kate was in flight school, having turned her travel agency over to her assistant. Taco was arranging the details of both the air and ground actions, and Soho was coordinating his men, procuring the passport for the Filipina housemaid, and waiting for them to come up with a layout of the house, so they could quickly locate Faiza without a second's delay.

Taco wanted $10,000 in advance, which took Morgan's savings almost to zero. They needed an enormous amount of money. The four men at $20,000 each, added to Taco's $50,000, plus various expenses, came to $130,000.

And that money was not going to manifest from angelic intervention. Selling the jewels on the black market was not an option. They were already violating Saudi Arabia's laws. Morgan wasn't going to defy her own country's too. They would sell the jewels later, when Faiza was back in the U.S. and could sign for them.

Morgan got a second mortgage on her house. With that money and a $25,000 loan from Linnie, she had raised the additional $120,000 still due Taco. Before the next meeting Morgan would convert it to one staggering cashier's check and place it in the hands of a man she would probably never know, in a gesture of either incredible trust or incredible stupidity.

Several times during the day and evening, Meredith checked her email for news from Sheena. The plan was to order robes and veils from Sheena's internet catalog. Presumably, if the underground could get a map of the house, it would arrive within the folds of the cloaks and veils.

Ashton and Morgan took charge of applications for visas, which required a formal invitation from the client who wanted to buy a Skybird. And Grady's friend, the Wolfman, had lined up a sheik who was interested in buying a jet. It amazed Morgan that they could find an individual who could pay for a forty-million-dollar airplane, but Grady said that was pocket change to a lot of those guys over there.

Morgan didn't talk with Grady often, but she thought about him a lot. And when she did hear his voice on the phone, she would feel those surges in her gut, just as she felt when he was kissing her.

Several times she started to ask Grady why he had changed his mind, but the question always got diverted shortly before it became an official utterance. Morgan was not sure why she was so hesitant to bring it up. Maybe she was afraid he would change his mind back. She felt more confident about this mission with him and Kate teamed up the way they were.

To keep their spirits up, Ashton and Morgan studied about Saudi Arabia. Her walls began to bloom with visuals, the most prominent a huge road map of the country, written in Arabic, a lovely language whose letters looked as if they were written to music.

They tacked up a Saudi Arabian calendar and a photo of the mountains that lined the western coastline, which Ashton thought looked like the California coastline near Cambria. They found a photo of a night scene of an oil refinery in Jubail, a city on the Persian Gulf. It looked like a skyline made of diamonds.

One morning Morgan woke up and saw that Ashton had taped a picture of Faiza in their collage, and below it a catalog photo of the Skybird V, poised over a glistening gold ocean. In the photo Faiza was smiling into the sun, her lush dark hair blown across her face as if she was wearing a veil. Her eyes sparkled through the dark strands.

Morgan was beginning to like this mysterious country they were headed to, and she realized how little she knew about it. For example, Mecca, the holy city that Muslims all over the world faced for daily prayers, was in Saudi Arabia. One of the tenets of Islam, she learned, was that all devotees must make a pilgrimage, called a hajj, to Mecca once in their life. Dressed alike in white robes, they streamed into Mecca hundreds of thousands at a time, by bus and train and camel, and in airplanes that landed at a special terminal reserved for pilgrims. Rich and poor, women and men, alongside each other, carrying the sick on stretchers, they packed themselves into the Holy Mosque. The Holy Mosque was a huge ancient stadium with rows of carved arches that look like the walls of a beehive.

At 830,000 square miles, Saudi Arabia was about the size of the United States from the East Coast to the Mississippi River. In 2000, it had fifteen million people, fewer than the state of New York. Basically, the country was one giant desert —possibly the driest country in the world. The amount of rainfall per year might not hit double digits. Some places in Saudi Arabia hadn't had rain in ten years.

In the southeast interior was the Rub al-Khali, which meant Empty Quarter, a two-hundred-fifty-square-mile area that was the largest sand desert in the world. On the east coast, on the Persian Gulf, a sand and gravel plain had a motherlode of oil under it.

Oil was discovered in Saudi Arabia in the 1930s. Major oil production began in 1946. The rest was the history of incredible overnight wealth, power, and world influence. In less than fifty years, a country that had existed in nomadic isolation was suddenly rolling in dough and prominence, strewn with oil refineries and airports and crisscrossed by television and high tech communication systems.

When individuals are plunged into such rapid growth —say, when someone wins the lottery—they feel disoriented, thought Morgan. Wouldn't a culture share a similar dissonance? With a foot in the future and one hand desperately clutching any thread to the past, it seemed to her there must be tremendous fear there, fear that the old traditions will be sacrificed to progress, fear that Islam will be lost. No wonder they clung to their traditional ways, she reflected—even when they seemed backward to the West.

She found Saudi Arabia intriguing, like the exotic spices and frankincense and myrrh that were traded there centuries ago. She felt a deep and very old connection to this place and to the people in it, a deja vu feeling of some dark, ancestral secret. As if everyone everywhere shared a piece of ancient history from those parched desert sands.

The Islamic calendar was not the same as the American one, which is based on how long it takes for the Earth to revolve around the sun. Theirs, which begins on the day the prophet Muhammed led followers out of Mecca, thus marking the beginnings of Islam, was based on a lunar year. One lunar month contained twenty-nine days and some odd hours. Each Islamic year started ten or eleven days earlier than the previous year, and the months were not coordinated with seasons.

The ninth month was Ramadan, during which Muslims abstained from eating, drinking, and sex from dawn to sunset. Though there were modifications for people who are weak or sick, this was an incredibly rigorous devotion, the purpose of which was to bring people closer to Allah through the exercise of self-discipline and self-control.

This year, Ramadan would start on December 8. During that holy time the sheik who wanted to buy the Skybird would refuse to conduct business.

But Ramadan was the least of their worries. They needed to get there long before that. If Faiza was accurate about when she became pregnant, she would be in her seventh month right now. If she was still pregnant.

Morgan realized they would have to get Faiza by the first of November. Otherwise it might be too late. If it wasn't already.

*   *   *

That night Morgan could not sleep. There was something on her mind that she couldn't shake, and there was no one she could talk to about it. But she had to know.

Was it even possible for a pregnancy to sustain itself in those horrible conditions? The darkness. The stress. Whatever the degree of nutritional and sleep deprivation? What if they were all in some sort of la-la land, imagining that Faiza was happily growing a baby bump and all they had to do was get to her on time?

Morgan found herself digging through boxes of old notes and notebooks. It took hours, and it was almost dawn before she found what she was looking for. The name and number of a woman she had interviewed several years before.

June was a midwife at a birthing center whom Morgan had featured in a story about alternative childbirth. At the time, something about June struck her. She'd felt warmth and authenticity, but also don't-mess-with-me energy in this woman who had brought hundreds of babies into the world outside the medical mainstream, and who seemed to know just about everything about moms and babies. And, most important, a woman Morgan sensed she could trust completely.

"Hi, I remember you," June said when Morgan called first thing the next morning. "You wrote a good story. How have you been?"

"Do you have a minute to spare?" Morgan asked.

"Of course," June said. "I'm actually off today, unless someone goes into labor early."

As succinctly as she could, Morgan told June the whole story. And when she finished, she asked, "Is there any possibility that a pregnancy could survive such horrendous conditions?"

June did not answer right away. Morgan waited in the silence. She was asking a lot and she knew it.

After a few minutes, June said, "First of all, I know about

something about Sharia law, and what your friend has done is a complete betrayal of family and religion and everything. She is in deep trouble. They will kill her. You are right to try to get her out."

Morgan shuddered.

Then June said, "But their love is stronger than all that."

"And the baby?" Morgan asked.

"This is a great love story," June said. "This girl is deeply in love. She knows your son is coming for her. She knows that he will do anything to save her. She knows that he will never give up. She knows that he will die trying to save her."

"So the baby can survive?" Morgan asked.

"Yes," June said emphatically. "She knows your son is coming, and that keeps her alive and her baby alive. She is that strong. The baby is that strong. They can both live."

CHAPTER FIFTY-THREE

Meredith came to Morgan's for a weekend.

She brought some good news. Maybe.

"The informant, whoever that is, has told Sheena that Faiza is no longer in the Woman's Room," Meredith announced the moment she arrived.

"What?" Ashton nearly shouted.

"The information is really fractured," Meredith said, "but from what I can decipher, they found out she is pregnant and have moved her to another secure room in the house."

Morgan blinked. "You mean they have just noticed this now?"

"It sounds as if this happened some time back," Meredith said, "like maybe even months. How they figured it out, who knows? But Faiza is also being seen by a female doctor. For whatever it's worth, it sounds like she is getting prenatal care."

Was that possible? It seemed too much to hope for, but truth be told, Morgan had been silently very worried about how anyone could sustain a pregnancy under that level of stress and in a dark tomb. And even if she'd been set free from the Woman's Room for now, chances were good that she would still be either back in that room or killed when the baby was born.

"We have get there as soon as we can," Morgan said. She walked over the calendar on the wall and opened a thick red marker.

"November tenth," she announced. She circled the date. "We go."

She turned to Meredith. "Now let's get to those catalogs. We need to order some coverings, and fast."

She and Meredith settled in front of the computer.

"It's so dissonant, Mom," Meredith said. "Here we are, on the internet, reading descriptions of styles and designs like it's a Spiegel catalog. But the whole concept is something out of the sixth century." Meredith clicked on a page.

"Look at this one." She read aloud: "This abaya, made of a silky synthetic, falls over the head and shoulders, and opens down the front with Velcro closures. For more closure in the front, see style number two."

Another picture showed several styles of burqa, black hoods with small thin openings for eyes. The caption said: "These are 100 percent cotton and cover the face completely, leaving only the eyes showing." The photo looked like someone peeking out of the slit in a bunker. Another style, called a nijab, was made of two layers of black. The top layer could be lifted up, to uncover the eyes if desired.

One design featured cuffs on the sleeves, so the woman could stick her hands out and "still be concealed" without having to wear long sleeves underneath. "Colors and prints available. Hand wash or machine wash cold."

In all the pictures, the women's faces, when uncovered by clothing, were blanked out by white ovals.

"But now, look at this," Meredith said.

In her daughter's blue eyes, Morgan saw the impish sparkle she used to get when she was small, right before she was going to play a trick on someone, or tell a joke. Meredith was such a smart and clever little kid, she thought, and had life pretty well figured out by the time she could string the words together to talk about it. Once, when she was not yet three, she came up with this joke: "What kind of bird has its wings on the bottom?" Answer: "One that flies upside down."

Meredith handed Morgan a printed catalog she recognized from a pile she'd meant to discard. It was the summer swimsuit edition from Victoria's Secret. The cover was dominated by a close-up of enormous cleavage, and strewn across the pages, an array of excruciatingly thin, airbrushed models posed with legs spread, backs arched, breasts thrust forward.

Morgan knew this catalog well, because she surreptitiously ordered bathing suits from them every year. She'd also written articles protesting how these magazines and advertisements created an impossible standard of beauty, a standard that was putting seven-year-olds on diets and sending an epidemic number of college women into bathrooms to throw up their lunches. She'd also heard many stories of beautiful young women getting breast implants for graduation presents from college or even high school.

The photos of Saudi women showed women how to cover. The photos of American women showed them how to strip. Their models looked out from behind heavy black cloaks with their faces blanked. The American woman looked out from behind silicone breasts and perfect photo-enhanced bare skin.

Both sets of images were telling women how they were expected to appear. And the orders, whether direct or implicit, came from men.

"They're kept covered, we're kept naked," Meredith said. "Who's the most oppressed?"

*   *   *

Dowd had business in Florida that weekend, and Morgan invited him to join them for dinner, something she did on the rare occasions when all four found themselves in the same geographical locale. They were, after all, still a family and inexorably bound together forever. They often shared laughs and memories, but always from a pale, safe place, a little more than casual but stopping short of intimate.

As soon as Dowd walked in the door, Morgan knew that the invitation was a mistake. The walls were plastered with the Saudi Arabian paraphernalia Ashton and she had collected, and the scene looked like a strategy room at the Pentagon. He knew something was up, and he was relentless until he pried it out of Ashton.

Then he blew up. Well, Dowd's version of a blowup. Coldly calm. Courteous. Blaming Morgan.

He fumed silently until he could get Morgan alone, outside.

"This is insane," he said. "How could you let it get this far?"

"Dowd, what else would you want me to do?" Morgan asked. Wrong question, of course.

"I told you before not to get his hopes up. And now you've launched a commando raid!"

"It's not a commando raid," Morgan said.

"I don't know what the hell else you'd call it," he said.

It's not a raid," Morgan said. "It's a well-planned rescue mission. And we've found some good, er, men to head it up."

"Who, for example?" Dowd demanded.

"I can't tell you."

"Oh, I get it," he sneered. "Top secret. James Bond. And you're going to storm in there and kidnap one of their citizens."

"She's a hostage," Morgan said. This debate sounded painfully familiar. She had already had it with herself a hundred times. Now the voice was Dowd's, parroting her own internal censor.

"Look," she went on, "there are thousands of children who've been abducted to foreign countries during custody disputes. In those cases, the parent in the United States has legal custody, the child is a U.S. citizen, and there is an arrest warrant out for the parent who's taken the child. And still the other parent can't get them back. A lot of countries, like Saudi Arabia, don't have extradition treaties with us. And the ones that have them don't honor them."

Morgan explained that a few years before, the U.S. had signed the Hague treaty, an international agreement that requires that children who have been wrongfully removed from their home must be returned. But many countries frequently violated that treaty, and Saudi Arabia didn't even sign it.

"It's all paper and ink if no one will enforce it," she said. "Dowd, if we can't get help for children who are United States citizens, there's not a prayer for Faiza."

"Aren't you making a lot of assumptions? How do you know she wants to get out?"

"I know," Morgan said.

"What, you've talked to her? And she's asked you to come and get her?" That was a rhetorical question, which Dowd often used when he wanted to be extra confrontational.

"I know. No one would choose to be locked up that way, or to be killed."

Dowd scowled. "You think you can decide what's right and what's wrong for someone else. You don't know that country. And you don't know her. Maybe when she got there, she assimilated back into her culture and she wants to stay there. The apple doesn't fall far from the tree, you know. She's an Arab woman, and maybe her life there is okay with her. What right do you have to interfere?"

"I don't know, maybe none," Morgan said, weary from the argument.

"What are you trying to prove, Morgan?" Dowd said. "That you've got the magic super-mother solution to everything?"

She shook her head and turned to walk inside. He caught her arm.

"It's guilt, isn't it?" he said. "You still feel guilty for walking out. You know how much you hurt him. And you want to make it up."

"That's bullshit, Dowd. It's you who's handing out the guilt trips."

"Look, Morgan, let's not dig up old issues," he said. As if she was the one who'd started it. She wanted to wring his neck, but it would have slipped right out of her grasp.

"You are putting Ashton's life at risk," Dowd said. "I can't allow that."

"Ashton is making his own decisions here," Morgan said.

"Oh, come on. You know that's not true. He looks up to you and thinks you have all this almighty power," Dowd said.

"This isn't about power, Dowd," Morgan said. "This is about saving Faiza's life."

"I care just as much as you do about Faiza," he said. "And I'm heartbroken about what's happened. But do you have any idea what would happen to you if you got caught?"

"I know it's dangerous," she said.

"Dangerous? Dangerous doesn't even touch it. Morgan, there was a special Congressional Human Rights Caucus in Washington recently, and a bunch of women testified about being in Saudi Arabian prisons. One was a Canadian, who was dragged from a shop by the religious police, searched, and thrown in jail. They kept her locked up and wouldn't let her call anyone. There was no water, no food. They tried to get her to sign confessions that she couldn't read because they were written in Arabic. She had the guts to refuse. She was one of the lucky ones. Another woman got sentenced to sixty lashes. She's disfigured."

The stories made Morgan shudder. And she began to doubt herself. Maybe he was right. Maybe she was acting out of guilt. Or from some exaggerated sense of mother omnipotence.

How did Dowd do it? He could slither inside, get to that place where she held her self-confidence, and sink his teeth in faster than a snake in a rabbit bed.

"That's why we need your help, Dad," said Ashton. He had been standing in the doorway.

Dowd covered his surprise that Ashton had overheard them. "You've got to call this off," he said.

"We're not calling it off," Ashton said. "Even if Mom did, I wouldn't. I'm going over there to get Faiza."

"Well, it's obviously two to one," Dowd said snidely. "Or

probably three to one. I assume Meredith is in on this too."

"She's not going," Morgan said, without explanation.

"How you can help, Dad, is to be our contact here in the United States. So if we disappear, there is someone on the outside who can tell the State Department."

"Oh, for god's sake, Ashton," Dowd said. "Stop talking like that."

"No, listen," Ashton said. "Meredith will know everything. But we need someone with a lot of clout in the government."

"You do know a lot of people, Dowd," Morgan added.

"I told you what the State Department said about all this. They aren't interested."

"But if we were arrested . . ."

"Stop it, son. You're not going to get arrested because you're not going."

As Morgan stood facing Dowd, his back to the living room, she saw Meredith quietly taking down the calendar with the red-circled date.

"Dowd, please," Morgan tried again. "We need help. It's help you can give us."

"The best way I can help you is to get you to stop," Dowd said. "And I'll do everything in my power." He turned to face Morgan. His eyes were as gray and unyielding as steel.

"Call it off."

CHAPTER FIFTY-FOUR

"You look different," Morgan told Kate, as she stepped, smiling, out of her car in Morgan's driveway. "Your face is, I don't know, lighter, softer."

"I'm having a lot of fun," she said.

Kate had dropped by to spend a couple of days on her way home from flight school in Savannah. As Grady had predicted, she had passed her flight check with ease and was now rated to fly the Skybird.

"Just like that?" Morgan said.

"And without my penis," she shot back, grinning.

"What are you going to do when you get back to California?" Morgan asked her.

"I'll fly for Baylor for a while, until we go, and after that I don't know," she said.

"Yeah, you do."

"Maybe I do," she said. "You know, Morgan, what's coming back are some of the smallest things about flying. Remember how cloudy the winters were in Indiana? Like the sky was aching to snow but couldn't quite get the right components together? So this gray-white aura would hang there, for weeks at a time sometimes."

"I remember."

"But you could get in an airplane and get above it, and see the sunlight again. And we'd go up and break through that mush and come out on the top, and the light would be so bright and so warm and we'd come back and tell everyone: 'We found the sun and it's still shining.'"

Kate hugged the kids, and the four made spaghetti and salad, and while they cooked, downed a very good Chianti. After dinner they went to the beach and all ploughed out into the water in their clothes, splashing Ashton until he was engulfed under a wall of water. It was a celebration of his healing, Kate announced, and an initiation back into the sea.

"To a future of surfing," Kate shouted, dousing him until he sputtered for mercy.

Meredith and Ashton went inside to change into dry clothes, and Kate and Morgan sat on the sand.

"Kate, do you think I really hurt the kids when I left?" Morgan asked.

"So, Dowd was here, huh?" she said.

"How'd you know?"

She shrugged. "You always get guilty when Dowd's around."

Morgan sighed.

"All kids are hurt by divorce," Kate said. "Yours included. You can't change that, Morgan. But what you can change is how you think about it. Children get hurt in lots of ways, and that's only one of them. Instead of trying to make that fact go away, why don't you change what you think about it?"

"I don't understand."

"Tell yourself, okay, I hurt them. And Dowd hurt them. And things didn't turn out like we promised ourselves, promised them. Can you allow that to be a fact, without making a judgment about it?"

Morgan looked at her questioningly.

"Try this," she said. "Let's say a huge storm comes up and an enormous tidal wave slams into this beach and covers your house. Your house is ruined, your plans are ruined, and your whole life changes. All because of the weather. You could really get angry at the weather. It would become a bad thing. But weather isn't bad or good. It's just the weather. Like waves.

They aren't good or bad, they're just waves. What makes them bad or good is our idea about them."

Kate scooped a handful of sand and sprinkled it over her toes as if she was dusting powdered sugar onto a pound cake.

"Morgan, what would your divorce be if you didn't have an idea about it?"

"You mean, stop judging Dowd?" Morgan asked.

"Yeah. And yourself."

"Hmm," Morgan said. "Maybe."

"Maybe's good." She laughed.

"Speaking of Dowd, he threatened to try to stop us."

"What could he do?" Kate asked.

"I don't know. Blow the whistle on us? Stop the flight?"

"He can't," Kate said. "When we leave here, all we're doing is taking off in an airplane. Nothing illegal about that."

"But it makes me nervous."

"Well, he must be worried as hell," she said. "And frankly, I don't think Dowd would do anything that would jeopardize Ashton, or you for that matter."

Suddenly Morgan laughed.

"What's so funny?" Kate asked.

"I was thinking, What would Dowd be like if I didn't have an idea about him?"

"Here's one," Kate said. "What would Grady be like if you stopped judging him?"

Morgan thought for a moment. "Probably still be an asshole."

*   *   *

Kate was ready to go back to California, and Ashton booked the same flight so he could travel with her. He needed to check on his apartment and take care of mail and bills. He was also meeting with Grady to put together a uniform for the trip. Grady thought Ashton should pose as a flight engineer, because anything else would look too suspicious. And with his blond surfer hair, he needed to wear a hat to look a little less conspicuous in that land of dark-haired men. So Ashton would put on the uniform hat anytime they left the plane.

Most important, Ashton was going to retrieve Faiza's passport from the safe deposit box. He also planned to pick out a few of her clothes to bring along on the mission. At the end of the spring term, Faiza had lost her room in the dormitory and Ashton had arranged to pack up her belongings and bring them to his apartment, where they waited in a wall of heavy boxes along one side of the living room.

"Um, aren't the clothes going to be a little small?" Meredith asked.

"I'll look for some loose ones," Ashton said. They all laughed.

"What is the proper attire for civilian raids on totalitarian countries?" Kate wondered.

"Well, basic black for women," Morgan said.

"I was talking about later," she said.

"Oh, I see. Then you'd be interested in our newest line of 'après-rescue wear,'" Meredith said, mimicking a French accent. She twirled toward Morgan's closet, pulled a light white robe from a hook, and slid into it, tying it with a long silk scarf.

"Zee soft lines and loose belt are paarrrrfect for zee relaxing flight home. Add a string of pearls, and thees ensemble screams out, I'm free, I'm free!"

"Nice feminism," Ashton said wryly. "We're planning this wild-ass mission, and you three are worrying about what to wear."

"Oh, dahhling," Meredith said, putting her hand on Ashton's neck and leaning coquettishly into him. "Zee clothes, zay make or break zee mish-awn."

*   *   *

The evening after everyone left, the space inside Morgan's house seemed to have holes in it, big empty spots that had not been there before. She was accustomed to living alone and loved it much of the time, but now that the space had been peopled with loved ones, their absence made her feel especially alone. It was as if their leaving had sucked some of the energy out, like a reverse wind.

There was plenty to do to keep busy. Besides the cleaning and shopping, she had an article due in three days. It was a profile of a woman plumber who had sued a whole bunch of suppliers for price fixing, on the grounds of gender discrimination. This woman had wanted to be a plumber from the time she was a toddler with a plastic Fisher-Price wrench, pretending to fix leaky pipes for her mother, a single mom. When she got old enough, she became an apprentice and eventually earned all the required certification, but most of the men never accepted her, and she was constantly contending with harassment and other nasty stuff.

Morgan couldn't imagine why anyone would want to be a plumber, but this lady was a real pistol. She now had her own small company, having given up on working for anyone else. It was an interesting enough story.

She sat down at the computer, and then got up again. The light wasn't right. And it was hot outside. So she shut the windows and turned on the air conditioner. As she was pulling the sliding glass doors closed, she noticed the moon was almost full. The light reflecting on the surface of the water glittered in a platinum path that quivered all the way out to the dark horizon. When she was a little girl, she thought a person could surely step right out on that silvery walkway and stroll right on out to sea, or beyond. And why not? It looked solid enough.

Morgan put some discs in the CD player and lit a candle. She turned on a favorite Eagles album, and the song that was playing was entitled "Love Will Keep Us Alive." She loved this song. It was this dreamy little piece, with lyrics like: "I was standing all alone against the world outside. You were searching for a place to hide. Now I've found you, there's no more emptiness inside."

She was singing along with a part that said: "I would die for you, climb the highest mountain. Baby, there's nothing I wouldn't do."

At that moment, there was a light tap on the door. Then another. Morgan drifted toward it, still humming, and opened it.

"I was in the neighborhood," Grady said, shrugging.

"How did you find my house?"

"Kate gave me directions," he said. "It's a layover. I only have a couple of hours."

He was still standing in the open door, and Morgan couldn't do anything but gaze at him. There was something she was supposed to do, like ask him to come in, or look surprised and wonder aloud why Kate didn't tell her. But she said nothing. Neither did he. He took her hand and drew her outside, and then held the door and let it gently close behind them.

Without a word, he led her down the wooden steps. Holding onto his hand, she followed his silhouette through the darkness around the house toward the beach. Never once did she have the urge to speak, or to ask him why he was here.

When they moved into the moonlight, he gazed back at her with eyes so full of passion and so dedicated to looking at her, she thought for a moment that she was seeing him for the first time. He paused for an instant, as if to give her a chance to reconsider, but she stepped up alongside him and they continued on to the edge of the water.

The sea was calm, with waves barely splashing up and over each other, and Grady drew Morgan into his arms. Starting with tender little nibbles, he kissed her like he had the first day she met him, soft and sweet, then deeper and stronger and more passionate as she relaxed into his arms. They kissed for a long time, maybe hours, maybe forever, and Morgan wished they never would stop.

Then he took her hand again and drew her out into the water. It was chilly, but seemed to get warmer around where they stood facing each other. As if he was trying to see how very slowly he could move, he gently lifted her shirt over her head and unfastened her bra and dropped them into the waist-deep water. Her shorts were clinging to her skin, but he slid them off tenderly, as if they were made of the most delicate lace. He began to touch her all over, slowly, slowly, as though he didn't want to miss a single inch. He made her feel as if he had never before in his life seen or touched a woman.

Morgan's clothes drifted aimlessly toward shore, and soon his with them, and they sank into the water. Against his body, her skin felt like precious silk.

It is true, she thought, what she'd believed as a child about the reflection on the water. Though she would never be sure, she thought she felt something under them, holding them up, and without ever speaking a word, they made love right on top of that shimmering ribbon of moonlight.

CHAPTER FIFTY-FIVE

The day after Grady's surprise visit, Morgan met an old reporter friend, Jacob Stoll, for lunch. The last time Morgan had seen Jacob, his hair was barely frosted with streaks of gray. Now, he was almost completely silver-white, and it looked good. He had aged, with more creases around his eyes and neck, but overall he actually looked younger. And definitely happier.

When they'd worked together at the *Dispatch*, they ate lunch together almost every day. This felt like old times, a sweet little slice of déjà vu, one of the few memories of the *Dispatch* that Morgan cared to revisit.

Jacob was a salty old investigative reporter, and when Morgan first came to the *Dispatch*, he'd taught her just about everything she would later know about newspaper writing. He could smell a rat a mile away, and he'd shown her how to cull through public records and virtually reconstruct a person's whole life.

Sitting in front of a computer screen for hours, Jacob could sort through records of property sales and traffic citations and divorce files and learn more about a person than you could learn in a hundred interviews. And in that profile, he could get inside someone's personality, deduce their likes and dislikes, how they treated their friends and family, where they might have slipped up, where they might be telling lies. He was ruthlessly ethical, however, and he never drew hasty conclusions or stuck anyone into a bad box unless he could back up every single allegation.

Morgan had lost track of him over the past couple of

years, but heard that he was now working for a television station. If that was true, it was even better, she thought. Television would be the best medium for getting their story into the public light.

"Do you know anyone in the press?" Larry Edwards had asked her.

"Of course."

"I mean, someone you can really trust," he said.

"Okay, that narrows the field. But yes, I know someone," she told him.

"A television crew filming your arrival would be ideal," Larry said. "You come off the plane with that young pregnant woman who was violently kidnapped out of her fiancé's arms and ask for asylum from the United States of America, right on camera."

"I can set that up, Larry," Morgan said. Later that day, she called Jacob and asked him to meet her.

"I love television," Jacob Stoll was saying. "It's a different scene and a crazy pace, but bottom line? You do the same stories in the same way; you just frame them differently. And it's great to have visuals to tell the story. You know I was never very good with words."

True, Jacob's brilliance was in the investigation, but he often lagged when it came time to sit down and make the story come alive at the keyboard.

"It suits you, Jake," Morgan said. "I wish I could see some of your stuff." The broadcast area where he worked was in a city seventy miles from where she lived, so she did not get his station's news.

"I'd say I'll send you some tapes, but you know how that goes." He smiled. "I probably won't."

Morgan understood. So many times readers called her and asked for copies of a story. She always promised to send them one. And rarely did. Later, she stopped promising and instead said she would "try" to send them one. That didn't happen either.

At the *Dispatch*, once a story rolled off the press you were already on to the next one with hardly a backward glance. Editors were like hungry little puppies, begging and sniffing around under the table mere seconds after they'd polished off a huge bowl of kibble. Don't they ever get full? the reporters would ask. No, and they're not cute, either.

Morgan told Jacob the whole story and, in the strictest of confidence, the plans to get Faiza out of Saudi Arabia. He polished off a club sandwich as she talked, and then pushed the plate aside and folded his hands, rubbing his thumbs together. She remembered it was the way he thought something through; so she waited. He stared at his hands, then shaking his head, looked up at her.

"Geez-us, Morgan. This is really dangerous," he said. "And so goddamm like you." He laughed. "Couldn't you stay home and write about it?"

"Jake, you know this is a good story," Morgan said.

"Shit, it's a great story," he said. "But there's a lot of good stories around."

Morgan picked a slice of carrot from her salad and wiggled it in front of his face. "National news. ABC. NBC. CNN. You know it," she sang. "And you want it."

"Sure. And I want to help you," he said. "But I have to tell you, if you get caught over there—shit, Morgan, no one can help you. Their justice system is—well, I'm not saying there isn't a system. But to a Western mind, it looks like they make it up as they go along. You can't get anywhere.

"First of all, the law is Islam, and none of you are Muslim; so what you say in court isn't even regarded as reliable. Second, those people cut off right hands for stealing a bag of dates. What do you think they do when you steal one of their women? And third, our American consulate over there won't be able to do jackshit, they're like geldings. And fourth . . . "

"Fourth?"

"And fourth, the Saudis don't give a camel's hump what CNN or anybody else says." Jacob leaned back and folded his arms across his chest.

He was her mentor and like a big brother, always pulling her back from the edge of somewhere, trying to keep her from going too far. He used to say that she could really write herself into trouble, but she always somehow managed to write herself back out again. Jacob was a serious fellow, and Morgan often thought her presence in his life allowed him to lighten up. Once they'd adored each other, and she could see that feeling still in his eyes.

"Morgan, I'll be there when you guys get off the plane, and I won't tell anyone about the story until I have word that you are into safe airspace. Can you call me from the plane?"

"You ought to see this plane. I can call you, fax you, probably email you," Morgan said. "And Jacob, I do appreciate how worried you are about this. But you need to stop thinking that way. There's some kind of unwritten rule with these spy guys. They don't talk much about what-ifs. We have backup plans and contingencies and stuff, but we don't dwell on what might happen if anything goes wrong. We assume it won't."

"That's denial," Jacob said.

"Maybe," she said. "But why focus energy on the danger? Won't that give it more power?"

He smiled.

"And anyway, you'll never let me rot in a Saudi jail."

"No. But it's gonna cost you some of your best racing camels."

Jacob opened a small notebook and flipped through pages littered with scribbles illegible except to him. He came to a blank page and jotted the date on the top, with the initials "MF." For the next hour he asked questions and listened as Morgan gave him full details of the story up to now.

Background complete, Jacob closed the notebook. Morgan told him she would call him when they were ready to leave, and if she couldn't reach him in person, she would leave a message with the code phrase: "The reception is on . . ." with the date and time of their departure. He would stand by for the next week, hopefully hearing from her within a few days.

After Grady had left her house the night before, in the brief exchange where they actually used the spoken word, he told her that Taco wanted to try to get in and out of Saudi in two days, three at the most. Taco had decided that the advantage they would gain by lingering and becoming a familiar part of the scenery was outweighed by the risk of arousing suspicion.

The arrangements to demo the plane to a sheik from Dhahran were nearly in place, and the required sponsorship letters were on their way to the Wolfman. For the business visas they needed, they had to be sponsored by a Saudi. That individual then became responsible for their conduct while they were in the country. Morgan hoped their sheik wouldn't get into too much trouble, but if he could buy a forty-million-dollar airplane, he could no doubt get himself out of the little pickle they were going to leave him in.

So, Morgan told Jacob, if the sheik showed up on time, they would be finished with their official business on the first day. If he showed up that day. That was the unknown. In Saudi, Taco had told her, business is not rushed, and people rarely arrived on time for appointments. Not just hours late, but sometimes days late. It was Bedouin standard time. Schedules were made to be broken, so they had to be prepared to wait patiently for the sheik to take it upon himself to mosey over. After that, they would quickly fabricate the second demo to a second businessman, played by Buck, and get the heck out of there.

"How soon will you be leaving?" Jacob asked.

"Within three weeks." The simple fact of saying that made the skin on her arms tingle. She was scared. No question about it.

"One more thing," she said as they were leaving the restaurant. She took Jacob's notebook and slipped the pen out of his shirt pocket.

"This is my daughter Meredith's phone number. If anything, well, if anything happens, stay in touch with her. She's the only person here who knows the whole thing. And . . ."

"I understand," Jacob said. "You know, Morgan, you've got . . ."

"Cojones?" She laughed.

"Whatever," he said. "You know something else?"

"What?"

"Goddd-dammm! I wish I were going with you."

CHAPTER FIFTY-SIX

The date was set, in three weeks: November 10. Morgan rarely talked to Kate or Grady, perhaps because they all felt that there was no more to talk about. They all just wanted to get on with the act of doing it.

Kate was flying for Baylor and trying to get as many hours as possible in the Skybird. Grady was finalizing the arrangements for the meeting with the airplane-buying sheik.

The application for visas to obtain entry into Saudi Arabia was complicated, but they had all received visas under the auspices of being part of the sales crew. Since they could not pose as Atlantic Aeronautical Corporation, they presented themselves as representing a private owner, which was of course not true. The plane was not theirs to sell, and they had to hope no one would find that out until it was all over. The Wolfman told the sheik that the plane was owned by a silent consortium, and everyone hoped this story would hold for as long as needed.

Morgan put together a uniform that would pass as a flight attendant, loose navy blue pants, white blouse, and navy blazer in a cotton blend that she hoped would be the right weight for warm days and cool nights. Because they were going in November, they might be spared the scorching, oppressive summer heat characteristic of the desert country. Everyone else would be dressing in similar garb, pilot and crew uniforms.

Off duty, they planned to pack modest, traditional clothes. The men would dress conservatively, but they weren't expected to adopt the Arab men's costume of thobes and headdresses. In fact, it was considered inappropriate for Western men to try to imitate Arabs.

The women, on the other hand, would be expected to keep as much of their bodies covered as possible. Short skirts and tight slacks, in fact anything tight, would be a no-no. And if they ventured out on the street, they didn't want to invite the harassment of the religious police, who might come over and yell at them or bonk them with a stick if they showed too much leg.

Morgan found some long black pants made of a lightweight synthetic. They tied at the waist with wide legs that fell loosely to the floor and looked almost like a long skirt. To be on the safe side and to avoid attracting any unnecessary attention, she and Kate decided to wear an abaya whenever they were out in public.

Meredith had received the abayas and veils she'd ordered from Sheena, and inside, as they had hoped, a pencil sketch of the inside the house. It was drawn on a half sheet of a light brown, coarse-textured paper. Meredith made copies and sent one to Taco by overnight mail.

It was spooky, Morgan thought, holding in her hand a picture of the house where Faiza was being held. The sketch was rough, one outline for the first floor and another for the second floor, with a small drawing in the corner showing the house from the front. There were no windows drawn on that picture, only a front door.

It looked as if there were about two dozen rooms. The drawing gave no indication of what those rooms were for, but a huge area in the middle of the house on both stories was probably an open courtyard typical of Arab homes. On the right corner of the second story, a section that jutted out from the main wall was marked with an "x." That had to be the room where they were keeping Faiza. But it didn't conform to the outer walls of the house. A balcony?

They looked closer at the front view. There was a dome on the top front of the house, probably a mosque-like decoration, and what appeared to be wide pillar-like extensions sticking up at each corner of the roof. The extensions, likely ornamental, looked big enough to be small rooms, and one corresponded to the section with the "x."

That meant the room where Faiza was being held was actually on the third floor, a special section on the top right rear corner of the roof, like a tower.

Like Rapunzel. Only this was no fairy tale, Morgan thought.

*   *   *

Morgan had not been on the beach for over a week, and she hadn't been swimming since the night Grady strolled up to her door and, just as effortlessly, into her body.

One morning she decided to go out and walk and walk and walk until she had sorted out her tangle of conflicting feelings. Her mind wanted a category for all this, a slot to tuck Grady safely into, a summary paragraph to close the chapter and put it all behind her.

But after a few miles that yielded no answers, she turned back and soon found herself in the water at the place where Grady and she had made love, going over and over it in her mind, basking in every delicious detail she could remember.

As Morgan walked back to the house, she studied the beach at her feet, wondering like a lovesick teenager if by any chance their footprints were still imprinted in the sand. So she didn't notice until she came upstairs that she had a visitor.

"Linnie!"

Linnie was sitting in a rocking chair out on the deck, a glass of iced tea in her hand. She set it down and jumped up to hug Morgan. Her hand was cold on her back.

"Where did you come from?" Though her bathing suit was still dripping, Morgan flung her arms around her friend. "I'm getting you wet," she said.

"That's okay. I saw you out there and almost jumped in with you, clothes and all," Linnie answered. "But you looked like you were in deep thought."

"More like deep doo-doo," Morgan said.

"Ewww," Linnie crooned. "Sounds like something about boys."

"Maybe a new book for you: 'Dangerous Currents.' Or 'Swim At Your Own Risk.'"

"I want to hear all about that. But first, we need to talk."

"Yeah, really. This is a great surprise. But what brings you here?" Morgan asked.

"I was in Orlando for a book signing. So I stayed over last night and rented a car and drove here this morning."

"Does Hal know you're here?" Linnie sat back down, and Morgan wrapped herself in her towel and pulled a chair closer.

"Yes, and that doesn't matter anymore," Linnie said, pausing for that to sink in.

"You've left Hal?" Morgan said, shocked.

"Not exactly," she said.

"He found out about your last trip over here," Morgan guessed. "And you had a huge fight."

"No. That's not it. I haven't left him in a physical way. But I've made a big shift."

"What happened?"

Linnie leaned back in the chair, hugging her knees.

"Morgan, it's like I've been a bird in a cage. Oh, it's a damn pretty cage. It has lovely, slender bamboo bars and flowering ivy woven through the top. I climbed into it voluntarily and stayed there voluntarily. Part of me was convinced that it was a nice place to be, and certainly a safe one. Another part of me thought that I couldn't get out, that the cage door was locked. And even if I did climb out, where would I go? I couldn't fly. So I stayed inside and wrote books. Books about the outside. Books about things that couldn't happen inside. And I convinced myself that I was as free as any ole bird out there."

"What changed?"

"I'm not sure when it happened. It has something to do with what you and Kate are doing. I've been looking for ways to help."

"Are you kidding, Linnie? You loaned me a fortune!"

"That doesn't seem like enough. And then one day last week I put together a first aid kit for you to take with you. You're going to need it. You've got a pregnant woman there, and who knows what kind of physical or mental state she might be in when you find her? And then it occurred to me, you really need a nurse. Someone who can examine her and give her meds or a sedative or whatever. My credentials are current."

"Those are good ideas, Linnie," Morgan said. "The plane will have a basic first aid kit, but not with all that special stuff."

"So then I started asking: Why can't I go? Why can't I go? And the answer was that Hal would have a shit fit. And then it hit me, how much I do and don't do to keep Hal from freaking out. To make Hal happy. To go along with what Hal wants. I've been doing this for so long, I can't tell the difference between what he wants and what I want. I don't even recognize when I'm giving something up that I really want."

"I've always thought you had a lot of freedom," Morgan said.

Linnie shrugged. "Freedom that he gave me."

"I thought you were making the ordinary compromises of marriage."

"Some were like that," Linnie said. "But my life, my actions, whatever I have done has always been maneuvering within the parameters of what's acceptable to Hal. And now I'm wondering, what would life be like without those limits? What happens outside those parameters?"

"Geez, Linnie. Have you said all this to Hal?"

"I tried," she said. "But right now, he doesn't get it. Maybe someday he will. In the meantime, though, I have to get out of the cage. You know, Morgan, Faiza is a true prisoner. That's one kind of cage. But most of our prisons are in our minds, of our own making. And those doors are never locked from the outside."

Linnie and Morgan sat and rocked for a while, and Morgan brought her up to date on the plans for the rescue. Linnie brought out the first aid kit and proudly showed Morgan the contents.

It was a small black canvas bag, small enough to carry with them if needed. It was stuffed full, packed with precision. Linnie had thought of everything from tranquilizers safe for pregnant women to a powdered drink to prevent dehydration in hot climates. There were antiseptics, bandages, scissors, pills for diarrhea and vomiting, and even a blood pressure cuff.

"I got to thinking," she said. "When you go to the house, what happens if she freaks out? What if you find her in a severely depressed state, where she can't move or react? She's been in a state of extreme deprivation. We need to be prepared for any possibility here."

"We?"

Linnie went right on, as if she didn't hear. "I've added one of those little waist packs to wear when you go to the house. It'll hold enough supplies to cover contingencies there. Definitely sedatives, and some basic first aid. And smelling salts."

"I don't know how to administer sedatives," Morgan said.

"I do," she said.

"So Linnie, what's that mean?"

She grinned. "It means, how long will it take for me to get a goddamn visa?"

CHAPTER FIFTY-SEVEN

Morgan couldn't sleep.

When she was growing up her mother used to say to her, "Morgan, you think too much." Morgan was never sure what that meant. If we only use ten percent of our brains as it is, she reasoned, how could a person think too much? She did analyze and ruminate, sometimes ad nauseum, but why should anyone else worry about it? It was her mind, her head, and she was the one trapped in it.

So this was how she came to be roaming the house, opening and closing the refrigerator, occasionally getting back into bed to try again, punching up the pillows to create a fluffy nest for her head, only to wriggle and twist, wide-eyed, kicking her legs like a fretting baby.

Only days remained before the mission was scheduled to depart. This was a time to be getting extra sleep, not wandering around in the dark, trying to find the answers to unanswerable questions.

The enormity of the risk they were taking, the extreme consequences if they failed, set her mind writhing in doubt and her insides reeling with fear. Where was her old chutzpah, the energy that usually propelled her forward? Hey mujeres, where's the old cojones?

The others? Morgan didn't dare call Kate or Linnie, or Ashton or Meredith. They were counting on her and believed she had gotten over her worst fears. What about Grady, Taco,

Buck, Crater, Soho, and The Bear? Did any of them feel the same misgivings, was their confidence leaking out, slowly deflating by little puffs, like a tire with a nail stuck in it? Probably not. They were all probably sleeping like little spy babies.

It was true, Morgan thought. She was out of her league here, and she shouldn't have involved her friends, let alone her son, for godssake. Dowd was right. As always. Dowd. The one who always knew best. Father knows best.

Would there come a point when she left all the doubts behind and plunged off the high dive and into the deep water? *Leave all the doubts behind,* her midnight mind chanted. *Leave the doubts behind. The doubts. The Dowds. Leave the Dowds behind.*

Find your fears, Grace said to her once. Find your fears. Usually your fears are not what you expect them to be. And as the night rolled on, Morgan realized that what she was really afraid of was that there was no meaning in what they were doing. That, as Dowd accused, this whole thing was nothing more than an ego trip, a crazy quest for danger and adventure to satisfy some exaggerated notion of her own significance. Thus the appeal of the spy guys—their aura of mystery and suspense and renegade daring. And was this what attracted her to Grady? That he was from this other world, where people actually had the guts to risk their lives? But why? Why were they doing it?

Why does anyone do anything? Why do people jump into oceans to save a man overboard? Why do people rush into burning buildings or dig in an earthquake's fallen debris while the ground is still vibrating to find someone they don't even know? Are these acts what define our lives, and give them meaning?

When Morgan was at the *Dispatch*, her stories did help a lot of people. But the outcomes never seemed quite enough. For all the Hazel Presleys she saved, there were always so many more. Thousands, millions, in the same predicament, people she didn't even know about. She was never satisfied. What she did was never enough.

Morgan remembered once when Dowd and she took the kids to the animal shelter to adopt a puppy. They joked that they were getting a used dog, "previously owned," as the car dealers euphemize. And it seemed so noble, saving one animal from being put down.

But when they got to this underfunded, rundown facility, with a hundred and fifty barking, howling dogs stuffed into less than one rusty fenced-in acre, Morgan couldn't stand it. She wanted to take them all home. She wanted to buy land and give it to the county.

The kids picked a little beagle they named Sparky. She was the sweetest pup anyone would every dream of, and she got to live ten bonus years. But she was only one puppy, and what about all the others? They had to leave them all behind, and so to Morgan, what they had done seemed smaller than a drop in a bucket.

You can't save the world, Dowd would say. Why not? Morgan would argue. But maybe he was right. Maybe it was arrogant to think anyone could save the world. Grandiose. Who was she to think she could march into another country and right the wrongs there? Okay, not all the wrongs. This one wrong. The wrong against Faiza.

What else were they supposed to do? Sit back and let it happen? Let her rot in that room, or die at the hands of some fundamentalist sword or fistfuls of stones? But if—*when*—they did get her out, what about the thousands they would be leaving behind? Was it enough to rescue one?

Please, please, just a short one-liner to explain it all. A little box of reason to put it in and tie it up, a neat philosophical package fit to mail to anyone. To no one.

But that didn't come. Morgan wondered if this was what had happened to Grady. Maybe he had wanted to save the world once. Maybe he'd tried and finally gave up and got cynical. Because it was all too big. You drop grain to feed one village, but there are hundreds more villages, millions more starving people. Maybe that's what Grady figured out. That you can't even make a dent in the suffering.

But he was, after all, going with them.

Before Morgan had a chance to censor herself, she had picked up the phone and was dialing his number. It must have been about three in the morning, his time.

"Hmmm, hello," he said, his voice thick and throaty from sleepiness. She told herself he was used to being awakened for flights.

"Grady, it's Morgan," she said.

"Oh, hi, Morgan," he said slowly. So this is what he sounded like in the middle of the night. Low. Tender. Sexy. He was making love to her with his voice and he wasn't even awake yet.

"I'm sorry to call so late, or early, I guess it is," Morgan said.

"That's okay. What's the problem?"

"I can't sleep. I'm scared."

"About what?" he asked, waking up.

Morgan pictured him pushing himself into a sitting position on the side of the bed and reaching for his cigs. She wondered what color sheets he had on the bed. She pictured a guy color, like chocolate brown. She heard the lighter click.

"Everything," she said.

"Buyer's remorse?" he asked. Morgan could see the smile.

"Not exactly."

"You worried about the flight?"

"Not really," she said. "Believe it or not, my fear of flying has given way to bigger and more terrible terrors."

"Listen, babe, I told you all along this was serious business," he said.

"You mean, not a place for girls."

"Yeah, that's what I thought," Grady said. "But you. You're different, Morgan."

When he said her name, she could feel his arms around

her, and ached for that.

He went on. "You've got a vision. It's a little screwed up, but the bottom line is, you care about what the hell happens to people and you're not afraid to do something about it."

"You don't understand. I am afraid. Terrified."

"You want to call it off?" Grady asked. There was no rebuke in his question.

"I don't know. Yes. No. Probably not." Morgan sighed. "I want you to tell me it's going to be okay."

"It's going to be as okay as we make it, babe," Grady said.

She pictured Grady leaning forward with his elbows on his knees, tapping his toes up and down, like she had seen him do when he was thinking about what to say next.

"Let me tell you something that happens when you're flying," he said. "You're getting ready to take off, and you're doing your run up, and you still can change your mind. Like if something doesn't sound right, or if you decide you don't want to fly after all. Then you're cleared for takeoff, but you can still tell the tower you're turning back. You start your taxi, and you can still abort the flight.

"But then there's a point where you can't stop, you can't change your mind. In a big airplane, it's called V1. You get there, and you're going too fast to abort, so no matter what happens, even if you lose an engine, you're committed to taking off. In a little plane, that point is pretty much when you rotate for liftoff.

"And Morgan, it's the damnedest thing. Your wheels lift off and you're in the air, and there is nothing you can do but fly that airplane. Once you leave the ground, there is only one way back to the ground, alive, and that's to land the goddamn airplane. You are committed."

"Like a teeter-totter," she said.

"Say again?" Grady said.

"Never mind."

"Your son knows that place I'm talking about" Grady said. "On the top of a wave, when the surfer decides to drop in.

He's gotta take the ride."

Morgan took a deep breath. "Grady, do you think we're at V1 already?"

"That's for you to decide for yourself," he said.

"C'mon, Grady. I need your help." She paused. "I want your opinion."

"Well, okay," he said. "I think you got to V1 months ago. Maybe before I even met you."

As he said that, Morgan felt something relax in her. The taut muscles softened their clasp on her bones, and her chest felt like there was more room inside her to breathe.

"Think we can get some sleep now?" he asked.

"Yeah, thanks," she said.

"See you in a couple days, babe."

"Grady," Morgan asked before they hung up. "Why aren't you scared?"

"Maybe I am," he said.

CHAPTER FIFTY-EIGHT

November 9, 7:00 p.m.

They gathered in Taco's hangar for one final meeting. The Bear, Soho, Buck, and Crater were not there. They'd needed a head start and were probably already in Bahrain, Taco said, maybe even into Saudi. Morgan's skin tingled and the joints in her wrists and shoulders ached, as if she were coming down with the flu, and she wondered if she was getting sick.

As they walked in, Grady put his hand gently on the small of her back, and that slightest touch pulled her back into the present moment, like when a hypnotist touches a subject's arm to bring the person out of a trance. Morgan drew in a deep breath from way down in her gut. During the next few days, she was going to have to remember to breathe. She looked at her son. His skin had regained its color, and his face looked fresh. This was the healthiest he'd looked in months.

Grady, Kate, Linnie, Ashton, and Morgan had rooms in a small, old-Florida-style motel in Kissimmee, five minutes from the airport. Grady and Ashton doubled up, as did Linnie and Morgan, but they gave Kate her own room. Everyone else could sleep on the plane, but Kate needed a good night's rest.

Kate and Grady would be leaving for the airport at dawn, to preflight the plane and file the flight plans. The others would follow in an hour, stopping for breakfast and last-minute supplies. A day's worth of catered meals would be delivered to the airplane that morning, but they still had a few items to pick up.

For example, Linnie insisted they bring several jars of peanut butter. You can survive for weeks on peanut butter, she said.

Taco sat alone at the familiar table. It seemed odd to be here without the four no-name guys, and Morgan wondered where they were right now. When she introduced Taco to Linnie, he smiled and waved them all to sit down. Grady had already cleared with Taco the plan to include Linnie. He'd agreed it was wise to bring along someone with medical expertise.

With no preliminaries, he began. "We'll arrive just before dawn on November eleventh, right guys?" He looked to Kate and Grady for confirmation. They nodded. They had approximately thirteen hours of flying time, plus the stop in Santa Maria for fuel, and the time in Saudi Arabia was eight hours ahead of Florida.

"We'll go to the hotel and return to the plane in the afternoon. The appointment to show the plane to the sheik is on the eleventh. This is cutting it close, but in Saudi, it's not unusual for business meetings to be delayed. Figure that the sheik will probably not arrive until late afternoon, or maybe not until the next day. I'll brief you later on how to act when he arrives; we'll serve him coffee and probably make an hour of small talk before we bring up any business or offer to show him the airplane. That's the Saudi way. Lots of foreplay." They all laughed. "Any questions?"

"Will he want to fly?" Kate asked.

"We'll be maxed out," Grady said, referring to the fact that pilots are required to take a certain number of hours off after completing a long stretch of flying. It was common sense, and it was also regulations.

"If he wants to go up we'll have him come back the next day," Grady said. "And in a way, that's good. It will establish us as going up for demos and so the next one, the one we fake the next day, will be just another routine flight."

"Remember," Taco said. "This country has private jets out the butt; a lot of princes and sheiks have their own planes. Shit, the Sultan of Oman has his own 747. We might be parked next to another Skybird or some other forty-million-dollar tube. Security will be tight because of these planes, but we also won't stick out as much as you might think.

"We won't see the boys, but they'll see us. As soon as we've shown Mr. Sheiko the plane, Buck will contact me. No screwing around. We go get the girl the next day. When we leave the airport, we casually mention to our security guard that we're going to be showing the plane to another client and his wife. When we come back to the plane, we'll have Buck posing as an Arab businessman and talking Arabic like a sonofabitch, with his wife walking demurely beside him, covered from head to toe. Thanks to this lady's ingenuity," Taco gestured toward Morgan. "Questions?"

They shook their heads.

"Okay," he continued. "The house." Taco laid the photocopy of the sketch in front of them. "You've all seen this. I'll finalize the time when I talk to Buck. The boys will get there before us. We'll know they are there, because there will be a white Land Rover parked across the street. We park and stroll to the front door like visitors. Two men, two women. Ashton and me, and you two," he said, pointing to Linnie and Morgan.

"What about Kate and Grady?"

"They'll stay on the plane. They'll have a flight plan filed to Riyadh and the engines running, and they'll be fucking calling the tower when we pull up to the gate," Taco said.

"Back to the house. We walk in, and the boys have the people sitting quietly in two rooms. We'll be going right before late afternoon prayers, so the men will probably be together in one of these rooms." He pointed to an area on the first floor. "And the women will be in the women's quarters, probably back here. Buck will watch the men; The Bear will cover the women.

"Crater will find the Filipino housemaid, who will take us to the room. Morgan, you're in charge of giving her the money and papers, and after she has a chance to hide them, Buck will tie her up. It will look like we found her hiding somewhere in the house.

"Soho cuts the phone lines and watches the street. In Saudi everything—shops, restaurants, even television in some places—shuts down during prayer times. That might buy us a little wiggle room."

"Will they be holding these people at gunpoint?" Morgan asked. "Because I still don't want any guns fired."

"They'll have big-ass guns," Taco said. There was a twinge of sarcasm in his voice, and Morgan felt she had been reprimanded. But then he shrugged and said, "We had a deal. We'll stick to it if we can. We're not going to get a fight from the women. They'll huddle there too scared to pee. And the men, if the boys have to put them down, they've got gas. We'll put them to sleep."

"How long do we have?" Ashton asked.

"Ten minutes, max, to get to the room and get the girl out. We're going for surprise and confusion. They won't have a clue what we've done. What we want is for you to get her and get out without them realizing you have her. They'll think it's a robbery and waste a lot of time looking for what's been stolen. That'll give us more time to get to the airport. The town is ten kilometers from the airport and there shouldn't be much traffic at that time, so figure twenty minutes max. Because we gotta go slowly and calmly. If we rush one little step, we send out vibes. And those vibes'll kill us."

Grady said, "When we see you pull up to the gate, we start the engines. You board as fast as possible without making a fuss. We'll be ready to roll when the door shuts."

"Why Riyadh?" Morgan asked.

Grady pointed to the map of Saudi. "It's about an hour southwest of Dhahran; it's the capital, and it's the only major city in that area. That would be the logical place to take the sheik for a ride. If we were on a demo we'd go there, land, maybe have a cup of coffee, and come back here. Except that when we get to Riyadh, we're gonna just keep goin'. Pedal to the metal."

"Will they know?" Morgan asked.

Kate laughed. "Oh, yeah," she said. "When we don't land at Riyadh, without any clearance to go on, let us say there will be much concern."

"Is that against the law?" Morgan asked.

"We'll be breaking international aviation regs," Kate said. "And when we get back, the FAA's probably going to have a little chat with us. But as far as Saudi is concerned, we're already breaking their law by leaving the country without a visa. And taking one of their citizens with us. I don't think flying four hundred miles without a flight plan ranks very high on that list of transgressions, do you?"

"So we're making a run for it?" asked Morgan.

"By the time they figure out we're not coming into Riyadh and call us back, we'll be less than an hour from the eastern coast, and in a few more minutes we'll be out of Saudi airspace," Kate said.

"Beatin' feet for Egypt," Grady said, grinning like an outlaw.

"All right!" Ashton said. "All right!"

CHAPTER FIFTY-NINE

November 10, 8:30 a.m.

As promised, that airplane shot up like a rocket. And it could be a rocket. Grady told Morgan that the plane's instruments and avionics were equal to what *Apollo* used to land on the moon.

There was a golf course next to the Kissimmee airport, and from the window Morgan watched it recede so fast it looked like a computer graphic that shrinks to the corner of the screen with a click.

They all stayed in their seats as they passed over the eastern part of Florida. A few minutes after they took off, Kate came on the intercom and announced they could get up and walk around now. But everyone stayed seated. Morgan thought they all must have needed time alone, to be quiet, to look out the window, to let the reality sink in.

This was it. They were on their way.

The Atlantic Ocean was clear and blue, and from their altitude of 39,000 feet, the coastline looked like a map, perfectly still, with no sign of wave motion, as if the water had frozen onto the beach.

And then they were out over the ocean, endless deep blue, "eternity blue" as Grace used to call it. Just a year earlier Morgan wouldn't have considered a flight like this. Seven hours to Santa Maria, a quick stopover, and another six to Saudi. But this felt fine so far. She had her son and two best friends on board, one at the controls, and a man whom she was beginning to believe she could trust.

The first few hours actually went by fast. Ashton located the VCR, and Linnie handed him a cloth bag embroidered with a pastel floral design. He untied the bag. It was stuffed with movies.

"Where'd these come from?" he asked.

"I brought them," Linnie said.

"Wow, *Vanishing Point*," he said. "And *Good Morning, Vietnam*. Good choices. Wait, *My Best Friend's Wedding*?"

"I picked a variety," Linnie said.

The labels were from Blockbuster video.

"Did you rent all these?" he said.

"Yeah," she said.

Morgan cracked up. "You went to Blockbuster to get movies for a rescue mission?"

"I'll be a little late getting them back," Linnie said. "But what the hell."

"It's gonna cost you a fortune!" Morgan said.

"Oh, yeah, like you're spending a hundred and fifty thou on a bunch of commandos, and you're worried about fines for late movies?"

Linnie burst out laughing, and when she did, it cracked something loose from all of them. Pretty soon they were clutching their stomachs and tears were running out of their eyes, and Ashton rolled over on his back on the floor.

"Aunt Linnie," he choked. "Did you get *Lawrence of Arabia*?"

"Yes!" she howled, digging into the bag, producing the box. Kate walked back into the cabin.

"What's so funny?" she asked, already catching it. They told her. She laughed. "Morgan, I'm taking a break. Grady wants to know if you want to come up front."

"Sure," Morgan said, turning to the others. "But call me when Lawrence blows up the train track."

Everyone howled again. Even Taco looked up from his newspaper and smiled. He told them they would have to hide the bag when the customs agent came onboard. In Saudi Arabia, books and videos that might contain any sexually suggestive material were routinely confiscated. There was a removable panel in a tool compartment in the aft section, where some other no-nos were concealed, namely, three rifles and four bottles of champagne, for the trip home.

"*Lawrence of Arabia*'s probably okay, isn't it?" Linnie said.

"What if they search the plane?" Ashton asked.

"Trust me, they won't," Taco said. "We'll get V.I.P. treatment. We're coming in on a hot shit plane. And we're here to see a sheik. We're wheels. Makes a difference."

Morgan slid into the copilot's seat next to Grady. The view out over the nose was an infinity of royal blue sea and over it, gray horizon fading upward into another lighter shade of crystal blue. Though the cockpit was small and compact and crammed with instruments and lights and gauges, it felt as though she was sitting right in the middle of the open sky with no obstructions, no limits.

"Hi, babe," Grady said. "How are you doing?"

"Good," Morgan said. Even though she'd had sex with Grady, there were times when she still felt awkward, as if she was meeting him for the first time. "Nice flight."

"Yeah," he said. "It's clear and calm and a real no-brainer."

"Where are we?"

"About five hundred miles from the Azores." He picked up Kate's headset and held it out for Morgan to put on. The headset muffled the sounds around them and placed his voice right there in her ear, as if they were alone in a private little cocoon. With nothing splatting against the windshield or whizzing by the side window, it was impossible to believe they were going over five hundred miles an hour. It felt like they were hovering there, hanging in the sky.

"Remember when Kate was explaining to your son about ARI, Aeronautical Radio Incorporated?"

"Control centers that track our path across the ocean," Morgan remembered.

"Right," Grady said. "Well, we've been reporting to New York center, but we're getting ready to change to Santa Maria center. I need to give them a position report."

"Do you want Kate back here?"

"Oh, no," he said. "I can handle it. I'd like you to stay if you want to."

"Sure," Morgan said.

Grady touched a control and some numbers lighted.

"New York, New York, Skybird Seven-Two-Three-Whiskey-Tango on six-five position."

Morgan heard a slight hum of static in the background, but the voice responding came through as clear as a telephone call.

"Skybird Seven-Two-Three-Whiskey-Tango, New York on six-five copy."

Grady said: "New York, Skybird Seven-Two-Three-Whiskey-Tango is at 35 North 50 West, flight level 390, estimating 35 North 40 West at 1950 Zulu; 35 North, 25 West is next."

"Roger, Skybird Seven-Two-Three-Whiskey-Tango." The controller repeated what Grady had said.

Grady: "Skybird Seven-Two-Three-Whiskey-Tango. That is correct."

Controller: "Contact Santa Maria on 8840 at 35 North 30 West."

Grady: "Roger, we'll contact Santa Maria on 88 at 35 North 30 West."

Morgan was not sure how long she stayed in the cockpit. Maybe an hour. Grady didn't talk to anyone for a while, and then he reached over and pressed another button.

"Santa Maria Santa Maria, Skybird Seven-Two-Three-Whiskey-Tango on 88 position copy New York."

Controller: "Skybird Seven-Two-Three-Whiskey-Tango Santa Maria, go ahead."

Grady repeated the report, the Santa Maria controller rogered him, and someone came on and said "Roger New York copies," and that was that.

"What does all that mean?" Morgan asked.

"I'm telling them where we are," Grady said.

"And where are we?" she asked.

"I want to see you again, Morgan," he said. "Like the night in the ocean. Only more. Not just making love. That and more."

"Well," Morgan said, looking back into the cabin. "We certainly have some of the same interests."

CHAPTER SIXTY

November 10, 7:00 p.m.

Morgan gazed out the window of the plane at the Azores, an archipelago of nine islands, with rocky peaks that jutted up from the sea. About 150 miles out, she could see the misty mountaintops, glowing gray-pink in the setting sun. She thought they looked as if they'd been strewn there in one graceful gesture, like a giant hand scattering rose petals.

When Morgan left the cockpit so Kate could get ready for the landing, Grady had told her to look out of the left side of the airplane for the best view of Santa Maria. Now, she could have sworn she had seen Santa Maria before, maybe in a wish or a dream about an island paradise. The coastline curved in and out with bays and inlets, as if God wanted to give more people a great view of the water. Grassy slopes dropped steeply into the lagoon-blue sea, dotted in places with white villages and lush green, terraced farmland that looked like hundreds of little steps coming up from the beach.

After one wide turn left and a breathtaking panorama, they descended rapidly to the airport. Linnie, Ashton, and Morgan scrambled to fasten their seatbelts before they touched down. Morgan thought she was going to have to do better if she was going to pose as a flight attendant.

They were on the ground for a little more than an hour, only enough time to stretch their legs. Not that they were cramped in this flying limousine. Hardly. But the fresh air felt good—not too humid, a warm breeze, a perfect seventy degrees. While the plane was being fueled, they walked around in a small terminal for private airplanes and finally settled out-

side on a short brick wall bordering a planter that was bloom-
ing with lavender and pink wildflowers.

As they reboarded the plane, Morgan honestly wished
she didn't have to get back on. The space around her began to
close in, pinning her arms, stealing the air. She hesitated on
the steps for a moment, hoping no one was noticing. Maybe
she could stay here. Maybe they could come back for her later.
She was starting to perspire as all-too-familiar anxiety seared
through her head, trying to explode out her eyeballs.

Then she felt the presence of a hand on the small of her
back, and Grady's voice speaking very softly, only for her. "It's
okay," he said. "I'm right here."

And it was okay; she found she could breathe again.

They took off at 9:30 p.m. and continued across the
North Atlantic. It got dark, really dark, like the inside of Mam-
moth Cave when they turn off the lights. They talked and ate
sandwiches and rehearsed their roles.

The more Morgan was around Taco, the more she liked
him. He kept to himself mostly and didn't join in on much of
the conversation. But he had a friendly presence, and a comforting energy of competence. He didn't volunteer a lot of
information, but when asked, he always seemed to know the
answer.

Taco tutored them on the use of the onboard coffee-
maker. Noting that the Saudis like their coffee strong, he
pointed out a special dark-roast Cuban blend he had brought,
along with an assortment of strong teas. He explained that
coffee and tea drinking was an important ritual for Saudis, and
as flight attendants, Linnie and Morgan would serve the sheik
and his interpreter when they came on board the plane.

Taco would pose as the intermediary for the plane's
owner, he said, and Grady and Kate would stay in the background until there were specific questions for the pilots. Grady
would answer those. In a country where a woman's testimony
in court is legally worth only half a man's, the word of their
woman pilot was not going to carry a lot of weight. Ashton

would be posing as flight engineer, and there would be no questions directed toward him.

"The sheik does not know how to fly," Taco said. "So there won't be any questions that will trip you up."

Once, during the night, Grady came into the cabin and stretched out in one of the recliners near the front. Everyone else was napping; Morgan moved up next to him, and they talked in hushed voices.

"I'm not keeping the money," he said.

"Why? You're earning it."

"No. I owe it."

"I don't understand," Morgan said.

"Look, babe, I'm not saying I feel guilty about flying the plane that took Faiza away. I was doing my job."

"I know. No one's blaming you," Morgan said.

"But let's just say this evens out the score," Grady said.

They sat in companionable silence, and he reached over and put his hand on hers.

Eventually Morgan asked, "Has there ever been anyone else? A wife? Someone serious?"

"No wife," he said. He was quiet for a while.

Then he said: "You know that story I told you about Crater and the flight out of Guatemala where he kicked the drug guy out of the plane?"

"Yes," Morgan said.

"Well, I lied to you about that."

"What do you mean?" she said. "The story isn't true?"

"It's true," Grady said. "Only it wasn't about Crater. It was about me."

Morgan leaned back and closed her eyes, and opened them once or twice to watch Grady sleep. Kate was in the cockpit, and Morgan could see the silhouette of her head. She drifted off into a weightless sleep, like a kid in the back seat of the car when your mother is driving. Warm. Cozy. Perfectly safe.

November 11, 5:15 a.m., AST (Arabia Standard Time)

"We're getting close to Saudi Arabia," Grady whispered, touching Morgan's arm. "We're over the Red Sea now. Thought you might want to take a look."

Just before dawn they were about one hundred miles from the Saudi coast. If that day's sunrise was any omen, Morgan told herself, then everything was going to be fine. The sky was perfectly clear, and the new day's light eased up in a luminous aura arching over the dark horizon. As the sky got brighter, it looked like a huge fire had broken out, sending miles and miles of smoke up into the sky, only the color of the smoke was pure canary yellow.

They crossed the Red Sea near its northern end and came into Saudi Arabia over Al Hijaz, the northwest coastal mountain range. The peaks were rocky and craggy—typically around three thousand feet, with some as high as seven thousand, and they looked like they dropped straight down into the sea.

Further south, in the Asir region, the coastal range got even steeper, reaching heights of ten thousand feet. Occasionally she'd spot shaded areas, with the barest signs of cultivation. Oases. They might be a welcome sight to someone dying of thirst, but as dots in the three hundred thousand square miles of parched desert, they looked no bigger than a puddle.

Under this dry, barren layer, Morgan reminded herself, lay the largest known deposits of petroleum in the world, and the source of Saudi Arabia's enormous wealth.

Kate and Grady began to slow the plane for the descent. They would be landing to the northwest, and about ten miles south of the airport they turned on the final approach and began to slope gently downward. To their right, Morgan recognized the island of Bahrain and the spectacular four-lane, seven-mile causeway that swept across the Persian Gulf connecting Bahrain to Saudi Arabia. She and Ashton had pinned a calendar photo of it to her wall at home.

Morgan was sitting in a seat facing Linnie and Ashton. She said to them, "In all my reading and studying about Islam, I noticed that whenever Muslims go anywhere or do anything or make any decisions, they say 'Insha'Allah.'"

"What's it mean?" Linnie asked.

"It means God willing. Literally, it means if Allah wills. In other words, this will only happen if it is what Allah wants."

"So do you think what we're doing is Insha'Allah?" Linnie asked.

"I think it must be," Morgan answered. "Islam is a very pure religion. It is based on the belief that God is everything. God is all there is."

"Isn't that what most religions believe?" Linnie said.

"I guess so, more or less," said Morgan. "But Muslims live every moment with this awareness. That everything that happens is exactly what God wants."

Ashton looked up thoughtfully. "What if Faiza's family believes they are doing the will of Allah, and we believe we are?" he said. "How does God decide?"

"Is it necessary for God to take sides?" Linnie asked.

The tires barely tapped the surface of the runway, and the plane slowed with a quiet, easy rumble.

Morgan smiled. "Not if she doesn't want to."

CHAPTER SIXTY-ONE

November 11, 9:00 a.m. AST

Morgan was aware that the spot on the map labeled Dhahran was actually three cities—Dammam, Al Khobar, and Dhahran—that had fused and intermingled over the years until there was now some uncertainty as to where one ended and the next began.

Hard as she found it to believe, just sixty years ago, before the discovery of oil in Saudi Arabia, Dhahran did not exist, and Dammam and Al Khobar were tiny fishing and pearling villages. The discovery of that oil in the early 1930s had led to the formation of Aramco, a joint venture between the Saudi government and Standard Oil of California. Aramco was responsible for the huge residential projects and compounds that housed the throngs of workers brought into the area, and the city of Dhahran was largely an Aramco creation, with residential areas made up of rows of white or light pink or butter-colored houses in what looked like a cheaper, sandstone version of southern California suburbia.

The Dhahran International Airport, partly commercial and partly a military air base, was built there by the United States in 1943. Though the Skybird was assigned a parking spot in a special fenced-in area reserved for private airplanes, Morgan noted a disturbing presence of men in uniforms with big, hulky assault rifles dangling at their hips, and fighter jets searing straight up over their heads.

Taco laughed and said not to worry, because a lot of the jets were "ours." The guard stationed at the gate into their assigned section was a Saudi soldier, however, dressed in khaki pants and shirt, with a red and white checked ghutra, the head-dress worn by men. The center of the soldier's ghutra bore a gleaming round pin, with the design of a single palm tree over two crossed swords with curved blades.

"That's the Saudi national coat of arms," Morgan told Linnie. "The date palm represents prosperity, and the swords stand for justice."

"The palm tree looks benign enough," Linnie murmured, as they watched him from the windows. "But I shudder at the thought of what short work those Saudi swords of justice might make of our little band of agitators if they knew what we were up to."

Everyone waited on the plane for about ten minutes before it was boarded by a man dressed in a light brown thobe and white headdress. In broken but decipherable English, he introduced himself to Grady as Fouad, an emissary and interpreter for Sheik Ahmed al-Khalid, the businessman who was interested in the Skybird, and their gracious sponsor to the kingdom.

In Saudi Arabia, the title of sheik was an honorific for successful businessmen and high government officials, but was never used for members of the royal family, who were called princes. Morgan asked Taco if it was good news that this guy was not in the house of Saud, thinking that they were about to hurl a big insult his way and perhaps it would be considered much more grievous if aimed at the royals.

Taco shrugged. "It probably wouldn't make much difference," he said. "There are hundreds and hundreds of princes, because anyone even distantly related to the first king, Ibn Saud, gets that title.

"Sheik Ahmed eez provided transpahtachun to your hahtel," Fouad told them. "When you passing cawstoms. Wait hee-ar."

It was another half-hour before a man in a uniform similar to the gate guard's climbed aboard, scanned the cabin, and began a summary perusal of everyone's luggage. Morgan, anxious to get off the plane, found the whole process inordinately long. But later, when they passed the customs building, where a swarm of a hundred sweaty people were squeezing themselves through a doorway meant for two, Morgan realized they had gotten VIP treatment. They were bigwigs, and the official didn't even give the closets a second look.

They also learned that in Saudi, it's best not to be compulsive about time. Delays were expected, the way of life.

"It's probably the heat," Morgan said.

From living in Florida, she knew how oppressive heat and humidity could be. It slowed life down. It baked you into indifference. But at least in Florida, the sand stayed in its place. Saudi sand seemed to penetrate everywhere. It blew in your face and up and in and through your clothing. It found cracks in the back of a jacket. It got through the molecules in closed car windows. Gritty sand made you feel hotter and stickier. No wonder no one rushed around.

Morgan did not want to presume that all Arabs looked alike, because they didn't; but the first three men they met did. They all had bushy black mustaches that joined up with close-cropped but bristle-thick beards, and rough skin that looked like the legacy of teenage acne or a scourge of sandstorms. Their dark eyes were distinctly expressionless. It wasn't exactly a blank expression, but more an inscrutable one, like: Don't even try to guess what I'm thinking.

On the way to the hotel, Fouad was friendly and chatty, talking and looking around at the group more often than he seemed to look at the road, but even when he smiled, his eyes didn't join in.   Their hotel, a very Americanized Sheraton, was on the Gulf in Dammam, about twenty kilometers from the airport.

This drive from the airport to Dammam and back would be the extent of their sightseeing for that day. Morgan studied her surroundings with interest. Greater Dhahran, like many cities she had visited, housed a conglomerate of old and modern buildings. In other cities, like Rome, however, there seemed to be a more orderly, gradual transition from old to new, over hundreds of years. The ambiance in and around Dhahran suggested a more sudden change—as if one day it was six thousand years ago, and the next day it was the twentieth century. There might be a stylish twelve-story apartment building in the foreground, and in the background, the ornate minaret of a mosque sticking up over the rooftops of city buildings.

Most of the buildings were modern, but the smaller ones were unkempt, with faded paint and mottled areas in the walls. The roads were paved, and on some of the narrower ones, small blockhouses crowded right up to the edge of the street. Pedestrians were mostly male, and Morgan thought their robes and headdresses seemed antithetical to the modern day, as if they'd just wandered into the city from the desert.

Much of the ride took them on congested, dusty two-lane streets with a has-been look Morgan had seen before when in the oldest part of a big city, scrunched amid a tangle of honking, terrible drivers. Fouad insisted on driving past one of Dhahran's architectural prides, the University of Petroleum and Minerals, a lovely sprawl of low, graceful tan buildings that connected to one another and looked as if they'd grown right out of the desert.

At the hotel they settled into their rooms, Linnie, Kate, and Morgan in one, and Grady and Ashton sharing another. Taco had his own room, in keeping with his practice of distance and aloofness. Curious about this, Morgan asked Grady why Taco had to remain such a mystery. She was sure that he must have a nefarious past.

"He's not that mysterious," Grady said. "It's the way he learned to operate. Outside the circle."

"How does he know so much?" Morgan prodded.

"He's been everywhere, done just about everything. And in the military stuff he did, he was effective because he didn't get into groups."

"He's a loner," she said.

"More than that, babe," Grady said. "He's nondescript. He fits in anywhere. He notices everything but no one ever notices him. He just shows up places. And you never see him come, and you never see him leave."

Grady was right. By the time the group convened in Grady's and Ashton's room, Taco had already rented an Izuzu van and gone out in it to locate the house where Faiza was held.

"You saw it?" Ashton said, clearly disappointed. He had wanted to go along.

"Sorry, son," Taco said. "Best I go alone. The streets are crowded and there're lots of foreigners around here, but we still need to maintain a low profile. We don't want to attract any attention, and we especially don't want any skirmishes with the local authorities. I mean, we kiss every Tom, Dick, and Abdul's ass, and we are as meek as mice. You girls wear your robes when we go walking around outside the hotel. We act like we are so damn glad to be permitted to be here, and we respect the shit out of everybody."

Taco added, "And another thing, son. Even though it's a big city, we have to consider that the meathooks who kidnapped your girl could be around somewhere. They've seen you before, and they could make you. So if you go out, stay out of the spotlight."

Ashton nodded, then asked, "What does the house look like?"

"Big. Like in the drawing. Wall around it, with an iron gate. It's gonna be okay," was all Taco would say.

CHAPTER SIXTY-TWO

November 11, 1:00 p.m. AST

After freshening up at the hotel, the group went back to the airplane to wait for Sheik Ahmed al-Khalid. Linnie and Morgan prepared coffee and tea, and found some little teacups in the galley, plain but better than Styrofoam. Kate and Grady went over charts, and later Grady left the plane and came back with good news. They could get the fuel they would need to fill the plane to the hilt and make a non-stop run for home.

Outside, playing his role as flight engineer, Ashton shadowed Taco while he checked out the plane. After a while everyone gravitated toward lounge seats, dropping the backs and closing their eyes. Ashton turned on the CD player, a nice Sarah McLachlan album. Morgan wondered if Sarah McLachlan would be censored by the Saudis.

They were all dead tired, but they couldn't leave the plane in case the sheik showed up. And Taco wanted them all to stay together. He wanted the guards to get accustomed to seeing them come and go in a big group, so that when they boarded the last day with the extra two, the size of the entourage wouldn't raise questions.

Linnie said the gate guard was eyeing the women, Morgan especially, probably because of her blonde hair. They decided to set up an opportunity for Morgan to flirt. Grady didn't like the idea, but surprisingly, Taco thought it might be smart to win an ally. Kate agreed.

While the plane was being fueled, Morgan walked out, ostensibly to talk to Grady, and then Grady left her standing there alone while he checked the fueling operations.

Saudi men and women did not mix in social situations, she knew, except with close relatives. When a man met a woman, he was not supposed to look into her face or shake hands with her. Women were not supposed to extend a hand for a handshake, and Saudi women could not initiate a greeting with a man outside her family.

But as a foreign woman, Morgan could get away with more. She nodded at the guard, and he dipped his head in response.

"Do you speak English?" she asked slowly.

"Yes, a little some," he answered.

"What is your name?"

"It is Rashad," he replied.

Rashad raised his eyes tentatively and eventually looked directly at Morgan. But even when he did, the eyes had that familiar absence of expression she had noticed with other Saudi men. Grace would call those "goat eyes." Because, she said, when goats look at you their eyes have a glassy vacancy. They just don't connect.

"My name is Morgan. I'm a flight attendant," Morgan said to Goat Eyes.

"Like stewardaize?" Rashad said.

"Yes."

"The women, they are also attendants?"

"Two of us are," she said. "The one with long dark hair. She is the pilot."

"The pilot?" He laughed. "I am being surprised."

"Are you a colonel?" Morgan asked.

Rashad laughed again. "Oh, no! No colonel."

"But you are important," she said, half question, half statement.

Rashad looked down. Morgan hoped she hadn't embarrassed him. But when he looked up again, she could see that he was flattered.

"You have a big gun," she said, pointing to the assault rifle at his side.

He shrugged. "Yes."

"I need to go back to the plane now. We are showing the airplane to many sheiks."

"I am not understanding," he said.

Morgan repeated. "Sheiks are coming here to look at the airplane. To buy it."

"Oh," he said, comprehending. He smiled and looked away, scanning his vocabulary for the right word. "Beautiful. Beautiful airplane. Like you."

Morgan smiled and lowered her eyes.

"I need to go back now," she said. "Rashad, you won't shoot us, will you?"

"Shoot? What?"

"With your gun," she pointed. "Do not shoot us, please."

"Oh, no." Rashad laughed, and there was the slightest of sparkle in the goat eyes. "Not to shoot you, beautiful lady."

From that time on, during their comings and goings to the airplane, Morgan always waved and shouted, "Hello, Rashad." And he would wave back. But his goat eyes never gave away what might be behind them.

November 11, 7:00 p.m. AST

By the end of their first day, Morgan had come to admire the quality she found most moving about this part of the world: the way the sun played on walls and buildings and mosques throughout the day, a yellow-gold reflection at sunrise, bright white light at midday, and a deeper gold at sunset. And of course on the plane she had witnessed the spectacular sunrise over the Persian Gulf, which on clear mornings turned the whole sky the color of the inside of a lemon.

They ate dinner in the hotel restaurant, everyone except Taco. He was driving back to the village near the house, to learn the exact time of the sunset call to prayer.

The menu had English translations and included a number of Indian and Pakistani dishes. Morgan ordered a chicken kabob with rice, which was rather spicy, but good. Everyone's appetite was suppressed from exhaustion, and the best part of the meal was chunks of seasoned bread, which they devoured.

"I'd kill for a glass of wine," Kate said.

"Me, too," Linnie echoed.

"Beer for me," said Ashton.

"We could sneak back to the plane and hit the champagne," Morgan whispered.

"No way," Linnie said. "That's for our going home celebration. And I'd hate it if we got caught over drinking some illegal booze."

Morgan eyed Ashton. Throughout the trip he had been rather undemonstrative, and she would often catch him staring off somewhere. But tonight he was engaging and talkative. He entertained them with surfing stories and wondered if there were any good waves in the area.

"Oh, right," Morgan said. "We'll be ready to leave, finally, after all these months, and you'll be out on a surfboard in the Persian Gulf."

Morgan could tell that Ashton and Grady were enjoying each other's company. Although she would have expected Grady to act fatherly and know-it-all, he actually treated Ashton more like a brother, an equal. Privately, he told Morgan that he thought Ashton was one of the bravest young men he'd ever known.

"I'm teaching this guy to fly," Grady said, scrunching Ashton's shoulder.

"No you're not," Kate said. "I'm teaching him. I saw him first."

"Hold it," said Morgan. "He's not going to have time. He's got a family to take care of."

Everyone got quiet, and they all looked at each other. In that moment, Morgan thought, What the hell had she done? Brought her only son into a country that would think nothing of letting him rot in a filthy jail cell if they knew he'd been intimate with one of their women. Lured her two best friends into a world where women were kept under lock and key, where they could be stoned in the streets.

So much could go wrong. Mujeres con cojones? They were seven thousand miles and about fifteen centuries away from that white van in Golden Gate Park.

And then there was Grady. He was happy as a pig in mud when Morgan met him, determined to keep his life just as it was, no more risking his precious neck for anything. She might never know what changed his mind, but here he was. He was finally taking a stand. For what, she did not know. But she was glad he was here, and she knew they had the best two pilots in the world.

"I'll drink to that," Grady said, raising his bottle of mineral water.

"To what?" Morgan said.

"To the new family."

They all clinked their bottles and took a swig. A new family was forming, right around this table. And in its midst, Morgan felt a wave of strength and courage so powerful that if Ashton had had his surfboard, he could have ridden that wave right on into the beach.

CHAPTER SIXTY-THREE

There they were, the three of them, sitting cross-legged on the beds like they were back in college. Kate was smoking a cigarette she had bummed from Grady, and Linnie was filing a broken fingernail. Only Linnie would think to bring an emery board to Saudi Arabia.

"It's weird," she said. "Here we are in this mysterious faraway place, and we're probably not going to get to do any sightseeing. Doesn't that seem sort of wacky?"

"I haven't thought much about sightseeing," Morgan said. "I'd like to go to a couple of shops and buy something for Meredith. But probably we won't have the chance."

"Maybe next time," Kate said.

Morgan shook her head. "Hate to tell you, kiddo, but I don't think we'll be invited back anytime soon."

"Yeah, we've sort of blown it here." Linnie grinned. "Anyway, I'm not sure I want to go walking around in a black cape. And doesn't it bother you that we can't even go outside without the men escorting us?"

"And we can't drive anywhere," Kate said. "I hate not being able to drive. In one day, I already feel like a prisoner."

"Doesn't this make you mad?" Linnie asked Morgan. "Don't you want to write some big exposé about all this?"

"You know, it's funny," Morgan said. "I used to get so angry about things that were wrong, about injustices. And that anger fueled my writing. It was very polarized. Black, white. Bad guys and good guys. The victims and the victimizers. And here, I don't even know anything about this uncle of Faiza's. Maybe he's a villain. Maybe he's not. Maybe he's just a Muslim version of a Christian fundamentalist, with a misguided idea of what the religion means. For some reason, all that doesn't seem to matter."

"How can it not matter?" Linnie asked. "This country is terrible to women."

"I agree," Morgan said. "But we aren't trying to make a big statement, or to change the country. We're trying to get one woman out of it. That's all there is to do. And we don't have to make everyone monsters to do it."

"But it is wrong, what they are doing to Faiza," Linnie said.

"It's wrong. It's hideous. But that's all it is," Morgan said.

Kate joined in. "I've noticed how the guys—Taco and The Bear and the others—they're not all caught up in a cause. They're simply doing a job."

"They're doing it for money," Linnie said.

"Yes, but they're still having to risk their lives," Kate said. "That Bear guy. He's got heart. You can tell. And Buck. It's more than money to him."

Linnie had stopped filing and was doodling star shapes on the bedspread with the emery board.

"What you said, Morgan," Linnie said, "makes me think about what happened with Hal."

"What did happen?" asked Kate. "You never told us."

"He was mad when I left, of course. He said he might not be there when I got back. And I was so pissed. I mean, what good would that do? Just make it harder if anything happened to me. But then I realized, it doesn't really matter what he does. I've shifted into a new place, and I don't have to be angry or make him a bad guy to do that. I can just go. Do it. I've seen something I want to change, and I'm taking action. It's what we said we would do thirty-five years ago. And now we're finally doing it."

Kate started laughing. "Speaking of cojones, Morgan, I can't believe you asked that guard not to shoot us!"

Linnie almost choked. "You said that? What did he say?"

"He said he wouldn't."

"Well, we've got that going for us," she said.

There was a tap on the door, and Kate got up to answer it. It was Grady, bringing an advisory from Taco.

"We'll leave at approximately seventeen-thirty—that's five-thirty p.m.," Grady said, "and arrive at the house at the start of prayer. We take the girl out during prayer time, twenty minutes max, faster if you can, and we'll be pulling away when the prayer break ends. We can't risk being on the street during prayer break."

"Why?" they all asked.

"Everything closes for prayer—shops, restaurants. Muslim men are supposed to go to the mosque. We'll be driving in a car with Buck dressed as an Arab, and his 'wife,' and we don't want to get stopped. And when we get back to the airport, we want your pal Rashad to be there to open the gate, not out on a prayer break."

"He's not my pal," Morgan said.

"You shitting me? The guy's got a big tent for you, babe," Grady said.

"I wouldn't be so sure."

"He can't keep his eyes off you, blondie. And you might as well play it for all it's worth."

"Maybe," Morgan said. "But I don't trust him."

"You don't have to trust him," Grady said. "Just keep his ass turned on until we're on the airplane."

Linnie changed the subject. "When are we going?"

"Depends on the sheik," Grady said. "He sent word that he would be at the airplane tomorrow in the early afternoon. That could mean one o'clock or it could mean five o'clock raghead time, or he might not show at all. But Taco says, if the sheik comes and goes by four, we'll go tomorrow. Can you be ready?"

"What else is there to do?" Morgan said. "Like, oh wait, we have to do laundry first."

"We need to get out of here," Grady said soberly. "When you go to the plane tomorrow, bring everything you need, and don't leave anything in the hotel that you want to keep. Hopefully we won't be coming back here."

"Well, there goes shopping," Kate said.

"We could mosey downtown to some shops in the morning," Grady said. "Of course, you females have to ask nice. You can't go without us men, you know."

"Enjoy it, you big bubba," Morgan said. "'Cause when we get out of this country, we're kicking your butt."

Laughing, Grady took Morgan's hand and led her out the door. In the empty hallway, he wrapped his arms around her.

"How you doin'?" he said.

"Okay, how about you?"

"I miss you."

He cupped his hands around her head and kissed her deeply, like the day in the motel, like the night on the beach. Morgan had to hand it to this guy. He would never brush her off with a peck on the cheek or a half-assed kiss. Even standing in the hallway of a hotel in the middle of a desert town in Arabia, he put his whole self into it.

"Are you scared?" he asked.

"Does a camel have humps?" Morgan said. He grimaced. Bad joke. "I'm worried about Ashton," she added, serious now.

"Your son's gonna be fine," Grady said. "How many guys get to risk their lives to rescue the woman they love?"

"You'd do that, wouldn't you?"

Grady shrugged and didn't say anything, but kissed her again, slowly, tenderly, as if they were all alone in their own little crystal pond, and it was clear, and it was safe, and it was forever. Then he opened the door to the room, and Morgan went in. She closed and locked it behind him, and turned to Kate and Linnie. They were both grinning.

"The things we do for love," Linnie sang.

"Okay, okay, knock it off," Morgan said.

"I almost forgot," Linnie said, digging into her flight bag. Smiling triumphantly, she waved a small pink votive candle. "Travel size."

They gathered onto one bed, and Linnie set the candle in an ashtray in the middle. Kate lit a match and then handed the book to Morgan, who lit one and passed the matches to Linnie. They touched their match tips at the wick, and the candle jumped into flame. They joined hands.

"Mujeres con cojones," Linnie said.

"Freedom," Morgan said.

"For all mujeres everywhere," Kate said.

Morgan met Linnie's eyes and then Kate's. "You're giving up so much," she told them.

"Don't you see, Morgan?" Linnie said. "It was never a trade, a husband for a cause. It was time to stand up and be the woman I started out to be thirty-five years ago."

"And it was time for me to find the woman I lost—no, gave up, when Jack died," Kate said. "And you, Morgan, what about you?"

"I'm just doing what mothers do," Morgan said. "Helping my kid get what he wants."

"No, it's more than that," she said.

"I guess maybe it is," Morgan said quietly. "I guess maybe it is."

CHAPTER SIXTY-FOUR

November 12, 10 a.m. AST

Morgan had no idea how many styles of abaya were available to women in Saudi Arabia, but the ones Meredith had bought for them were definitely high end. Made of a soft black silk, big as tents, they had little hand openings designed to allow the woman to extend her arms without revealing them.

The robes for Linnie and Morgan were open at the front, so they had to hold them closed. They could wear them as a cape around their shoulders or pull the edge up into a hood over their heads, and the folds still fell evenly to the floor.

The robe that Kate wore, which would be the one they later put on Faiza, had an embroidered edging with small snaps to close the opening. Meredith thought that since they didn't know the state they would find Faiza in, or what she would be wearing, this was the best style.

Fashion tip, Morgan told the others: When you are fleeing a country for your life, wear an abaya with a front closure, so your hands are free.

That morning, for their little shopping expedition, they hid their hair under scarves and hoods, but did not wear veils, because the travel books said that Western women were not expected to cover their faces. Later, when they went to the house, they would veil completely, as a safeguard and to match Faiza. With Ashton and Grady as their escorts, the five took off on foot toward the center of Dammam, about a mile walk.

They all agreed they needed the exercise. Morgan felt conspicuous, like a fugitive from a church choir. But no one paid them much attention. So instead of sticking out like a sore thumb, they were actually rather invisible.

Most of the men were dressed in traditional white dishdashas with red-and-white checked ghutras and sandals. They looked like the characters in the *Story of Jesus* Golden Book that Morgan's Southern Baptist grandparents gave her for Christmas when she was growing up. Except in those books, you could see the women's faces. That day they saw only a few women, and most were completely veiled. They looked like black chess pieces, bishops, gliding steplessly as if on rollers.

"Customs, shmustoms," Linnie said, as she shuffled along, trying to keep from stepping on the bottom of her robe. "This is all about power and control."

"The frigging Stepford wives," Kate said. "If we had to stay here very long, I could never keep my mouth shut."

"No problem there," Linnie said. "We won't be lingering."

A refreshing breeze from the direction of the Gulf stirred up little whirlpools of sand and gave the atmosphere a yellowy amber haze. Along the main streets, greenery and trees were abundant, with an occasional small flower garden and clusters of palm trees that looked like ones in Florida. The side streets were narrow and devoid of plantings. Morgan had read in one book that the wealthier homes and palaces often had lush gardens inside the walls.

They found a bank at the corner of King Saud and Dhahran Streets, and exchanged one-hundred dollars into riyals. It wasn't exactly shop-till-you-drop, but they only had a couple of hours to spare.   Shops were grouped together by wares, so they went for broke and chose the ones selling gold. The first, a narrow and rather dark cubby, was operated by two Indian men. No women worked in shops, and most of the men were Indian, Pakistani, or Filipino. Grady said, with his trademark sarcasm, that Saudis rarely lowered themselves to shop-keeping unless they had to.

The back wall of the shop looked like the inside of a treasure chest. Chains in thick clusters cascaded down like glittering golden curtains, and in front of them, ornate crafted pieces the size of a fist hung on trains of gold rings and multiple strings of golden wafers. Morgan guessed these to be wall hangings, and under her breath Linnie said that if you wore one of these creations around your neck, you wouldn't have to wait until old age for a dowager's hump. A glass display case gleamed with rings and bracelets and trinkets and pins, and it was from these riches that they picked out three thin bracelets with varying but lovely, distinct etchings.

One of Morgan's travel books said it was the Arabian way to haggle the prices when shopping, but this particular shopkeeper reported the price to her in a very disengaged manner, as if he couldn't care less whether they bought anything or not. Morgan, always too codependent to be a good bargainer, pulled Kate over and asked her opinion on the bracelets. Kate shook her head and said, "Oh, no, don't pay that, that's too much."

Morgan shrugged, and as she turned to walk away, the shopkeeper raised his finger and said something incomprehensible that was followed, Morgan thought, by the word riyal. Again Kate pursed her lips and said, no, she didn't think so, but she reached out and slipped one of the bracelets on her wrist, examining it more closely. This went on for a respectable time, until they bought the bracelets—for what price, Morgan had no idea, but less than where they'd started.

The next two shops were similar, and each one they entered looked like Morgan imagined the king's tent in *Arabian Nights*. In one glass case they found some sweet little metal and glass perfume bottles with gold designs and lids that were shaped like minarets. They cost about thirty American dollars apiece. Morgan thought one would be a perfect gift for Meredith, so they lingered a while, trying to decide which ones to buy. The shopkeeper must have taken this gesture as hesitancy and several times reduced the price. Linnie called it "body language bargaining."

Morgan settled on a roundish bottle with a royal blue background and gold stars, and Kate and Linnie got slender ones with delicate gold and silver embossed stripes and tops that looked like crowns. They paid fifteen dollars each, and they were almost out of money and time. Morgan asked Ashton if he wanted to buy something. He said, grinning, he would pick up his souvenir later.

The shopkeeper was pointing to a place down the street where they could buy perfume for the bottles, when the call to prayer came. All over the city, criers sang from tinny loudspeakers on the tops of mosques, not exactly in unison, but all within about one minute of each other, and the call came out in a scratchy cacophony that sounded like dozens of announcers all talking at once on bad microphones.

"Please come back more," the shopkeeper said, smiling, as he shut the doors.

Morgan was glad to be outside. She had read that sometimes tourists would get stuck in a restaurant or shop and couldn't leave until the prayer was over.

"Let's head back to the hotel," Grady said. "It's getting late."

On the walk back, she saw fewer male pedestrians. The robed men had all gone to the mosques, and the faceless women had disappeared also. Outside the closed shops, the shopkeepers, mostly non-Muslims, stood in small groups, laughing and drinking coffee until the prayer time was over and they could reopen their doors.

"I know they have oil and money and airplanes and all this nineties technology," Linnie said, shaking her hooded head. "But this place is like another planet."

November 12, 3:10 p.m. AST

Sheik Ahmed al-Khalid boarded the Skybird with the flourish of a president getting onto Air Force One. He was dressed in a crisp white robe and the same red checked head-dress worn by others. Like most Saudi men they had seen so far, he was immaculately groomed, with not a wrinkle in his outfit, and the headdress appeared to have been ironed with starch.

The sheik's body was large, with bulky shoulders, and his head was huge, as if it had muscle on it. He had a dark mustache and beard, closely cropped, and that same glassy, non-committal look as Goat Eyes at the airport. When he walked by Morgan, a very pleasant odor of expensive aftershave wafted in his wake.

Fouad, the emissary, padded behind the sheik and acted as interpreter, first introducing him to Taco, who was using the alias Capt. Robert Lane, then to Grady and Ashton, whom he referred to as "the crew," failing to mention Kate as one of the pilots, though she was uniformed like Grady. Linnie and Morgan were not introduced at all.

"Well, kiss my ass," Linnie muttered to Morgan as the men proceeded to seats in the aft cabin, where they had set up a table with coffee cups and related amenities. "I ought to put a kinky hair in his tea."

"You ought to keep your mouth shut," Morgan said, biting back a laugh. "If you get arrested here for being a wise ass, we don't have any more money to come back for you. We're fresh out of family jewels."

"I don't care," she said. "This place makes me want to convert to solar energy."

"So what's the title of your next book?" Kate whispered. "*No Exit?*"

"Not a bad idea," Linnie whispered back. "But I think Camus or Sartre or one of those guys already used that one. How about *The Invisible Woman*?"

Morgan and Linnie pasted on demure smiles and served the men tea. Then the three women sat in chairs up front near the galley and did what was expected of Saudi women: Stay separate from the men, sit quietly, and wait. Kate stole some peeks at her watch, and when four o'clock rolled around, shook her head. They were missing their deadline, which meant they would have to stay another night and plan the rescue for to-morrow.

"Damn," she whispered.

From what they overheard of the men's conversation, the first hour was spent in idle chitchat, not once mention-ing the airplane. Through his interpreter, Sheik Ahmed asked Grady how he enjoyed his view of the Gulf, the hotel, and what he had seen so far in Dammam. Then they talked about res-taurants and food and an archeological museum in town.

Apparently, this was the Saudi way. Meetings began with polite conversation and it was considered rude to jump right into talk about business. *Not a bad idea,* Morgan thought. *Some of our hyper, type-A overachievers, pacing on the golf course with their cellphones stuck to their ears and one foot in the cardiac ward, could learn a thing or two here.* But from her standpoint that day, it was maddening. When were they going to tour the plane? Negotiate? Was the sheik going to request a demo flight?

Finally the sheik rose, and the others stood up with him. At this point they began a tour of the inside of the plane, with Taco leading and quite unhurriedly answering most of the questions. The women stood aside while the men moved for-ward and into the cockpit area, and then repositioned them-selves at the back of the cabin. As Grady was pointing out fea-tures on the controls, Taco moved out of the way and walked back to where Morgan, Kate, and Linnie stood.

"Got a problem," Taco said, speaking low.

"What?" they asked.

"He wants a demo flight," Taco said.

"Today?" Kate asked.

"No, that's the problem. He wants to fly tomorrow afternoon. Which could mean late tomorrow afternoon. Who knows when he might show up?"

"Can we set a time?" Kate asked.

"No, that's not done," Taco said. "And if we demo him tomorrow, that puts the rescue off another day. Don't want to do that. We need to get out of here."

"What are you going to do?" Morgan asked.

"I need to talk to Buck. But I can't leave. I'm sending Ashton off to make contact with him. To get things going for today."

"Ashton? Alone?" Morgan asked.

"Robert!" Grady motioned for Taco to join the group, which was heading out the door to look at the outside of the plane.

"Gotta go," Taco said, walking backwards. "He'll be okay. It's a place not far."

"Shit," Morgan said. She hated the idea of Ashton off by himself in some secret desert rendezvous.

"He'll be okay," Taco repeated. "You all just get ready to go."

CHAPTER SIXTY-FIVE

November 12, 4:45 p.m. AST

"We've got to stay calm," Linnie said, as she gathered up coffee cups and scooped napkins and wet tea bags into a trash bag. "We need to recheck our supplies."

From a storage compartment in the rear of the cabin, they retrieved their flight bags containing the abayas and two fanny packs. Inside one, Morgan had packed the cash for the maid, and the passport and papers she would slip to her. Besides staying alive, the role as courier was Morgan's main job.

Linnie had assembled first aid supplies to take into the house. She was prepared to revive or sedate Faiza, depending on how they found her. If Faiza had indeed been held in a Woman's Room, then she would be emerging from months of total darkness, complete sensory deprivation. Would she recognize them? Struggle? Scream? Would they have to carry her out?

"She'll be fragile, no question about that," Linnie said. "Otherwise, I'm not sure what to expect. If she gets hysterical, I'll give her a shot of Valium, low dose. Then we'll wrap her in the abaya and veil. Light will be a shock. The veil will help shield her eyes. And it'll be sunset, so she won't get slammed with bright sun."

Kate went into the cockpit to make sure all the charts were in order. Morgan, Linnie, and Kate talked quietly, reviewing the plan one more time, but the big question hung there, conspicuously unspoken.

What if Faiza was insane? Men trained in combat had been driven insane by lesser incarcerations. Seven months without a sliver of light or even one other human sound, and worse, without the barest touch from another living being, was a horror none of them could imagine. Obviously the punishment was intended to drive a person crazy, but how long did it take? One month? Six months? Years? What happened to a person's sense of time?

Did Faiza have the psychological and emotional stamina to cling to her sanity? If she was still pregnant, that would surely help. There would be constant change in her body, growth, something to mark the passage of time with no awareness of mornings and no evenings, just one long endless dark night. The presence of life inside her, movement, perhaps would keep her company. And give her hope.

Morgan recalled what June, the midwife, had said. That Faiza would never give up, and that would keep her and her baby alive and well.

And there was always the hope that their intel from the spies inside the house was correct, and that Faiza had been released from the Woman's Room.

Morgan clung to that hope.

November 12, 5:30 p.m. AST

Ashton wasn't back yet. The sky was beginning to soften into the glow of approaching sunset, and the sunlight falling in the thick, round windows made rose-gold streaks that turned the cabin amber.

Taco tried to check his watch surreptitiously, but Morgan could tell he was getting concerned. She stationed herself on a small couch near the door, so she could see Ashton coming through the gate. Grady sat down next to her and put his arm around her shoulders.

"Where is he?" Morgan said. "He should have been back a half hour ago."

"I'm sure he's fine," Grady said.

"But what if he gets picked up?"

"Morgan, you've seen this place," Grady said. "It's not a

war zone. It's just another city. The same streets, the same shops. Yeah, they're kind of weird, but there's no Gestapo. And so far, we haven't done anything against the law. No one knows what we're planning."

Morgan nodded, and he put his fingers through hers, squeezing her hand. She looked into his eyes; they were serious. She thought, for an instant, that she might be looking in a mirror. All of the loneliness of the past many years, loneliness she didn't even know was there before now, seared through her. And she wondered, was it all wasted time, or was it perfectly planned, all leading up to this moment?

November 12, 5:45 p.m. AST

"Why don't you go out and chat with your pal Rashad?" Taco said.

Morgan shook her head. "I'd be too nervous. It would show."

"We need to tell him, casually, that we're going to demo the plane. So he'll be cool when we come back," Taco said. "Go on, you can do it."

Morgan walked down the steps. The air had cooled considerably, and though there was no breeze, it felt almost refreshing. She took a deep breath and waved to their gate guard.

"Hello, Rashad," she said.

"Hello," he said. "You are liking your day here?"

"Oh yes," Morgan said. "We went to shops today."

"Shops?"

"The souks," she said.

"Ah," he said, understanding. "Are you buying some thing?"

"Yes, we bought jewelry. Bracelets." She pointed to her wrist. "Gold."

"Ah, gold." He smiled. "Americans are liking gold?"

With Rashad's stuttering English, the two made a semblance of small talk. Then, Morgan told him that they entertained the sheik today, and that they were taking another sheik for a ride.

"Oh, the sheik returns?" he asked.

"No, a different sheik," she said. "Two sheiks."

"Ah," he said. "One more sheik."

"This sheik is bringing his wife."

Rashad raised his enormous eyebrows. "Wife. On the plane?"

"Yes," Morgan said. "This sheik wants to bring his wife. To see the plane." She made a sweeping gesture toward the plane. "We are flying tonight, with the sheik and his wife. To Riyadh."

"Ah, Riyadh. Pretty airport."

"Yes, I've heard that," Morgan said.

"Pretty airport. Like you, pretty lady," Rashad said.

Morgan sensed he was still confused. He peered at her from behind his black goat eyes.

"Soon, we will go to the sheik and bring him back here," she said.

"He has not a driver?" Rashad asked.

"Oh yes," Morgan said. "But we are invited to his house."

Suddenly, this felt like too much information, and Morgan decided to end the conversation before Rashad got significantly curious. Just then she saw Ashton rounding the corner of the building and walking toward the gate. Her heart was racing, and she wanted to run up and hug him and scream with relief, but she had to act cool. Rashad recognized Ashton and opened the gate. Morgan walked with Ashton back to the plane, waving at Rashad as they boarded.

"That was a bad idea," she told everyone.

"Looked like you were chatting amicably enough," Linnie said.

Morgan frowned. "I don't know. I think I might have made him suspicious."

"I think Grady's right," Linnie said, reassuring her. "With this Rashad guy, you can do no wrong."

"Maybe," Morgan said. "But something still doesn't feel right. I don't trust him."

Ashton slumped into a seat.

"Sorry for the delay," he said. "But Buck wasn't sure he could put it together on this short notice. So he left me at a coffee shop while he checked with the guys. I drank about a hundred cups of that coffee. It's so strong, it's like drinking pure adrenaline."

"Did he come back?" Taco asked.

"Yeah," Ashton said.

"Can they do it?" Taco said.

"Yeah," Ashton said, clenching his hand in a victory fist. "He said they will be there as planned, and they'll see us when the sunset prayer call goes out."

Taco checked his watch. "We gotta haul ass, but act like we've got all the time in the world. Gather your stuff. We need to be in the car in twelve minutes."

Morgan felt sick and short of breath as Linnie and she buckled on their fanny packs and wrapped their abayas around their shoulders. They would put on their veils in the car. Morgan bundled the extra abaya and veil for Faiza, and held it under her own.

They all gathered at the door of the plane and faced each other one more time. Kate took hold of Morgan's hand and Linnie's hand, then cradled them into her chest.

"Good luck, you two," she said. "We'll be here when you get back. Ready to roll."

Grady pulled Morgan toward him, and with the other hand squeezed Ashton's shoulder. "Don't get ahead of yourself, kid," he said. "Take it slow and easy."

"I will," Ashton said.

Grady gave him a thumbs-up. "Go get that woman of yours out of that house and into my airplane. And we will f-ing rock and roll."

CHAPTER SIXTY-SIX

November 12, 6:45 p.m. AST

The drive from the airport to the house where Faiza was held captive would take twenty minutes—if there were no traffic jams or no one blasted into the side of their car. Taco took it slowly, muttering about the lousy Saudi drivers.

It did seem to Morgan that the traffic on the streets and highways moved with a sort of frenetic recklessness, which didn't match the lazy indifference of life in the hotel and in restaurants and shops. But this was a country of incongruities. After all, they were on their way to a contemporary mansion with a medieval dungeon.

Ashton, still wearing his flight engineer's garb, sat in the passenger seat next to Taco, who wore his pilot's uniform. Morgan and Linnie spent most of the drive securing their veils. They were made from panels of thick black netting, with strips for tying around the crown of the head. The netting was in two layers. The first, a thicker one, had a narrow, half-inch slit across the eyes, allowing just enough space to peek out. The top layer, a thinner mesh, could be worn back over the head or over the face for complete coverage of the eyes.

"This is sort of like a bridal veil," Linnie said, pulling the second layer down over her face.

"Hardly," Morgan said.

"You look like Darth Vader," Ashton said.

They turned onto an unpaved street on the outskirts of town, in a small, ancient village that had once been a caravan stop. The mansion stood alone on the right side of the street, surrounded by a high concrete wall. The color looked like a light rose, though at sunset it reflected lavender hues.

Morgan wondered if this was an old historic house, refurbished, or a brand new structure. It was difficult to tell, because the style was traditional Arabic, featuring stark, imposing walls with narrow slits for windows, to keep out the sun's raging heat. The doorways were set in deep arches, and flowering bushes flanked the center gate, which was made of black iron bars and topped with an ornate design.

Just as in the maid's sketch, a small minaret rose in the center of the roof, and the corners bore fat, squared turrets, big enough to contain small rooms.

"There's the car," Taco said.

Around the corner was a white Land Rover, pulled over to the side. One man sat behind the wheel. Morgan squinted, trying to make out the driver. It looked like Soho, but from behind the veil, objects were shaded and indistinct. It reminded her of trick or treat on Halloween, peering out of the tiny mask holes, stumbling in the dark from house to house, trying to navigate without any peripheral vision.

Taco stopped the car directly in front of the gate, which was slightly ajar. So far there were no other cars in the vicinity. They had heard the prayer call just minutes before turning onto the street. *Oh God, Goddess, Allah, or whoever, let us get away with this,* Morgan prayed silently. *Please let us get away with this. And please, please, don't let anyone get hurt.*

They entered the gate like couples coming to call; Taco escorted Linnie, and Morgan walked alongside Ashton. If they had been real guests, they would have parted company inside the gate, and Linnie and Morgan would have diverted to the women's entrance that led to the women's quarters.

Morgan's heart was thumping so hard she was sure it was beating aloud, as though they were marching to a big kettledrum. The telltale heart. So she clutched Faiza's abaya bundle to her chest to muffle the booms.

The front door was open, and inside, Crater stood holding an assault rifle casually at his side. *Shit, please please don't fire it,* Morgan thought. *Please nobody shoot.*

As agreed, no one spoke. Crater pointed to his right and whispered, "The men are in there. Buck has them. Women, there." He gestured left, toward the back of the house.

They were standing in a massive entry hall. The floor was made of white and black marble tiles in a checkered pattern, and through the veil, the walls looked to be a light color. There were wall hangings in gold frames and perhaps some rugs or tapestries on the walls, and several period chairs in gold and green velvet. If this were the time and place for humor, Morgan knew what Linnie would say. That it looked like Louis XIV goes to Hollywood.

Ahead of them the foyer opened into a courtyard, lush with small palms, clumps of little ornamental trees, and explosions of flowers. Morgan could hear the sound of water splashing on marble or stone, perhaps a fountain. Toward the back of the foyer, an enormous marble staircase with a gold-trimmed banister towered, like an emperor holding court.

They walked swiftly, tiptoeing on the marble, toward the stairs. As they passed the room where Buck was holding the men, Morgan glanced over. She noticed that Buck had grown an Arab-style heavy dark beard and mustache since she'd last seen him at Taco's. He certainly looked like a local now.

Buck must have herded everyone into one room. There were maybe eight or ten men, most in thobes and ghutras, and two or three in the long nightshirts worn by servants. They all sat on the floor, their backs to the door, and Buck braced his rifle with both hands.

On the opposite wall, the one the men were facing, Morgan saw a beautiful gold table with what looked like carvings or icons. She wondered if this was the prayer room and that was some kind of altar. If so, the men were facing the right direction toward Mecca, and maybe they wouldn't even miss their prayers.

None of them looked around, or even moved, as the

group walked by. Morgan didn't think they knew of the strangers' presence.

The stairway was so wide they all four walked up it abreast. Ashton squeezed Morgan's arm and looked at her, but of course she could cast him no expressions of reassurance. His face was set and his jaw jutted in and out, as though he was gritting his teeth. Morgan's breath, trying to pant, collected in a hot, dry pool inside the veil, and she felt stifled, taking in the same air over and over.

From the stairs she could see a long, gleaming white-tiled hallway off to the left, and The Bear standing inside a doorway. The women's quarters. The Bear raised his fingers in a wave, then grinned and gave the thumbs-up. Morgan prayed, to whomever might be listening, that none of the women would get hurt. To the women, Morgan silently said, Don't be frightened. Please forgive us for scaring you.

So far no one in Taco's group had spoken one word. When they reached the top of the stairs, they were met by a small, timid Filipina with straight dark hair, wearing a long green frock that looked like a muumuu. Her hands were clasped over her mouth, and her black eyes were misted over with fear.

Taco approached the woman, and Morgan guessed that this was Maria, the informant, the one who had drawn the map, the one whose passport Morgan carried. She looked so terrified, Morgan wondered how she'd had the courage to do what she had done so far. Morgan had expected someone a bit more brazen. Maybe, like Morgan, Maria was a lot bolder in the rehearsal, but jelly when it was really show time. Well, she could feel whatever she wanted. Morgan loved her for her guts, and for being the only one who would stand up and do something. Morgan prayed she would get out safely.

Taco held his hand out to Morgan. She fumbled in her fanny pack, producing the passport and bundle of U.S. bills, and handed it to Maria. The papers jiggled as they were passed from trembling hand to trembling hand. Then Maria turned

and motioned them to follow. They headed down a long hallway, which then turned left. Maria stopped opposite a closed
door, made of some highly polished wood, like oak or cypress.

"In here," she whispered. "That door is locked. I have no
key."

Taco nodded and took a small satchel off his belt.

"Wait," Maria said. "You must tie me up."

"I will," Taco whispered. "When we come down."

"No, now, please," she said. "I am afraid."

"You must wait," Taco said. Turning to the others, he
explained. "The servants' quarters, her room, are probably on
the first floor. We can't take the time. We'll have The Bear do it."

Maria protested, but Taco was already kneeling by the
door. It was dark at the end of this secluded hallway, and Taco
flipped on a small flashlight. Ashton also turned his on and
aimed the narrow beam at the door's lock.

The door was secured with two huge padlocks, one near
the top and one near the bottom. In the middle of the door was
a metal plate, about twelve inches by four inches, held with big
wingnuts. A pass-through for food, Morgan guessed.

"Goddamm!" Taco said. He knelt down and began pry-
ing the lower padlock with a small instrument that looked like
a brass toothpick. "Goddamm," he repeated.

Morgan's mouth was so dry that her tongue was actually
sticking to the roof of her mouth, and she wondered if anyone had remembered to bring water. She took hold of Ashton's
arm, and Linnie clutched hers, and there wasn't a sound from
their breath, or from anywhere. It was as if the whole house
suddenly fell silent, so everyone everywhere could hear the
tapping and scratching of Taco's little tool on the padlock.

Then there was a crunch, and Taco whispered, "Got it.
Let's hope the other's the same."

He went to work on the top padlock, and it broke free
in seconds. He tugged on the long brass handle, and the enormous door rasped open. It was at least six inches thick, and
lined on the inside with some kind of padding that felt like

boxing gloves.

One at a time they passed through the doorway. It was like stepping into an old attic that had been closed up for fifty years. Morgan untied her veil and took a breath through her nose. There was an odor, but not as terrible as she had expected. It smelled unventilated and stale, with a trace of stench, like the smell that stays on the bottom of the kitchen garbage can when you take out the plastic bag.

The room, about ten by twelve, was dark, but not pitch. Near the top of one wall, much too high for a person to look out, was a small sliver of a window, and still enough daylight outside to cast a dim, grayish glow into the stale air. From somewhere overhead came a faint sound like a fan motor, but no movement of air that Morgan could detect.

This was not the Woman's Room.

At least those prayers had been answered, and Faiza had been moved from the pitch black, padded, soundless isolation. But this room was still a ghastly prison.

They all huddled together near the doorway for what seemed like minutes, though was probably only seconds. Morgan did not think any of them could have ever prepared for what they were seeing. The room, its size, the desolation, the confinement. The knowledge that Faiza had been locked up for seven months.

Morgan heard someone choking back a sob.

In the corner opposite the door there was a silhouette, crouched on the floor, bundled in a cover. *Oh God, don't let her be dead. Please don't let her be dead.* Taco lifted his flashlight just enough to cast dim filtered light in that direction. The bundle stirred.

"Son," he said to Ashton. "Go to her."

In two strides, Ashton was kneeling at her side.

"Faiza," he whispered. "It's me. Ashton."

Taco moved the light to illuminate Ashton's face. When he did, Morgan caught a glimpse of Faiza. She had covered her head and face, as if she were wearing an abaya, and her eyes squinted. Very slowly and gently, as if she might shatter into a million pieces, Ashton touched her shoulder.

"It's me. Ashton," he repeated.

Faiza raised her head slightly, but her expression was blank, with no sign of recognition. Ashton looked over at Morgan, shaking his head, his eyes pleading, *Please, no, don't let it be too late.*

"We came to help you," he said. "I want you to come with me now."

Then there was a tiny whimper. And another. And then a small pale hand slipped out of the cover and, in that same way Morgan had seen once before, when they stood together in her kitchen, Faiza reached up and touched Ashton's cheek with her fingertips. She began to sob, and said some words that Morgan didn't understand, probably Arabic.

"We must go quickly," he said to her. He began to gather her up in his arms. She started to sob as she wrapped her arms around his neck. She spoke some more words.

"What?" he asked gently.

"Ashton," she said, in a voice as soft as a baby bird's. "I believed you would come."

CHAPTER SIXTY-SEVEN

November 12, 7:05 p.m. AST

"Can you walk, sweetie?" Linnie whispered as Ashton lifted Faiza to her feet.

Faiza nodded weakly.

"Mom is here," Ashton said.

Morgan touched her arm, but didn't say anything. She wondered how long it had been since Faiza had heard a human voice. Did their whispers blast into her ears like sonic booms, the words clattering and screeching on raw, chaste surfaces?

"We've got to move," Taco said.

"Faiza," Ashton spoke just above a whisper. "Mom has a robe. Let them help you get it on. Then we are going to walk out together."

"Oh, no!" she cried.

"It's safe," Ashton said. "We have men downstairs to protect us."

Faiza gasped, and slumped into Ashton's arms. Linnie moved forward and held her from the other side. Ashton had turned his flashlight back on, holding his palm over the beam. In the added light, Morgan saw that in the corner of the room there was a low cot, some crumpled rags, and two metal buckets. Morgan unfurled the abaya and held it out to her.

"Faiza, dear, you need to wear this. To hide you," Morgan murmured.

Faiza clutched the blanket more tightly around her. She

was so utterly confused.

"Please," Ashton said. "Trust me."

He took her fingers and gently loosened her grip on the blanket, then eased it off her shoulders as Morgan wrapped the silk robe around her. During the exchange, Morgan could see that Faiza was wearing a knee-length white shift, made from muslin, yellowed and thinning. Her hair was long and matted into thick strands, as if she had been braiding it, and her body smelled musty. She was hugely pregnant. Her head came just to the top of Ashton's chest, and as he leaned over to kiss her forehead, he looked at her as if he could scoop her up and tuck her completely into his heart.

Linnie tied the veil around Faiza's head; then they fastened their own.

"I'm a nurse. I'll take care of you," Linnie said.

Taco went first, followed by Ashton and Faiza. Ashton had both arms around her, but she was taking steps on her own. Morgan and Linnie stepped out of the room, and as they had been instructed, they quietly shut the door and replaced the padlocks. The longer it took for the household to figure out what had been done, the more time they had to get away.

They hurried down the narrow stairs and closed the second door. What Morgan really wanted to do was to toss some gasoline up those stairs and torch the damned place. Gasoline made from their fucking oil.

Linnie lifted her veil from her mouth and put her lips close to Morgan's ear.

"She's definitely with child," Linnie said, and Morgan could hear her smile.

"How far along, do you think?" Morgan whispered.

"Let's put it this way. If she doesn't take a deep breath, she might make it to the car."

"You're kidding!"

"Yeah, I am," Linnie said. "But it's close. She's nine months if she's a day."

"*Ssshhhh.*" Taco put his finger to his lips, and they

dropped their veils back over their faces.

As they descended the staircase, Morgan saw that Crater had taken Buck's post at the door to the men's room, and Buck was walking toward them from the back of the house. Later, Morgan learned that after Maria stashed the money and passport under her mattress, Buck had tied her to the bedpost and wrapped a scarf over her mouth.

Buck shouted something in Arabic to the men in the room, instructions to stay where they were until told to move. The plan was that Crater and The Bear would hold their hostages for thirty minutes, enough time for the group to drive to the airport and get airborne. After that, if no one had seen them in the house, there still might be time before anyone realized they had taken Faiza out.

The walk across the foyer took a millennium. Every step felt to Morgan like slow motion, like a dream where she was trying to run but the ground was quicksand and she was trying to pull her feet through the thick muck. They strolled across that entry hall toward the front door like kinfolk who come to call on Sunday afternoon. Ya'll come back now, y'heah?

Morgan honestly didn't think any of the men or women in that house knew they had been there.

Still, she had a feeling that they were being chased, that someone was right on their heels. It reminded her of when she was a little child and went down into the basement alone. She always felt that some shadowy stranger was lurking behind the furnace or in the damp concrete corner under Daddy's workbench. The light was at the bottom of the stairs, a plain bulb with a thin chain pull, long enough for a kid to reach. And the kids were supposed to turn off the light before they left the basement. That meant that after you pulled the chain and the basement was swept in darkness, you still had to go all the way up the stairs.

So Morgan would pull the chain and then tear up the stairs, taking two at a time, like a fly darting out from under a flyswatter, but on the way up she could feel a presence right behind her, its big hairy, gnarled hand open and poised at her heel, and on the last step, she'd leap out of its reach just before it grabbed her foot.

Taco opened the front door and held it as Ashton, Faiza, and Buck stepped into the dusky sunlight. Morgan and Linnie were right behind them. A few more steps and they would be out of the house.

But suddenly there was pressure on Morgan's arms, as though someone was hugging her from behind. Linnie? What was she doing? Morgan wriggled against the hold and started to turn to her, when she saw Linnie's robed form a few feet ahead. The hug got tighter and more fierce. *What the hell?* And then her arms were pinned at her side and she couldn't move forward, and a hoarse male voice was spitting angry words into her right ear, unintelligible and muffled through the heavy veil. Morgan struggled, trying not to cry out, pulling and tugging to wrench herself from his violent grasp.

Where was Crater? The Bear? And then came the thought, instantaneously, that this was one of them. One of them wasn't who he said he was. A traitor. No, that couldn't be. She trusted them. She knew them. No she didn't. She didn't even know their names.

Linnie turned back toward Morgan, her face hidden behind the dark veil. She kept walking, backing tentatively toward the open door. Then she turned again and hurried toward the opening, reaching out to get Taco's attention.

Taco looked back at Morgan, then raised his arm, like a signal to someone outside. Morgan tried to muffle her own grunts as she hunched over, kicking and flailing against her attacker. What was going on?

Suddenly she sensed confusion all around her, and terror and disaster as she sank to the floor. A two-ton sandbag pushed her under its weight, and the abaya piled up around her like a crumpled black tent. And she knew that this was it. She was caught, and so everyone was caught. It was all over. They would never get out.

Somebody help me. Get this awful thug off me. Please. Get us out of here. Morgan clenched her fists, bracing for the sound of a gun, fearing it, then hoping, wishing, praying for it.

Then there was a sound; but it was not a gun. It was a hiss, several short bursts, like someone pumping an aerosol can that's almost empty. The arms gripped her tighter for a moment, then relaxed, and she felt the weight come off her back and slump to the tile beside her.

"Sh-h-h-h-h," whispered Crater, as he stooped down in front of her and held out his hands to help her to her feet.

"What happened? Who . . ." Morgan whispered.

"The guy was hiding somewhere," Crater said.

Through the veil, Morgan could see that Crater was actually grinning. He gave her a little shove toward the door, and she hurried out. Linnie and Taco were waiting at the gate.

"It's okay," Taco said. "He gassed him."

"Gassed him?" Morgan said.

"You said no guns, boss lady."

CHAPTER SIXTY-EIGHT

November 12, 7:15 p.m. AST

"We're running a few minutes behind," Taco said as he steered the car into a U-turn and back out to the paved road. His voice was easy, which Morgan found comforting. She was so numb from acting calm when she really wanted to scream that she wasn't even sure she had a voice anymore.

Ashton held Faiza bundled in his arms, and talked to her quietly. Once in a while she nodded her hooded head.

"We are going to an airplane," he said, very slowly. He explained that she must walk with Buck to the plane. When he said this, Faiza protested.

"It's part of the plan," Ashton said. "I will be right behind you."

When they turned onto the street that led to the airport, traffic stopped. Horns were blaring and the cars ahead were bunched together in what looked like an impromptu tailgate party. Buck, sitting in the front seat, craned his head out the window.

"Is it a wreck?" Morgan asked.

"I can't tell," Buck said. "I don't see any police. It might just be an ordinary day on Saudi streets. Organized chaos. Everyone cuts everyone else off at the same time."

"Shit," Taco said.

They waited two minutes, five minutes. The guys in the house had given them thirty minutes. How much time had they already used up? Had the skirmish with the guy who grabbed Morgan triggered a big confrontation in the house? A shootout that would alert the neighbors and the police? More cars came up and wedged in behind them, and it appeared they couldn't move forward or back. Buck got out of the car and disappeared into the fray. More minutes went by. Finally Buck returned.

"It's a wreck," he said.

"We can't wait," Taco said.

"I saw a back street." Buck pointed.

They were blocked by other vehicles, but Taco inched the car forward and then back, forward and back, like he was maneuvering out of a tight parking space, and finally got them free from the gridlock.

"Over there."

Taco jumped the car onto the sidewalk and drove for about a half block, and then bounced into what looked like a narrow alleyway. It wasn't an official roadway, rather a sand strip between two buildings. They emerged on another street, and Buck glanced out the back window.

"Clear behind," he said.

As two American guys, an Arab guy, and three Darth Vaders on the streets of Dhahran, they probably blended right in, Morgan thought. But it seemed to her that they couldn't be more conspicuous if the car was painted Day-Glo red with a big neon hand on the roof that said: "Cut me off, I've stolen your woman."

"I've never been so scared in my whole life," Linnie whispered to Morgan.

"You're the one with the Valium in your pack," she whispered back.

*   *   *

When at last they pulled up to their terminal, Morgan thought the Skybird was the most beautiful sight she had ever seen. She wanted to grab its sleek, shiny fuselage and give it a big kiss, like sailors do when they throw themselves down and kiss the dry land.

"Take it slow," Taco said.

Morgan needed the reminder. She, for one, would have bounded out of the car and right up the steps.

In a voice barely audible, Faiza said something to Ashton.

"What?" he asked her.

"I have no shoes," she said faintly.

"Oh my god," Linnie said, pulling Faiza's robe up from her feet. They were bare.

A Saudi woman would never let her feet be seen in public. Although the abaya went to the ground, there was a chance that a toe might stick out when she walked.

"We've got to find something to cover her feet," Morgan said.

"Here," Ashton said, pulling off his shoes. "She can wear my socks. They're dark."

Taco stalled, repositioning the car in the parking space, as they scrambled to cover Faiza's tiny shoeless feet. Morgan and Linnie removed their veils, because Rashad was accustomed to seeing them come and go in Western dress.

Buck got out of the car and opened the door for Faiza, whom they had placed in the back seat on the right. During the drive, she had sobbed some, and spoken Ashton's name aloud over and over again. Now it was time for her to walk to the plane alongside Buck, her fake husband.

Saudi men and women don't walk in public with their arms around each other; so Faiza would have to make the distance on her own power, in a stately manner. Just as she was getting out of the car, her legs gave way under her, but she regained her balance. Morgan couldn't see her face, but she could feel her determination.

Like an actor effortlessly on cue, Buck nodded formally to Faiza and proceeded slowly toward the gate. With every timid, labored step she took, Morgan could feel her exhaustion and weakness, and worried she might pass out and her body would crumple under a heap of black silk on the tarmac. But Faiza held herself steady, as if she was balancing a crystal vase on her head.

Go, Faiza, go. Slowly. Walk. One step at a time.

Before they reached the gate, Buck greeted Rashad in Arabic, and the guard had the gate opened before they arrived. Faiza stepped through behind Buck, and when they reached the airplane, he extended his arm to support her. But she didn't need it. She took the handrail and climbed one step at a time, her hooded head never wavering.

Ashton followed a respectable distance behind, and as he ascended the stairs, only the most astute observer would have noticed that he was wearing no socks. But on Faiza's last step, the bottom edge of her abaya caught on the railing, disclosing one black and red men's argyle.

Morgan's heart leapt, and she quickly glanced at Rashad. Maybe he didn't notice.

But there was a flicker of recognition on his face, and Morgan knew that he had seen the sock sticking out under Faiza's robe, screaming the truth, betraying them all, the betrayal of a betrayal.

CHAPTER SIXTY-NINE

November 12, 7:35 p.m. AST

Rashad reached out and took hold of Morgan's arm, stopping her forward progress through the gate.

"You are flying now?" Goat Eyes asked, revealing nothing.

"Yes," Morgan said. "To Riyadh."

"This night?" Rashad's woolly eyebrows arched up.

"Yes. The sheik wants to go to Riyadh." Morgan shrugged, like she was just as mystified.

"You returning this night?" Rashad said.

Morgan shrugged again.

"You are returning," he said, half question, half rather commanding statement.

Morgan heard the whine of the engines starting, or what she thought were the engines. As planned, Grady was supposed to start the engines when their car pulled into the parking area.

"Maybe this night, maybe tomorrow," she said.

Morgan knew what he was thinking. Why doesn't the flight attendant know the plans? She cocked her head slightly, tossing him a flirtatious smile, the best she could do under the circumstances.

"Good-bye, Rashad," she sang out. "See you later."

He did not let go of her arm.

Morgan looked directly at him. For the first time since she'd met him, his dark eyes were opened deeper, revealing something, but she didn't know what they were telling her.

Terrified, she started to speak, then silenced herself. But

her thoughts wouldn't quiet. His gaze pierced through her and into the place where she held all her secrets.

Images tore through Morgan's mind, of angry police marching them all off the plane, of arms and legs in shackles, of a black prison cell, of fear and isolation, of Faiza gasping for breath, of a baby being torn from her grasp. If Rashad could read her mind, they were dead. *Stop, stop,* she ordered her thoughts, but they wouldn't stop, they were tumbling out into the unspoken space between the two people, revealing Morgan, betraying them all, and if Rashad could read them, the whole mission would be ruined and they would be dead.

"Who are these people?" Rashad asked. His English was clear, schooled, and Morgan realized that he had been faking his bad accent, and all along had understood more than he let on.

"As I told you, a sheik, and his wife," Morgan answered. "They—he—is interested in buying the airplane."

"What is his name?" Rashad demanded.

"Uh . . ." Morgan stumbled. She didn't trust her skimpy knowledge of Arabic enough to make one up. If she did, and came up with some outlandish guess, some Arabic gibberish, a name that no one had ever heard of, they were dead.

"I don't know," she answered.

"You did not meet them?"

"Yes, I did meet them. In the car. But I have forgotten." She shrugged, feigning embarrassment.

"My Arabic is very poor," she said.

From the corner of her eye, she could see Taco in the hatchway, his eyes begging her to hurry up.

"I think I must talk to your captain," Rashad said, in flawless English.

"He is on the plane, in the cockpit," Morgan answered, gesturing toward the plane, whose engines were humming.

"Then the man in charge," Rashad said sternly.

Morgan took a deep breath and realized that everything was going to happen in the next moment. They were on the teeter-totter, suspended in the middle of the ride, at the place where the weight could shift one way or the other, with the weight of just one hair, of one movement, of a single wrong word.

Morgan looked straight into Rashad's eyes. Of all the brave and gutsy things she had done in the past many months, this was the moment she knew that she needed the most courage, more than she had ever needed anytime during this crazy mission, anytime in her whole life. It was the courage to not speak, but to allow him to see all the way inside, and to trust that there was a place in him that could see, could know, could understand. With all her strength, Morgan opened her heart to him. Without speaking a word, she told him everything. And silently she pleaded. *Please. Please. Let us be. Let us go.*

Taco was now motioning with his arms; the engines were revving.

Please, please. I know you are a good man. You have love in you. I know you have love in you. Please.

For seconds, minutes, hours, Rashad stood without making a move. He didn't even blink, and his dark eyes locked into Morgan's. His held his body like a statue, so still he could make the guards at Buckingham Palace look like wriggling two-year-olds.

And then he spoke. Two words, maybe three. In Arabic. Morgan did not understand. But she would never forget them.

"Allah Ma'ak," was what Rashad said, before he turned and briskly walked in the other direction.

CHAPTER SEVENTY

November 12, 7:40 p.m. AST

Morgan climbed aboard, and with Linnie, pulled up the stairs. They secured the hatch and yelled, "Okay!" into the cockpit.

Taco was crouched behind the pilots. Buck was helping Ashton get Faiza to a seat in the back of the cabin. Morgan saw them buckling themselves in. Ashton's arms were wrapped around her.

Morgan looked into the cockpit and caught Grady's attention. She mouthed the word "Hurry!" What if she was wrong about Rashad? What if he had a change of heart and was on his way to an office to call the police? There was not a second to waste.

Then she noticed. Grady was in the right seat. Kate was in the left.

"Did you see that?" Morgan said to Linnie.

"What?"

"Kate's in the left seat," Morgan said. Linnie didn't understand the significance. "She's pilot in command."

"Is Grady sick or something?" Linnie asked.

"He looks okay," Morgan said.

There was no time for questions, or to go back to talk with Ashton and Faiza. But they looked fine. Faiza had removed her veil and abaya, and Ashton had wrapped her in one of the plane's soft brown blankets. Her head was burrowed into Ashton's chest.

Linnie and Morgan took seats at the front. The right engine was rumbling steadily. They waited for the left engine to roar into service. Morgan could see the backs of Grady's and Kate's head; both leaned toward the instrument panel. Taco was standing up now, peering over their shoulders. Morgan unbuckled her seatbelt and stood next to him.

"Hit it again," Grady said. Kate hit the starter switch once more. And once again, the left engine was silent.

"Shit. Try again," Grady said, calm but urgent. Kate hit the switch. Nothing. They scanned the instruments for a clue.

"Maybe it's the starter shaft," Taco said. "Sheared."

"Can't be," Kate said. "There's nothing on the ammeter."

Grady turned and saw Morgan.

"In an airplane," he explained, "when the starter is turned, there is an initial drain of amps, which shows up on the ammeter. If the starter was sheared, it would be activated but not rotating the engine, and the result would be little click sounds. But here, there's nothing. Not a sound."

"We're not energizing the starter," Kate said. "There's no discharge, no rotation, no nothing. Damn."

"We've gotta move," Taco said, looking at his watch.

Earlier, Kate and Grady had filed the flight plan, and as Linnie and Morgan were closing the hatch and Kate was hitting the switch for the left engine, Grady had radioed the tower for clearance to Riyadh. The tower controllers responded, clearing them to taxi to the runway. And they were now failing to taxi in an expeditious manner.

The tower called. "Skybird Seven-Two-Three-Whiskey-Tango, are you intending to taxi?"

Kate looked at Grady and shook her head. They could taxi with one engine, but they couldn't take off. But if the tower learned that they couldn't start an engine, the flight would be aborted and they would be called back to the terminal.

"What could it be?" Grady said. "What the fuck could it be?"

"Let's roll while we think about it," Kate said.

Grady pressed his mike button. "Roger, Skybird Seven-

Two-Three-Whiskey-Tango taxiing to runway three-two."

Kate edged the plane forward smoothly. An ordinary observer would not have been able to tell that they were motoring merrily along with only half their oars in the water.

The tower came back. "Skybird Seven-Two-Three-Whiskey-Tango, is there a problem?"

"Negative," Grady answered.

"Roger. Proceed to runway three-two."

"Taco, what do you think?" Grady said.

"I don't know, man," Taco said. "It's dead as a rock in a road."

"Wait a minute!" Kate shouted. "You just reminded me of something. Something from ground school."

"What?' Taco said.

"A little peccadillo of the Skybird," Kate said. "I heard of it one day, this very same scenario. It could be a bus tie breaker." She turned to Taco. "The instructor said that if everything's as flat as a dead man's dick, you've probably blown a bus tie breaker."

Taco explained to Morgan that a bus tie breaker is a giant fuse, about four inches long, intended, as most fuses are, to prevent electrical overload. It was located in a large circuit box behind some panels in the tail of the airplane.

Kate continued taxiing. "Grady," she said. "Call the tower and buy us some time."

"Dhahran ground control," Grady said into his mike. "Skybird Seven-Two-Three-Whiskey-Tango, request permission to pull over for a brief time."

"Skybird Seven-Two-Three-Whiskey-Tango," the controller repeated slowly and more emphatically. "Do you have a problem?"

"Negative, sir, we have a minor technical difficulty in some navigational equipment."

"Roger, Skybird Seven-Two-Three-Whiskey-Tango, pull into the taxiway off your starboard wing."

Taco had already streaked to the back of the plane. He

pulled a large red toolbox out of a side compartment and was frantically taking screws out of the wall panels as Kate steered the plane over and stopped. Ashton tightened his grip on Faiza and tried to conceal his fear.

What time was it? Surely by now, Crater, Soho, and The Bear would have released the hostages and fled in their own escape plan. Maybe the family thought it was a robbery. Or maybe they had already searched upstairs and found Faiza's prison empty. And if so, wouldn't the airport be the first place the police would check? And then this sticks-out-like-a-sore-thumb crew in the Skybird would look so obvious. So easy to catch.

Three minutes. Five minutes. Taco removed the panel and opened the circuit box, inspecting it. Eight minutes.

The tower called again. "Skybird Seven-Two-Three-Whiskey-Tango, do you need assistance?"

"Negative," Grady said.

"Found it!" Taco yelled up to the pilots. "It's blown."

"Skybird Seven-Two-Three-Whiskey-Tango," the tower called again. "We are sending a courtesy truck out to assist you."

"We can't let them do that," Kate said. "We've got to fix it ourselves. We can't let anyone on this airplane."

"Taco!" Grady shouted. "Can you replace it?"

Taco searched the tool compartment and the toolbox.

"No. There isn't a spare," he yelled.

"Can you fix it?" Grady yelled back.

Out the window, Morgan spotted a small white vehicle turning onto the taxiway, heading in the direction of the plane. It had a rotating yellow beacon on the top. In the twilight, she could see the outlines of two people on the inside.

"I'm gonna jump it," Taco shouted. "When I tell you, hit the starter."

"Ready!" Grady said.

Morgan looked at Buck, searching for some sign that everything would be okay. But his expression was stoic. She didn't fully understand the technical drama that was going on, but she did realize that Taco was about to jump-start a forty-million-dollar airplane, like the guys in high school used to do when their '57 Chevies wouldn't turn over.

Morgan didn't dare look at Ashton and Faiza. Linnie grabbed her hand and together they whispered, "Go go go, hurry, hurry, hurry. Please start. Please start."

"Ground control, Skybird Seven-Two-Three-Whiskey-Tango," Grady calmly told the tower. "Thank you, but we decline the assistance. We are correcting a minor technical problem in navigational equipment."

"Skybird Seven-Two-Three-Whiskey-Tango," the tower said. "Please proceed with your taxi or return to the terminal."

Taco yelled to Morgan to bring him a towel. She did and stayed aft with him, kneeling on the floor. He picked up a big wrench and a pair of insulated pliers, then wrapped the towel around the handles of both. Then he stuck both tools into the circuit box. The ends of the tools crackled and sparks flew out like a Fourth of July sparkler.

"Hit the damn starter!" Taco roared. Grady flipped the switch.

There was a whine and a *tick, tick tick, tick* sound from the engine. More sparks from the circuit box. *Tick, tick, tick.* Morgan held her breath. Then, all of a sudden, there was a whoosh and a rumble, and the engine thundered into life.

"Yeee-haw!" Taco yelped. "We're outta here!"

"Ground control" Grady spoke coolly into his mike. "Skybird Seven-Two-Three-Whiskey-Tango ready to taxi to runway three-two."

"Roger, Skybird Seven-Two-Three-Whiskey-Tango, cleared for taxi."

Morgan peered out the window. Before, she had been afraid to look. Afraid she would see a bunch of army guys with big rifles in jeeps speeding out to intercept them. Afraid a police helicopter would set down right in front of their nose.

But there was no one. Just an ordinary runway and some rundown terminal buildings and a couple of palm trees in the background of her last look at Dhahran International Airport. The courtesy car had turned back.

The plane turned onto the runway. "Skybird Seven-Two-Three-Whiskey-Tango. Ready for takeoff on runway three-two."

"Roger, Skybird Seven-Two-Three-Whiskey-Tango, cleared for takeoff."

Kate eased the throttles, and the plane sprang forward as if fired from a slingshot. Taco and Morgan had forgotten to sit down, so they both hung onto seat backs and braced themselves as the plane rocketed almost straight up into the sky.

Up in the cockpit, Grady put his hand on Kate's shoulder. He turned on the intercom, so everyone in the cabin could hear.

"Way to go, Captain," he said. "Nobody ever would have thought of that."

"Thanks," Kate said.

CHAPTER SEVENTY-ONE

November 12, 7:55 p.m. AST

The Skybird leveled off at 43,000 feet. It was dark now, but at the higher altitude, a dim sunset glow remained. Then as they traveled, a full moon illuminated the sky, as if the Universe was calling forth all its resources to light their way.

Still, they weren't out of danger. They had the entire country of Saudi Arabia to cross over, which, in this plane at mach speed, would still take over two hours.

Morgan wanted Faiza to feel safe. She knelt by her seat. Linnie walked back and sat on the floor next to Morgan. Linnie had the first aid kit, a bottle of water, a jar of peanut butter, and a half loaf of bread in a bag knotted at the end.

"Hello, Faiza," Morgan said. "How are you doing?"

Behind the tears, Faiza's exquisite dark eyes sparkled with love and hope and gratitude.

"I'm okay," she said, tightening the blanket around her head.

"Is the noise hurting your ears?" Linnie asked softly.

"Not hurting," she said. "It's just, well, so much."

"Can you eat or drink anything?" Linnie asked.

"I would love some water, please."

"Peanut butter?" Linnie offered.

Faiza looked up at Ashton and began to smile. Then she started to giggle.

"Peanut butter?" she said. "Peanut butter." And her

shoulders shook with laughter. Morgan wondered if this was the first time she had laughed in seven months.

"You don't like it?" Morgan said.

"I love it," Faiza said. "It's so ... American."

"Well, you're in the ole U.S. of A., now," Ashton said.

Faiza looked at him questioningly.

"This airplane," he said. "It's registered in the United States. So no matter where we are, in this plane we are officially on U.S. soil."

"So we are safe?" Faiza asked.

"Almost," Ashton said.

Sitting on the floor, Linnie began spreading peanut butter on slices of bread. "We all need to eat something," she said. "When we get out of the country, we'll get out some canned stuff in the galley and have a feast."

Faiza reached for Morgan's hand.

"I know I will thank you many times, for the rest of my life. It will take that long to tell you all of my gratitude. So I will start now. Thank you. Thank you."

Morgan took Faiza in her arms. From the corner of her eye, she could see Buck and Taco watching them from where they stood in the tail section.

"There's something else, Morgan," Faiza said.

"What, sweetie?"

"When I was in that room, in the dark, sometimes I could feel your presence. Like you were there. Giving me comfort. And hope."

*   *   *

Faiza asked if she could use the bathroom, and if there was some soap and a towel. But when she started to get up, she slumped back down into the seat.

"There's plenty of time to wash up," Linnie said. "You need to take it slow."

"Did you say that you were a nurse?" Faiza asked.

"Yes," Linnie said.

"I'm pregnant," Faiza said.

Linnie smiled. "We know."

"Um, but I'm feeling strange. Heavy. A little dizzy. It's like cramps."

Linnie turned to Ashton and Morgan. "Could I have a little time alone with her?"

Ashton stood up and walked with Morgan toward the front of the cabin. He wrapped his arm around her shoulders and said, "Mom, I love you. Thank you."

"We're not out of the woods yet," Morgan said.

"I know," he said. "But we're off the ground. And she's out of that prison."

Morgan peeked into the cockpit. They were still very busy.

"Nice driving, Kate," she said.

"Thanks," Kate called back.

Grady turned around and smiled. He was having the time of his life.

There was something about this airplane. When they were on the ground, cranking a dead engine and taxiing along one minute ahead of disaster, Morgan had felt numb with fear. But now, in the air, she felt like they were on their own little tubular planet, blessed by some invisible hand, or hands. Maybe it was angels, who knew? But in this moment, it seemed as if no one but angels could touch them.

Linnie motioned Morgan back. She had a stethoscope around her neck and was loosening a blood pressure cuff from around Faiza's upper arm.

"How is she?" Ashton asked.

"She's fine," Linnie said. Then she looked at Morgan and grinned. "Geez, girlfriend, you sure put on a helluva thrilling tour!"

"What is it?" Morgan said.

Linnie placed her hand on the small mountain that was Faiza's abdomen and announced, "This beautiful young woman is going to be a mother."

"We know," Morgan said.

"I mean soon," Linnie said. "She's in labor."

CHAPTER SEVENTY-TWO

November 12, 8:35 p.m. AST
They were about one hundred miles west of Riyadh, the point at which they would begin their descent if they were actually landing at Riyadh. Which they weren't. But Riyadh didn't know that.

They had filed a flight plan to that city, and Riyadh was expecting them. Airplanes are supposed to stick to their flight plans and go where they say they are going. Otherwise, air traffic controllers, and many other officials, get very upset.

When the Skybird didn't land in Riyadh, but instead headed out across Saudi Arabia, they would be violating international aviation regulations.

Why didn't they simply file a flight plan to the United States and then leave the country with Faiza hidden in the plane? Morgan had asked in an early planning session. The reason was that visitors cannot leave Saudi without exit visas. If they had stated their intention to leave the country, they would have had to request permission, which would have opened them to official scrutiny.

They simply had to leave without asking.

*　　　　*　　　　*

Taco had stationed himself outside the cockpit door and kept the rest apprised of what was happening.

The Skybird was cruising at mach .85, about 550 miles an hour, he told them. The plan was to pass by Riyadh and head straight west toward the Red Sea. The east side of the Red Sea was Saudi Arabia's airspace; the west side was Egypt's. The flight plan to Riyadh was a decoy, and once they got past there, they would be outlaws until they traversed Saudi Arabia and crossed over that line into the safety of Egyptian airspace. At that point they would file another flight plan with Universal Flight Service.

From the standpoint of Egyptian air traffic control, it didn't matter where they had come from. Air traffic control was not going to ask the pilot: Are you by any chance escaping Saudi Arabia with one of their women? But time was critical. Once Riyadh figured out they weren't landing, suspicions would escalate, and the Saudis' hospitality would come to an abrupt halt. The flight from Riyadh to the Red Sea would take about an hour.

*   *   *

Nearing Riyadh, Taco allowed Morgan to listen outside the cockpit door. The pilots received a call from air traffic control.

"Skybird Seven-Two-Three-Whiskey-Tango, you are cleared to descend to flight level three-three-zero for your approach to Riyadh."

Kate looked over, and Grady shrugged. "I didn't hear anything, did you?"

"Nope."

Several minutes passed. On the ground, Riyadh air traffic control, which was tracking the plane on radar, would have begun to wonder why the Skybird was not descending. Or responding. They called again.

"Skybird Seven-Two-Three-Whiskey-Tango, please begin your descent to flight level three-three-zero for landing at Riyadh."

The pilots said nothing. Every minute they stalled got them ten more miles further along, and closer to the border.

"Skybird Seven-Two-Three-Whiskey-Tango, are you descending?"

Kate nodded to Grady, and he answered. "Riyadh, control, Skybird Seven-Two-Three-Whiskey-Tango, that is negative, sir."

"Skybird Seven-Two-Three-Whiskey-Tango, you are scheduled to descend for landing at Riyadh. Repeat, are you descending?"

"Riyadh control, that is negative," Grady said.

"Skybird Seven-Two-Three-Whiskey-Tango, do you have a problem? Repeat, do you have a problem?"

"Riyadh control, Skybird Seven-Two-Three-Whiskey-Tango, that is negative," Grady said.

The controller's voice was angry, and the louder he shouted, the more pronounced his accent.

"Skybird Seven-Two-Three-Whiskey-Tango, why have you not descended?"

Grady answered, calmly, "Skybird Seven-Two-Three-Whiskey-Tango, we have changed our plans, sir."

"Skybird Seven-Two-Three-Whiskey-Tango, you cannot change your plans. You must land at Riyadh."

"Copy, Riyadh control," Grady said. "We will not be descending."

"Skybird Seven-Two-Three-Whiskey-Tango, please explain!" the controller shouted.

"Riyadh control, Skybird Seven-Two-Three-Whiskey-Tango," Grady said, cool as a gambler with a straight flush. "We have changed our mind."

November 12, 8:50 p.m. AST

Kate and Grady ignored any more communications from Riyadh control. The damage was done, and they were officially renegades. In less than an hour, hopefully, they would be out of Saudi airspace.

Fifteen tense minutes passed. Linnie and Morgan stayed near the front, sitting across from Buck. They left Faiza and Ashton alone in the rear of the cabin, though Linnie walked back to check on Faiza every few minutes.

"She's doing fine," Linnie reported. "The contractions come and go, with no pattern. Which means she has a long way to go."

"Is she going to be okay?" Morgan asked.

"As far as I can tell, it all looks real normal," Linnie said. "Which is amazing, considering what she's been through. I can't imagine how she survived, with a healthy pregnancy to boot. But she's got incredible resilience. She told me they did have a doctor checking on her."

Morgan went to the cockpit and told Kate and Grady.

"I always wondered what the stork looked like," Grady said. "It's a fucking jet."

"Smart ass," Morgan said. "At least if the baby is born on the plane it will be a U.S. citizen. But what if there's a problem? Can we land?"

"Not here!" Kate said.

"We could go into Egypt, or Greece," Grady said, checking the charts. "But it'll be a mess. So much to explain. Can't you do some medical thing to make it wait until we get home?"

"What, Grady? Have her cross her legs? You guys all need to have one baby. Just one."

"Keep us posted," Kate said.

Grady glanced out his window, then leaned closer, pressing his nose to the glass.

"Uh, oh. We've got company," he said. "Go get Taco. Tell him to look off the starboard wing."

*   *   *

Taco cupped his hands around his eyes and peered out the cabin window. "Damn."   Morgan followed Taco back up to the cockpit. "What is it?"

Taco said to Grady, "What do you think? F-15's?"

"Looks like it to me," Grady said grimly. "Two of them."

Morgan, Linnie, Taco, and Buck all crowded around the windows. In the night sky, the planes were dark gray silhouettes, like fighter-jet ghosts. They stayed right beside the Skybird, two shadows, never wavering from their position. The moonlight illuminated the emblem on the tail of the plane closest to them. A palm tree and two swords. Like on Rashad's cap.

"That's the Saudi Air Force?" Linnie said.

Taco nodded.

"They sent the goddamm Air Force after us?" she said.

"Do they know we have Faiza?" Morgan asked Taco.

"I doubt it," Taco said. "Probably scrambled when we skipped Riyadh. Checking us out."

"What if they knew what we have done?" Morgan said.

Taco thought that was unlikely. It would mean first, that Faiza's disappearance had been discovered and somehow connected to them. That would take time. Then, someone would have to make the connection between them and the plane that didn't land in Riyadh. Long shot. To merit the Air Force, someone in Faiza's family would have to exert considerable influence in the government. Also not likely. In the U.S., what daughters would rank an Air Force rescue? Maybe the Bush twins, or some Kennedy kids.

The planes continued to flank them with their eerie precision. In the cockpit, Kate kept the pedal to the metal, and she and Grady simply ignored the radio calls from the Saudi planes.

"Skybird Seven-Two-Three-Whiskey-Tango," came the radio call, in English with a deep baritone Arabic accent. "Please identify yourself."

Grady monitored the channel they were calling on, but did not respond.

"Skybird Seven-Two-Three-Whiskey-Tango," the pilot repeated. "What are your intentions?"

Kate and Grady looked at each other and shrugged.

"Skybird Seven-Two-Three-Whiskey-Tango," the pilot said. "Do you have a problem?"

"Yeah," Kate muttered. "You guys are scaring the shit out of us."

The Saudi pilot advised them to turn back and land in

Riyadh.

Kate and Grady continued to ignore him.

The Saudi pilot offered to escort the plane back to Riyadh.

No response.

"Are they going to shoot us down?" Kate finally asked.

"No way," Grady said. "We're a U.S. registered civilian airplane. What? They're going to start a fucking war because we didn't land in Riyadh?"

"Then why don't they go away?"

"They're trying to muscle us into landing," Taco said.

"Do you think they know we've got Faiza?" Kate asked him.

"I doubt it," Taco said. "If they knew, they probably would have said something."

"Ignore them," Grady said.

"Shit," Kate said, a mischievous smile breaking through her seriousness. "I've never been chased by fighters. I usually fly by the rules."

"Well, you're way outside the lines now, babe," Grady said.

November 12, 9:10 p.m. AST

Taco spread a navigational chart out on the floor. "This is our approximate location right now," he said. "About thirty minutes to go."

This whole flight is otherworldly, Morgan thought, distorting time and distance, and with it, reality. They were moving hundreds of miles an hour, and yet it felt as though they were not moving at all.

They had half an hour to safety. The length of a television sitcom. The time it takes to make a pizza. Half a CD. How many half hours went by in our lives that we didn't even notice? And during this one, their lives would either go forward or take an unspeakable downward spiral. Yet, for some reason, Morgan's fear had completely vanished. She wondered if there was a zone, right on the edge of real danger, where the fear is neutralized. Maybe the moment of death was like that. You were seeing it so close up you no longer feared it.

She walked back and knelt next to Faiza. "You kids doing okay?"

Ashton said they were fine. He was keeping Faiza in the back, sheltered from the drama unfolding in the cockpit. She was still very disoriented; also full of fear. She sensed their escape was not yet sure—that Saudi Arabia was not yet behind them.

"Are we going to get away?" she asked Morgan, her voice weak and shaky.

"Yes," Morgan said. "It's a little, well, tenuous until we get out of Saudi Arabia."

"You are in so much danger," she said. "You have risked your life. And all these other people have too. I am so grateful, yet I don't understand."

"It's really pretty simple," Morgan said. "Everyone wanted you to get free."

Faiza took hold of Morgan's hand and held it to her cheek. "Ashton told me about the jewels," she said. "I am sorry you were not able to use them, but when I get home, I will use them to raise the money. My father would be very happy. He, too, wanted me to be free."

"Faiza," Morgan said. "There's something I want to ask you. Before he let me go, the airport guard said something to me in Arabic. Would you tell me what it means?" Morgan pronounced the phrase as best she could.

"Allah Ma'ak," Faiza repeated softly. "The words mean: God be with you."

"Taco!" Grady shouted from the cockpit. "We've got more company. Off the port wing."

CHAPTER SEVENTY-THREE

They all crowded to the window. It looked like a mirror image of what was on the other side. Two more planes, flying alongside, as though they were stuck to the Skybird's shadow.

Taco studied them for a while. Then he said, "It's the good guys."

"Who?" everyone asked.

"Our guys. The Air Force. Probably F-16s," he said, as if it was nothing to be flying along flanked by fighter planes.

"The United States Air Force?" Linnie said. "Our Air Force? What are they doing here?"

"Keeping an eye on us," he said.

"Where did they come from?" Morgan asked. She and Taco moved toward the cockpit.

"We have a huge military presence in Saudi Arabia," he answered. "They were probably scrambled to check things out. By now, everyone knows that there's a civilian plane up here that's not exactly playing by the rules."

In the cockpit, the pilots got a call from the new arrivals.

"Skybird Seven-Two-Three-Whiskey-Tango, this is U.S. Air Force Strike Flight leader. Do you copy?"

The voice was steady and composed, definitely American, with a slight Midwestern twang. These supersonic jet pilots always had such a flat affect when they talked on the radio, Morgan thought. Like when they called from the moon, with this impassive tone of voice, as if they're checking in to see if anyone wants them to pick up anything from the grocery store.

"The Air Force!" Kate said. "Ours?"

Grady leaned forward and looked past her out the window. The planes flashed their landing lights, joining the full moon in illuminating their outlines and the round, striped insignia on the fuselage with the words United States Air Force.

"F16s," Grady told her. He pressed his mike button. "Strike Force, this is Skybird Seven-Two-Three-Whiskey-Tango. We copy."

"Whiskey-Tango, we have been advised that you were supposed to land in Riyadh and have not. Is everything okay?"

"Affirmative, Strike Flight, we are okay," Grady said.

"Whiskey-Tango, do you realize you are overflying your destination and are in violation of international civil aviation regulations?"

"Affirmative, Strike Flight, we realize that," Grady said.

"Whiskey-Tango, what are your intentions?" the Air Force pilot said.

"Uh, Strike Flight, we plan to continue on," Grady said.

"Whiskey-Tango, do you have a problem? Are you being hijacked?"

"Strike Flight, that is negative." Grady said.

"Whiskey-Tango, do you need any assistance?"

"Negative, sir. We are leaving Saudi airspace."

"Whiskey-Tango," the pilot said. "Do you have any Saudi nationals on board?"

Kate sucked in her breath and looked at Grady in alarm. He pressed the mike button and spoke without hesitation.

"Negative, Strike Flight, we are all American citizens."

* * *

The Saudis, monitoring the radio frequencies, would have heard the transmissions between the Skybird and the U.S. planes. So they tried to make contact again, demanding that the pilots respond and requesting that they follow their planes and land in Jeddah.

Kate and Grady continued to ignore them and continued merrily on, surrounded by four military jets that could fly circles around them, with missiles that could vaporize the Skybird with one flip of a switch.

"We got us a con-voy!" Grady drawled, when Morgan poked her head in the cockpit door.

"What if we start a world war?" Morgan asked.

"We might," Kate said. "If anyone in the world cared about one woman's life."

"She's right," Grady said. "Even if they knew what we'd done, they're not going to blow us out of the sky. We're Americanos. And they can't exactly pull us over."

"How long will they follow us?" Morgan asked.

Taco was standing right behind her. "They'll escort us out of Saudi airspace, and then be on their way."

"How can you be sure?" Morgan asked.

"What? Saudi military airplanes are going to follow us into Egyptian airspace? You wanna see a fucking war? Now that would be one."

Grady turned and winked at Morgan, and in his eyes she saw reassurance, tenderness, and love. And she hoped that he saw something also in hers. She wanted him to see her gratitude, her growing love, and most of all, her respect. He deserved it. This man, whom she had once seriously misjudged, had really stepped up to the plate.

"Stan Grady," Morgan said. "Thank you."

Then she put her hand on Kate's shoulders.

"You're the best," Morgan said.

November 12, 9:35 p.m. AST

Taco crouched by the charts and pointed to their current location. On the chart they were less than an inch from the coastline, less than fifteen miles from the safety of the Red Sea. At that point, they were as good as out of Saudi airspace.

In the cockpit Kate and Grady were counting the miles. Suddenly the two Saudi Air Force planes dipped their wings, and in a split second their lights disappeared, as though a genie had just poofed them out of sight.

The next transmission was from the U.S. plane.

"Skybird Seven-Two-Three-Whiskey-Tango, this is Strike Flight. Do you copy?"

"Strike Flight, this is Whiskey-Tango," Grady said. "Copy."

"We see that you are coming out of Saudi airspace. If we cannot be of any further assistance to you, then we bid you good evening and wish you a good flight."

"Roger, Strike Flight. Thank you. Good evening."

November 12, 9:55 p.m. AST

What they heard next was Kate's voice on the intercom.

"Mujeres con cojones. Ladies and gentlemen. We have just received clearance from Cairo air traffic control for our flight over Egypt."

There was a pause. Then she continued.

"Feel free to walk around the cabin. Or to pour some champagne. Or to twist and shout. We have left Saudi airspace."

And cheer they did. Linnie brought out the champagne. Buck popped the cork, which hit the ceiling with a thud. While Linnie talked with Faiza and checked the progress of her early labor signs, Ashton got up and retrieved the CDs and movies from the storage compartment where Morgan and Linnie had stashed them.

"We need some music," he said.

"Oh, I thought you were going to watch *Lawrence of Arabia* again," Morgan said.

"Cute, Mom," he said. "What do you want? Enya? James Taylor? Grateful Dead?"

"How about the Beach Boys?" Linnie shouted.

"You got the Beach Boys in there?" Morgan said.

"You bet," Linnie said. "Let's hear 'Surfer Girl.'"

Leaving Kate in the cockpit, Grady walked back into the

cabin for a moment, long enough to give Morgan a hug and meet Faiza face to face. From inside the blanket, she extended her hand and her dark eyes filled with tears.

"I heard that you are the one who made this happen," she said.

"Morgan made it happen," Grady told her.

"You are the pilot captain."

"Actually, I'm the copilot. Kate's the captain," said Grady.

Morgan looked at him questioningly.

"It was her turn to fly," he replied. Then he asked Faiza, "How are you feeling?"

"Okay," she said. "I'm ... we're ... going to have a baby." She gazed at Ashton.

"I heard," Grady said.

"Soon," Faiza said.

"I heard that, too."

Morgan noticed Taco was in the front, hanging up the telephone. She had not heard it ring. He turned to the group and said quietly, "The men have arrived on the island of Bahrain."

Soho, Crater, and The Bear were on safe ground. Everyone cheered again. Linnie was filling glasses with champagne. She had brought a bottle of the non-alcoholic kind, for the pilots and pregnant ladies, she said. Grady took a glass up to the cockpit for Kate.

"To freedom!" Linnie said, raising her glass.

"To new life!" added Morgan.

"To us!" Kate said, over the intercom. "And to our fuel tank, which has enough in it to take us all the way home to the U.S. of A.!"

Everyone cheered and hooted.

"What an adventure," Linnie said.

"Adventure?" Morgan asked her.

"You said it yourself, Morgan," she said.

"What did I say?'

"That adventure is about taking action," Linnie answered. "We took a stand. We stood up for something and faced off against a little piece of injustice. What else is adventure?"

"I know one thing," Morgan said. "I don't think I'll ever be afraid of anything again."

Linnie sat down next to her.

"Morgan, one day not long ago I heard this woman on CNN. She was a Holocaust survivor. The interviewer asked her what she had learned from all that horror. And she said, simply, 'Pay attention, get involved, and never ever look away.' That's your life, girl. You live that, you know?"

Linnie circulated throughout the cabin, refilling glasses. Music blasted over the speaker system. It was the Eagles CD Morgan had been playing the night Grady showed up on her doorstep. Linnie and Morgan grabbed each other's waists and sang along. Then they reached out and pulled Taco and Buck into the line, swaying back and forth with the music.

Ashton and Faiza looked on. Her smile was so broad it barely fit on her face. Morgan noticed that there were tears in her son's eyes.

"I would die for you. Climb the highest mou-ouuuntain. Baby, there's nothin' I wouldn't do-o-o-o."

"Now I've found you, there's no more emptiness inside. When we're huuunnn-gry, love will keep us alive."

Never in her life had Morgan felt so strong.

And so free.

EPILOGUE

It was the very middle of the night, the point furthest away from going to sleep or waking up, and a handful of people stood near the small north terminal building at the Kissimmee airport. The tower had long since shut down for the night, and the runway and taxiways were dark and soundless.

An airport where everyone has gone home is like a stadium after hours. The stillness is more than still, the space is emptier than empty. In a few moments the airport manager, who had agreed to roust himself out of bed on this particular night, would illuminate the runway lights on number 33. He didn't have to do this. The usual airport tower hours were seven a.m. to dusk, and after that, pilots wanting to land there would activate the runway lights using a radio signal.

But tonight it was the press asking, and it seemed like a good story, so the manager agreed to open the gates and unlock the terminal for this entourage to come in and await the arrival of a Skybird jet from overseas.

The group who had come there, however, chose to wait outside the terminal building on the ramp. The night was typical of November in Florida—cool, low humidity, with just enough breeze to move the tops of the trees—and a full moon cast a bright silvery band right across the airfield, like a shimmering welcome mat.

They huddled together, talking softly, watching the sky. Occasionally one or two would sit on the pavement and lean against the chain link fence. One man crouched down next to a large video camera, which he occasionally picked up and heaved onto his shoulder to line up some shots. Two metal stands held high-intensity bulbs with tinfoil hoods. The photographer checked the lights once, aiming them toward the area where the plane was expected to stop, creating a field of illumination like spotlights on a dark stage.

Besides the cameraman, there was Jacob Stoll, a reporter for channel 15 television; Meredith Rivers, the daughter of a woman on the plane; and her father, former Indiana state senator Dowd Rivers. Also present was a woman named Alex, who was a representative from Amnesty International.

Parked nearby was a white van, no lights, and inside the van were two U.S. Customs officials and a drug-sniffing dog, who would all board the plane when it arrived, the legal procedure when planes from overseas come into uncontrolled fields. Next to that van, a Sunrise Health Service ambulance with two paramedics aboard idled softly with only its interior overhead bulb glowing in the back. The Skybird pilot had called Sunrise to request the ambulance, for a female passenger in labor.

"What time is it?" Meredith asked Jake.

He pulled his shirtsleeve back from his watch. "Two thirty-five," Jake said.

Meredith cupped her hand over her mouth and yawned. It wasn't a yawn of boredom. She was exhausted. She had barely slept for the past four nights.

"There's something!" the cameraman shouted, pointing to the eastern sky.

It looked like a star. Jake held his thumb in front of his eyes to create a bearing. Sure enough, the star passed his thumb, creeping closer and closer. It had to be them. Jake motioned to the cameraman, and the lights flipped on. Jake stepped in front of the camera.

"For channel 15 news, this is Jacob Stoll, and I'm at the airport in Kissimmee, Florida, where we are awaiting the arrival of a U.S. jet returning from Saudi Arabia. We are told that on this plane is a Saudi Arabian national, a woman, who was reportedly imprisoned there. A group of civilians, including her American fiancé, organized a covert mission to rescue her. We have also been told that the woman is pregnant with the child of her fiancé."

As the airplane eased toward the ground, the lights from its landing gear jiggled against the dark horizon, inching nearer and brighter until the plane touched down at the far end of the runway, the roar of its engine shattering the night's quiet. Then it slowed, and the engines whined as the tail glided around and the plane came to a stop right in front of the terminal where the tiny welcoming committee stood, the sleek white fuselage gleaming in a luminescent mixture of moon and electric spotlight.

The paramedics got out of their truck and hurried toward the plane.

The hatch opened, and the first person out, a woman with blonde hair, smiled and squinted into the lights.

"Mom!" Meredith met her mother at the bottom of the steps and threw her arms around her.

"This is Morgan Fay, one of the organizers of the mission," Jake said, the cameraman alongside him. "What can you tell us?"

Morgan kept her arm around her daughter. She smiled at Jake.

"We have with us a woman who was kidnapped while she was in the United States as a university student. She was taken back to Saudi Arabia against her will and imprisoned there by people we believe to be radical fundamentalists," Morgan said. "For a time she was locked in a room with no windows or sounds, because she was pregnant with the child of an American man. We also believed she was in danger of being killed as punishment for breaking Islamic law. So we went over there and got her and brought her back."

Morgan waved the paramedics on to the plane.

"What is her condition now?" Jake asked.

"She is doing fine; but we want the paramedics to check her out," Morgan said. "We are concerned that this woman is at risk for deportation, so we have asked a representative of Amnesty International to be here. If it is necessary, we will ask that organization to assist us in obtaining asylum for her, on the grounds that her life may be in danger if she returns to her country."

"Who else is with you?" Jake asked.

Morgan responded evenly. "We have two pilots, my son, and a woman who is a nurse."

She did not mention anyone else because, somewhere, somehow, before the officials would board the airplane, the two men nicknamed Taco and Buck would have disappeared into thin air.

"Oh, and we have one other," Morgan said, looking up the steps.

Ashton appeared in the hatchway, holding a small, dark blue blanket bundled closely against his chest. He made his way cautiously down the steps. When he got to the bottom, he lifted a small portion of the blanket.

The cameraman stepped in closer, tipping the lens toward the tiny face, eyes closed, skin rosy with newness, a miniature rosebud mouth crinkling in and out.

"She was born just an hour ago over the Atlantic Ocean, aboard a U.S. registered airplane. That makes her one of our newest American citizens," Morgan said.

"Meet my granddaughter, Ashley Salah Rivers."

--- END ---

Made in the USA
Columbia, SC
30 March 2022